W. K. Tweedie

Earnest Men

Their Life and Work

W. K. Tweedie

Earnest Men
Their Life and Work

ISBN/EAN: 9783337058906

Printed in Europe, USA, Canada, Australia, Japan

Cover: Foto ©Raphael Reischuk / pixelio.de

More available books at **www.hansebooks.com**

EARNEST MEN

THEIR LIFE AND WORK

BY THE

REV. DR TWEEDIE.

Lady Russell taking Notes at her husband's trial. Page 309

THOMAS NELSON AND SONS,

LONDON. EDINBURGH AND NEW YORK.

EARNEST MEN:

THEIR LIFE AND WORK.

BY

W. K. TWEEDIE, D.D..

AUTHOR OF "THE EARLY CHOICE," "SUCCESS IN LIFE," ETC.

LONDON:

T. NELSON AND SONS, PATERNOSTER ROW;

EDINBURGH; AND NEW YORK.

1872.

Preface.

—o—

 BOOK has been published in our day by a distinguished nobleman, Lord Lindsay, under the title of "Progress by Antagonism." The thought expressed by that title is presented in many lights, and with great fertility of illustration, and embodies what seems to be a general law in our world. It operates in the conduct of moral agents with the universality of gravitation in material things, and the following pages tend to illustrate the law, in a popular form, from many different points of view.

In consequence of its operation, feeble minds are worthless in stirring times, or at any important crisis. What would Cicero, great orator as he was, have been, had he stood alone, wailing and weeping like a woman, when calamities assailed him, or actually hastening to stretch out his neck for his assassins to smite? What would Melancthon, the timid, scholarly trimmer, have been without a bolder nature at hand to uphold him? Or what would Cranmer have been amid the trials which assailed him for the truth, and under which he more than faltered in his steadfastness, had not a higher power than his own raised him after his fall?

But energy or decision of character may be educated like any other attainment. Those who are familiar with the self-discipline of such men as Ignatius Loyola are well aware of that fact. Every successive generation may be thus trained by studying the examples of those who have gone before; and an attempt is here made to promote such study. The contents of many volumes are condensed into one, to meet the requirements of our rapid age; and by accustoming youth to fix the eye steadfastly upon those who have done great deeds—struggling, but yet victors—many more may learn to go and do likewise. In the rude collisions which virtue must encounter in a world like ours, or amid the hostility to which philanthropists and other benefactors of men are often exposed in their efforts to do good, it is sometimes difficult to realize the actual progress of man upon the whole. Yet that progress is real; and it is equally opposed to Scripture and to fact to "say that the former times were better than these." The lives which follow both attest and explain that progress, and they are commended to the study of the young, that the coming generations may learn to be wiser, better, and nobler than the past.

Contents.

— o —

EARNEST MEN.

CHAPTER I.
Principles.

"But of our souls, the high-born loftier part,
Th' ethereal energies that touch the heart;
Conceptions ardent, labouring thought intense,
Creative fancy's wild magnificence;
And all the dread sublimities of song
—These, Virtue, these to thee alone belong.
Chilled by the breath of vice, their radiance dies,
And brightest burns when lighted at the skies;
Like vestal lamps to purest bosoms given,
And kindled only by a ray from Heaven."

LORD GLENELG.

The temptation and fall—Brief examples of decision—A prodigal turned miser
—The decision of Camillus—A Roman embassy—Julius Cæsar—Calvin—The
battle of Marengo, Dessaix—Buonaparte—Religious decision—Athanasius—
Luther—A female martyr.

HE who deliberates about doing what is wrong will most probably do it. Our safety and our strength lie in instant and decided rejection. Satan's victory was already half won when Eve listened to his flattery, and asked him to conduct her to the tree where the serpent said he had acquired the power of speech. The words,—

"Indeed! Hath God then said that of the fruit
Of all these garden trees ye shall not eat,
Yet lords declared of all in earth or air?"

really involved the fall, when Eve consented to hear them

without an instinctive recoil; and it has been the same with myriads of her sons and daughters since that fatal hour. To parley with the wrong is wrong. Hence the need of energetic and instantaneous decision—of flight rather than parley, and of a determined struggle rather than yield. The history of the world furnishes many illustrations of the effects of decision. If we refer to a few, they will best define and briefly explain the object of the following chapters.

He who has perhaps acquired the best right to address us on the subject of "Decision of Character,"* has recorded the case of a youth who had wasted his patrimony in profligacy and folly. His associates, who gathered round him, like flies round a decaying carcase, as long as he had the means to pamper and indulge them, forsook him and fled when he had become a penniless beggar. He was reduced to utter want, and suicide became his choice in preference to the degradation into which he had sunk. On the way to a secret spot whence he could rush, unhindered and red with his own murder, into the presence of the Judge, his eye chanced to wander over the wide domains which he had once called his own. He could not leave the scene, and after hours of self-communing, he rose from the earth, where he lay in his abjectness, with the resolution formed in his mind that these domains should one day be all his own again.

And action followed resolution, as shadow follows substance in sunshine. That prodigal instantly proceeded to carry his purpose into effect. He stooped to become a menial and a drudge. He hoarded every farthing he could earn, and sometimes approached the verge of starvation ere he would expend any part of his earnings even upon necessary food. No occupation however mean, no degradation however deep, could make him swerve from his purpose. It took possession of his whole soul. The gains of one adventure were made a

* John Foster.

stepping-stone from which to rise to higher and still higher things, till at last the resolute man accomplished his object. He added unit to unit, ten to ten, and thousand to thousand, till the patrimony of his fathers was recovered, though in recovering it he had become an inveterate miser. He died at last worth £60,000 ; and such is a lucid illustration of the power or the results of decision—not certainly of an elevated kind, but not the less fitted to show what man may become when his whole soul is concentrated upon one master object. An undecided man proclaims by his indecision that he was meant to be possessed by others; his conduct must be that of a satellite at best; while a decided man as loudly tells that he was meant to command. He will not submit to events; on the contrary he will make events submit to him.

The history of Rome abounds in examples of intense decision.—The city was besieged by the Gauls in the time of the Republic, and so hard was it pressed that the Romans consented to purchase immunity with gold. But while they were in the act of weighing it, a legend tells that Camillus appeared, threw his sword into the scales instead of the ransom, and indicated by that action that he at least would not purchase peace—he would win it. A battle was accordingly fought; the siege was raised, and the enemy were triumphantly swept from the sacred soil, all in consequence of the decision and the promptitude of one bold man—the second Romulus of the city.

Again; about one hundred and seventy years before the Christian era, Antiochus Epiphanes invaded Egypt which was then under the protection of Rome. Application was made to the Romans for assistance, and an embassy was sent which met Antiochus not far from Alexandria. The ambassador who was selected for that mission haughtily requested the invader to withdraw. He gave an evasive reply, but with his sword the Roman, on the instant, swept a circle

round the king, and insisted on an answer before he dared
to cross that line. By this decision the invasion was brought
to an end, war was prevented, and the ambassador gave one
proof more of the effects which man can accomplish when
he gives himself wholly to realize some cherished result.
Without such energy of decision men may be pretentious
or grandiose; they can never be great.

Further; Julius Cæsar was marching with his triumphant
legions along the shores of the Adriatic, and reached the
Rubicon which there formed the boundary of Italia—the
sacred and inviolable. For a time he paused upon the
northern bank, for even he faltered at the thought of invad-
ing a territory which no general might enter with an army
without the permission of the senate. Such was the state
of matters that the alternative which Cæsar had to face was
this—Destroy myself, or destroy my country! But he was
not slow to resolve. "The die is cast!" was his prompt
exclamation, and Cæsar crossed the Rubicon at the head of
one of his legions.—This also was the deed of a bold decided
man. It was an act which involved the life or death of
thousands. It led to battle after battle—it may even be
said to have decided the current of the world's history from
that day to this. Had Cæsar been undecided, while he gazed
across that little stream, the whole future of the nations
might have possessed a different aspect; but to his other gifts,
the man who was at once a general, a statesman, a lawgiver,
a jurist, an orator, a poet, an historian, a mathematician and
an architect, and great in nearly all of them, added a promptitude which sometimes made an action a flash. "I came,
I saw, I conquered," aptly describes his decision.

But this man's history supplies many other examples
of determination. He landed in Britain, and was boldly
opposed by its people. Though not a match for Roman
legions led by Julius Cæsar, the men of our island were even

then determined to let no foreign power be dominant here, if their blood could prevent it. Cæsar soon saw what spirit reigned, and to commit his soldiers to victory or death, it is well known that he burned the ships which had borne them to our shores.—It was once more the action of a man determined to carry out his purposes at all hazards, and enlisting even desperation in his cause, and such an action is a key to the triumphs and the character of Julius Cæsar. One can believe that such a man would not scruple to cause the death of two millions and a half of human beings, as Cæsar did, to slake and gratify his ambition. The union of an earnestness which is almost passionate with practical sagacity, renders a man fit for any thing human; and Cæsar possessed both of these properties. In him, they seemed to say, as one has said, "I am linked to my determination with iron bands; it clings to me with the tenacity of my fate." The untameable power of such decisiveness, illustrated in the life of Columbus in one aspect, and in that of Loyola in another, invests a soul with a grandeur such as little minds can never gage. What the feeble may attempt in paroxysms, or under intense excitement, the great do as a calm habit, and they sometimes wonder why other men admire what the decided could not help doing.

Again, at the siege of Pampeluna, early in the sixteenth century, when he was still a gay cavalier, Ignatius Loyola had his limb factured, and was long confined to his couch by the wounds which he had received. The broken bone was not well set, and threatened to disfigure him for life—a thought which he could not easily endure, and with the calm fortitude of a strong-willed soul, he broke his own limb once more that the new setting might afford another chance of elegance. The second fracture threatened to end in death, but it was the act of a bold, decided nature—such a nature as superstition might first mould, and then employ for the most daring and energetic designs, as we know was eventually the case.

Again; it is well known that Calvin's efforts to advance the Reformation in Geneva led to keen and violent opposition. A profligate faction, called "The Libertines," caused many troubles in the city; and on one occasion it was understood that some of the men who acted in that manner, designed, in spite of their atrocities, to partake of the Holy Communion. Calvin learned their purpose; he threw himself across their path, in the Church of St. Peter, and declared that if they dared to approach such a solemnity while steeped in guilt, they must do so over his dead body. By that act of intrepid decision the evil was averted.

In modern times examples of a similar kind abound. It is well known that at the battle of Marengo, the French army was defeated during the earlier part of the day, and Buonaparte and his staff were assembled to consider their next move, when Dessaix, who subsequently fell on that field, suggested that there was yet time to retrieve the disaster. On the spot, he counselled a renewal of the action; it was renewed, and won, for the Austrians were driven with great slaughter from the scene where they had so lately triumphed. That general was decided, and such decision was the harbinger of victory, though also of his death.

In another engagement, fought during winter, Buonaparte saw some of his enemy's forces crossing a lake which was frozen at the time. In an instant he resolved upon an easy victory—and though it was the decision of a diabolical spirit, it accomplished its object. He commanded some heavy artillery instantly to play upon the ice; it was done, and the columns perished at once by fire and water, when the fragile bridge which bore them sank beneath their feet. That resolute will which subdued to itself nearly the whole of Europe, was all concentrated in that destructive command. Multiply such actions by a thousand, and we have the rise and the grandeur of Buonaparte: his fall and his littleness, suggest other thoughts which are not at present to be pursued. Self-made men of every class, from those who vault into a throne and found a dynasty as Buonaparte did, down to those who become millionaires, like Astor, or Girard, all possess this decision. By seizing the tide at the full they are floated " on to fortune," while those who are born to rule, rule with glory under the guidance of such a principle. Such, for example, was the inflexible resolution of Queen Elizabeth of England that in her family, her court, her Church, and her kingdom, she was equally mistress: she scarcely tolerated a second near her throne.

But it is in the domain of religion that we may expect to find the most satisfactory examples of decision. It is not left merely to the appeals or the poetry of men to plead with us, " Be wise to-day, 'tis madness to defer :" the only wise God is no less urgent. " To-day, if ye will hear his voice ;" "I have set before you life and death, blessing and cursing, saying, choose,"—are the counsels of the Supreme ; and the Bible abounds with maxims which enforce them. " If the Lord be God, follow him; but if Baal be God, then follow him," calls on man to decide and not to falter or halt between two opinions. " Give thyself wholly to these things ;" inculcates entire consecration. " What thy hands find to do, do it with all thy might," indicates the energy which should be concentrated upon what we undertake. " He that is not with me is against me," unequivocally shows that indecision is hostility, when that indecision relates to him who is the truth. " One thing I do," tells that the man who employed the words had discovered how unwise it is to let our powers run to waste amid distracting pursuits. " Would thou wert either cold or hot !" expresses the earnest longing of Him who came to save us. And further still, the first and great commandment, "Thou shalt love the Lord thy God with *all* thy heart, and *all* thy soul, and *all* thy strength and .mind," proclaims as from his very throne, what should be first, last, and supreme in the soul—the one overmastering, all-absorbing principle. The man who is actuated by that great command has one thing to do : he does it, and that is decision.

Once more : " It is good to be zealously affected in a good thing," shows how the heart is to be thrown into what we undertake, if we would do good in our day and generation. But, above all, the following words seem to concentrate and condense all that can be said on this subject. " Behold this selfsame thing, that ye sorrowed after a godly sort, what carefulness it wrought in you, yea, what clearing of your-selves, yea, what indignation, yea, what fear, yea, what vehe-ment desire, yea, what zeal, yea, what revenge !   In all things ye have approved yourselves to be clear in this matter." Here we have some of the most commanding principles that reign in man's heart employed to reinforce his religious decision. A place is found in the soul even for revenge—revenge upon sin for the multiform sorrows which it has occasioned to man.

For an example of such decision we may quote the case of Athanasius.   He had welcomed the truth as his guide, and though he expressed it in language which *all* would not adopt (if the creed called by his name be his) he was illustrious as a defender of truth.   For his steadfast-ness, however, he was deposed from his bishopric by a Coun-cil, and banished to Treves by the Emperor Constantine. But that emperor, two years thereafter, ordered Atha-nasius to be restored to his charge, where his flock would not receive him.   After other two years he was again re-stored, but only to be again banished by Constantius, and obliged to flee into the desert. Having subsequently returned he was once more banished under Julian the apostate, then recalled by Jovian, then banished once more by Valens, and after all, he was recalled from his fifth exile to his home in Alexandria. Now, did these things shake the confidence—did they at all modify the convictions of Athanasius? Nay, he continued steadfast and unmoveable amid them all. It was "Athanasius against the world," so widespread was the defection from truth, and so determined his adherence to it.

Another example is found in the case of Luther. He was cited to answer for his opinions before the Diet of Worms, and proceeded thither under the protection of a passport, which many believed would not secure his·safety. He was implored not to go; the case of John Huss was quoted to scare him; for that reformer, with such a safeguard in his possession, was burnt to death for his religion. Luther, however, was not to be deterred. He had chosen his path, and was determined, God helping him, to pursue it. His well-known exclamation was, "I am called in the name of God to go, and I would go, though I were certain to meet as many devils in Worms as there are tiles on the houses."

The same energy may be seen not seldom in weak womanhood; perhaps the grandest display of decision which the world has witnessed has been made by her. On the margin of a bleak bay in what was then a bleak part of Scotland, there were assembled, nearly two hundred years ago, a band of bloody men—the tools of still fiercer persecutors. They had fastened two women to stakes to die for their religious convictions, in such a position that the flowing tide would slowly drown them. One of them was aged, and the other youthful, and in the hope of shaking the constancy of the girl, her companion was placed nearest the ocean that she might die first, and under the eyes of the other sufferer. That girl's only crime was refusing to let men dictate to her conscience regarding Him whom she honoured as her re-

deemer; and was she shaken in her purpose either by the
death of her fellow sufferer, or by the surge threatening to
engulf herself? Did she blanch before either her murderers or
the sea? Nay, the heroine held fast by her heroism, and though
rescued when half drowned, in the cruel hope that she might
then recant, she resolutely refused. " I am Christ's; let me
go!" was her cry, when tempted by the offer of life to commit what she held to be a sin, and that also was decision—
decision amid the horrors of a terrible death, in a girl who
was only eighteen years of age. We do not speak here of
the secret of her decision: it was God-given and mighty in
his strength; we refer only to the fact, and it illustrates well
the more than mortal energy with which the mind is nerved
when it is " thoroughly persuaded."

Such, then, is decision of heart, and soul, and life in some
great and worthy object. He who counselled his friend to
"do something—do it—do it—do it—and do it at once,"
exactly defined the spirit of a man who is decided in upholding the right; but the instances already glanced at
are d igned merely to announce what is meant by such
decision, or to intimate the energy which is needed if we
would do good. When the Highest dwelt among the
sons of men, His life was one long effort—one long self-
denial—one august self-sacrifice. He passed without repose
from place to place, by sea, by mountain, in the desert, in
the city, everywhere working the Father's work, till the
life-long struggle was completed by the noblest work of all
—by suffering unto death. Now that is the all-embrac-
ing model, and the examples which follow in detail, are designed to show how much depends upon the possession of
such a spirit of calm determination, whatever we pursue.
" We are not careful to answer thee in this matter," was the
quiet reply of a servant of the Great King when a despot
threatened him with death by the lions, because conscience

refused to call a creature its Lord; and that answer embodies the unruffled spirit of the man who has learned to fear God, and have no other fear. To be thus decided for truth and to continue so amid trials, or even torments, is a sure presage of real grandeur. How serene might life become —how rapid the progress of men in the path to that glory which the world can only counterfeit, were such decision common—the decision which seeks to do everything for the truth and nothing against it!

But in such a cause there is only one solid basis for decision, the strength of the Unchanging One. All else is like a dream when one awakes—a building on the sand. Kingdoms rise and fall—kings occupy a palace to-day, to-morrow they are without a home. Man's truth this hour is man's lie the next. The right on one side of a mountain or a river, is the wrong upon the other: only the word of the Lord endureth for ever, and that is the basis of all religious decision. We must there confront the scorn of the haughty, and the mirth of the fool, the hatred of the malignant, and the opposition of the stupid or the blind. But just as Cæsar burnt his ships, to cut off all hope of retreat, or just as some when they draw the sword, cast the scabbard away, or just as some nail their colours to the mast, determined to conquer or to sink with their ship, we should intrepidly confront what impedes us in the heavenward way. Daniel and Nebuchadnezzar's decree, Luther at the Diet, Huss at Constance, Tyndale at Vilvorde, and a " great cloud" before their murderers, are our models here; and in their footsteps, the tame may be roused to energy, the feeble to decision. In carrying out her bloody convictions, many an Indian widow has joyfully mounted the funeral pile of her husband, and made it also her own. Now she did it for an earthly end,—a dread delusion. What shall we do for heavenly truth? The lives of some of its heroes may reply.

CHAPTER II.

Heroes for the Truth.

IT is a formidable thing to enter a city like Lucknow, or Delhi, or any other stronghold, when it is held by a numerous enemy, fanatically fierce, and counting it paradise to die in the cause for which they fight. Loop-holed walls on the right and on the left, an enemy with a musket at every aperture, and friends falling fast beside you—all these test a soldier's courage. If ever he may reasonably be a coward at all, it is when his antagonist is, for the most part, invisible, and when nothing or little is seen but the muzzle of a weapon ready to lodge its contents in the unshielded person of the soldier.

And yet there is something which has tried the courage of men far more than such peril. Amid the noise and the excitement of war, man is roused to resistance—he has no alternative but to contend, and that to the death. But in moral warfare the case is altered. To defend the truth which most men dislike, to uphold the cause from which multitudes are open deserters, or to which they are secret enemies, to resist the sneer, or the pity, or the laugh, which often waits on those who stand up for truth and the right, may demand an amount of calm courage which is not needed amid the garments rolled in blood of the battle-field. Some have found it more difficult to resist the force of a sneer than to face a legion; some have proved cowards before ridicule who have marched against thousands without one beat of the pulse the more; some have yielded to the smiling enticements of wickedness who could never have been terrified by any sight of danger—not the rack, the dungeon, nor the stake.

But, on the other hand, there have been many who stood courageously up for truth, even when it seemed to have fallen in the streets. They were not daunted by the opposition of ignorance; they could not be silenced by gainsayers; they refused to compromise what they believed to be divine, and felt to be mighty, whether for comfort or alarm; and they moved forward unchecked amid all opposition. Flattery and frowns, blandishments and dungeons, king's palaces and a cross or a gibbet had no power to turn them from their steadfast way. They were what they were by the help of God; and their faith in Him made them strong.

The following sections are meant to sketch the lives of some men who were valiant for the good and the true, and who wrought out their purposes with unswerving persistency. The greatest hero of our age, or at least the most signal conqueror, is reported to have said to a minister of religion that his "marching orders," the Bible, should form his only guide,—and many a soldier in what Bunyan has depicted as "The Holy War," has honestly consulted, and heroically followed his marching orders amid much that threatened to retard or harass him. It is the heroism of these men, their unflinching determination to do good, that is here presented as a model, in the various departments of life.

And the age—our country—the world needs such men more than ever. Evil has been developed till it has become gigantic; the huge Upas which has blighted the earth never

shot forth its branches or diffused its poison more widely
than in our day. How, then, is it to be counteracted? By
the diffusion of the pure and the true; and that can be
better done by presenting models than by abstract maxims.
We have seen Thorwaldsen in his studio at Rome, busy
upon a group of statues which were designed to adorn
a royal palace in his native land.   The figures stood
before him, slowly emerging into life and beauty under his
hand and chisel. He had models beside him, and he consulted them: but he had a more perfect model in his own
mind. *That* he could not entirely reach, but on he wrought,
by blow after blow, by touch after touch ; now the contour
more rounded, and now the expression more life-like, indefinitely approaching his ideal. The great sculptor eyed
his handiwork from this point, from that, from many; he
retreated to a distance, he came nearer, and his eye, deep-
lored in the beautiful, created fresh attractions even where
all had seemed symmetry before.

Now would we thus work out moral beauty? Setting
some standard, not ideal but actual, before us, would we go
on unto perfection, and leave our mark upon our age,
so as to be missed when we die? Then be it ours to study
model men, and mark what made them what they were.
Testing all by the only perfect model, be it our business to
note how men stood, or how men fell in the battle of life.
So shall we find stepping stones through the rapids which
might otherwise sweep us away, or help in hours of weakness when we might otherwise falter, or hope at times when
we might despair, and either sink into feebleness, or have
power only for evil.

Every human being is a centre of influence for good or for
ill. No man can live unto himself. The meshes of a net are
not more surely knit together than man to man. We may
forget this secret, silent influence.   But we are exerting

it by our deeds, we are exerting it by our words, we are
exerting it by our very thoughts,—and he is wise with
a wisdom more than that of earth, who seeks to put
forth the highest power for good, be his home a hut or a
hall, a cabin or a palace. True, all this may have nothing
heavenly in it. It may never rise higher than a few feet
above the level of the earth. But would we ascend into the
region where our influence stretches into eternity? Would
we not merely soothe the sorrows of the mortal, but, moreover, promote the joys of the undying? Then Truth must
be lodged deep in the soul. The right arm of the All-power-
ful must be grasped by the hand of faith, and *then* the child
of the dust is invested with a portion of Omnipotence. He
becomes a fellow-worker with God, and some examples of
this heroism and decision are here to be submitted.

I.—BASIL THE GREAT.

A.D. 316—379.

"Immortal Truth! make known
Thy deathless wreaths, and triumphs all thine own;
The silent progress of thy power is such,
Thy means so feeble and despised so much,
That few believe the wonders thou hast wrought,
And none can track them but whom thou hast taught."

COWPER.

Basil's era—His parents—His studies—and travels—Becomes acquainted with Julian the Apostate—His trials begin—Firmness—Persecuted by Julian—Other troubles—and successes—The Emperor Valens assails him—Basil's intrepidity exemplified—Closing scenes—His character, life-work, and death.

THE question has been asked, Whether do great events call forth great men, or great men occasion great events? The partizans on either side of the alternative can support their views with many specious illustrations: they can make it appear that had certain combinations not occurred, there would have been nothing to call forth the energies, or develop the powers of the men of those times; or, on the other hand, they can show that these combinations might have happened again and again, and passed unheeded after all, had there not lived a Christian, a hero, a statesman, or a patriot fitted to turn them to account.

But, in truth, neither of these views can be exclusively maintained. They belong to a mixed class of topics, where there is neither an absolute standard, nor the possibility of always reaching a demonstrable result.

Enough, then, to know that when great occasions arise, some will be raised up to profit by them; when a gifted agent appears, aiming at something higher, purer, better than the present, he will find or create a sphere for his energies. It may be true that "some mute inglorious Miltons" have passed unknown through life; or that some Cromwell has lived and died "guiltless of his country's blood;" but while the world is under the guardianship of Omniscience we may be sure that the Mighty Ruler will adapt the man to the times, and the times to the man: they act and re-act like the ocean wearing away the land, yet the land, after all, bounding the ocean.

Basil called THE GREAT, was one whom his times most probably made what he was. It is believed that Cæsarea in Cappadocia, or Neo-Cæsarea, was his birth-place, and his parents and ancestors were noble. He was born about the year 316, and died on the first of January 379. At that period, superstition was rushing into the Church like water into a leaky vessel at sea. Anchorets were hastening away in thousands to dens, and caves, and deserts. Simple truth was not then sufficient for men, — they must mingle their own devices with it, and the foundation of many corruptions had thus been laid, long prior to the birth of Basil. Legends are accordingly mixed up with his life which are to be utterly discarded. They are the fictions of wonder-seekers, and not the facts of history—excrescences on his character, not vital parts of it, and dismissing all these, the lessons of Basil's life will show us what one resolute man may accomplish—what heroic principle directed to right results may achieve, either in preventing evil, or in promoting good among the sons of men.

From his youth, Basil had before him, in his parents, an example of undaunted devotedness. They passed through times of hot persecution, during which unprecedented woes were endured, for the malignity of paganism was then doing its worst. Exile, and all its miseries, and want in many forms were their lot; but none of these things moved them, and the father, Basil, with the mother, Emmelia, both endured these hardships in their own persons, and taught their eldest son and second child to prize what they valued beyond country, home, and life itself.

After spending five years in acquiring elementary knowledge at home, he proceeded to increase his stores abroad. Antioch, Cæsarea in Palestine, Athens, Constantinople, and other places were visited, and Syria and Alexandria in Egypt are mentioned among those where he resided. The philosophy of their schools, then famous, was mastered, but even then he appears to have been devoted to what is, in truth, the flower and crown of all the sciences—the science of salvation, the knowledge of that plan which came from heaven to guide men thither. At Athens, Basil became acquainted with Julian, afterwards the apostate Emperor, and had for his teacher a famous sophist whom the Emperor Constans sent to Rome where a statue was erected to his honour, bearing the proud inscription, "Rome, the Queen of cities, to the King of eloquence."

But Athens did not meet the mental wants of Basil: its happiness he called "a hollow felicity;" it was the happiness of mere learning without the supreme knowledge. At Antioch, he began to plead causes as a lawyer, but that also he found to be uncongenial work, and the Holy Scriptures now became his master study, so that his whole life and history takes its character and hue from them. Nor was he long without some trial of his firmness and decision. Julian, whom Basil, we have seen, knew as a fellow-student at Athens, was now the Roman Emperor. He had renounced Christianity, and declared himself a pagan, and yet he invited Basil to his court with a suspicious show of toleration and indulgence. The zealous man was not, however, to be moved even by imperial blandishments, and declined the invitation making, at the same time, no secret of the

reason,—his pain at the apostasy of his former friend. Julian
now haughtily rebuked him for the audacity of such a course,
and, moreover, fined him in a sum equivalent to nearly
£40,000 of our money.

It was by such means that the renegade Emperor sought
at once to gratify his resentment, to repress the Christians, and replenish his treasury. Withal, however, Julian
did not know the power which guided Basil, nor the resolution of that calm but indomitable man. The apostate
had no line long enough to fathom the depths, no skill
profound enough to gage the motives, which swayed a soul
like that of Basil, whose moral heroism was mightier far
than the imperial sceptre; and his reply to the Emperor's
rescript was felt to be quick and pungent. "You have
exposed yourself," he said in substance, "to the condemnation
of wise men. Seduced by the evil one, you have exalted
yourself against God and his Church; you have belied the
promise of your youth, and as to the fine, you need not
expect much from one who has not food for a single day,
whose house is a stranger to a cook, and whose fare is herbs
and a crust with wine which is both sour and vapid."*
Julian soon appeared more and more in the true character
of an apostate, and because the Christians at Cæsarea dared
to uphold their religion or obey their conscience, he persecuted them with rigour; he fined, imprisoned, and tormented.
Basil was one of two who were supposed to be reserved for a
public death, had the tyrant returned alive from his Persian
wars.

Such was Basil's first trial, the first flash from the flint
struck by the steel; at least it was this collision with an

---

* During this correspondence, Julian, imitating the first Cæsar, wrote in
reference to Basil's remonstrance: "I have read it, considered it, condemned
it," to which Basil rejoined, "Though you read, you did not understand, for
had you understood, you would not have condemned." That is the explanation
of all infidelity (John vii. 17).

imperial persecutor which first showed his decision in defence of the truth, and the eager agitations of his day soon tested him more and more. But though resolute against external assailants, he was averse to contention among Christians themselves, and rather than be drawn into unseemly strifes, he withdrew to solitude and a desert. Acting too much in the spirit of the age, he was there much engaged in planning schemes for monastic retirement, and unwisely encouraged and fostered a system which was then rising like a flood to overflow the Church. But he soon discovered that the desert afforded no guarantee for peace. "He had shifted the scene, but had not changed his state: he had fled from Cæsarea to avoid noise and contention, and only met with vexations and disquietudes nearer at hand." Charge after charge was heaped upon him by some of his enemies: he was compelled, in spite of himself, to act in self-defence, but once more he displayed the same resoluteness in repelling a faction which he had before evinced in combating an Emperor.

Though excessively and ignorantly attached to the life and habits of a monk, because the strong current of the age swept him along in that direction, Basil was forward and bold in defending every portion of the truth that was challenged in his day. He everywhere helped to unmask deception, and though this brought him into collision with another Emperor, the Arian Valens, he would not swerve, on that account, from his own decided convictions. As a resolute and dexterous champion, or like one who, in years long subsequent to the era of Basil, did not fear the face of man, he had to confront hostility in many forms, from the purple to the populace, but remained undaunted amid it all. Abuses were corrected, and his daily assaults on the enemies of the truth drove them at times discomfited from the field. Though not yet exalted to any high dignity in the

Eastern Church, he already directed many of its affairs, and with equal energy and sagacity, promoted whatever could advance the interests of truth. In many respects, he was the model of a Christian man, loving, prompt, tender, resolute, fearing God, and having no other fear.

The Emperor, Basil's enemy, having triumphed in a war against the Goths, now determined to press upon his subjects the adoption of his own religious views. Holding that "the only wise God our Saviour" was a creature, he wished to compel others to hold his blasphemy with him; and one of his prefects attempted, by promises first and then by threats, to bring Basil over to the side of error and the Emperor. But the attempt was vain. He stood unmoved alike by frowns and smiles; and for a time he was spared, though it was only to encounter a sharper trial in the end. About this time he was made a bishop, and troubles soon thickened around him. Factions raged, enemies assailed, but still he would not yield. In spite of envy and opposition, he held on his way. Truth needed a firm defender, and he was steadfast. It became manifest that he knew how to act upon the advice of a friend, and "maintain his ground like a rock in the midst of the sea."

But Valens at length attempted to carry out his design of corrupting the Church without leaving room for difference of opinion. On that errand he came to Cæsarea, where Basil abode, and as he had baffled the imperial endeavours before, will he yield to them now? Are truth and Basil to fall together? On the contrary, he boldly confronted the agents of the emperor, and gave place, no not for an hour, either to empurpled oppression, or to official insolence. The emperor's prefect demanded of Basil why he presumed to oppose the imperial religion, when all others yielded? His answer was that a higher Emperor hindered him. "I can never worship a created God," he said, "since I may

myself be a partaker of the divine nature; commands like
yours are nullities."

The rejoinder of the prefect was characteristic: "Is it
not an honour to have us on your side?" and Basil loyally
replied, "I grant you to be governors and very illustrious
persons, ... but Christianity is to be measured not by
dignity of persons, but by soundness in the faith." The
prefect, irritated and incensed, exclaimed, "What! are you
not afraid of the power we are armed with?" And Basil
calmly asked in his turn, "What can I suffer?" "All that is
in my power," was the retort. "But what is that? Confiscation of goods? Banishment? Tortures or death? If
there be anything worse, threaten it, for of these none can
touch us." Amazed by such boldness, the prefect asked
for explanation, and Basil answered, "That man is not
afraid of confiscation who has nothing to lose unless you
want these tattered clothes, and my books, my whole estate.
Banishment I regard not, for I am tied to no place .... The
whole earth is God's, whose pilgrim and sojourner I am.
As for tortures, what can they do? .... Set aside the first
blow, and there is nothing more in your power. And then,
for death, I shall esteem it a kindness and a benefit; it will
but sooner send me to God." ....

Such a spirit was Basil's—brave to intrepidity in the face
of danger, and the cause of truth. Though assailed by
threats, as well as tempted by promises, he had felt the
supreme fear,* and all besides was feeble. Basil is ranked by
some among the greatest orators of antiquity, and his closing
appeal to the prefect makes the opinion probably correct.
"When the cause of God and religion is at stake, we overlook all else, and fix our eyes only upon Him. In such cases,
fire and sword, wild beasts, and instruments to tear off the
flesh piece-meal are a pleasure rather than a torment to us.

* Isaiah viii. 13.

You may therefore reproach and threaten us; do your plea-sure, and use your power but let the emperor know you cannot conquer us, for you shall never prevail to make us confederate with Arians; no, though you should threaten worse things than you have yet done. And as for the advan-tage which you proposed, and the favour of the emperor, offer these things to boys or to children, who are wont to be caught with such gaudy baits. .... I highly prize the emperor's friendship, when I can have it with truth, and the favour of heaven, but without that I look upon it as pernicious and deadly."

This man was told, like one far greater than he, that he was mad; but his resolution was impregnable. He wished to be more mad still, and the report to the emperor was that no threatening could shake Basil, no argument could move him, no promises allure—he must either be vanquished by force or not at all. For a time, therefore, he escaped again, out at last a decree for his banishment was obtained from the emperor, and Basil's steadfastness was now tested to the uttermost.

And all this came upon him because he would not abate one jot of the truth—literally a single jot.* He would not sur-render even *that* when it involved the mind of God, and he was therefore resolute beyond the power of imperial majesty to shake him. A time-server would have yielded without a struggle in a thing apparently so small. A man who did not know the truth, or did not prize it, would have surrendered it without compunction. But Basil would not : he would die rather, and the Church will be his debtor till time shall be no more. He knew the power, some have called it the omnipotence, of words; his heroism was therefore employed to prevent man from giving currency to one which embodied

* Had he been willing to use the word ὁμοι-ουσιος, instead of ὁμο-ουσιος, of *a like* nature, for of *the same* nature, most of his sufferings might have been escaped.

death, and in his case inflexibility became the highest virtue. Superstition all apart, he was a hero indeed.

But no sooner had one trial terminated than another began, and we give one example more of Basil's heroic firmness. There was at Cæsarea a widow, rich, and well-connected, whom one of the high officials of that city desired in marriage. He was both powerful and importunate, but she was determined to remain a widow, and in the spirit of her day, sought a sanctuary in the church from the persistency or the persecution of that official. She was next demanded by the governor from Basil as the guardian of the sanctuary, but he refused to surrender one who had fled to him for an asylum, and pled the sacredness of her retreat, fenced as it was by the laws of those times. The governor stormed, and sent officers to search for her whom he designed to make the victim of oppression. He even commanded Basil to appear before him as a criminal, and treated him there with violence and indignity. Amid threats and brow-beating, however, Basil was firm ; he could suffer, but he would not do wrong ; and once more he testified the power of his decision. He himself escaped uninjured, and the person whom he so resolutely defended was also set free. In Basil's case, a calm judgment had acquired the power which belongs to strong passion—his decision for good and his fortitude in enduring were resistless, and hence attacks against him recoiled upon their author, even though he were an emperor.

But although he escaped from these troubles, Basil was soon plunged into others by his attempts to check the prevailing abuses of his Church. Into these matters, however, we do not enter here. He was accused of deserting the very cause of which he was the chief supporter ; and though assailed with rancour, he bore it all, knowing that the truth would triumph, and for three whole years he was mute, under some of the most violent of the charges which were advanced against him. The sharp arrows of bitter words which pierce not a few, were not much heeded by this man; at least, he waited for the "time to speak," though he sometimes had occasion to doubt whether there was honesty to be found among the sons of men. For more than eight years did he thus struggle against keen opposition, that is as long as he was Bishop of Cæsarea. He tried to live so as to make the world better; but his good was repaid with evil, his love, often with persecution. All this, however, only added one name more to the long roll of those who have persisted in doing good to men in spite of themselves, and Basil's death came at last to soften the minds of many. They soon discovered what a father, or what a friend they had lost, and so great was the concourse at his funeral that several were crushed to death in the crowd.

And such was one whom God raised up in a declining age, to help forward his cause on the earth. Basil, we have seen, was not superior to some of the corruptions of his day, but in other respects, he was one of the heroes of the truth. He was perhaps the most learned man of his age, and had attained, one says, "the utmost empire in all polite and useful learning." But though he laid it all, with himself beside it, on the altar of truth, that did not free him from the life-long battle, nay, it dragged him daily into the contest for the good against the evil, where all his force of character was needed to bear him up and on. Men of "steeled foreheads" chose to rise up against him, but he fearlessly met them all. In his eloquence, one of his friends records, "he seemed to speak nothing but life." Men confessed they were overcome by his fascinating persuasiveness and his power, yet no temptation could bias him, as no danger could terrify. A minister of state, nay, the imperial master of the Roman world, might assail Basil; but still he was steadfast, and triumphed. Though he had sometimes to stand alone in defending the cause which he loved, he never prized it the less because few befriended it. And though humble, calm, and peaceful by nature, yet as strife was forced upon him, he manfully faced it—that is, he "earnestly contended for the faith which was once delivered to the saints,"—and at last some of his very enemies were at peace with him.

Nor was this calm but energetic man left without other rewards. While many assailed, not a few admired; and so great was the veneration in which they held him that some weakly imitated even his bodily imperfections. His wasted, pallid looks, his gait, his sparing speech, his apparel, the style of his home, in short, his life became *the fashion* to some. This was a tribute which he did not desire, but which his powers, his strong-willed decision and his heroism extorted. When men read his books against the errors of his age, they seemed to see the flames of Sodom reducing those errors to ashes, or the tower of Babel falling upon those who impotently attempted to build to the skies. But eulogy apart, his actions are his best character, and these show him to have been bold, uncompromising, and fearless wherever the right was concerned. His life-work was to help to establish some of the truths which are at once most momentous to man, and yet most resolutely denied; as well as to retard the progress of some of the growing corruptions of his age, and whether we trace his first impressions, and his subsequent decision to his mother Emmelia, or his grandmother, Maorina, or to both, the result is the same, —Basil the Great now stands ennobled till time shall be no more, among those who were valiant for the truth—who did not count even their lives dear to them, that they might advance that cause which involves both peace on earth, and glory in the heavens.

II.—COLUMBA OF IONA.

About A.D. 521.

" Lo! darkness and doubt are flying away;
No longer I roam in conjecture forlorn;
So breaks on the traveller, faint and astray,
The bright and the balmy effulgence of morn.
See Truth, Love, and Mercy in triumph descending,
And Nature all glowing in Eden's first bloom!
On the cold cheek of death smiles and roses are blending, ·
And Beauty immortal awakes from the tomb."

BEATTIE.

Columba's birth—His early choice—Abounding corruptions—His boyhood—
Leaves his native country—Arrives at Oronsay—Then at Iona—The isle of
the Druids—Opposition to his landing—Open hostility—Yet firmly established in Iona—His life-work commences—Successes—His devotedness—The
Scriptures copied and spread—His ascendency—A missionary hero—Other
institutions, Abernethy and elsewhere—France, Switzerland, Germany, Italy,
all visited—The secret of his power—A mother's power—Tests—His illness
and death—Conclusion.

" WHY are you so troubled?" said a Mohammedan convert at Delhi to his weeping wife, when he was within a few minutes of his martyrdom, during the great Indian rebellion. " Remember God's word and be comforted. Know that if you die, you go to Jesus. And if you are spared, Christ is your keeper. I feel confident that if any of our missionaries live, you will all be taken care of, and should they all perish, yet Christ lives for ever. If the children are killed before your face, oh, then, take care that you do not deny Him who died for us. This is my last charge: Oh, God help you !"

Such were among the last words of a modern martyr—of one whose life of faith, and whose death of atrocity make it manifest that the truth of God is as quick, and his grace as mighty now, as they were eighteen centuries ago, and we are next to trace the history of one who had welcomed the faith which prompts such devotion, and embodies it in deeds, one who was as decided as that martyr in upholding and spreading the truth. He did not indeed die a martyr, but for half a century and more he held his life in his hand, ready to surrender it rather than forego what his God had taught him to prize and to propagate.

In the year 521 there was born somewhere in Ireland, a child who was destined to leave the impress of his mind for centuries upon the countries where his influence was known. It was COLUM, better known as COLUMBA, the son of Feidlimyd, the son of Fergus, and reputed the descendant of an Irish king. By his mother, he was connected with some of the early rulers of the western parts of Scotland, and was thus, according to tradition, related to the royalties of two kingdoms. But Columba was happily one of those who know that there is something to be won which is better than the crowns of earth. He had learned to weigh such things in the just balance, and when offered some position of honour or of wealth by Sigbert, king of France, the devoted man was able to decline it, and say, " It is not right that one who has relinquished his own riches for the name of Christ, should accept of the wealth of others." He had early caught the spirit of Moses when he sojourned at the court of Pharaoh, and made his choice between the shadow and the substance, and prizing the cross of Christ more than royal blood, or a golden diadem, he resolved to devote his life to eternity and not to time.

When Columba appeared among those who chose the better part, the Church of Christ was sinking fast into those corruptions which at length all but extinguished the heavenly light. It was the Church, and not the Saviour, that was becoming the prominent object of man's confidence or regard. It was the priest, and not the truth. It was forms and ceremonies, not the grace which came by Jesus Christ, that had become the hope, or the religion of many in every land. Columba saw this, and, to a considerable extent, escaped from the corruptions of his age. There *was* superstition mixed up with his creed, and even in him we can trace the vitiating effects of the practices which were becoming rife. In many respects, however, he stoutly resisted the growing corruptions. He became a light shining in a dark place, even a burning and a shining light, and it may exhibit the beneficial effects of religious decision, as well as illustrate an otherwise dark period of our national annals, if we glance at the chief incidents in the life of this unwearied friend of truth—this man as prompt and decisive in action, as he was holy and grand in his aims.

While still a boy, Columba obtained from one of his teachers the name of saint, and his youthful decision appears to have been indeed remarkable, even though we make a large allowance for the partiality of admiring biographers. The wild times, and the wild land in which he lived, helped to render him more and more decided in pressing along his chosen path, and his early zeal was whetted by a residence in the monastery of Clon on the banks of the Shannon. While there, his mind was strongly turned towards the western parts of Scotland. He accordingly left his native country, perhaps about his twenty-seventh year; but even then his energetic character had stamped itself on all with whom he had held intercourse: indeed, his fame had already spread over a great part of Ireland, and he left behind him there some lasting traces of his power.

It was not likely that one so prompt and so emphatic even in youth, as to resign the pomp or the power of royalty for the sake of doing good, would be long without an object on which to concentrate his energies, and Columba soon

found a congenial outlet for them all. Moved, we know
not how, he resolved to visit his mother's native land,
with the design, it is believed, of making the gospel more
extensively known in those parts. It was about the year 563
that, after attempting to settle in Oronsay, he reached the
island of Iona, which had long been known as the isle of
the Druids. It was in such lonely retreats along the shores
of our island, that those pagans practised their bloody
rites, and some remains of those ages still attest that Iona
was one of their asylums. Thither, at least, Columba was
conveyed in a frail bark formed of osiers covered with the
hides of wild beasts. His arrival took place in the year
564 or 565. He and his twelve friends, whose names are
carefully preserved along with his own, found some of the
Druids still existing there, and those fierce islanders employed both art and menace to prevent him from settling in
Iona—soon to become I-colm-kil, the island of Colum's cell.
The rude natives also resisted the missionary on the adjoining mainland, and more than once endangered his life. The
king, a Pict, further attempted to repress him. On one
occasion a village, where Columba was resting for the
night, was set on fire, and on another a savage rushed upon
him with a spear, with the design of destroying him. But
Columba had a mission : he *would* perform it, and though,
like all who would do good, he had to advance through
antagonism to success, he did advance till his zeal, his devotedness, his prudence, and the truth which he taught,
secured his triumph alike over the ferocity of the savage,
and the wiles of the Druids. The shores of Iona became
vocal at length with hymns to the glory of the Deliverer
who came out of Zion to turn away iniquity from men.

Such was the progress which Columba made, amid difficulties which would have caused less decided men to quail,
that he soon obtained a grant of the island from its Pictish

king, and there laid the foundation of an influence which is
scarcely yet exhausted. Indeed, we may question if any
spot on the face of the earth, so insulated and sequestered,
ever sent forth such streams of light, such showers of blessings, as did that lonely island—but let us notice how
Columba proceeded to lay the foundation for such results.

First, in regard to his own deportment, he was resolute
in carrying out the purposes of his youth. So devoted was
he that it is recorded he was "second to none after the
apostles." He slept on the ground with a stone for his pillow,
to "keep the body under;" and though some of the results
of the papal superstition, then struggling for the ascendant,
might appear in certain of his doings, he shone conspicuous
for his graces yet more than for his royal lineage. In
season and out of season he was zealous in advancing what
his heart was set upon, and in that work, "He prayed and
read; he wrote and taught; he preached and redeemed the
time." He visited from house to house, and even from
kingdom to kingdom. The Pictish king, who had before
been Columba's enemy, was converted, with many of his
people. Manuscripts of the Scriptures and other books
were conveyed to Iona. A school of theology was founded
there, and, ere long, a bright missionary spirit breathed
over the place, the blessed result of one man's devotion, his
earnestness and energy in his great life-work. Iona, in
short, is fast becoming "the light of the western world." A
speck, scarcely visible above the surface of the sea, is about
to be made the Jerusalem of the west, for God on high had
guided thither one man who was as resolute for eternity as
others in general are for time.

Nor is this very wonderful. Columba, we repeat, carried
his energy of character into his devotion as well as his
public life. Whatever he undertook, it was in a spirit of
the meekest dependence. When starting on a journey he

always "took God with him." If he saw what was destined for the food of men, he paused to bless it as it passed,
and a barn stored with grain was sure to draw forth the
thanksgiving of this good man. In brief, by sea or by
land, when meeting his friends, or when parting with them,
every deed was consecrated by devotion. When he gave
counsel to those who asked it, he never omitted what alone
could render his advice really profitable,—namely, prayer
to the Great Wisdom. Thus guided by the truth of God,
and firmly declining every counsellor who opposed it, Columba
walked in the light of Heaven. The way which he took was
that of safety and assured triumph ; and if it be true that he
sometimes added the night to the day in studying revealed
truth, we see in that at once an illustration of Columba's
character, and an explanation of his success. He was a
man of prayer, and, therefore, a man of power.

It is often noticed that superstition lays its hand on its
victims at their birth, and never leaves them till they are in
the grave—if possible not even then. Popery, for example,
takes its stand by the cradle of infancy, as well as haunts
the bedside of the hoary-headed—nay, even beyond death, it
does not relax its terrible grasp. And Hinduism, in like
manner, enters into the very existence of a Hindu. He
is so fenced round by it, that if he swerve from its iron
laws, he is forthwith deserted by those who love him best.
Father, mother, wife, child, brethren, all forsake him, or
give him up as dead. To touch him, and still more to eat
with him, is degradation—so completely is the whole man,
body and soul, subject to that dire idolatry. Now, what
superstition thus does for its victims, Columba tried to do
in regard to truth. He sought to mix it up with all that he
did. It was to him an all-pervading, ever-present influence ;
and is not that just pure and undefiled religion ?

Or again, if we look for yet more exact details, they may

be found in Columba's endeavour to spread the Scriptures of truth in the regions where he dwelt. Upon that the energies of his mind were intensely bent. There was no printing then, and no copy of the word of God could be obtained, but such as had been copied by men's hands. Columba himself became a devoted copyist of Scripture, both that he might set an example, and that the words which make men wise might be more open to all. He transcribed, we read, no fewer than three hundred books with his own hand, a work which may be said to exceed the labour of *composing* as many, of a certain class, in our day. To the end of his life this true philanthropist continued thus employed, and only a few hours before his death, he was engaged in copying the Psalter. In consequence of these and similar measures, so great did the influence of Columba at last become that princes were his fast allies. He was an arbiter in their disputes, and on one occasion, was chosen to place the Scottish crown upon the head of Aidan. He, in short, was one of those who knew no fear that could quell him, or no favour that could bribe him. His eager aim was to bring man's mind into contact with God's truth; that done, Columba felt that a heavenly influence was employed to promote a heavenly result, and no favourite occupation—neither his acquirements as a poet, nor his likings as a writer, were allowed to interfere with this master object of his life. "Give thyself wholly to these things," was obeyed by Columba, if ever by any.

And the plans of this man were as comprehensive, as his firmness and decision in carrying them out were praiseworthy. He was one of those rare souls who win, or who awe all that come within the sphere of their influence, and who can use as instruments what other minds might encounter as enemies. Under the fostering care of such a man, Iona became so famous as a place for study, that youth from all parts resorted thither, many of whom, like himself, were employed in copying books, while, as the result, Christian missionaries went forth to diffuse the light of heaven among the dark surrounding places. They not merely pervaded Scotland, but penetrated far into England; and if we bear in mind the age, the hindrances and trials of this man's lot, there is scarcely a greater wonder in the history of the past than the influence of Iona under its great missionary Columba.

But all humanizing influences, as well as those of literature and religion, were employed. The orchards of the island produced abundance of fruit—the fields were covered, and the barns were stored with grain, and while we read of such things in such an age, and at such a place, scepticism begins to question, Is this not the creation of fancy instead of the reality of fact? Yet, all these were the undoubted result of the personal ascendency of one wise spirit evermore seeking to promote the chief end of man. It is of such men that patriots are made, and whether it be to discover unknown shores, to tame savage hordes, or spread the hope of glory where the shadows of the second death prevail, the influence which went forth from Columba and his sacred isle was just what was required; he attempted great things and he succeeded. By firm determination on the one hand, and invariable gentleness on the other, he made his strong will felt wherever his power was put forth. Often, amid his attempts to spread the light, he was thwarted by the ignorance, or repelled by the coldness of those to whom he sought to do good. But as he did not live for man's smile, but God's, he could endure all things, and move calmly forward to fulfil his high embassy from heaven. Severe against sin, but gentle to all besides, he held on his intrepid way till he saw the darkness of paganism superseded by the radiance of truth.

And who, in our land of free thought, does not connect
all this devotedness with the zeal which truth produced at
Iona? Its sages knew nothing of the more modern figments
of Romanism, and would not submit to Rome. Prayers for
the dead, mid-day tapers, auricular confession, and similar
corruptions, were either utterly unknown or steadfastly resisted. It was the Bible and not the priest that was the
light of that lonely isle, and with the brightness of the
Aurora, but with far more than its steadfastness, did
Columba and his companions spread the truth which they
all loved so well.

It is time, however, to gather up the fruits of this good
man's labours. So bent was he on making the world better
by his sojourn in it, that his hand was open as day to
deeds of charity and compassion, and one who was at once
so gentle in his affections, and so unflinching when the
truth of God was concerned, left footprints behind him
which it is easy to trace.

When death drew near, it found Columba copying the
Psalter. He had just written the words, " They that seek
the Lord shall not lack any good thing," when he suddenly
paused. His work was nearly finished, and the last sentiment which he transcribed from the book which he loved,
was true of his own life.—The first aspect in which we
may regard him is that of a great missionary hero. He
knew what could do good to a sin-laden world,—the truth
of God, and sought, with all his heart, to spread it. Like
other God-sent men—the stars of the spiritual firmament,
as the Saviour is the Sun—Columba's devotedness and zeal
dispelled clouds of ignorance, and superseded despair by
hope. In spite of incipient corruptions then creeping into
the Church, he spread the light almost as untainted as when
it issued from the great central Fountain. From the parent

Institution at Iona others arose at Abernethy, Lochleven, St. Andrew's, Brechin, Dunblane, Kirkcaldy, Culross, Melrose, Inchcolm, and elsewhere,—each in its turn a centre of influence for good,—nay, far beyond these limits that influence is well known to have spread. Orkney felt it, and even in snowy Iceland traces of the ascendency of Iona, its great missionary and his followers, were found. Different parts of the British Isles were thereby won to the truth. The Saxons of Northumberland, as well as the inhabitants of other places felt the spell of that island of the west; and, not content even with such spiritual conquests, missionaries went to the continent of Europe, where such was their activity that they were compared to hives of bees, or to a spreading flood—"From the nest of Columba these sacred doves took their flight to all regions," were the terms in which the dispersion was described.

And even hoary hairs did not mitigate their ardour. One of the missionaries set out for Italy when he was about seventy years of age, and another who was to exert a wide-spread influence in England, could scarcely have left Iona till his eightieth year. France, Switzerland, Germany, and even Russia, are described as profiting by its school, and scarcely anything recorded in history could more clearly manifest the supremacy of the moral over the material than the case of Columba and his successors. It was a maxim with them not merely to enlighten, but, if possible, to plant an institution like their own, in order to perpetuate the light; and Seckingen on the Rhine, Brisgau in the Black Forest, Warzburg in Thuringia, St. Gall in Switzerland, and other places are mentioned among those to which the hallowing power of truth was thus extended. It was, indeed, a goodly sight to see men issuing from their humble abodes, built, perhaps, of turf, or of osiers, in that little island, and proceeding to the north, the south, the east, and the west, to spread the

glad tidings which had come from heaven to earth, to guide
men from earth to heaven; and all this, we repeat, is to be
traced up to the life, the example, the energy, and the faith
of one self-denying man—

> " Slow, step by step, he won his winding way,
> And reached the top, and stood up victor there."

The Moses of Iona, who refused to take his place among the
royal, and preferred a home among the ransomed, was ever
the presiding influence; and had he grasped at the earthly
in preference to the heavenly, none of these things could
have happened. Had he been content to cast in his lot
with those who dwell in king's palaces, his name might have
been wrapt in perpetual oblivion twelve centuries ago. But
Columba chose wisely; he decided to follow up his choice
with firmness, and was able to found a school whence missionaries and martyrs were to convey the richest gift of
Heaven to thousands of their fellow-men. Not till about
the year 1126 were the traces of Columba swept away by
the rising tide of Popery. What he had established had for
some time, and at some places, been undergoing a gradual
corruption, and the distinction between his system and
that of Rome became fainter and fainter till, about the
time just specified, the latter triumphed. The Culdees, who
were the religious successors of Columba, were suppressed
or compelled to lurk in dens and caves, to escape from the
persecutions of that power which never yet was confronted
with the truth without attempting to weaken or obscure it.
But this noble Christian so far triumphed that his influence
spread to many lands, and for four or five centuries " the
memory of the just was blessed."

But can we read off the secret of this man's success?
Taking our place by the little *currah* or wicker boat which
landed at Iona about the year 563, contemplating the thirteen men who stepped on shore from that crazy vessel, and

tracing their leader down through several centuries and to
many lands, can we explain his influence, or tell how Columba became greater than a king? He honoured God, and
that explains the whole. With singleness of aim and simplicity of confidence he took Heaven's truth for his, and
then nothing is too great for man to dare or to accomplish.
He believed that salvation was a fact, and, in the depths of
that conviction, found impulses high and manifold to carry
him through a thousand perils, or to render him decided
amid a thousand enemies. It was the force of truth, then,
that made Columba great. It was devotedness to it that
made him repel mortal errors, yet love the souls whom these
errors ruined. Calm and resolute as he was, the energy of
conviction in that man's soul wrought like a passion, and
the result was a deathless name to Columba here, and heaven
made sure to multitudes hereafter.

We say that truth had the force of a passion, and yet he
was calm and temperate in adopting the measures which
were blessed to secure his moral triumphs. In selecting can-
didates for his missionary work, one of Columba's tests was
to ascertain the character of their mothers. He wisely judged
that if the truth which he loved so much had been early
planted in the heart, it would yet bear fruit; and when to
that inquiry he added tests which he adopted to ascertain
the aptitude and zeal of his missionaries, we obtain one
glimpse more of his sagacity, his determination not to be
thwarted in his high undertaking, if pains and prayer could
prevent disappointment. In that spirit, and with these aims,
so resolute yet so peaceful, did this devoted benefactor of
man live and labour till he was about seventy-seven years of
age. He died on the 27th of June 596.—Superstitious biographers have narrated not a little that is fabulous concerning the close of Columba's career. But dismissing such idle
legends, we only notice that in dying he evinced the same un-

swerving devotedness to duty which had signalized him from the time when he withdrew from a palace to occupy a cell. At midnight he resorted, as he was wont to do, to the church for prayer, and while there he was seized with the illness which terminated his labours and his mortal life. He had led a life of unresting earnestness,—a life which was, indeed, like one long hymn to God for all his blessings—and his last recorded act partakes of the same character—it was a persistent imitation of Him who went about doing good, and who, in the last hour of mortal conflict, exclaimed, "Father, forgive them; they know not what they do."

Such, then, is the history of another zealous man, and by his grave, if he sleeps in his own chosen isle, we may exclaim,—

> ".... They go, they triumph, they repose:
> Erewhile they fought and conquered."

—So great, indeed, was the power of Columba that he made his island-speck another Athens or another Tarsus. At the distance of more than twelve centuries, the thought of him and the effects which he produced extorted eulogies from one who was not much addicted to praise, but who exclaimed, "That man is little to be envied .... whose piety does not grow warmer among the ruins of Iona .... that illustrious island which was once the luminary of the Caledonian regions, whence savage clans and roving barbarians derived the benefits of knowledge, and the blessings of religion."

We have said little regarding the encouragement which Iona gave to science, or the stimulus to study which the example of its scholars supplied. Upon that subject some men may have entertained exaggerated notions, yet it would be difficult to over-estimate the blessings which Columba imparted by his residence there. Greece is but a speck on the map of the world, yet, from its territory, a thousand influences have gone forth to refine the sons of men while sun and moon endure. The Holy Land was but a narrow strip not two hundred miles in length, and only a few leagues in breadth—from the Jordan to the Great Sea—yet has not that country been the theatre of doings whose effects stretch into eternity, and will intensify the blessedness of the ransomed there? And so of Iona. By the untiring energies of one man, results were accomplished there over which all eternity will rejoice. The highest authority in such matters has said, "The Judaical sacerdotalism which was beginning to extend in the Church, found no support in Iona. They had forms, but not to them did they look for life. It was the Holy Ghost, Columba maintained, that made a servant of God. When the youth of Caledonia assembled around the elders on those savage shores, or in their humble chapel, these ministers of the Lord would say to them, 'The Holy Scriptures are the only rule of faith. Throw aside all merits of works, and look for salvation to the grace of God alone. Beware of a religion which consists of outward observances; it is better to keep your heart pure before God than to abstain from meats. One alone is your Head, Jesus Christ.'" *

Now all that began when Columba decided that whatever others might do he would live for eternity; and were such decision more common than it is, man would be more blessed, and the world less dark. It is not its stately ruins, it is not its fabulous library, it is not the tombs of forty-eight Scottish kings, of eight monarchs from Norway, of four from Ireland, and one from France, whom legend upon legend describes as buried there, that render this island illustrious. It is the fact that the indomitable Columba made it his home, and the glory which has radiated thence is of the kind which never fades away.

M. D'Aubigné.

As we wander along the gloomy galleries of the catacombs near Rome, and try to recall the scenes which have been witnessed there—the misery endured, or the consolations felt —strange memories rise up before the mind. The senseless babble of attendant monks, or the disgusting spectacles got up by modern superstition, may repel for a time. But when the mind has become self-possessed in such a place, and has adjusted itself, like the pupil of the eye, to the medium around it, crowding recollections come up from the past: it is one of the scenes where mind signally asserts its superiority over the body. There some men became more bold and decided for truth, while crowds in the daylight world above were thirsting for their blood. There one utterance of Him whose words were spirit and life, separated men from the perishing, as if by a great gulf, and nerved them to endure till even persecution grew weary. There many were "laid to sleep in Jesus," many found death the birth-moment of eternal life, and rose triumphant above all the agonies which malignity could inflict. Now, how blessed the resurrection of such men! How different the scene amid which they will awake from that amid which they "fell asleep!" But, over the whole world, there will be a similar resurrection, and Iona will, doubtless, send forth not a few to take their place among the white-robed. And will such a place be *mine?* The resurrection of the saved? or the resurrection of the lost?

III.—JOHN HUSS.

A.D. 1369—1415.

"And when recording History displays
Feats of renown, though wrought in ancient days;
Tells of a few stout hearts that fought and died,
Where duty placed them, at their country's side;
The man that is not moved with what he reads,—
That takes not fire at their heroic deeds,—
Unworthy of the blessings of the brave,
Is base in kind, and born to be a slave."

COWPER.

His birth—His studies—And first work—His purposes—The influence of Wickliff—Huss's difficulties increase, and his firmness—He is summoned to appear before the pope—Indulgences—Huss is laid under the ban of Rome—He retires from Prague—His writings—His resolution—Returns to Prague—Proceeds to Constance—His treatment there—Imprisonment in Castle of Gottleben—His trial—His deportment—His degradation—And death.

SOME of the fairest scenes in nature have been rendered revolting by association with human ferocity, or vileness. The lake and city of Constance belong to that class. Few can visit that mouldering city, which now contains only about an eighth part of the population which it counted in the fifteenth century—5300, instead of 40,000—without admiring the calm beauty of the present, and lamenting the atrocities which stain its past.

JOHN HUSS, a reformer before the Reformation, and the martyr of Constance, was born on the 6th of July 1369. His birth-place was Hussinetz, a village of Bohemia. His parentage was humble, and his early toils and privations formed the school in which he was trained for future hardships and sufferings. He studied at the university of

Prague; and some of his teachers were men somewhat in advance of their age. In the year 1396 Huss received his master's degree, and began to lecture in his university in 1398. In 1400 he was appointed Confessor to the Queen of Bohemia; and in 1401 he became President of the philosophical faculty of Prague. The corruptions of his day, especially among the Romish priesthood, early suggested deep thoughts to this ardent man, and he found a few who were like-minded with himself among those who resided at Prague. Some of these entered into an arrangement for spreading truth as purely as it was then known; Huss was chosen their preacher, and there, in a place appropriately called "Bethlehem," or the House of Bread, he "refreshed the common people with the bread of holy preaching." The impression which he produced was profound. A fervent love, a holy life, glowing appeals, and a gentle manner, all helped to make him a master in grace, but soon brought him into collision with dark, mediaeval minds. He came into close contact with the people's wants on the one hand, and the worse than worthlessness of the reigning superstitions on the other; and a nature already ardent and intrepid became more ardent and intrepid still. It is the early decision of John Huss that no corruption shall be spared. False miracles, unholy lives, with all the lying vanities of that age, shall be swept away, if by any right means he can free his fellow-men from bonds.

Here, then, is another decided and heroic man who has entered the ranks of the friends of truth. He will have much to do and much to endure,—his patron will become his persecutor, and his friends will cast him out,—if he is to assail the corruptions of the year 1400. But Huss was not the man to be damped by danger. His only inquiry was, What is duty?—he will do it at all hazards, and let us consider how; for in considering it, we see another example of

the need of heroic decision in a world like ours, if man
would really benefit his brother man.

Huss, then, attacked the lying wonders of his Church with
withering power, and exposed them with merciless honesty.
He took his appeal to the eternal standard—God's—in every
disputed case. Pilgrimages he helped to put down. With
Augustine to guide his studies, and Wickliff to quote in the
pulpit, he waxed bolder and bolder; and as a close connection then existed between England and Bohemia,—for a
princess of the latter was married to Richard II.,—he was
encouraged and countenanced by those who resorted from
Oxford and elsewhere to Prague. As early as the year 1391,
the Bohemian reformer was studying the works of the great
Englishman of that age; and all these things helped to urge
him forward in the path in which he resolved to move.
An archbishop might thwart him, and try to put him down.
A whole university might oppose some of his measures.
Wickliff's books might be burned, and loud remonstrances
be heard. As a result, students, variously estimated at from
5000 to 44,000, might forsake the university of Prague. But
unmoved by such commotions, Huss went boldly forward.
He wished the truth of God to be paramount in his native
land, and neither priest nor potentate could stay his resolute
endeavour. Firm, yet gentle,—decided, yet calm,—he was
not to be daunted by any mortal power, and he thus became
the fit harbinger of a spiritual revolt from an oppression
which was both dark and grinding.

But intrepid as he was, Huss needed all his intrepidity.
One of his friends was first thrown into prison, and then
banished for his boldness; and Huss had to appeal to the
archbishop, the chief agent in the persecution. "What is
this," he cried, "that men stained with innocent blood,—
men guilty of every crime,—shall be found walking abroad
with impunity, while humble priests, who spend all their

efforts to destroy sin, ... are cast into dungeons as
heretics, and must suffer banishment for preaching the
gospel?"   But Huss will soon have other reasons for indulging such righteous indignation.   He has entered the
arena to contend against the corruptions of the clergy, and
he must suffer—he must die.   What else could any man
expect, who dared to preach that Rome was the seat of
Antichrist, and that her priests were too often a blot and a
disgrace?

This eager advocate for truth was silenced, that he might
no longer mislead the people ; and the authority of a papal
bull was the pretext.   Wickliff's books were burned by the ·
Archbishop of Prague, Huss all the while opposing that step
with all his might.   "Such burning," he said, "never removed a single sin from the hearts of men ;" and as that
was now the chief end of his labours, the violent procceding
of his enemies pained, without, however, repressing him.
Having taken his stand avowedly on the authority, the
example, and the word of "The Truth," this decided man
grew more and more resolute from day to day.   Fighting
with worldly men for a pure revelation, Huss had solemnly
to say, ". . . . I avow it to be my purpose to defend the
truth which God has enabled me to know, and especially
the truth of the Holy Scriptures, even to death." . . . "And
if the fear of death should terrify me, still I hope in my
God, and in the assistance of the Holy Spirit, that the Lord
himself will give me firmness."   The deep presentiment of
death was long rooted in his mind, as if he had felt
assured that he could not both hold the truth which saves
and be tolerated by men who were ignorant of its power, or
sought to extinguish its light.

But matters at length reached a crisis.   Cardinal Otto di
Colonna was empowered to try the case of Huss, who was
summoned to appear before the pope at Bologna ; and all

Bohemia was roused by that step. The future martyr was
not permitted to go—it would have been to sacrifice his
life. Meanwhile Queen Sophia used her influence on his
behalf. The king wrote to the pope and the cardinal in his
favour. He demanded liberty for Huss to preach, and insisted that all actions against him should cease, so that for
a while the persecution was stayed. But at last Huss was
pronounced a heretic ; and now he is one stage nearer to
Constance and the funeral pile. On the way, however, he
could exclaim, " Where I see anything at variance with the
doctrines of Christ, I will not obey, though the stake were
staring me in the face." That was his maxim all through
life; and in such an age such heroism in such a cause was
the harbinger of death.

At one stage of these life and death struggles, Huss had
to do battle against a whole theological faculty; and that
and similar contests trained him to a boldness and decision, which was constantly growing. But he had now to
separate, for the truth's sake, from friends whom he had
prized through life. His pathway, indeed, is gradually
becoming more narrow, as well as more rough—he is one
of those who must often walk alone. The hateful things
called Indulgences were now attacked by him in public dis-
putations. Declining to make the Church supreme, Huss
placed himself on " the immovable foundation, the corner-
stone . . . . . our Lord Jesus Christ," and is accordingly in
unconscious collision with the whole Romish system. His
pleading was in direct opposition alike to its creed and its
practice ; and he was either a marvellously bold or a marvellously ignorant man, thus to throw himself across the path
of a proud mortal who claimed to be higher than the Highest. The bull of the Pope regarding Indulgences was publicly burned at Prague, after being paraded through the city
in an indecent procession. Huss had a queen for one of his

disciples, and an adherence of nobles, knights, and others, who were counted by thousands; but such boldness as his could not be much longer endured, and he must first suffer, and then die.

About this period some of his friends were condemned to death because they objected to Indulgences, and Huss took up their cause. He hastened to the Senate House, and pled for the three condemned men. He made their danger his own, and declared that he, the teacher, not they, the disciples, should die. In spite of his efforts, and in violation of promises given that no blood should be shed, his three friends were hurried to execution; and what could be the result of that step, but a more intense antagonism, a more resolute decision? On a subsequent occasion, accordingly, Huss appeared before the king and his Council, to defend what he reckoned the right. He offered, with characteristic ardour, to be bound to die at the stake if he did not make good his views, provided his eight opponents would do the same. But all other struggles were soon merged in the great conflict with Rome itself. The pope had determined to put down Huss, and he was excommunicated with the most terrible of papal forms. If he did not submit in twenty days, the ban was to be proclaimed against him in all churches: all who harboured him were to be laid under an interdict, and Huss himself was to be burned according to law.—She who has often been drunk with the blood of the saints is surely preparing to lap !

Parties in power now assembled to seize Huss and demolish his church, as they were ordered to do. But the measure was too bold. "They feared the people," and for a time he escaped. He appealed from Rome to "the one incorruptible, just, and infallible Judge, Jesus Christ;" and this he boldly announced from his pulpit, though at the time no sacraments could be administered, no burial permitted, no

church function performed in Prague, owing to the pressure
of the ban against him. Attempts were made to heal the
breach, but in vain, for Huss was not to be swayed by anything but the word of God. Strong behind that breast-
work, he resisted a papal interdict, the royal urgency, and
all the pleadings of the officials of Rome.

The King of Bohemia had urged Huss to leave Prague
for a time, in the hope that peace might thus be restored.
He complied, and, like Luther in the Wartburg, in the Castle
of Kozi-hradek wrote some of his most important works.
Never was more determined courage displayed by any man
in similar circumstances than by Huss in that castle. In
spite of danger, he drew the line between Christ and Antichrist more broadly than ever, and though he was only
erecting his own scaffold, or heaping up faggots to consume
himself, he did not flinch from following wherever he was
led by truth. He is making it plainer and plainer how the
world must be won to God if it is ever won at all.

Huss has hitherto been led by a way which he scarcely
knew. He had no purpose to cause a disruption in the
Romish Church; yet he is every day drifting nearer and
nearer to that result, and must soon be confronted with
her terrific powers, leagued to crush him and his cause. So
clear are his views upon many points, and so bold his mode
of presenting them, that we are saddened by the thought
that so little progress has been made during the past four
hundred years, in developing the right idea of the Church,
beyond what Huss had reached. But having reached it, he
calmly and intrepidly took up his ground. "I will resist
to the death," he vowed, "all agreement with falsehood. Let
the world flow on as the Lord permits it to flow; a good
death is better than a bad life. One ought never to sin
through fear of death," and that defiant speaker will soon
be put to the proof. Yet in the prospect he remained un-

ruffled. "I assure you," he wrote to a friend, "that persecution would not trouble me . . . . if my sins did not."
Indeed, the whole demeanour of this intrepid man is such
as to strike a reflective mind with awe, at the sight of so
much calmness amid such agitations—such decision amid
so much that might have overwhelmed him.

From his hiding-place Huss often went abroad, and
preached to the crowds who flocked to hear him; but the
Council of Constance is now at hand, for we are referring
to the year 1414, and he is to proceed thither under a safe-
conduct from Sigismund, Emperor of Germany, with the
assurance that if he could not submit to the decision of the
Council, the emperor would send him back unharmed to
Bohemia. This was an opportunity for which Huss had
longed. He would now, he thought, deliver his message and
uphold the truth before assembled potentates, and proceeded
to Prague to prepare for the Council.* He there publicly
challenged all his opponents to convict him of error if they
could, and proved that he was valiant for the truth as long
as he was free.

Huss set out for Constance on the 11th of October 1414,
with two faithful knights to protect him by the way. Even
in Germany he was cordially welcomed by many. He
courted opportunities of making known his views, and at
Nuremberg, in particular, he enjoyed such an opportunity
to the full. He reached Constance on the 3d of November,
where his enemies were busily employed, and he was
speedily posted as a vile heretic; indeed, it was soon made
plain that if he was a bold, intrepid man, he needed it
all. Officials from the pope, who was then at Constance,
desired him, as an interdicted priest, to abstain from the

---

* It should be carefully observed here, that the Emperor guaranteed to Huss
a safe journey both to Constance and from it. The words of the document are:
" Ut et transire, stare, morari, redire libere permittatis."

Church services; but he would not compromise his liberty, and declined to comply. Had he chosen even to equivocate, he might have escaped; but Huss was not the man to trim. Such a course was formally proposed to him; but though he was far from being buoyed up by false hopes, he resolutely and without hesitation declined all under- hand suggestions: he would uphold the truth, but that was all that he would do. "I fear nothing," he said; "for I hope that, after a great conflict, will ensue a great victory, and after the victory a still greater reward to me, and a still greater discomfiture to my enemies."

Huss was not kept long in suspense. He sought various opportunities of proclaiming his views: but these were all denied him. Intrigue and cunning devices were employed to deprive him of the privilege—and moreover, on the 28th of November, he was made a close prisoner. His enemies had endeavoured to entrap him, but that was resisted by his friends, and he himself at length determined to accompany the cardinals and others who had come on the treacherous errand. He dared anything when truth was at stake, and consented to place himself in their hands.

He was now confined under the care of men-at-arms. Insults began to be heaped upon him, and one of his faithful knights hastened to the Pope in the vain hope of securing the liberty of his friend. But for eight days, Huss was kept in durance, and on the 6th of December was thrown into a filthy dungeon, the victim of insult after insult. The Emperor interposed, indeed, and threatened to free him by force, but the power of the Church soon awed the Emperor, and the prisoner's trial must begin: he will need all his firm- ness now—in truth, he is already condemned. "Let the Lord Jesus be my Advocate, who also will soon be your Judge," was one of his first appeals to his persecutors, when he saw that his case was foreclosed. Enfeebled by a fever caught in his fœtid prison, and otherwise ailing, the heroic man might have succumbed. It was feared, indeed, that he would die in his dungeon, and yet, so remorseless were the men into whose hands he had fallen, that he had to prepare his defence in fetters! Never did he appear before any of his accusers without being assailed in the harshest terms, and, though he often prayed for these bitter enemies, it was not easy to subdue his ardent nature and quietly submit to be ignominiously assailed. His expressed resignation, however, was nearly perfect, while the certainty of the final triumph of truth made him brave. He would subject his mind to no trammels. He would submit to no base conditions. He protested against the whole proceedings of the Council, and took his stand once more upon the rock of truth. " The Law of Christ" was the rule which he avowed, and gloried in, however men might hate him, or hunt him to death.

It is well known that the pope fled at last from Constance, and when Huss subsequently fell into the hands of the bishop, he was removed in chains to the castle of Gottleben. By night and day he was kept chained there, and all was done that was likely to bow down, or to break the undaunted man. But though one form of disease after another assailed him, no wavering thought was harboured, no wavering word escaped: all his sorrows only led him deeper and deeper into the truth which he prized so well, and, in the face of crowding dangers, his resolution actually became more and more fixed and heroic.

The cruel mockery of justice at Constance was carried on by tribunal after tribunal; but the victim was steadfast and unmovable. Now, gleams of hope broke forth for him and his friends, and then, darkness gathered round them once more; but Huss found one thing unchanging, the word of his God—and when the Council met in the Franciscan convent, which had become the martyr's prison, formally to try

his case, they cruelly attempted to prejudge the matter
without hearing him at all. But the Emperor interfered,
and Huss appeared before them, ready to retract whatever
was contrary to Scripture, but whenever he attempted to
plead, a savage outcry arose around, till the voice of truth
was drowned in the din. On the 7th of June, he stood
forth the second time before the Council, · but it was a
wrangle rather than a solemn trial, for Huss would not
abate one jot of his convictions, except as the Scriptures
condemned them. Cardinal, and bishop, prince, and chancellor, might assail him. In some cases, his statements as
to the Redeemer's supremacy might be received, as they
were, with laughter and scorn, but the victim was still unshaken.

On the 8th of June, his third examination took place,
but it was another wrangle marked by bitter persecution on
the one side, and corresponding firmness on the other. Huss
was told, at the close, that if he would suppliantly submit
and retract opinions which he declared he never held, his
judges would be lenient—otherwise, his danger was obvious.
He was thus asked to confess his errors, to swear that he
would never more preach them, and publicly recant; but he
constantly refused such terms, unless he were convicted by
the word of God. Even the Emperor pled with him to yield;
his judges also urged him, and professed a desire for his
escape; but he was not to be moved, and must therefore hasten back to his cell, an outcast heretic in chains.
If he would recant, he would be permitted to live—but
little more, for imprisonment for life was to be his lot. But
little did those judges know either the man whom they
held in their grasp, or the principles and the power
which bore him up. He could die, but he could not be
anything but a true man, and loyal to Him who is the truth.
In the pulpit, in prison, in chains, before kings and prelates,

as well as among his friends, that truth was Huss's rock and fortress. An Emperor's safe-conduct was found to be a worthless thing, and "Trust not in princes" was a portion of the word of God which Huss learned thoroughly to understand. Though unshaken still, he must now prepare to die, and such unflinching firmness amid so much that was fitted to daunt, or to bewilder, can be ascribed only to one origin, and that a heavenly one. On the other hand, the Jesuitism, and the absence of common honesty in some who urged Huss to recant, indicate too plainly into what evil hands he had fallen. And was it not strange that that very Council deposed its demigod, the pope, shut him up in prison, and treated him more contumeliously than Huss had ever done? "The head is cut off; the earthly God is in chains, accused of sin; the fountain is dried up; the sun is eclipsed; the heart torn out . . . ." Such was the language of Huss; and was he wrong in seeking to reform a system presided over by such a head, or supported by such members?

It was with unruffled self-possession that Huss gave himself to martyrdom. As he had never abandoned the Romish Church, he calmly engaged in its functions preparatory to his death, and even chose for his Confessor one of his most envenomed persecutors. Indeed, some touching scenes were witnessed in his prison—he unshaken—his friends, his very enemies weeping like womanhood beside him. Deputation after deputation visited him—one of them from the Emperor himself—and recantation was constantly the burden of their pleading. But Huss would not recant except upon conviction; and on the 6th of July he appeared once more before the Council, where the Emperor was present on his throne. Many of the judges were Huss's bitter personal enemies, for as he had assailed the measureless corruptions of their order, that was an unpardonable sin. Besides,

history is careful to tell that bribery was largely employed
to make sure of his destruction—and now the last act of the
dark tragedy has arrived.　No further defence was permitted to Huss, yet he uttered one solemn appeal—"O
Christ, whose word is by this Council publicly condemned,
I appeal to Thee anew—to Thee who, when thou wast ill-
treated by thine enemies, didst appeal to thy Father, and
didst commit thy cause to that most righteous Judge, that
we, following thy example, might, when oppressed by injustice, take refuge in Thee."　Once and again he prayed for
his enemies.　Being clothed in his priestly robes, he was
stripped of them by seven bishops, while he still persisted
in holding fast his convictions, except as the truth of
God could be shown to condemn them.　"We give over thy
soul to the devil," were the atrocious words of his persecutors; and his rejoinder was, "I commend my soul, Christ
Jesus, into thy hands, as it was by Thee redeemed."　The
mask of his tonsure was next removed, and that with great
cruelty.　A cap daubed over with the figures of demons was
then placed on his head, and thus the heroic martyr of
Bohemia was led forth to be burned in the name of religion.

At the place of execution Huss prayed, and often repeated
the words, "Into thy hands, Lord, I commit my spirit."
When compelled to rise from his knees, he still appealed to
the Saviour, and prayed for "a strong and steadfast soul" to
endure that shameful death.　He declared that he willingly
wore his chains for Christ, who wore yet heavier bonds, even
after he was placed at the stake, and had actually been surrounded by faggots.　With his last breath he repelled a
temptation to recant, and when the fire was kindled he
began to sing with a loud voice, "Jesus, son of the living
God, have mercy upon me."　When he was repeating the
words for the third time, his voice failed; he was stifled by
the flames, and soon reduced to ashes.　These ashes were

cast into the Rhine—like Wickliff's into the Swift—and one witness more is under the altar on high—

> "Is there a God in heaven? A great white throne?
> Shall truth yet triumph? Shall the first be last?
> Then, Huss, for glory wait: *He* shall thee own
> Whose flashing justice shall thy butchers blast."

Thus perished one of the noblest men who ever walked our world. The measure of light which he had reached could not be tolerated by Romanism, and potentate and priest must therefore combine to extinguish that light. They did not, however, succeed. Oppression might persecute Huss, and priestly hatred might hurry him to the stake, but the intrepid man continued to be zealously affected in a good thing in spite of all assailants, and laid his life at last a noble and a free-will offering on the altar of truth.

Nor can we have any difficulty in gauging the unbending decision of this man's steadfast soul. First, he rose up undaunted against the corrupt practices of his age and Church. Secondly, he resisted unchristian power in every form, from that of royalty down to superstition, when truth took hold of his conscience. Thirdly, he declined to be silenced even by the ban of a Pope, and that at a time when nations quaked before it. Fourthly, he withstood the repeated solicitations of an Emperor. Fifthly, he confronted a whole Council of churchmen clamouring for his blood. Sixthly, he braved all their anathemas, and clung to the truth. Lastly, he faced the fire, and the stake, and death, and his case is another proof of God's mighty power. It tells what even weak man may become when the truth of God is his guide, and the Son of God his strength. Huss asserted what he never could enjoy in the Church of Rome,—namely, liberty of conscience ; but he manfully upheld what he claimed, at the price of his blood.

IV.—WILLIAM TYNDALE.

A.D. 1484–1535.

" Who brought the lamp that with awaking beams
Dispelled thy gloom, and broke away thy dreams?
Tradition now decrepit and worn out,
Babbler of ancient fables, leaves a doubt.
But still light reached thee. . .

" But Rome with sorceries and magic wand
Soon raised a cloud that darkened every land,
And thine was smothered in the stench and fog
Of Tiber's marshes and the papal bog."

COWPER.

The Bible—William Tyndale—Ascendency of Rome—Gloucestershire—Stinch-comb—Oxford and Cambridge—Little Sodbury—Tyndale's mission—His debates—Cited to answer for his opinions—Removes to London—Preaches—Goes abroad—Hamburg—Translations—Denounced at Canterbury and in London—Cologne—Alarm of heresy—Press stopped—He flees to Worms—Prints—His motives—Books landed in England—Interdicted—Burned—Persecution—Search on the Continent—Tyndale works the faster—Flees to Marburg—Patrick Hamilton—Strenuous efforts to seize Tyndale—His labours increase—John Fryth — Tyndale entrapped — Imprisoned — Strangled and burned at Vilvorde—His character and achievements.

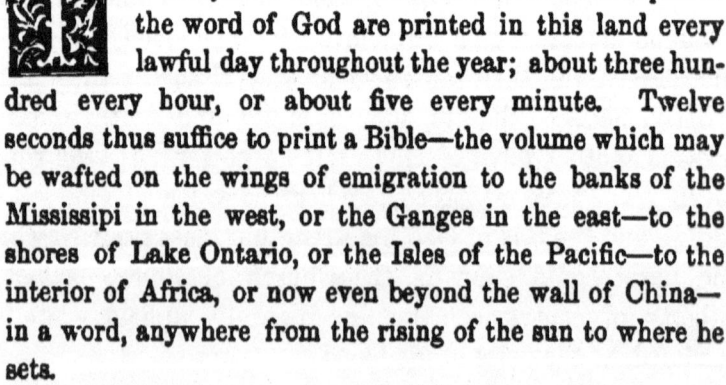

T is computed that at least three thousand copies of the word of God are printed in this land every lawful day throughout the year; about three hundred every hour, or about five every minute. Twelve seconds thus suffice to print a Bible—the volume which may be wafted on the wings of emigration to the banks of the Mississipi in the west, or the Ganges in the east—to the shores of Lake Ontario, or the Isles of the Pacific—to the interior of Africa, or now even beyond the wall of China—in a word, anywhere from the rising of the sun to where he sets.

Was it, then, always so ? Has the Bible been at all times
so accessible ? Nay, there was a time when millions who
professed a form of our faith had never seen the word of
God. It was carefully withheld from them as "poison,"
just as it continues to be from millions still. A dark superstition sealed up that Book which would at once, as if by a
flash of light, annihilate all human corruptions. They are
doomed by it to destruction ; and hence, in self-defence, men
silence or seal up what has come to shed the light of heaven
on the dark places of the earth.

But a man was raised up to break both the silence and
the seal, to spread abroad the perfume of the precious alabaster box, and we are about to trace the career of that
man from his birthplace to his stake. He was indomitable
in resolution, powerful in speech, enterprising in spirit, and
not to be repressed or turned from his purpose, by the frown
of the persecutor, or even the terrors of death.

WILLIAM TYNDALE was born about the year 1484,
when Rome was ascendant in this island, for though
Wickliff and his followers had greatly disturbed the followers of the pope, no effectual check had been given to
a system whose beginning, whose middle, and whose end
is death. So far from being curbed, the agents and upholders of Rome were never more bold than about the
period now mentioned. Under Henry VIII. and Cardinal
Wolsey, the Papacy may be said to have been enthroned in
England : Rome was enriched from this country, and the
popes deemed England "a garden of delight, an unexhausted
well." Romish priests farmed out the one, they poisoned
the other, and kept the nation, financially and religiously,
in a condition akin to serfdom. The Annate, or first-fruits
payable by all ecclesiastics, eked out the papal exchequer.
There was the appeal to Rome, and the dispensation from
it—with the Indulgence, the Legantine levy, the mortuary,

the pardon, the Ethelwolf's pension, the Peter's pence for every chimney that smoked in England, the pilgrimage, the tenth, besides the sale of relics and other trash from Rome, all taxing at once men's means and their conscience, all pressing upon them from birth, baptism, and the cradle, to the sick-bed, the moment of death, the grave, and even the eternal world.

As one example, we may point to Gloucestershire and Worcestershire as the very centre of Popish influence, because they were then among the richest regions in the land. From the year 1497, to the year 1534, the bishops who ruled there were all Italians—four of that nation in unbroken succession there extorted wealth, and bore it off to Rome. And not merely was wealth extorted—it was done in a manner which augmented crime, which degraded men, and turned the realm of England into a match for Italy itself in corruption. There was, in truth, a bounty offered upon crime by the facility with which pardon could be purchased.

A man was needed, then, to resist these agencies of death. He must be at once daring and prompt, gentle and wise— awing by the one, attracting by the other; and exactly such a man appeared. In France, Lefevre; in Switzerland, Zuingli; in Germany, Luther—had arisen and begun to break the spell of Rome, and one like-minded with them arose in England. His native county, it has been said, " had fallen like a ripe fig into the mouth of the eater," an Italian bishop; and just while things were at the worst or the darkest, William Tyndale was born at Stinchcomb, or more probably at North Nibley, within the Hundred of Berkely. His origin and parentage it is somewhat difficult to trace with precision, nor does our purpose require it. Enough to know that at the set time he appeared, and his coming realized in a nobler sense than the monkish saying meant,

that God was in Gloucestershire. Efforts have been made
to connect William Tyndale with some of the nobles of our
land, but his truest patent is to be sought in his work.
His forefathers had taken part in the wars between the
houses of York and Lancaster; but we need not trace his
lineage: it is with himself we have to do; and we shall
forthwith find that he was precisely a man for his times, at
once acted on by them and acting upon them in return. He
was, indeed, a hero of the highest type, for why should that
title be reserved for warriors alone? The truth has its heroes
as well as the sword, and Tyndale was one of them.

He was educated at Oxford, where he began his Scriptural studies, and not merely welcomed the truth in some
degree himself, but, moreover, instructed others in the more
excellent way. True, he had to stand alone and unfriended,
but, in the right sense, he was self-upheld and self-guided, a
man of inflexible perseverance from his youth up, and needing it all. His zeal, however, soon carried him in advance
of Oxford toleration. He was in consequence exposed to
danger, and removed to Cambridge, where he resided for
some time; but had to flee from it as he had previously
done from Oxford. Competent judges pronounce his
attainments in Greek and Hebrew to have been just such
as were required to fit him for translating the Scriptures.
Altogether, Tyndale was in advance of his age; he was
marking the signs of his times—at least from the year 1517,
when he lectured at Oxford, and had to leave it for his
opinions—so that he unconsciously walked abreast with
Luther and others in the mighty work of rescuing the
nations from that incubus which pressed them down to the
second death—the superstition of Rome. He retired from
the universities, and became for a time tutor at Little Sodbury, where he diligently pursued his chosen career.

And what was it? What was the master object of this

man's life? He was one of those energetic men who are as
sure to leave their mark upon their age as the seal is sure
to impress the molten wax. What, then, was the special
direction which the energies, the decision, and the inflexible
perseverance of Tyndale had taken? It was to translate
the Scriptures, especially the New Testament, into English.
He had marked at Sodbury and elsewhere how the people
were kept in ignorance of the truth, as he himself had had
to abandon Oxford and Cambridge on account of the discoveries which shed light upon his mind. At the mansion where he resided, abbots, achdeacons, and deans were
wont to visit, and with them and others he debated, and
not seldom exposed the abuses which prevailed. "To con-
fute their errors and confirm his sayings, he often appealed
to the great, but then dishonoured arbiter, the word of God,"
and at last, the future martyr's views caused these dignitaries
to be less frequently invited to Sodbury Hall. As that was
ascribed to his influence, it combined with other things to
exasperate and provoke them. The storm, in short, is gathering, and the bold man will soon need all his boldness.
"A thousand books," he said, "they would rather see put
forth against their abominable doings and doctrines, than
that the Scriptures should come to light . . . . which
thing only moved me," he adds, "to translate the New
Testament." He saw that unless the people had the Scriptures in their mother tongue, they could be led captive by
superstition at its will. The manner in which the priests
"juggled with the text," deepened the conviction, and fortified the decision of Tyndale—the Scriptures must be translated, and he prepared to do it.

Having thus taken up a position full in front of those
enemies of the truth, Tyndale was not long left unmolested.
He was warned to appear before the Chancellor of the
diocese of Worcester, and now he must either recant or

become bold as a lion. On his way to the tribunal, he, Luther-like, cried heartily to God to give him strength to stand fast in the truth. He had hitherto been "turmoiled," he says, but now a crisis appears to have arrived, and he must throw down the gauntlet. Is he ready?

Quite. The Chancellor might threaten and revile him; he might be "rated as though he nad been a dog;" but Tyndale's mind was made up. He knew what he had believed, and Dr. Thomas Parker, the Chancellor, surrounded as he was by "all the priests of the country," could not shake the steadfastness of one who was apparently unfriended and alone. The bishop of that diocese was Julio dei Medici, afterwards Clement VII.—and with such a master, the servants were fiery and zealous. Their victim, however, was firm. His life-purpose was formed, and the doings of that day confirmed it more and more. "I defy the pope," he said, on a future occasion, "and if God spare my life, ere many years I will cause the boy that drives the plough to know more of the Scripture than you do." But this only increased the murmurs of the priesthood, and Tyndale must therefore take another step in advance. He knew that his life was now in jeopardy, and resolved to leave Sodbury to seek some safer spot, where he might give himself to the only work equal to the wants of the times—the translation of the Word of God. He knew by anticipation,—

> "That Indian dreamers tell of animals
> On which the world rests, while yet, in earnest truth,
> It rests upon a Book—the Book of books."

Tyndale, at least, rested there. He had perhaps already begun the work of translation, and now proceeded from Sodbury to London, to seek the counsel of Tunstal, its notorious bishop, the friend of darkness and all superstitions.

Tyndale's sojourn in London was the means of preparing him more and more for his work. As the truth was then

rising in its influence, those who loved God's simple word
began to be hunted out as heretics. Men in power thought
once more of burning not merely books, but their authors;
and at such a time Tyndale could not be safe. Yet he
preached for some time at St. Dunstan's in the west;
and while there, a neglected and an obscure individual,
who would have thought that he was soon to agitate the
hierarchy of England,—that he was to rouse the wrath of its
imperious king, and shed the light of heaven upon the darkest places of the land? Such, however, was the work given
him to do. He was one of the men who choose their course
wisely, who enter on it firmly, who pursue it steadfastly,
and refuse alike to be quelled by opposing enmity, or diverted
by secondary cares. We shall see how God blessed him in
his deed.

As dangers thickened, Tyndale retired beyond seas, his
heart still fixed, and his hand still engaged in his life-work,
that of giving the Scriptures to the people of England, in
the tongue which they could read. He proceeded most probably to Hamburg, and there for some time prosecuted the
work with as much dispatch as numerous difficulties and
hindrances would allow. The Gospels of Matthew and
Mark were first ready, and were published before the rest
of the New Testament; but if Tyndale was zealous, his antagonists were not less eager. The Archbishop of Canterbury,
and the Bishop of London denounced his translations as
early as the year 1526, and so diligent was the search that
was made for them, so frequent the flames which consumed
them, that only one copy of these books is known to exist in
a perfect state.

Leaving Hamburg, Tyndale's next residence was at
Cologne. This was early in the year 1525, and with characteristic promptitude he began to print his New Testament in that city. Not far had he proceeded, however,

when an alarm of heresy was raised, and the work was interdicted. Collecting the sheets he had printed, Tyndale
hastened up the Rhine, to Worms, already half Lutheran,
there to carry on his work with diminished risk to it and to
himself. His zeal was not damped, nor his resolution
affected by these persecutions. On the contrary, it is believed that he now printed two editions of the New Testament instead of one. John Cochlæus, whose enmity to
Tyndale and his work was fierce and fiery, tried to check
him, and seemed as bent upon preventing translation as
the Englishman in promoting it. The Romanist, in the
spirit of his order, gloried in his enmity to the diffusion of
truth in any vernacular tongue. Attack after attack was
published, for he assailed with fury all who dared to make
"the way of life" more patent. The English "apostate,"
as Cochlæus tells us, designed to publish six thousand
copies of the New Testament, but was contented with
three thousand, for the incensed devotee had influence to
stop the printing, though not to silence truth. By bribing
workmen, and by the potency of wine among officials, he discovered the plans which had been formed for sending the
truth of God to down-trodden England; and for a time
appeared to triumph in suppressing it. The king, Cardinal
Wolsey, and the Bishop of Rochester, were warned to "take
care lest that most pernicious article of merchandise (meaning the Word of God) should be conveyed into all the ports
of England."

But the word of God was not bound. On his arrival at
Worms, Tyndale did not lose an hour in prosecuting his work.
He had to change the size of his New Testament because an
edition had been detected, described, and put under priestly
ban; but that was a slight inconvenience to one so devoted
as Tyndale, and in spite of all prohibitions, of hostile mani-
festoes, and even Archbishop Warham's keen denunciation,

followed by that of Bishop Tunstal, these translations were
known, read, and rejoiced over, both in Scotland and in England, during the year 1526. Two editions passed through
the press at the same time, for this man of God thoroughly
understood the importance of His Word, alike to nations and
to individuals. At a period somewhat subsequent to that to
which we now refer, when men were hunting for Tyndale
over the Continent, he made it known to the English ambassador that if Henry VIII. would "grant only a bare text
of the Scriptures to be put forth among his people, he would
immediately make faithful promise never to write more."
But, failing that promise, this untiring man knew from the
Book which he loved so well, that we must obey God rather
than man, and, with his life in his hand, he determined thus
to obey.

One of his fellow-labourers and fellow-martyrs once
said, "If you will not grant this liberty to circulate the
Scripture, then will we be doing while we have breath,
and show in few words, what it doth in many, and so
at the least save some." Such was the spirit of Fryth
the martyr, and decision so firm was not to be put
down. Though such men should be reduced to ashes to-
morrow, they will circulate the Scriptures to-day. Their
zeal was yet more burning than the persecutor's pile,
and urged on by the one they could disregard the other.
Neither perplexity nor vexatious toil, neither the snares
of the crafty nor the violence of the powerful, could daunt
William Tyndale. He might have occasion to complain
of "very necessity and combraunce" (encumbrance) occasioned by the hostility of men who loved the darkness.
He might have to "beseech the learned to consider that he
had no man to follow as an example (in translating into
English), neither was holpen of any that had interpreted the
same, or such like thing in the Scripture beforetime." But

neither could these check his aspirations to spread the truth. He had given himself to that work, and he did it against all assailants.

But his motives should be described in his own words of power.—"The causes which moved me to translate," he says, in his first Address to the people of God in England, "I thought better that others should imagine than that I should rehearse them. Moreover, I supposed it superfluous; for who is so blind as to ask why light should be showed to them that walk in darkness where they cannot but stumble, and where to stumble is the danger of eternal damnation ; either so despiteful that he would envy any man (I speak not of his brother), so necessary a thing; or so bedlam-mad as to affirm that God is the natural cause of evil, and darkness to proceed out of light, and that lying should be grounded in truth and verity, and not rather clean contrary, that light destroyeth darkness, and verity reproveth all manner of lying?" This is surely the language of common sense. Strange that such sentiments should be gainsaid by any, and especially by those who profess to be exclusively the Church of Christ! But men in Tyndale's day were not to be deceived. They had once been thralls to the papacy themselves, and, after their escape, no sacrifice was too great, not even life was deemed too costly a price to pay, that the system of Rome might be unmasked, and its victims rescued. *

It was thus that Tyndale began a new era in our country; he laid the foundation of its greatness upon the truth of God. But no sooner did his books arrive in England than

* For example, Tyndale once said, "What a trade is that of the priests: they want money for everything: money for baptism, money for churchings, for weddings, for buryings, for images, brotherhoods, penances, soul-masses, bells, organs, chalices, copes, surplices, ewers, censers, and all manner of ornaments. Poor sheep! The parson shears, the vicar shaves, the parish priest polls, the friar scrapes, the indulgence-seller pares—all that you want is a butcher to flay you, and take away your skin."

they were seized wherever men could. They were condemned by Henry, by Wolsey, by Warham, and by Tunstal.
The sea-ports were guarded against their introduction.
Cochlæus and others had sent earnest warnings on the subject: but they had a spirit still more earnest to cope with.
No siege, it has been said, which Britain has ever conducted,
could furnish the tenth part of the incident, or evince half
the courage, by which this island was then assailed. From
Antwerp, or down the Rhine from Worms, through Holland,
or by some other route, bales of books were conveyed,
contraband of man, but blessed of God. They found their
way to the metropolis, to both the English universities, and
over the country at large. Merchants trafficked with them.
Students read them in secret. Earnest souls drank there
from the stream of life, hitherto a frozen mass or a stagnant
marsh to them, and in spite of fire and faggot, ban and
murder, William Tyndale's books spread in the dominions
of the ferocious Henry, if we should not rather say of the
voluptuous and unprincipled Wolsey. In truth, a fierce
crusade has begun. The atrocities of Nero and Diocletian
are to be renewed; men must be afflicted, tormented, and
slaughtered, because they *would* take their religion from
their God, and not from their fellow-creatures.

Amid all this, not a few loved not their lives unto the
death, and held by the word of God, as seamen hold by
their sheet-anchor in the storm. Bilney the martyr, Lati-
mer the martyr, Barnes the martyr, and many more woke
up from the darkness of Popery, and though the seed thus
sown bore death to the body as its fruit, the end was life
everlasting. Books were burned; so were men: but the
blood of the martyrs was the seed of the Church. A
royal mandate ordered all translations to be burned "with
further sharp correction and punishment against the
keepers and readers of the same," and it was obeyed to

the letter. After all, however, it was imbecility in collision with Omnipotence, and the result was sure. The Book was daily burned, yet it seemed daily to multiply.

In these circumstances, then, the search for the contraband Volume was transferred to the Continent, to prevent, if possible, the outflow at the fountain. Two editions of the New Testament from Worms, and a third from Antwerp were either in circulation or in the flames, and the king urged the destruction of the whole. He wrote on the subject to the Princess Margaret of Brabant, the aunt of Charles V., for it was understood that in her dominions much of the dreaded evil arose. The British envoy to those parts pressed the same suit, and the princess who " could not (she said) sufficiently praise King Henry's virtuous intentions," commanded her officers to search her dominions for the hated books, " utterly to destroy them and bring them to nought," and to proceed with all rigour against those who spread them.

Such were the great swelling words of vanity by which princes and their creatures combined against the truth of God. Wolsey lent his willing help, and copies of the Bible were dispatched to the Continent to guide the hunters in their search. Archbishops, nobles, and many of the people joined in the cry, so that the war of extermination was thickening fast. So determined were men to extinguish the light, that the British envoy actually proposed to Wolsey to " buy up all the books, or as many as he could find, and send them to him, to do his grace's pleasure." The men of Antwerp would not kindle fires so furiously as those of London desired, and the proposal, therefore, was to buy instead of burning. Antwerp, Bergen, Zealand, Ghent, Bruges, Brussels, and Louvaine were eagerly searched, and all the books that could be found were destroyed. Hackett, the envoy, told Wolsey, in one of his letters, that he had made " a good fire " of the Testaments.

But, amid these things, how was Tyndale employed? Had
the hot haste and the fiery zeal of his enemies succeeded in
repressing his exertions? On the contrary, he was issuing
edition after edition. From Henry downward all were in
full pursuit of him; but passing from one hiding-place to
another, he was despatching bale after bale to his native
land—a kind of merchandise which has enriched our island
with the produce of every country under heaven. Indeed,
the darling desire of Tyndale's heart was now in large
measure fulfilled. While yet at peace in his native country,
he had expressed the conviction that nothing but the Scriptures in their mother tongue could really establish the
people in religion; and, with all his high-souled energy,
he is trying to establish them. So early as the year 1527,
when an exile at Worms, Tyndale laid his account with
martyrdom in this cause; he said, "Some men will ask,
peradventure, Why stake the labour to make this work, (a
work entitled "The Wicked Mammon") inasmuch as they
have burned the gospel? I answer, In burning the New
Testament they did none other thing than that I looked
for; no more shall they do, if they burn me also, if it be
God's will it shall be so." Strong in that conviction, he laboured, translated, and hoped in God. No crafty jugglers,
he said, were to move him. He sent forth his winged messengers, which the very flames helped to spread, and England was moved by this poor, persecuted exile, as the leaves
of a tree are shaken by the wind.

Amid his toils, Tyndale was sometimes made merry by
the doings of his persecutors. Warham, the English archbishop, at one period purchased translations, to the value
of about £1000 of our money, on purpose to burn them. But
the profits just enabled the friend of truth to proceed more
vigorously with his next edition. Meanwhile the diocese of
London was searched, as if Tunstal had designed to sweep

it clean of the pestilent Bibles, but still the printing proceeded. Even when the workmen were imprisoned, Tyndale found others to take their place; and thus amid obstructions of every kind he pressed forward to accomplish his heart's desire. It was William Tyndale against the banded princes, but there was One with him who is more in might than even great sea billows, and the hated man was triumphant. He might have said, amid his own sleepless urgency, and his crowding enemies,—

> " Paul did not wait ; you trust in numbers, I
> Trust in One only."

While hatred to Tyndale and his labours was deepening from month to month, he was ever fleeing from place to place for safety. Hamburg, Cologne, Worms, and Antwerp had already been the exile's asylums ; but another flight was now necessary, and he removed to Marburg, an inland town on the Lahn, in Hesse Cassel, and famous in ecclesiastical history for the deeds and discussions which there took place. It is now easy of access; but three hundred and thirty years ago it was retired, and rarely visited. Thither, then, did Tyndale now retreat. He was governed by two master feelings—first, the love of the Bible, and secondly, the love of his country; and he laboured to make the one acquainted with the other. While at Marburg, Tyndale had for his fellow-labourer, Patrick Hamilton, the proto-martyr of Scotland, who perished in the year 1528. Drawn together by common likings and common aims, these two congenial spirits helped for a season to brace each other for the death which each had before him. Looking back over the centuries which have intervened, and imagining the converse of such men under the shadow, perhaps the roof, of the antiquated castle which crowns the heights of Marburg, or amid the woods which cover the surrounding slopes, the mind is stirred by conflicting emotions. How Satanic

thus to hunt and persecute these heroes of truth, these benefactors of humanity! How noble they, above the nobility
which kings impart, to continue steadfast amid the scorn,
the hatred, and the "deaths oft," which formed their only
reward from those whose welfare they desired! Such men
have been called the greatest benefactors of Britain, and to
this hour their works are following them in Britain's greatness—in her Bibles, her Sabbaths, and ner "great cloud" of
witnesses to the power of truth. When it is recorded that
Tunstal, Bishop of London, actually went in person to Antwerp to buy up the translations, and paid down money to
get them into his possession for the flames, the antagonism
which Tyndale had to face, and the determination which
signalized him may be better understood. And yet, Tunstal's own diocese, as well as Oxford, Cambridge, and many
of the quiet rural scenes of the land were all supplied with
the hated Bibles. The fiery persecutors were effectually
baffled.

And if Tunstal was so zealous abroad, it is not to be supposed that he would be remiss at home. Nay, with an
ardour that would not be cooled, he proceeded to search out
the Bible-readers. Forty of them were betrayed by one
man, in London, and as many more in Essex, all of whom
had often read the Bible in their mother tongue — for
that was their offence. Fact after fact was now elicited
to show how successfully Tyndale had laboured; and we
learn to wonder more and more how one proscribed and
hunted outlaw could so convulse a kingdom. Some of
the detected recanted, and betrayed "their friends, their
brethren, their nearest relations, and those that themselves
had brought into those opinions," but still the work advanced. Tyndale and his fellow-labourers overmatched
Tunstal and his twelve selected "Tryers"—nay, the mightiest
in the kingdom. Wolsey and More, each of them a Lord

Chancellor of England, passed away, like withered leaves in
autumn, before the power wielded by that detested yet
valiant man.

It was now more than time, however, that decisive attempts should be made to seize the arch-heretic. His persecutors were only lopping off the branches; the root was
still firm; and it must now be assailed. Tyndale and some
of his assistants were accordingly denounced more boldly
than ever; and the British envoy was now directed to apply
to Margaret of Brabant to seize them, that they might be
sent to England. But the despotism of our dark Britain
was not responded to upon the Continent. Men could not
be sent off merely as prisoners—they must be examined first.
Moreover the Inquisition must be consulted; and amid these
tender mercies of the wicked, Tyndale continued for some
time longer at large. He was now busy with the Old Testament, that it also might be read in the mother tongue of
England; and while death by fire began to be prepared for
him, and the toils of his persecutors were drawing more and
more closely around him, he was, with all his former ardour,
persisting in sending the whole word of God, if he could, to
the land whose rulers had cast him out. A translation of
the five books of Moses, along with some productions of
Tyndale—for example, his " Practice of Prelates," and similar treatises—were in circulation, while their author was
found to be more than equal to cope with both Wolsey and
More, who had only despotism, darkness, and superstition
on their side. Tyndale's desire now was to open up the
whole truth of God—be that done, and no danger, no prospect however dark could turn him from his path. On he
marched to achieve his mission, borne up by the consciousness that he was doing what God would have him to do,
but most probably unconscious that he was doing what will
cause his name to be revered till time shall be no more. It

was not *his* name, it was God's, that this heroic soul sought
to glorify; and if he must fall in that cause, we have seen
that he was ready—"ready to be offered up."

Meanwhile, and till the night came, Tyndale would work.
He was labouring in opposition to a power which never
sleeps—that power which, with threefold boldness, arrogates
not merely the name of Church, but moreover calls itself
Holy, Apostolic, and Catholic. He therefore plied every
instrument within his reach. He appealed to the king and
the rulers of England. Book after book was published, but
the chief apparent result was a proclamation in which the
translator was expressly named, while men were incited to
" detest his books; to abhor them; not to keep them in their
hands; to deliver them to the superiors such as call for
them. And if by reading of them theretofore anything
remained in their heart of that teaching, they were either to
forget it, or by information of the truth, to expel it." Moreover, the king's desire to seize the person of Tyndale
increased from day to day, and he was now pursued on the
Continent more eagerly than ever. How he was able, amid
so many snares and perils, to issue edition after edition,
as he did, continues a marvel to this day; but once engaged in the work, he pressed it forward with unresting
earnestness, as if aware that his time was short. Two
special envoys were sent about this time—1531—to the
Low Countries, one, at least, of whom was charged with
explicit instructions regarding Tyndale, and attempts were
made to entrap him to England. He had more than one
interview with Vaughan, one of the emissaries, and the
high-toned appeals of the noble man, as recorded by his very
enemies, remain to attest the grandeur of his character.
He pled with no common pathos for the circulation of the
Bible in the English tongue. "As I now am," he said to
Henry's creature, "very death were more pleasant to me

than life, considering man's nature to be such that it can
bear no truth," and what he preferred was fast coming.
When Cromwell was urging the agents of Henry to be alert;
when even More wrote against the friend of the Bible;
when John Fryth was burned at the stake for his adherence
to the simple truth of God, who could be safe ? Tyndale
wrote to that young friend in prison; but our translator's
own mind was so agitated by the woe, that he needed consolation nearly as much as the martyr. The last sentence
of his letter relating to the wife of Fryth—one who was
worthy of such a husband—enables us to comprehend the
magnanimity which grace can impart. Tyndale wrote : " Sir,
your wife is well content with the will of God, and would
not, for her sake, have His glory hindered."

Tyndale's own day of doom was now at hand. Early in the
year 1535, he was seized by a mean stratagem on the part of
some of his English pursuers, and imprisoned in the castle of
Vilvorde. He was examined at Louvaine, and it was soon
apparent what would be the result. But did he relax in his
endeavours ? Was his imprisonment equivalent to fettering
the word of God ? On the contrary, three editions of the
Scriptures which he had translated were published during
the year in which he was seized, and he could not be much
longer endured by truth-hating and misguided men. His
trial was hurried on ; he answered for himself; but his sentence was sure; and William Tyndale was condemned to
die. On Friday the sixth day of October 1535, he was led
forth to execution. Having reached the place, he was fastened to the stake, where he prayed with a loud voice, " O
Lord! open the eyes of the king of England," and after having been strangled, he was reduced to ashes—a martyr, if
ever there was one, to the simple truth of God, as it repu-
diates and disowns all error—all that is polluting and all
that is offensive to the Holy One who gave it.

"And thus much," one has written, "thus much of the life and story of the true servant and martyr of God, WILLIAM TYNDALE, who for his notable pains and travail may well be called the Apostle of England, in this our latter age." His life was signalized by so remarkable a unity, that it is easy to indicate his master object, his one great design; and we need not name it. He was pre-eminently a man of one idea, but it was so comprehensive, that a multitude of others clustered around it, like steel dust clinging to a magnet. He never for a day, as far as we can notice, swerved from his high pursuit, nor ever sacrificed truth for favour. Though loyal to his sovereign, some would say to excess, he feared his God yet more, and died rather than compromise the rights of conscience, or the place due to the Truth. For twelve years he contended, all but single handed, against the most formidable antagonists then upon the earth; but wielding that mightiest of all human agencies, the press, to diffuse that mightiest of all moral powers, inspired truth—Tyndale fought on, and though he fell fighting, he triumphed even in his fall. A Vicar of Croydon, speaking for the priesthood, had once said, "We must root out printing, or printing will root out us," and Tyndale believed that vicar's words. He printed— he printed especially the word of God in the mother tongue of England, and when he passed up to glory from the precincts of the old castle of Vilvorde—about half-way between Brussels and Malines—it was rather as a conqueror than a victim. In the very year of his death, at least nine editions of the New Testament issued from the press. During his twelve years of labour, only about one edition annually had appeared; but, from whatsoever cause, the year on which he sealed his testimony with his blood, was nearly as prolific as the whole of his former career. And, strangest of all, Henry's own printer in London issued an

edition of Tyndale's Bible in folio, in the very year in which
the martyr perished! It was a singular revolution. Can
we connect it with Tyndale's dying words, "Lord, open the
eyes of the King of England?"

Though this martyr thus fell, we are not to suppose
that he fell prematurely, for he was immortal till his
work was done. While struggling against fearful odds, he
had seen enemy after enemy fall. Two chancellors, one
archbishop, at least four bishops, besides others ignominiously dismissed, had all passed away; while the God-
guarded man lived and laboured, till even royalty bloated
with crime must succumb. In truth, Tyndale made his
times what they were by his indomitable perseverance, and
there is not a soul in our land that does not profit still,
in some degree, by the travail of this martyr. It was
once said of him and his coadjutors, and we adopt the
saying, The writings of Tyndale contain "not only matter
of doctrine to inform thee, of comfort to delight thee,
of godly example to direct thee, but also of special admiration to make thee to wonder at the works of the
Lord.' These things made him a felt power among the
peoples.

Let no one suppose, then, that this other king of men
was disappointed in his great life-work. We may have to
trace him from hiding-place to hiding-place, or read his
books by the blaze which was consuming the friends of
truth. But the single and sublime object of his life, was to
win his native land to the faith of the Redeemer. By
God's blessing he did it, and in a few years after his death,
a Protestant king sat on the throne of England, for the
corruptions of men had been largely swept away by the
force of truth. Upon the whole, his life and death supply
another example of the process by which God's purposes
for good are wrought out on earth. It is progress by anta-

gonism, and the final day will declare what myriads Tyndale has been the means of helping forward.

These conclusions would be confirmed were a contrast drawn between Tyndale and Wolsey, his contemporary. The one all for God, the other all for self, and self-aggrandisement. The one frugal, abstemious, humble, and never accused of any crime but one, that is, the circulation of God's word; the other gross, godless, a voluptuary, and an oppressor. The one loving the light, and living and dying to unveil it; the other hating the light, and giving himself soul and body to extinguish it. The one honoured now by millions throughout the world, the other a hissing and a proverb to all who have learned to apply the only standard of right to man's conduct. These lights and shadows make Tyndale's greatness greater still, and show us how God over all may exalt the man of low degree, while he pours contempt upon princes, so that they wander where there is no way.

Nor should we fail to notice the moral grandeur which environs both this man and his mission. A solitary individual, humble in station but undaunted in heart, conceives a purpose, and with him it soon acquires a sacramental sacredness. In the manor house of Little Sodbury the truth wells up. It becomes a little wandering rivulet, sometimes flowing softly, it has been said, like the waters of Siloah, and sometimes about to be utterly dried up by the fierce heat of persecution. On, however, it flows, winding and meandering; now hid from view, and anon flashing in sunlight; till, in our day it is refreshing millions, and rolling on to gladden millions more. All these results were wrapt up in the indomitable purpose of William Tyndale, to give the Bible to his countrymen. Bitter enemies might gainsay. That greatest of enemies, Rome, whose name is legion, might assail. But firm as a rock, and fixed in purpose beyond the power of mortal arm to quell him, Tyndale held on his way. It was the heart of a hero bent on achieving the work of a martyr, and it was achieved. The Bible is open to perhaps a hundred millions in the English tongue, and much of that as the result of a blessing from the Omniscient on the labours of a man who would not be turned from his purpose, though fire and faggot closed the vista of his earthly pilgrimage.

And such is a glimpse at the career and the labours of William Tyndale. Like Columba and others, he selected a noble life-object. He pursued it with a stanchness which never shrank, and an intrepidity which quailed at no danger. Is decision to be praised? Tyndale was decided. Is truth to be clung to whatever it may cost? Tyndale did so. Is heavenly wisdom more precious than rubies? Tyndale acted like one who was fully convinced that it was. He incurred all risks to spread that wisdom abroad, and though his ashes were scattered to the winds, his record is still on high—in all respects he was a model. Though often likened to the apostle John in meekness, Tyndale was daring as well as generous and genial. He feared no danger, and shrank from no toil, might he only advance his cherished purpose—the Scriptures in English for the English people. Inflexible in that aim, he moved forward in his great work, as Columbus moved over the great deep, undeterred by murmurs or by mutiny. His eloquence, his quick wit, his gentle nature, as well as his unflinching ardour, were all consecrated to the highest, noblest ends, and would we walk in his footsteps? Then let the same wisdom guide, the same ardour impel, the same love constrain, and all is well.

> "He liveth long who liveth well;
> All else is being flung away:
> He liveth longest who can tell
> Of true things truly done each day."

—The verdict is true, "Tyndale did not take his seat on a bishop's throne, or wear a silken cope; but he mounted the scaffold, and was clothed with a garment of flames. In the service of a crucified Saviour, this latter distinction is higher than the former." *

* M. D'Aubigné.

V.—HANS EGEDE.

1686—1758.

———" Far above
Where mortal footsteps ne'er may hope to rove,
Bare granite cliffs, whose fixed, inherent dyes
Rival the tints that float o'er summer skies;
And the pure glittering snow-realm, yet more high,
That seems a part of heaven's eternity.
There is no track of man where Hamlet stands;
Pathless the scene as Lybia's desert sands."
MRS. HEMANS.

Attracted to Greenland—Proposes to go—Deterred—Alternatives—Trouble of mind—Appeals made against his proposal—His purposes shaken—New difficulties—Resigns his charge at Vogen—His interview with Frederick IV.—Increased difficulties—Hope deferred—The heart sick—Tokens for good—Fresh disappointments—New friends—The king favourable—Subscriptions flow in—Ship bought—Egede embarks for Greenland—Perils by sea—Lands—First trials—Hopes—Disappointments—Disease ravages Greenland—Death of Mrs. Egede—Egede leaves Greenland—His new sphere—Results of his labours—The influence of one man—Conclusion.

EN have done much for gold. They have braved all climes, and encountered all perils. They have dived into the depths of the ocean, and climbed to the most inhospitable heights. They have snapped every human tie, and made their hands red with human blood. Now, when we behold the sacrifices thus made, the sufferings thus endured, and the perils thus encountered, one is prompted to conclude or to fear that the being who is swayed by motives so low must be incapable of being controlled by any lofty considerations at all.

And yet he *is* capable. He can be so transformed by a heavenly power as to manifest a spirit more akin to the divine than the human; and the devoted man at whose

fervid intrepidity we are next to glance, will exemplify at
once the majesty and the tenderness of that love which has
in it more of heaven than of earth.

HANS EGEDE, a lowly, yet a noble man, was born in the
year 1686, and was educated for the Christian ministry.
He was settled at Vogen, in the south of Norway, about the
year 1707; and soon thereafter, or in 1708, had his attention
turned to Greenland and its spiritual darkness. So early as
the eleventh century, the Norwegians had sent a colony to
that country, and for about three hundred years they continued in some vigour there; but from an early period of
the fifteenth century the settlement had been lost sight of—
if any survivors remained, they had relapsed into paganism.
Egede, however, had heard or read of that colony,—his
interest was awakened,—and as he was one of the men who
follow out, as far as they can, any inquiry which they may
have raised, he forthwith began to gather information on
the subject.   Bergen was the town where he was most likely
to obtain the needed intelligence, owing to the employment
of many of its inhabitants in whale-fishing.   In that place,
accordingly, Egede began to institute inquiries; and his
interest was deepened by what he learned.   What had at
first been only a vague longing, now took a definite shape;
for the fact that the Greenlanders were of the same nation,
appeared to give them a strong claim on the Christian sympathies of other Norwegians and Danes.   The first impulse
of Egede was to proceed to Greenland in person, there to
tell men that a Saviour had come to earth from heaven, in
order to rescue the perishing; but for some time he was
perplexed and at a loss as to the path of duty.   On the one
hand, the dark-souled were perishing; on the other, Egede
had occupation and tender ties at home.   He had a family
to support.   His way was beset by dangers, and, concerned
as he was, he could for the present proceed no farther.

He waited for light, and watched lest he should be tempted
to plunge himself and his family into ruin by any rash or
unwarranted step.　It was not precipitate ardour, then,
but calm principle, and cautious consideration, that guided
Hans Egede at the outset of his career.

And here is a guiding idea lodged in the soul of a man
who must either follow it out to its legitimate results, or
sink self-condemned beneath the burden.　It is such an idea
as cannot be commanded away from the mind.　It is a
leaven to ferment.　It is a seed to grow.　It is a power to
propell; and how does it influence Egede?

His first resolution was to address the king of Denmark
regarding the conversion of the neglected Greenlanders.
Egede's mind was ill at ease amid the delay which was taking place.　He could not dislodge the thought which had
taken possession of him, but hoped that if he could enlist
royalty in the cause, the object on which his heart was set,
and for which he was now to live and to die, would be
gained.　Afraid, however, lest an appeal from one so humble
might be overlooked or fail, Egede forwarded a memorial to
Randulph, Bishop of Bergen, and Krog, Bishop of Drontheim,
imploring them to second and enforce his address to the king.
They favoured his views, and he began to feel at rest, as if
the work which had fired his soul were now in wiser and
more powerful hands than his.　He thought that he had
left his cause with God, and tried to be at peace.

Still, the question must be solved, the battle must be
waged, in that man's own mind; he could not delegate his
felt responsibility to another, not even to a king.　Hitherto
the thought had lain concealed in Egede's own bosom.　He
had not disclosed the secret even to his wife; but the letters
which he sent to Bergen and Drontheim soon made his
proposal public, and now began his trials—it is about to
be made plain whether he is to live the mere creature

of circumstances, or whether he is one of those God-sent men who make circumstances bend to their firm will. Some of his friends assailed him for his foolhardy proposal. His relatives appealed to him on the ground of the misery he would entail on those whom he was pledged to cherish. The love of notoriety, the desire of riches, and other charges, were advanced against him; and such remonstrances, enforced by the anguish of his wife, shook him for a time—at last, he consented to remain at home, engrossed with the pleasant employment of his charge at Vogen. It then appeared as if he had exhausted his duty to the Greenlanders; and for a time he seemed like one who had escaped from some great snare.

But that was not peace; it was only temptation yielded to. The thought of Greenland soon intruded again upon the calm which Egede seemed to be enjoying, and it came now like a plumed arrow or a loaded spear, not to be withstood. The words, "He that loveth father or mother more than me, is not worthy of me," were heard and *believed* as the utterance of his Redeemer, and Egede could rest no longer. He had a fire in his bones; he had a truth not obeyed in his conscience; and, as the result, he became wretched—day and night the poor Greenlanders lay heavy on his soul. His wife added to his misery by her chiding, and he became all but desperate. Friends and kindred —indeed, all who knew him—seemed to oppose his purpose, and if ever a mortal was in a strait as to his path, it was Egede. Shall he carry light, and hope, and help to Greenland; or shall its darkness be unbroken by him? That was the question which was now to be solved, amid a hundred difficulties; and how did he solve it?

It was not long till the darkness began to clear away. The assaults and accusations, the lies and calumnies of some of his neighbours, but, above all, the free and full consent of

his wife—obtained in consequence of these very calumnies—
made Egede's path plain. She now felt a desire like his
own to proceed to Greenland. After seeking counsel where
the believer will not long seek it in vain, she became as
thoroughly convinced as he was—an heroic helpmate for an
heroic man—one who fed the flame, instead of trying to
quench it. " Magnanimous," is the epithet which history
couples with her name.

This was one difficulty surmounted, but it was only one.
The earnest man now began, however, to agitate the question more freely. Bishop after bishop was addressed by
him. The College of Missions at Copenhagen was memorialized; but as his country was then involved in war, this
servant of the Prince of Peace must wait, and year after year
thus rolled away. Hope deferred made the heart sick,
for the thought of the Greenlanders perishing in darkness still kept possession of Egede's tender soul. Indeed,
instead of damping, delay roused and stimulated him, and
he now resolved to apply in person to those who could promote his views, or make rough places smooth before him.
The pent-up passion must have vent. The words, " He that
loveth son or daughter more than me is not worthy of me,"
were such as Egede could not evade. Nay, they were
indelibly written on his conscience; and there they became
a power.

But a new difficulty arose. It was rumoured, and not
without cause, that a ship from Bergen had been wrecked
on the coast of Greenland, and that the crew were not
merely murdered, but devoured by the barbarous people.
For a time such statements startled the Egedes. Yet should
such things prevent them from carrying out their purpose?
On the contrary, they calmly concluded that He who made
duty so constraining, could support them even in a land
of cannibals. Like the dying Haliburton, Egede could

say, "I am pained, yet without pain; without strength, yet
strong;" and undeterred alike by rumour and by facts, he
resigned his charge, and threw himself on the good providence of Him whose cause and glory the single-aimed man
was trying to promote. His parting with his flock was one
of many tears; but the resolution was formed, the tie was
broken, and one hero more stands on the side of truth.

Hans Egede had first begun to think of Greenland in the
year 1708. It is now 1718, and he is on the way to Bergen
to seek the means of reaching the land of his adoption. In
that city he was regarded as a wonder; by some he was
treated as an enthusiast, by others as a devoted man. But
war again frustrated his hopes, and delay followed delay as
before, till the death of Charles XII., at Frederickshall, in
Norway, held out the prospect of peace; and Egede hastened
to Copenhagen, there to press his proposal in person, and, if
possible, open a door of hope. The king, Frederick IV.,
admitted him to an interview, smiled on the proposed
undertaking; and since this zealous man has so far risen
above his difficulties as to stand before a king, his trials
may now perhaps decrease.

At this juncture—or in November 1719—the king sent
orders to the magistrates of Bergen to ascertain whether
any of the merchants of that city were willing to trade to
Greenland from that port. Fearing, however, lest they
should be asked to visit such inhospitable shores, the pilots
and captains who were appealed to, gave an unfavourable
reply to the king's inquiries, and Egede was once more disappointed—this time to be reduced to the verge of despair.
He even murmured against Him who doeth all things well,
when scheme after scheme was blasted; and though he
never let go the conviction that he was in the path of duty,
or swerved from his purpose to discharge it, he was tried
and buffeted, no doubt, that he might be prepared for the

heavier trials which, as a Christian hero, he has yet to face
and to master. He was called to a great work, and God is
making his instrument great for the occasion.

Distressed, but not in despair, Egede next spoke to some
opulent individuals, and urged them by all the arguments
he could devise to aid the cause he had at heart. He had
now some hopes of success; but it was once more to be
made plain that the work was not to depend on man.
When all seemed fair and promising, untoward events
occurred, which threw the whole arrangements into confusion again. Egede, however, was not to be repressed
even yet. Woe was unto him if he now drew back his
hand; and like another devoted missionary, who knew
that prayer and pains could do everything, this unflinching friend of Greenland resolved to persevere against all
opposition. Indeed, opposition was only the whetstone
of his zeal; and though the close of one difficulty was just
the commencement of another, the indefatigable man pressed
on—he sought the welfare of Greenland, as the devotees of
earth seek the gold which they covet. He may die in the
struggle; but he will persevere, in the spirit at once of a
hero and a martyr.

Having thus been baffled in several attempts, Egede now
resolved to try a different plan. Home affection had repressed him for a time. War had stood in his way at
another stage. The timidity of the men whose aid he
sought had further retarded and tried him. At last, however, he invited a band of earnest men to meet him and
consider his proposals. Moved by his indomitable zeal,
they met; and his remonstrances, his tears, and entreaties,
secured their pledge to aid him. On the spot he himself
subscribed three hundred rix-dollars, or about £60. Some
hundreds of dollars were subscribed by others. The bishop,
the clergy, and the merchants now responded to his appeal,

and a sum of eight or ten thousand dollars, or about
£2000, was raised. Though that was not adequate to the
undertaking, Egede determined to embark in his long-
cherished enterprise without longer delay. A ship was purchased to carry him to Greenland. Two other vessels were
freighted in connection with the high embassy. Meanwhile
the King of Denmark caused information to be conveyed to
Egede that he had granted him a salary of three hundred
rix-dollars, and subscribed two hundred more to aid in his
equipment for the enterprise. The missionary can now lay
himself afresh upon the altar, a willing sacrifice to the glory
of his Lord, and he does it with brightening hope.

Thirteen long and weary years have come and gone since
this humble, yet dauntless man first thought of a mission
to Greenland. During all that time, he has been, to human
eyes, contending with difficulties which threatened from day
to day to overwhelm him; but now, victory seems at hand;
all the initial impediments are surmounted, and Egede will
soon be on the sea seeking the haven and the tribes which
he had so long desired to visit. At evening time it is light.
The weak are made strong. "Things that are not, are
chosen to bring to nought things that are." A model
is set up, teaching us at once that where good is to be
done opposition may be expected, but that at the same
time, God will enable his chosen instruments to do it.
To flesh and blood, Egede was a weak, impulsive enthusiast.
To faith, he is a believer in Him who is Lord of all hands,
and all hearts, and all agencies; and strong in that might,
this hero's work is to take its place among

> "The deeds of men, unfriended and unknown,
> Sent forth by Him who loves and saves his own;
> With faithful toil a barren land to bless,
> And feed His flocks amidst the wilderness."

Rather than that such work should be left undone, the king

of Denmark shall lay an impost on all his subjects, known as the Greenland Assessment.

From Bergen, from which Egede sailed in May 1721, with his wife and four children, the voyage to Greenland occupied about eight weeks, and the perils on the deep were scarcely fewer than the delays on dry land had been vexatious. On reaching the Greenland seas, the drift ice was so abundant and so closely packed along the coast that the captain thought of returning to Bergen, and after cruising off the coast for about three weeks, the ship was run into an opening which promised a safe harbour. But instead of being safe, it became ice-locked, and high gales, dark fogs, and crashing bergs threatened the destruction of the ship. The vessel which accompanied Egede's was dashed upon the ice and sprang a leak. Both vessels were in imminent peril, and the captain even warned the Egedes to prepare for death, as escape seemed hopeless. But the tempest which wrought so fiercely really proved to be their safety. It swept away the ice, it left the sea comparatively open, and the party landed safely in Greenland on the 3d of July, 1721.

It has cost this man, then, thirteen years and more to find his way from Vogen to Greenland, and it will yet cost him weary years, and many woes, to win the souls of the Greenlanders. He and his companions had, first of all, to erect a house of turf and stone to shelter them. The savages were friendly for a time, and then somewhat hostile, but from the foundation of the mission, the work of Egede was very re markably a work of faith. The natives grew jealous of the Kablunaks or Europeans, and employed their Angekoks, or wizard-priests, to answer the strangers by incantations and otherwise; at length, however, the steadfastness of the missionary overcame these attempts, and such was the confidence reposed in him, that some of the people actually led him to a grave that he might raise the dead. It was, in

spirit, a scene identical with that in which Paul was nearly
worshipped as a God, and seemed a high barrier to the
truth. But love is inventive, and Egede prepared pictures
of Scriptural subjects, by means of which he tried to
attract and impress the natives, as young Doddridge's
mother impressed him, while a feeble little child. The
effect, however, on these rude tribes was rather ludicrous,
and such means were not long employed. Indeed, they
seemed hopeless in regard to a people who heartily despised
their visitors as men who loved "to stare at a book, and
scrawl with a feather."

Meanwhile, the trade which the king of Denmark had
connected with the mission was not successful, and in
the month of May 1722, the colonists resolved to leave
Greenland, in order to avoid death by starvation. Shall
Egede, then, flee along with them, or shall he face the
threatening peril of famine, and brave it for the sake of
the degraded Greenlanders? It was just at this point
that the faith of her who had once seemed likely to
thwart or to impede his plans, shone out with singular
vigour. Amid the bustle of preparation to forsake the
colony, she was herself unmoved, and was the means moreover of establishing Egede. At last, amid hopes deferred,
and after many a gaze at the wild North Sea, which seemed
to grow darker every day, two vessels hove in sight. They
brought supplies from Bergen, and announced that the king
was resolved to support the mission, as well as the merchants
to continue the trade. They had surely some encouragement,
when their missionary opened up new seas for whale-fishing,
the result of his intrepid explorings.

Thus delivered from immediate danger, Egede persevered
in his life-work. He dwelt in the filthy abodes of the
natives, along with themselves, that he might learn their
tongue. He fed upon their food, loathsome as it generally

was. He took part in their employments as far as he could, and showed how far love can sink to rescue its objects, when it is enkindled by Him who loved us and gave himself for us. Never a more perfect self-denial. Never a more conspicuous example of taking up the cross. Never a closer copy of the example of him who became all things to all men, though, in return, Egede's services were often drowned in the noise of drums, and in other ways rudely interrupted. Yet as the result, his persistent love was in some degree rewarded. Some Greenlanders began to wait on him for instruction, though they were often weary of such restraint. The wild adventures of the seal-hunt, and the stirring incidents of the canoes in which the amphibious natives delighted, had more attractions than either knowledge or truth, and no impression, or little, was made on the minds of the savages. It was one of Egede's sorest trials to see that the work to which he had dedicated soul and body made such little progress. But success is not the rule of duty; the word of God alone occupies that rank, and Egede continued to labour, and was encouraged by the arrival of a second missionary in July 1723. The unwearied philanthropist made a long and perilous voyage to gratify his king, and, if possible, to find more ample means of subsistence for the Greenlanders. He was, in truth, a man who sowed beside all waters, and hoped even against hope, though sorrow was often his reward.

In the year 1726 fresh difficulties arose. There was then a famine in the colony, and Egede and his friends were reduced to the greatest extremities. Indeed, it would be difficult to name the form of opposition to which he had not already been exposed; and he must now undertake a voyage of two hundred and fifty miles in the hope of procuring a supply of food. After all, he could deal out to those whom he guided only an eighth part of what was needed;

and his heart was wrung with anguish when he saw those whom he loved emaciated by famine, and verging on the grave. The murmurs of the colonists added to his other troubles, and even when a vessel did arrive from Norway, its freight furnished rather a respite than an adequate supply. Surely this good soldier of Jesus Christ needs the whole armour of God, to equip him for his arduous task! Perils on the deep were added to perils on the land, and it seems as if he were placed in circumstances, where everything but faith on the one hand, and self-preservation on the other would have faltered, and broken down.

But other forms of sorrow were yet in store. The king of Denmark, Frederick IV., now resolved to render the colony more permanent, and sent some officers and soldiers to Greenland to construct a fort. They were accompanied by two missionaries, but soon after their arrival, disease broke out in some of its most disastrous forms. It supplied a fresh field for the exercise of faith, but in all other respects it threatened to annihilate the colony. To crown the calamity, Christian VI., when he became king of Denmark, issued orders to break up the settlement, and Egede now felt as if his hopes were to be blighted for ever. He had, indeed, the option of continuing in Greenland if he preferred that course; but government would aid him no further, and he must either return, or remain with such of the colonists as he could persuade to continue with him. None would consent, but the Governor, at Egede's request, reluctantly named a few seamen to remain, and then the whole colony, including even the other missionaries, forsook the unpromising shores, while murderous plots among the natives, mutiny among the soldiers, in short, cross upon cross tried Egede.

And what is his deportment now? Does he droop or despond? On the contrary, he laboured on, and now at last, he had his reward. In 1732, the king, after all, sent a ship

with supplies, and devoted 2000 rix-dollars to the support
of the Mission. But in 1733 fresh difficulties arose; indeed,
the ravages of disease, and other causes once more threatened to destroy the enterprise. So wide-spread was the
mortality that the living did not bewail the dead,—they
rather thought them happy in their escape from the sorrows
of life. Amid these testing scenes, Egede still laboured up to
and beyond his strength; and his kindness won the affection of savage men during the epidemic which raged for a
year and more. "Thou hast buried our dead," they said,
"who would have been devoured by the dogs, the foxes, or
the ravens; thou hast instructed us in the knowledge of
God, and of a better life to come;" and even this much, in
some degree, cheered the indomitable man.

About this time, the first missionaries from Herrnhut
reached the shores of Greenland. Egede's eldest son soon
followed, a youth who had been trained for missionary
labour, but his father was now so enfeebled by cares, and
watching, and work, that he resolved to proceed to his
native land, not forsaking Greenland, but to rouse men, if
possible, to an interest in its darkness and spiritual death.
It is another example of the power of faith, unflinching and
ardent amid a thousand things which threaten utterly to
quench it; but to add to his other sorrows, the year 1735
saw him bereft by death of her who had so long helped to
cheer and uphold him; and his own account of his mental
misery at that juncture is one of the most touching in the
history of woe. Paroxysms of grief, and despondency akin
to despair came upon him. He was bowed to the earth.
He preached his farewell sermon, and in August 1736, left
Greenland after fifteen memorable years of privation, of
hardship, and of danger, carrying with him the mortal remains of his wife, and an affection for the people uncooled
by all that he had endured.

His mission to the mainland was successful. He was admitted to an interview by the king, and various measures were adopted to revive the Greenland Mission. Egede was made superintendent of an Institution for training missionaries for that bleak and frozen land. A salary of five hundred rix-dollars was assigned to him by the king, and there he laboured as before for the welfare of the embruted Greenlanders. As bearing the image of God defaced in the first Adam, Egede knew that the Second could restore it to them again. The faith and the hope of that result created a sunshine in his soul; and, waiting for the perfect day, he toiled and endured as before.

He lived and laboured till the year 1758, for he was above seventy-two years of age when he died. He thought that he had spent his strength for nought in Greenland; but during the three-and-twenty years which passed away between his leaving that country and his death, tidings after tidings came of the conversion of the savage people to the faith of the Saviour. Not merely tens, but hundreds of the once senseless and degraded, listened to the glad tidings of great joy. The Moravian missionaries, the most devoted, perhaps, of all the sons of men, followed up the efforts of Hans Egede and of Paul his son; and these labours of the Moravians are known to constitute one of the most remarkable chapters in the history of man. It were difficult to decide how much of their success was owing to the labours of Hans Egede, and the translations of Scripture, with the Dictionary and Grammar of the Greenland language prepared by Paul. But he who runs may read of the marvellous devotedness and heroic persistency of this man of God. He had his foibles. He committed errors, for he was human. But with his eye fixed on the terminus —the winning of souls to Christ, and his heart aglow to reach it, in spite of every obstacle, Egede pressed forward

Neither could affection allure, nor peril scare him from his selected path.

"In that drear spot, grim Desolation's lair,"

he believed, he laboured, he suffered, he wept, he prayed, and now his works do follow him. He is a beacon-light amid wide wastes of danger; and were every Christian in his sphere, however humble, to do as Hans Egede did, how speedily would the world assume a new aspect! Would not the moral desert blossom as the rose, and myriads be raised from their death-like degradation?

But in presenting this other example of a noble and disinterested decision, we should not fail to notice that all that has been described as achieved by Egede was achieved by a man of very ordinary powers. There was no brilliance about him; he had no remarkable gift, except that of simple faith and glowing love. And yet, mark what he accomplished! Strong-willed as he was, his courage rose with his difficulties. Concentrating his energies upon one single pursuit, he mounted up from obscurity to stand before kings. He repelled all that would have held him back from his self-sacrifice. His profound convictions were not dependent either on human smiles or human frowns. With the word of God for his light, and the love of the Saviour for his motive-power, Egede became something more than a conqueror over a thousand antagonists; and our path might be more bright or more blessed did we, in all simplicity, take hold of the same strength and yield to the same love. Egede was a man of God thoroughly furnished, because he looked to God alone to furnish him, and who may not go and do likewise? Who, for example, may not imitate the poor widow of Iona, concerning whom traditions tell that she made her cottage a light-house, for guiding the frail vessels of her day? That cottage stood in sight of the sea, on a rugged and a perilous coast, and her heart was sometimes agonized by the sight of drowned corpses, or the cries of men in danger. Her lamp in her window was thought of, and employed as a beacon; and there it stood during all her nights, at once a warning and a guide. Now Egede did for the souls of the Greenlanders what that poor widow did for the bodies of the rescued seamen; and may not the lowliest learn from such examples? Is there not something for every man to do, to diminish the evil and augment the good of earth? Surely when the truth of God is fully lodged in the minds of men, they will learn to be zealously affected as Egede was, and as all would be had they caught the spirit of Him who went about doing good!

VI.—CAREY, MARSHMAN, AND WARD.

1761-1837.

" In her own light arrayed,
See Mercy's grand apocalypse displayed;
The Sacred Book no longer suffers wrong,
Bound in the fetters of an unknown tongue;
But speaks with plainness art could never mend,
What simplest minds can soonest comprehend.
God gives the word, the preachers throng around,
Live from His lips, and speed the glorious sound;....
'Tis heard where England's Eastern glory shines,
And in the gulf of her Cornubian mines."

COWPER.

Influences—Carey's infancy and tendencies—Examples—Bound an apprentice—
His painstaking as a shoemaker—His deep poverty—His conversion—Begins
to preach—Efforts to rouse men to an interest in heathendom—Difficulties—
Persistency— Success—Difficulty of reaching India—Sails—Arrives—First
efforts—Poverty—Finds employment and access to natives—His danger of
deportation—A translation of the New Testament ready—Ward arrives in
India—Marshman — Persecution—Driven to Serampore—Labours there—
The first convert—Prolonged trials—Progress and repression — Success—
Carey's habits and labours—Lord Minto, and his efforts to suppress the
missions—Translations multiplied—Missionaries driven from India—Labours
continued—Illness—Death —Summation.

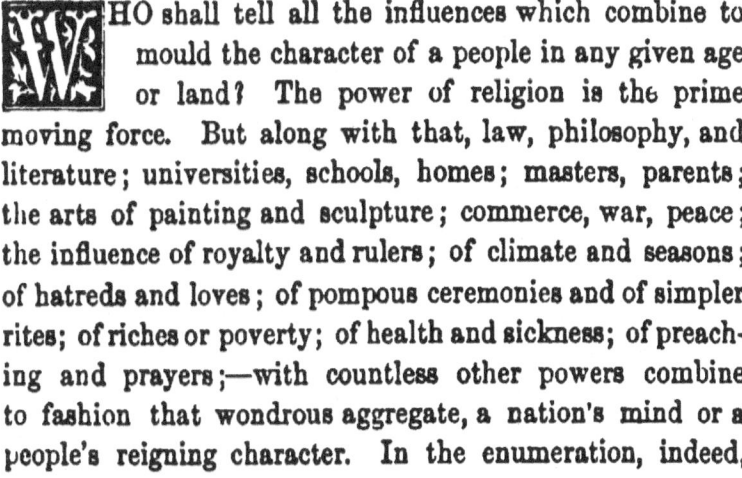

HO shall tell all the influences which combine to
mould the character of a people in any given age
or land? The power of religion is the prime
moving force. But along with that, law, philosophy, and
literature; universities, schools, homes; masters, parents;
the arts of painting and sculpture; commerce, war, peace;
the influence of royalty and rulers; of climate and seasons;
of hatreds and loves; of pompous ceremonies and of simpler
rites; of riches or poverty; of health and sickness; of preaching and prayers;—with countless other powers combine
to fashion that wondrous aggregate, a nation's mind or a
people's reigning character. In the enumeration, indeed,

every moral force might be named, from the Bible and the immediate blessing of Almighty God, down to the minutest incident which happens in the bosom of a family or an individual soul. Just as raindrops swell the brooks, and brooks the rivers, do these multiform and manifold influences tend to elevate or else degrade—to mould a nation into manliness and virtue, or debase it down to slavery and spiritual death.

But while these effects are ceaselessly and in silence produced, as certainly as time moves onward, there are events which exercise an unwonted influence upon a nation's mind. We can then actually see its growth, or its development in some definite direction, as some allege that they have seen the palm-tree in the very act of growing.

Such an epoch was inaugurated by WILLIAM CAREY, JOSHUA MARSHMAN, and WILLIAM WARD. They did not create any new moral forces, but they called into action some which had long been dormant and neglected. They roused the Churches to address themselves to duties which had for centuries been unknown to millions; and while these devoted men were themselves, more or less, the result of influences which were at work in their day, their labours, their ardour, and a persistency which bore them forward in spite of a thousand obstacles, helped to speed on a reviving interest in heathendom, till it controlled many minds with the power of a passion.—Their lives are a study from which much may be learned of the force of truth upon the one hand, and the power of resolute and devoted men upon the other. Science alleges that, according to the atomic theory, the effect of a pebble thrown into the sea on the shores of America, *must* be felt on those of our island, notwithstanding the fathomless depths or the thousands of miles which intervene; and something similar to that exists in the moral world.

As this is not a volume of biography, the lives of these pioneers of missions in Bengal are not to be sketched in detail, but only in so far as may be necessary to indicate the effects of decision of character, of well-directed ardour, and of efforts wisely concentrated upon a worthy or an ennobling object.—The energy of William Carey was very early evinced; for during his very childhood, he never allowed himself to be checked by difficulties—whatever he undertook, he completed. Early in life his love of books appeared; and when, in his humble sphere, he passed up to the study of science, his persistency in searching by hedge-rows for objects of natural history, to which he was devoted, in collecting specimens, and otherwise enlarging or correcting his knowledge, gave token of what the man might become when the boy was so energetic. He borrowed a Latin vocabulary; he committed it nearly entire to memory; he studied the grammar prefixed to it, and thus initiated himself in studies which gave a character to his life. But disease and the poverty of his parents repressed this ardour, or for a time prevented its full effects. At the age of fourteen, young Carey was bound an apprentice to a shoemaker, and thus appears doomed to hard labour as his lot.

But though that repression might impede, it could not crush his spirit of enterprise. His energy found or forced outlets in spite of all impediments. Among the books of his employer, Carey found a Commentary on the New Testament, which contained some words in Greek characters; and with the assistance of a weaver who had been taught Greek, he so mastered the alphabet as to be able to enter on the study of that language. Never, perhaps, was knowledge pursued under greater difficulties or by a more circuitous path; and never did any man, who subsequently left his mark deep upon his age, commence the great enterprise of life in circumstances so unpromising. While working

as a shoemaker, Carey attracted the notice of Scott the
commentator, then a minister in his vicinity, who, after the
humble workman had become famous, often pointed out the
home where he had laboured as a shoemaker, as " Carey's
College."

About the same time religious impressions came, at once
to solemnize and exalt young Carey. He found out that he
was a sinner, and must either be pardoned or lost. In
the new bent which such convictions gave to his energetic mind, he displayed much of the ardour which that
solemn crisis of life, Conversion, demands; and though the
measures which he adopted were not always according to
the wisdom which comes from above, they were such as
might be expected in a character like his, when roused
by the power which makes all things new. He soon thereafter adopted the views of the Baptists, and began to preach
in that communion at the early age of eighteen—though
while preaching to others, he was, on one occasion at least,
obliged to fast a whole day, because he had not the means
of purchasing a meal. Amid such difficulties, however, he
persevered in his studies. He received a call to act as
pastor to some scattered little flocks, and while doing duty
to them, he was married. He still carried on business as
a shoemaker or shoe-mender; but at the same time he
could now read the Scriptures in Latin, Greek, and Hebrew.
He had to travel from place to place to dispose of his goods,
in order to procure a bit of bread; for a congregation to
which he ministered at Boston " was not able to raise
enough to pay for the clothes worn out in their service," and
Carey was rescued from starvation only by the self-denying help of a brother. Sickness followed in the wake of
other ills, and it seemed as if this earnest worker were soon
to be cut down. Even his decision could not bear up against
poverty and its attendant evils.

Amid tastes like those of Carey, it is not difficult to believe that he never became an accomplished shoemaker. He had energy enough even in that pursuit; for once every fortnight he might be seen walking from his home to Northampton, a distance of eight or ten miles, with a wallet of shoes on his back, and returning with a fresh supply of leather for future engagements.* But he sought more excellent things, and in order to prepare for *all* he had to do, he very resolutely adopted a systematic economy of time, to which he adhered through life, and which largely helped to make him what he was. As an example, it was by such determined economy of time that he was able, amid increasing labours as a pastor and a teacher, to master the Dutch language. A friend presented him with a folio volume of sermons in that tongue. Carey borrowed a grammar and dictionary, and was soon able, in his turn, to present his friend with a translation of a portion of the volume.

With such tendencies, and such training, then, we may now inquire, what was to be the life-work of this man, and in what spirit did he address himself to it? That he was energetic, onward, and decided, we have already seen. Amid pecuniary difficulties, and hard drudgery, and something which often approached to want, he formed plans such as no other man of his age is known to have originated, and from one so signalized by his magnificent conceptions, lessons may be learned which are rare as his own energies. What, then, was Carey's life-work?

It was when reading Cook's Voyages round the world, and instructing some pupils in geography, that the attention of William Carey was first turned to the moral and spiritual condition of heathendom. While pondering it, the idea of

* Thirty years after this, when Carey was dining with the Governor-General of India, the Marquis of Hastings, the missionary overheard a general officer in the drawing-room asking an aide-de-camp whether Carey had not once been a shoemaker, and stepped forward to say, "No, Sir, only a cobbler."

a mission to the heathen took such possession of his mind
that all else seemed now to fade away before the greatness
of such a work. In his little shop, Carey had a map of
the world suspended before him, inscribed with all the
knowledge he could collect regarding the peoples, and while
making or mending shoes, his eye often wandered from his
last to his map. His eye thus affected his heart, as his
mind roamed over the wide realms of spiritual death, and
thought of means for sending thither the living water; and
when Wilberforce exclaimed in the British House of Commons that "a sublimer thought could not be conceived than
when a poor cobbler formed the resolution to give the millions of Hindus the Bible in their own tongue," he was only
giving utterance to a sentiment which all subsequent years
have re-echoed and confirmed. The power which could
grasp, and the principle which could carry out such a plan
at such a time, and in such circumstances as those amid
which Carey lived, stamped him as one of the benefactors
of the race—a man to be studied, that others may become
wise like him.

But he needed all his energy. When he first ventured to
draw attention to the duty of converting the heathen, even
a grave, devoted, reverend man hastily ordered him to sit
down, and sarcastically said, "When God pleases to convert
the heathen, he will do it without your aid or mine." Such
was the dense ignorance which then prevailed, and such the
indifference to the chief work of the Church on earth which
Carey had to face. But he was not to be daunted. He
was the rock—other men were the stream, and he pressed
the work upon their consciences with all the force of his
own deep convictions. Amid all the reluctance even of
great-souled men like Andrew Fuller, Carey proceeded with
his plans—unchecked, though often grieved—and prepared
an address at a time when "he and his family were in a

state bordering on starvation; and passed many weeks without animal food, and with only a scanty supply of other provisions." His mental energy rose superior to all such clogs, so that he was actually preparing to do battle with the grim gods of heathenism, at a time when gaunt famine was hanging on the skirts, or had penetrated to the very heart of his own family.—This is a phenomenon. The youngest may wonder; it requires a sage to fathom or explain it—a poor half-starving man planning, nevertheless, the conversion of millions to the Saviour!

Even when he had become a pastor in a larger sphere, at Leicester, Carey had still to labour with his own hands in addition to all his other duties, in order to secure a livelihood for his family. The record of a week's work at this period is preserved, and it might suffice to prove how indomitable was the spirit of this great missionary, how fitted in heart and by habit for the work he had to do. "On Monday," he says, "I confine myself to the study of the learned languages, and oblige myself to translate something. On Tuesday, the study of science, history, and composition. On Wednesday, I preach or lecture, and have been more than a year on the book of Revelations. On Thursday, I visit my friends. Friday and Saturday are spent in preparing for the Lord's day, and the Lord's day in preaching the word of God. Once a fortnight I preach three times at home; and once a fortnight I go to a neighbouring village in the evening. My school begins at nine in the morning, and continues till four in winter, and five in summer." We need not wonder to be told that a man of such energy, when he found his Church overrun by errors which refused to yield to ordinary treatment, formed and executed the bold resolution to dissolve "the Society," and constitute it afresh, carefully excluding the tainted. His manly decision, and withal his generous nature, rendered such a resolute

measure a great success, and his Church arose from its moral
ruins with its waste places restored and revived.

Still, however, Carey turned with deep longings to the
dark homes of the heathen.   Nothing could divert him
long from what was in truth the pole of his affections, the
centre to which his soul evermore tended; and he was able
at last to secure the attention of some devoted men to his
absorbing topic.   In the year 1791, at a meeting of ministers, he urged the adoption of some decided measures, and
though more than a year must elapse ere success begin even
to dawn, *something* was done.   Men refused to pledge themselves to actual efforts, in spite of all his earnestness; but
they, at least, listened to his wide-reaching proposals, and in
the year 1792, after Carey had preached with contagious
ardour on the subject, the minds of some were fairly won to
the cause of missions.   "Expect great things from God :
Attempt great things for him," thenceforth became the
watch-cry of the friends of that cause.   Carey's energy
sought and found a full, free vent in preaching on the subject; and though all his efforts sometimes appeared likely to
be baffled, he at length prevailed; a resolution was formed,
and the Baptist Missionary Society was virtually founded.
William Carey's decision did it : a new era in the history of
the Church has commenced.

After he had succeeded in removing many difficulties, and
persuading some of his friends to obey the last injunction of
the Saviour, a subscription was raised.   It amounted to £13,
2s. 6d.   Thirteen pounds two shillings and sixpence to convey the gospel to eight or nine hundred millions of heathen
in India and the world!—such was the commencement of
this great enterprise.   But faith is not to be defeated
when it is divine : Carey and his associates felt the truth
of the promises, and the authority of the commands.   They
grasped the one, they obeyed the other, and the cause has

grown from that day to this. True, it had many difficulties yet to encounter, much lukewarmness to overcome, or transform into ardour. In London, for example, only a single minister could be found to countenance Carey's new enterprise. But he would not put truth to the vote, or peril the world's salvation upon either the applause or the coldness of men; and though some leading religionists advised others not to commit themselves to such undertakings, that only stimulated Carey the more—he knew whose cause he was trying to promote, and threw himself into it with heart and soul. With thirteen pounds two shillings and sixpence in the exchequer, that noble man was prepared to embark for any country to which he might be sent. His soul had measured the grandeur of the enterprise : he knew whose work it was, what mighty results hung on the enterprise, and while the timid or the doubting stood aloof, he hastened with all his heart into the mission field. John Newton cheered him. Andrew Fuller stood by him; but few besides, and none of any eminence, would encourage him with their help. It was Columbus travelling from court to court to beg permission to discover a world. It was Galileo demonstrating a fact which superstition as boldly denied.

And we can scarcely wonder. It was about that time, or the year 1796, that the General Assembly of the Church of Scotland voted missions to the heathen unscriptural and revolutionary. Parliament was still more hostile, so that Church and state were harmoniously agreed in discountenancing such proposals as Carey was upholding. First the Governor-general, Lord Cornwallis, and after him, Lord Minto, then Henry Dundas as a politician, and then the Court of Directors as rulers, all vehemently opposed such undertakings. Bishops, ignorant of the Bible, and old Indians, themselves utterly Indianized in principle and practice, scouted the proposal of Indian missions as alike enthusiastic and useless. But Carey, the cobbler, knew a power which was more than a match for them all, and he firmly grasped it, and triumphed. Wilberforce pled for him. Charles Grant was zealous; Dundas somewhat meanly equivocated; Pitt was politic; but not among men was the progress of Indian evangelization to be speedily patronized. The measure must visibly begin on high, and be dependent on the Highest; and never was that rendered more manifest than when He chose one still weaker than "the worm Jacob" to overcome the mighty. In short, it was apparent once more in his case, that—

> "Not to the many doth the earth
> Owe what she hath of good;
> The many would not stir life's depths,
> And could not if they would.
> It is some solitary mind that moves the common cause—
> To single efforts Britain owes her knowledge, faith, and laws."

Yet friends gradually gathered round William Carey. His path to India is opening up: a colleague was found for him, and when they met, Carey actually rushed to embrace him; they fell upon each other's neck and wept.

But trials were not over, they were only beginning. Mrs. Carey—a feeble, timid woman—now declared that she would never leave her native country : yet even that could not shake the indomitable man. Those whom he loved the most might weep to hinder him as if they would break his heart; but he would follow where he believed his God was leading him, and return for his family when the first difficulties of the mission were surmounted. "The sense of duty," he said, "is so strong, as to overpower all other considerations. I could not turn back without guilt on my soul," and he resolutely held on his way.

At this stage, however, a most important question arose: How was he to reach India? At that period, none could proceed thither without a license from its Directors, and such a document no missionary could obtain; nay, the whole of British India was a forbidden territory to such men; and, daring to land there, they would be imprisoned, deported, or treated as vagabonds and invaders. Nearly twenty years after the date of Carey's first proposal, that state of matters still continued; and when he boldly embarked, even without a licence, to incur all hazards, he was compelled to unship his baggage and return to our island. He was distressed but not despondent—he trusted in God, and was not put to shame. In the year 1783, it had been enacted by parliament that any British subject proceeding to India without a lawful license, would be liable to fine and imprisonment. He was contraband. He was an invader. But as that law was a violation, in Carey's view, of a direct command of heaven, he felt that it had no force on his conscience, and in due time was able to proceed to India in a Danish vessel, the *Kron Princessa Maria.* As he approached the shores of Hindustan, his conceptions of the work became more vast, and his eagerness to plunge into it greater : nor did he lose any time in embodying his desires in deeds. His energy has gained one victory, and he must aim at another and another.

But all his decision, all his calm intrepidity were needed now. The want of means compelled him to move from place to place, seeking the humblest home. He became dependent for a time on the bounty of a generous Hindu— and the missionary's distress, at this stage, actually surpassed what he and his family had endured when destitute of food in his native land. He was without a friend or a farthing, and, in such a case, the heart of any ordinary man would have sunk in despondency, or abandoned the work in despair, especially when to his other woes were added the murmurs of his wife. He had frequently to return to his wretched home from missionary tours, only to hear her up-

braid and inveigh.   Even he was driven almost to distrac-
tion by such complicated sorrows, and had to write to England saying, " I am in a strange land, alone, with no Christian friend, a large family, and nothing to supply their
wants," but it does not appear that he ever regretted his
great undertaking, or doubted whether he was in the path
of duty.   On the contrary, while trial crowded upon trial,
he never relaxed his great work—but we should hear his own
sentiments as they were recorded at this period.   " Though
the superstitions of the natives," he writes, " were a thousand times stronger than they are, and the example of Europeans a thousand times worse; though I were deserted by
all, and persecuted by all, yet my hope, fixed on the Rock,
would rise superior to every obstruction, and triumph over
every trial.   I feel happy in this, that I am engaged in the
work of God, and the more I am employed in it, the more I
feel it a rich reward.   Indeed I would rejoice in having
undertaken it, even though I should perish in the attempt.
. . . . I feel a burning desire that all the world may know
this God, and serve him."   Now this man belongs to the class
from which martyrs are chosen.   In truth, he was a living
one, and from the jungles of Bengal, opened up the channels
along which the waters of life were to flow.   A friend was at
length raised up to Carey.   At some distance from Calcutta
he laboriously reared a few huts to shelter himself and his
family; and while procuring food by shooting wild hogs,
deer, and fowl in the jungle, he still cherished the hope of
at length enjoying " daily opportunities of conversing with
the natives, and pursuing the work of the mission."   It was
his ruling passion, ascendant in spite of much that might
have counteracted it, or rather it was a bold pioneer employed by the Highest to prepare a way for His truth.

Here, then, did this intrepid man, amid the upbraidings
of his wife, and the wild beasts of the eastern wilderness,

plant a mission in India. He had surmounted the ills of poverty. He had borne up under the disquiet of domestic vehemence. He had braved the hostility of men in power. He had traversed fifteen thousand miles to reach a sphere where he could embody his love and his convictions in deeds —and even in the jungle he was ready to live and labour for the Redeemer and the souls of men. There was death, however, and not life in such a place as poverty had driven him to select, and he was, in providence, soon enabled to abandon that region of miasma and tigers. Meanwhile he had made it plain that to him "no land was strange, no ground unholy; every coast was Jewry; every town Jerusalem; every house Zion," for God was there.

It was the generous proposal of a friend that rescued Carey from starvation and disease. He was invited to occupy a sphere where he could at once secure a livelihood, and operate upon the natives, and all that he could earn, after supporting his family, was devoted to the Christianizing of India—indeed he resolved to continue poor till the natives possessed the Bible in Bengalee and Hindustanee. A fourth, and often a third part of his income was thus devoted to missionary objects, while William Carey gave one proof more of the concentration of his mind upon the grand object of his life. Fever might assail him; a child might die; his wife, amid the agitating scenes through which she passed, might lose her reason; but Carey pressed on, for life or death eternal was dependent on his enterprise—an enterprise which the wisdom of this world despised, but on which the God of heaven smiled.

Measures had lately been adopted for deporting all unlicensed parties from Bengal, and as Carey belonged to that class, his position became more and more precarious. By the help of friends, however, he was tolerated, though little more, but in a short time he was again reduced to pecuniary

straits—in plainer terms, to dependence verging on want.
His zeal, however, was still unabated. That was not to
depend either upon fulness or scarcity of bread, and measure after measure was therefore adopted to promote the
grand object of his heart's desire. He had laboured without ceasing at the work of translation, by the help of all
whom he could find means to enlist; and in the year 1797,
or four years after he sailed from England, Carey could
intimate to friends at home that he was ready to begin to
print a translation of the New Testament. He had persisted
in that work of faith with intense devotion, and now the
manual labour of printing must be pushed forward with as
much ardour as the mental process had been. A printing
press was procured, and set up, and was regarded by the
wondering natives as an European idol. It was only another trophy to the perseverance of William Carey.

Though these measures animated him amid his toils, his
want of success among the natives tried him to the uttermost. For more than five years he had laboured for their
good, but still no fruit. With incessant activity and un-
flagging zeal, amid indescribable discomforts, he had sown
the seed; but still hope deferred made the heart sick. He
persevered, however; he preached in season and out of season, and did all that a loving mortal could do to win the
perishing to the Redeemer. If he confessed at this period
of trial that his hopes sometimes passed away like a cloud,
we surely need not wonder. Let us wonder rather at that
indomitable ardour which carried him over a hundred hindrances. " I still hope in God, and will go forward in his
strength," was his determination, and at last his resolution
was crowned with success.

Moreover, the zeal which Carey had been among the first
to display was increasing in Britain, and in the year 1799 he
was cheered amid his Indian trials, by the arrival of William

Ward, a like-minded labourer, who toiled in the same cause, and manifested a similar ardour till his dying day. He also was of humble origin—the son of a carpenter—but passed through a training in his youth somewhat superior to that of Carey. Before proceeding to India, Ward had been for several years the editor of a newspaper; but after he had devoted himself to his life-work, so complete was the consecration, that he did not read a publication of that class till after he had been ten years in India. Conscience, he said, commanded him to go, and under its orders he denied himself in a hundred ways. He encountered privations not a few, but at the same time he helped to forward that mighty revolution in public opinion which has made India through all its borders open to the gospel. Ward wrote to Carey, "It is in my heart to live and to die with you, to spend and be spent with you," and he fulfilled his resolution with a decision which never faltered.

About the same time Joshua Marshman, another heroic missionary, resorted to India to engage in the same undertaking. He was the son of a weaver, and for some time had himself followed that business; but he had other work to work in his time, and in the course of a few years, joined Carey and Ward in Bengal. We have thus three men brought together, differing considerably in gifts and tendencies, but one in heart and in devotedness. They were soon knit together by a common ardour in beckoning souls to the Saviour; and amid a thousand difficulties and trials, the noble triumvirate pressed forward that work which must at last be recognised as the greatest that is given to mortals to accomplish.

It were tedious to detail the vexations to which these three men were exposed ere they could find a place of rest, or rather a sphere of toil, in India. Plan after plan was formed, and attempt after attempt was made to expel them

from the land. It is well known that they were compelled
to take refuge at Serampore, a Danish settlement, where
they dwelt in safety, though not without molestation, under
the protection of the Danish king and his flag. Efforts were
made to dislodge them—they were even ordered to quit
India; but Lord Wellesley, the Governor-General, on his
own responsibility, granted them permission to remain.
Their movements, however, were circumscribed; their freedom of action was abridged, and every inch must be contested if they were to make progress in the cause on which
their heart was set. Indeed they were fenced round as if
they had gone avowedly to enlist the natives in a rebellion
against Britain; and prisoners on the Andaman islands can
scarcely be more strictly watched than Carey, Ward, and
Marshman were, in the asylum which they had found at
Serampore. It was as if men had revived the old popish
scandal, that the Bible is a " pernicious poison."

Yet they toiled on against all opposition. A press was set
up. With the exception of two books of the Old Testament,
the whole Bible had now been translated into Bengalee, and
the printing of it was commenced. From day to day the
heathen were addressed, and by circumscribing the light, its
enemies had just made it more conspicuous or more bright
where it shone. Schools were opened; tracts were circulated
by means of the press, and even environed as they were by
thousands of watchful enemies, the three undaunted missionaries proceeded with their work—they held, as they
believed, a commission from on high, and were determined
to perform it. The native languages were mastered with
all possible dispatch; and the persistency of these men, each
in his peculiar sphere, gave happy presage of what was yet
to be accomplished. At times even Lord Wellesley took
alarm at their proceedings—for example at the proposal to
issue the New Testament in Bengalee. But quietly, unob-

trusively, yet firmly, they proceeded with their work—and after seven years of labour and watching, of teaching, translating, and printing, their first convert from Hinduism entered the Christian Church! They had been tried by the apostasy, or the indecision of some; but hailed the first-fruits with exceeding joy. A mob arose and threatened violence to the convert. A missionary, who had sometimes co-operated with the three, and sometimes vexed and thwarted them, became delirious. Mrs. Carey, in a similar state, at times poured forth the most painful shrieks—and impediments such as these might have unmanned less devoted or less enterprising men. But they had chosen their part and their path, and they hastened forward like those who know that " the night cometh."

Nor were these their only trials. Friend after friend, or fellow-labourer after fellow-labourer, died. Four out of seven were carried off in two years—and these things, added to the fact that their proceedings were watched by the jealous eyes of men who were ready to assail them on the first appearance of what was deemed offence, kept the brothers ceaselessly anxious. Still more, perhaps, were they pained by the fact, that about this period, or in the year 1802, they had to intimate to their friends in England that the Government of India went, by deputation, to make an offering to the bloody goddess Kali, in the name of the Company. The success of our arms was the occasion, and five thousand rupees were presented as a peace-offering to superstition—a mockery of the true God; a dark spot in the history of the past; a source of anguish to the men who had left their homes fifteen thousand miles behind them, in the hope of seeing such debasing practices vanishing away. They *will* vanish, but the unprincipled doings of Britons have often been a buttress to an idol.

A boarding Institution, presided over by Mr. Marshman,

was now yielding a yearly income of about £1000, but he took only £34 for the personal expenses of his family. The press, under Ward's management, yielded a considerable sum, but his share was only £20 per annum. Carey had now an income of £600 as teacher of the native languages in a Government college, but £40 was the yearly allowance for himself, his wife and family, with other £20 to meet expenses occasioned by his duties at the Government college. The rest was employed in advancing the work of the Mission; and never, perhaps, in the history of man, was a stronger evidence given of the devotedness, the determined purpose, and concentrated zeal of any three men. A sum of not less than £1500 was annually contributed by them for advancing a cause to which whole communities in Britain did not then give a third of that sum. *

But the buoyant minds of the three devoted men were made equal to all emergencies, and ready for every form of sacrifice. Harassed as they were by the unmitigated hostility of the Court of Directors and their agents in Bengal, it required at once the wisdom of the serpent and the harmlessness of the dove to carry them through their difficulties. At one time, the Government seized some innocuous papers which the missionaries had circulated, and endeavoured to extract from them charges of sedition, republicanism, and other grounds of accusation. When Lord Wellesley left India, they lost a large-viewed friend, while his successor, instead of repressing the violence of the prejudiced, weakly fanned the flame. Hitherto the three had with difficulty stood their ground in spite of all their decision, but now the storm threatened to sweep them utterly away. What were

* The self-denial of these men might become a proverb. They found, for example, a nauseous substitute for beer, which cost only about the thirtieth part of that beverage. This they used owing to its cheapness, and when a tumblerfull of it was brought to Carey, as he sat at his desk with his translations, he would drink it down at one draft, simply to get rid of it. What was thus saved was expended upon missions.

they about? Were they a band of felons? Were they seeking to upset governments? Were they there, like comets, with fear of change perplexing nations? On the contrary they were there doing the work of the Prince of Peace. They were trying to restore Eden to our poor world; and yet for that they must suffer as if they had been plotting desolation. They were committed, however, to a mighty enterprise. Calmly and deliberately they had entered upon it. "India shall know the truth" was their maxim, and, in carrying it out, their earnestness of purpose was equalled only by their energy in action. Feeble or time-serving governors might find willing instruments to check, and thwart, and harass. But Carey, Ward, and Marshman confronted hostility with a wisdom which was majestic, and a determination which sometimes awed, till at last they triumphed by a power mightier than man's.

For the work grew. On some of their missionary tours, they were stopped by the Magistrate of the district. His authority was reinforced by that of the Collector, and the missionaries were compelled to leave the scene of their labours—the people would have heard them, but the rulers were afraid: their own ease might be marred, and, in comparison with that, what was the salvation of souls? Yielding to constraint, then, the missionaries sought another outlet for their zeal. Yet there was a point beyond which they would not yield. Danger might be conjured up at some places; at others there was none, and however great might be their respect for the Governor-general, they were determined to carry on missionary work, and take the risk of all that might follow. It was a collision between the Saviour's command, and human interference, and Carey was not the man to hesitate as to his choice: he both chose and acted, and though still hunted from district after district, he and his fellow-labourers persisted in carrying out the objects for which they were self-exiled from the land of their fathers. Slowly, and without much observation, the work advanced.

In the year 1806, they had made such progress, amid a host of difficulties, that a preaching-station was opened in one of the most debased and crowded quarters of Calcutta. It led to considerable excitement among the people when they were actually addressed by a converted Brahmin upon "the new religion," and, as sermon after sermon was preached, the excitement increased. But the civil authorities interfered, and forbade the missionaries to show any disrespect to the prejudices of the natives. This was afterwards explained to mean that the missionaries were not to preach to the natives—not to employ converts to preach—not to distribute tracts—not to permit others to distribute them; in a word, they were not to take a single step, by conversation or otherwise, to induce the Hindus to become Christians. It seemed as if the rulers of India thought that they could command the tides not to flow, or the Ganges to roll back to its fountains; but while the missionaries determined not to give needless offence, they were as resolute in following up their purpose to plant mission-stations wherever actual force did not prevent them. It was the case of Daniel and the other worshippers of God, when persecuted by the despot; and the same God guarded his servants at Babylon and in Bengal.

The hostility with which the three had to contend at this period was deepened by the mutiny at Vellore in the year 1806. That sad event assumed a religious aspect, as everything in Hindustan must do, because the Hindus are steeped in superstition from the cradle to the grave. Hostile parties were not slow to embrace that opportunity to damage the missionary enterprise; especially as the boldness of Carey now demanded decided measures, unless he is openly to triumph. The loss of five hundred lives at Vellore was imputed to alarms occasioned by efforts to convert the natives, and to preserve the lives of thirty thousand Europeans, it was deemed needful to suppress all such endeavours. Violent men denounced these efforts as the certain forerunners of rebellion and of massacre. The Governor-general, Sir George Barlow, interposed on behalf of what he deemed safety and order, and the little Chapel of the missionaries must be shut up, else the Indo-British Empire would be overthrown! But while men, as dark as the heathen themselves, were thus in terror of the truth as a power for evil, the three were not less confident in its power for good. A measure of freedom of action was extorted from their rulers. The previous prohibitions were modified, and the friends of truth really pushed forward amid much that threatened to throw them back, or even to drive them from India. For the present, they determined to endeavour to rouse England to a sense of the iniquitous opposition which they encountered in spreading the religion of mercy and of peace.

But about this period, some new missionaries arrived at Calcutta, and were there placed under restraint. When Carey applied to the rulers on their behalf, he was contemptuously treated by the magistrate, and every effort was employed to harass and silence the missionaries, or even to drive them entirely from Hindustan. The account of these proceedings forms a dark chapter in the history of religion, one, perhaps, of the very darkest; but the three men were not to be discomfited. They had been taken under the protection of the Danish flag, and, ere they could be driven from India, violence must be done by British rulers to a friendly power. It was thus that the friends of truth were hunted and harassed by men who were utterly ignorant of its power, and bent upon sweeping away whatever seemed to them to imperil their sway or their riches: but it was

thus also that two or three men, who were weak in themselves, by calm persistency at last chased a thousand. At
the close of 1806 they had baptized ninety-four natives,
and had ten native itinerants whom they sent out, two
and two, to a distance of many miles, in spite of all human
prohibitions (Acts iv. 19; v. 29). They had stations at Dina-
gepore, at Cutwa, and Malda. They rejoiced that nothing
had been found against them, except in the matter of their
God, and wisely but resolutely continued to sap the power
which would have crushed them if it could, till in the beginning of the year 1807, Carey was made a professor, with a
salary of 1000 rupees a-month, instead of a teacher with
only 500,—a step in which he rejoiced as bringing a large re-
venue to the mission. In addition to this, Ward again opened
a chapel in a great thoroughfare in the native quarter of
Calcutta—in a word, every opening was seized, every opportunity was embraced for carrying on the work; and it may
well be mentioned as a fact all but unparalleled, if not
entirely so, that so early as the year 1822, the whole Bible
had been printed in six languages, while the New Testament was either printed or in course of being so, in no
fewer than twenty-seven, all under the care of Carey, at
whom a Sadducean divine had so cruelly sneered.

But even these public enterprises do not fully exhibit the
indomitable spirit of Carey. His labours were at times incredible, and the following quotation * will furnish a specimen of what consecrated zeal can achieve. Carey, it is said,
"rose at a quarter before six, read a chapter in the Hebrew
Bible, and spent the time till seven in private devotions.
He then had family prayer in Bengalee with the servants,
after which he read Persian with a moonshee who was in
attendance. As soon as breakfast was over, he sat down
to the translation of the Ramayun with a pundit till ten;

* From Marshman's "Life and Times of Carey, Marshman, and Ward."

when he proceeded to the college and attended to his duties till two. Returning home he examined a proof-sheet of the Bengalee translation of Jeremiah, and dined. After dinner, with the aid of the chief pundit of the college, he translated a chapter of Matthew into Sanskrit. At six he sat down with the Telinga pundit, to study that language; and then preached the English sermon to a congregation of about forty. The service being ended at nine, he sat down to the translation of Ezekiel into Bengalee; .... at eleven the duties of the day closed, and after reading a chapter in the Greek Testament, and commending himself to God, he retired to rest."—The man whose activities were so intense and so untiring was sure to leave his impress deep upon his times. It was the heroic age of missions, and Carey over-topped even the heroes, as Saul of old did the people around him.

It was in the year 1807 that Lord Minto proceeded to India as Governor-general, and efforts the most decided were speedily renewed to quash and extirpate the mission. Carey's domestic trials might have crushed any ordinary man, for his literary and biblical labours were carried on with an insane wife raving wildly in an adjoining apart-ment: but to that domestic woe, trials of a public nature were added. Spies were employed to watch the proceedings of him and his colleagues. A pretended inquirer went to endeavour to ensnare them, and much occurred to put it beyond a question that missionary efforts were, if possible, to be now suppressed. To defend the truth of Christianity against Hinduism or Islam was deemed an intolerable offence. The dread of rebellion was again the watchword, and after surveying the perilous position of the Indo-British Empire, in consequence of preaching the gospel and spread-ing tracts, the Supreme Council actually agreed that the Government was bound by every consideration of general safety and national faith to extinguish the efforts of the missionaries. It was again the effort of puny creatures to resist Omnipotence, or roll back a flowing tide; but that effort was made, and here is the sentence in which it was announced to Carey : "The Right Honourable the Governor-General in Council deems it necessary to desire that the practice of preaching .... be immediately discontinued." The press must be placed under Government control, and all Christian appliances must cease.

It was well that the prohibition was so complete, for it was impossible to comply with it on the one hand, or enforce it on the other. Active resistance to the blind determination were hopeless, on the part of men so feeble and unfriended, but it could be confronted with a resolute will on the part of men who had learned to be still and know that God is God, and it was so. The co-operation of the Danish governor of Serampore was invoked by the British authorities to promote the exterminating measures, and Carey wept like a child at the attempt, not with the tears of weakness, but of very woe. The Danish governor, however, declined to comply with a demand so arrogant. He resolved rather to strike his flag and leave the settlement, than expel the missionaries, and the King of nations made that the defence and the safety of His servants. At last the extreme measure recoiled on its inventors, and the three self-sacrificing men, after many fears and much to harass them, were able to say that they had reached a better position than they occupied before these deep troubles began. While every letter, every order, every dispatch breathed hostility to the greatest of causes, malignity in Europe responded to hostility in India. Vulgar abuse was heaped upon Carey, and all was done that was likely either to scare or to drive him from his purpose towards India. But he persisted without flinching, and his onward movements, seen in the mellowing light of time, remind us somewhat of the march of the elephant in the jungle, prostrating by his bulk and power all that threatens to impede his progress.

But trials of a different kind were also employed to test the faith and the firmness of Carey. He had a son—Felix —who had studied medicine, and who went to found a mission in Burmah, where he had an opportunity of commending the truth by some cures which he wrought in the families of high officials. In August 1814, he embarked at Rangoon, in the viceroy's pleasure-barge, to proceed to Ava with the design of inoculating some of the royal children. The vessel upset, however, during the voyage, and young Carey's wife and children perished, while he himself narrowly escaped. Next day he proceeded, a melancholy man, to Ava,—a voyage which occupied about four weeks. The king sympathized with him in his sorrows, and was so much captivated by the young physician that he appointed him his ambassador on a difficult embassy to Calcutta. Thither young Carey proceeded with Oriental magnificence, holding the rank of a prince, dignified with the Red Umbrella, and other insignia of Burmese royalty. The humble office of a missionary was thus abandoned for the flaunting gauds of Eastern pomp; for young Carey lived in the highest style of Oriental splendour, and greatly grieved his venerable father. It was a sad and a humbling close to a promising career. It was the world ascendant where better things might have been expected, and, perhaps, that burden pressed as heavily on the father as either the hostility of Governors or the indifference of the heathen.

But the trials of Carey and his colleagues have not yet been all described. Money raised in their name was spent without their sanction. A crusade against their evangelizing operations was persisted in for several successive years. Moreover, internal troubles arose. Turbulent spirits ap-

peared among the younger missionaries sent out to reinforce
the fathers whose rules of abstinence and order of toil and
self-denial were too stringent for less devoted men. But
their resolution rose with the opposition which they encountered; it derived fresh ardour from every new difficulty. Instead of being scared or daunted by what he
suffered, Carey's views as a missionary expanded from year
to year. Bengal, Burmah, China, Siam, Nepaul, Cochin,
and other places all rose in succession before his wide-
ranging mind; and while he tried to mollify hostility by
gentleness, he never yielded a tittle of his conviction that
the world must be won to the Saviour, cost what it may.
At first, Carey would have been content to die when he saw
the Scriptures translated into Bengalee; he said that in
contemplating that result, while it was yet future, he would
have been willing to exclaim, "Lord, now lettest thou thy
servant depart in peace!" But he lived not merely to see
that work done, but also to see portions of the Bible printed
in Orissa, in Sanscrit, in Hindustanee, in Mahratta, in
Canarese, in Telinga, and Punjabee, with a beginning made
in Burmese and Chinese translation. Vast as his labours
were, he deemed them still but a trivial offering on the altar
of redeeming love, and humbly ranked himself below his
two like-minded colleagues. Yet with the eye fixed on what
Carey achieved, all who are competent to judge can decide
how much steadfast zeal, yet judge-like calmness, he threw
into the work. To carry it out, he determined to bury
himself among the natives, and passed six years of his life
surrounded by them alone,—surely a most costly contribution
to the elevation of the degraded, and one which, so far,
explains his success—a success which casts a stain on all
the plumed pomp of potentates.

It may here be observed, that there is something in open
and determined hostility which rouses us to confront it

with boldness, while to bear up against dull and sluggish indifference is at once more trying to faith, and more exhaustive to patience. That indifference, however, Carey had to encounter in very many forms. The superstition which pervades a Hindu's whole nature renders him impassive to all but Omnipotence. But hear one of themselves after his conversion, "Consider," he says, "the grand, wonderful superstition which penetrates and pervades all the Hindus. It has, indeed, become a part of their nature—a pious instinct of their soul—superstition is in their body, in their dress, in their food, in their doings.... In fact the life of a Hindu, from his cradle to his grave, is but little more than a round of ceremonies. He talks ceremonies, he eats and drinks ceremonies, and he dies a ceremonial death." Now when the dread resistency implied in such a condition, is reinforced by the hostility of Governors or the contempt of magistrates, we can estimate the heroism that is needed to confront it all.

Nor, in estimating the power of such men, should we fail to notice again and again the sums which they contributed to the mission. In the year 1811, Mr. Marshman's income amounted to about £2000 from his school, and after reserving about £100 for the expenses of his family, the balance was devoted to the mission. Up to the year 1817, the three had received about £50,000 for their labours, in various forms, and after retaining the veriest pittance for themselves,—sums so paltry as to seem almost incredible,—the rest was consecrated to the work in which they had embarked with all their soul. Even when their whole premises, their presses, books, paper, and property in every form were consumed, on one occasion, by fire, they did not yield to unavailing complaints. On the contrary, they once more rose to the emergency, like a vessel breasting the waves in a gale. In less than six weeks much of the damage was repaired. Funds were supplied by friends, and the vital force of the religion which they taught had largely imparted its energy to those much-tried men. In England such was the zeal in relieving them from their straits, that eight hundred guineas were offered on one occasion for Dr. Carey's likeness.

Now the disasters which thus befell furnish us with an arithmetical gauge for the result of Carey's decision and devotedness. But a few years before, he stood alone in all England in regard to the duty of the Churches to heathendom. With difficulty could he find one like-minded man to aid him. Now, however, that earnest man and his friends have lost mission property to the value of more than £7500, while, to compensate for the loss, the nations competed in liberality. India contributed about £1000, America sent £1500, Britain supplied £10,611 in seven or eight weeks, and the British and Foreign Bible Society voted stores of paper for the use of the mission. All these things followed in the train of a divine idea first lodged in the mind of a friendless, moneyless mechanic; then expanding as God's truth ever expands, and ending by subduing hundreds to itself, as fire subdues the fuel which feeds it.

But amid this chequered state of things, the Government hostility to missions was revived, and that in a form more rancorous than ever. On the 17th of June 1812, the Supreme Council issued an order expelling two missionaries from the country, and in the course of a few months, the banished, including the Serampore missionaries, amounted to eight in number. But acrimonious as this persecution was, and bitter and determined as was the hostility of the Indian rulers to the truth, all these things were only the expiring efforts of malignity—in another year, India was to be open to the gospel. Lord Minto unworthily lent himself to these endeavours on the part of his secretaries to quench the light, and some devoted men were deported. But such things just hastened the reflux, and though the missionaries were exposed to truculent attacks from old Indians in parliament, though their defenders were even in danger of being challenged to fight duels for their sake, and though their cause was like to be borne down by the combined force of prejudiced and blinded men, a triumph was at hand; Carey and his friends persisted in doing good, and they were not left alone. Amid angry controversy and hostile attacks, amid bitter accusations and many deceptions, amid disheartening opposition and unparalleled misunderstandings even among friends, a spirit of Christian fortitude faced all, endured all, and triumphed by enduring. Labours, called Herculean without exaggeration, still continued to be carried on, for Carey's promptitude was equal to every emergency.* His systematic distribution of his time made a day much longer to him than to most men, and hence his wondrous achievements in translations, in grammars, in dictionaries, in preaching, and in science, in spite of the relaxing effects of climate, or the eager antagonism of those who sought to extinguish the light as resolutely as he tried to spread it. †

The difficulties of the Serampore Mission during the last seven years of its existence were as great as those which marked its commencement. The indescribable misunderstandings and intense opposition to which the three were

---

* An example: He was pleading with an audience of Hindus to abandon their lying and nameless abominations. It was denied that such things were sins at all—they were the doings of the Hindu gods and not of Carey's hearers. Well, since it is so, was his reply, come home and eat rice with me—break caste —and that also will be the sin of the gods. Of course, the audience were not convinced.

† Dr. Carey published a Bengalee Dictionary, in three volumes, in 1825, " A noble monument of erudition and industry, which did that for the Bengalee language which Dr. Johnson had done for our own." Indeed, his labours in translating, composing, and otherwise operating on India through the press, render Carey's life one of the most amazing instances of consecrated industry, persistency, and zeal which the history of the past supplies.

exposed at the hands of some friends in England, remain
among the most humbling things recorded in the history
of the Church. Funds were withheld, or doled out with
niggardly hand. Cruel imputations were cast upon men
who had joyfully contributed thousands to their Mission.
But it is not our object to detail these struggles and sufferings, except as they serve for a background to manifest more
distinctly the noble devotedness of Carey and his friends.
His ardour was not to be repressed : even while engaged in
sore conflicts, in the year 1832, a new mission was planned,
and new translations were made. His own income was
still devoted to these undertakings,—but a financial crisis
through which India passed in 1833 dried up all their
resources : the missionaries were actually left without provision for their own immediate wants. They were obliged
to contemplate curtailing their work, and so violent was
the shock to Carey, that his colleagues feared they might
have to lay him in his grave. He could bear want,—he
could smile at obloquy, or repay it by prayers, but this
hero for truth could not brook the thought that his missions
should be abridged.

But his labours were drawing to a close. In 1833 he had
been repeatedly ill. In 1834 the effects of forty years of
labour and of suffering in an Oriental climate became very
apparent,—and after completing his last revision of the
Bengalee translation, he felt that his work was done. His
dread of " becoming useless" was great; and he was spared
the pain, for, amid a serenity which formed the consistent
close of such a life, the father of modern missions died on
the 9th of June 1834, in the seventy-third year of his age.
He had early selected his sphere, and pursued it through
life with unabated ardour. The renewal of the East India
Company's charter in 1813, and still more in 1833, had
opened India to all that Carey longed for, so that, in *that*

point of view, his highest aspiration was gratified. That
aspiration was sublime. Even yet, after the lapse of more
than half a century, too few are alive to the grandeur of
his conceptions; but though he had thus outstripped his
age, his deep piety and unswerving persistency made him a
power: perhaps it would not be too much to say that no
man of Carey's day contributed so much as he to the progress of the world. When he had fairly made up his mind,
difficulties only served to confirm his purpose to succeed,
and urged on by his master passion—the desire to supply
the Oriental people with the Scriptures—he knew no rest,
as he succumbed to no difficulties till that work was well
accomplished. Happy in like-minded colleagues, and im-
movably conscious that he was engaged in the noblest work
of man on earth, he pressed on, alike unawed by parliaments and by governors; and when he caused this inscription to be placed over his grave,

> "A wretched, poor, and helpless worm,
> On Thy kind arms I fall,"

he indicated to us the secret of his strength. That man's
life was "hid with Christ in God," and there no mortal
power could touch it. He went quietly home to enjoy his
new-birth-right of immortality.

And such was the man, the eldest of three, to whom we
are indebted at once for the Serampore Mission, and for a
model of calm yet manly decision of character. Round
that "consecrated cobbler" the war of opinion raged for
many years, for if, in one point of view, he was a centre of
noble influences, he was, in another, the point against which
a thousand assaults were made. The tours of Carey and
his colleagues, their tracts, their translations, their preaching, their converts, their schools, all became, in succession
or together, the war-cry of enemies; but the men held on
their way unscared, appreciated by such men as Lord

Wellesley and Lord William Bentinck, though lampooned and maligned by hundreds of others. Wilberforce in parliament pronounced their eulogy when he said that they were signalized by "zeal combined with meekness, love with sobriety, courage and energy with prudence and perseverance." "In fourteen years," said one who knew them well, "these low-born, low-bred mechanics have done more towards spreading the knowledge of the Scriptures among the heathen than has been accomplished or even attempted by all the world besides." But, in truth, encomium is incompetent: it is needless to praise. Yet we may *learn;* learn the blessedness of being guided to a right choice; learn the duty of addressing ourselves with heroic firmness to promote noble ends; and, finally, learn from one example more that decision of character based upon truth, and guided by "the True Light," is the surest path to glory even here.

The grand study in this man's life, and what renders his character sublime, is his unwavering devotion to one sovereign idea. Country, family, friends, and all that is merely earth-born, must take their place in his mind far below that idea. Carey became great, just because his eye was "single." There was no overstrung intensity in his case, but just the calm purpose of a soul which felt that God had given it a work to do, and with him scorn, opposition, suffering, hatred, all became means to an end, for they threw him more upon his God. Hope deferred or blighted, the climate with its fever, and the people with their callousness even unto death, tried, but did not repress, William Carey; and now that his example has been bequeathed as a legacy to the Churches, they will prosper just in proportion as they imitate his energy of purpose and his unswerving decision.

VII.—DR. CLAUDIUS BUCHANAN.

A.D. 1766–1815.

"O how comely it is, and how reviving
To the spirits of just men long oppressed,
When God into the hands of their deliverer
Puts invincible might
To quell the mighty of the earth, the oppressor,
The brute and boisterous force of violent men."

SAMSON AGONISTES.

E see all nature lying dormant and apparently dead in winter, till the breath of spring returns, and bids it once more make ready to display the beauties of summer.

We see many a precious truth lying long concealed, or unnoticed, as if it were actually interred, till some crisis in the world's history occurs which fastens attention on that neglected maxim, or that unheeded element of power. It then becomes the watchword perhaps of thousands; nation may vie with nation in giving it free course.—It was thus with the truth which overthrew slavery, and banded the nations of Europe against it, at least for a time.

We see many a man living in obscurity unnoticed and unknown, and perhaps not deserving to be noticed, on account of his sins and his folly, till some emergency arises

which draws forth the powers which were latent or choked
before, and sends the neglected one forward on some career
which is bright with blessings to thousands. The history
of the world is stored with the names of men who have been
thus aroused, thus transformed into public benefactors, and
not merely rescued from obscurity, but signalized by such
immortality as mortal man can bestow.

In illustrating the wholesome influences of decision alike
in an individual and the world at large, we are now to fix
attention upon one who ranks among the world's best
benefactors, and who was honoured at least to renovate
and largely extend, what will continue to grow till time
shall be no more. Having once taken up his ground,
or chosen his path for life, this man pursued it with
the energy of his whole mind. He enlisted the influential; and taught hundreds, nay, thousands to sympathize
with him in his aims. He roused not a few alike in
Europe and America to promote the work which is now
deemed the chief end of the Church on earth, though
many millions still give, as a yet larger number then gave,
no heed to the enterprises now referred to. The history
of CLAUDIUS BUCHANAN affords a fine illustration of the
effects of decision at once upon the individual character,
and in its results on the wide arena of the world,—calm,
intrepid decision, without aught that was either boisterous,
or fitted to overmaster.

He was born at Cambuslang, near Glasgow, on the 12th
of March 1766; and some members of the family had first
learned to live according to the truth of God during the
remarkable Revival of religion at that place, under the
preaching of George Whitfield and others. Where truth
was so powerful as it then was, we may well believe that
young Buchanan would be carefully trained,—and he was
so. Even in his early years he sometimes felt the sharp

pungency of truth in his conscience; but he never became
so decided as to give the heart to God.—A man may have
intense decision and an iron will for evil, while he continues
a cowardly time-server for good.

At the age of six or seven he was sent to a school at
Inverary. About seven years thereafter, when he was only
fourteen years of age, he became tutor to two youths,
and continued in that office for about two years. His
religious impressions from time to time revived; but for
years he continued undecided as to the concerns of eternity,
trying to accomplish what is impossible, that is, to be the
friend at once of the world and of God. He now began to
study at the University of Glasgow,—and for several years
Buchanan was alternately a student and a tutor. He resided for some time in the island of Islay; and a course of
life so full of change gave little token as yet of that energy
which lay folded up in that mind, so persistent, yet so calm.
It lay fallow for a rich harvest.

If the next incidents of his life betoken decision, it is
decision in evil ways. Young Buchanan had read the " Life
of Oliver Goldsmith," and learned that he had made the tour
of Europe with few resources but such as his flute and his
musical powers could command. To read of such a thing
was to admire it, and to admire, in the present instance, was
the first step to imitation. Buchanan accordingly formed
the romantic resolution that he also would make the tour
of Europe, supported mainly by what the music of his violin
might extort or entice from his listeners. Though educated
for the ministry of the Church, the solemn nature of his studies had not yet impressed him, or made him feel that God
and truth are realities; and as no way was open for his leaving Scotland, except by secretly withdrawing, or else openly
proceeding against the wishes of his parents, he adopted
the middle course of feigning that he was engaged to go

abroad as tutor to the son of an English gentleman. With
this lie in his right hand, and its sin upon his conscience,
this enterprising youth set out for the south—on foot, and
designing to travel over the continent of Europe in the same
humble way. Who would have expected an end so blessed
as we shall see his to have been, from such a commencement ?

In the month of August 1787, with his violin under his arm,
he started for London. As soon as he had reached a part
of the country where he thought he would not be recognised,
the stripling began to exert his musical powers, and called
at every abode where he thought he could obtain money,
food, or a lodging for the night. Travelling thus, he tells
us that he sometimes received a whole crown, sometimes
only half that sum, and at others nothing but his dinner for
his music. Occasionally he was pressed to remain for some
time at the places which he visited, for the people were
attracted either by his conversation or his violin; but the
fear of detection urged him forward, and after wandering
thus for about a month, he reached the English border.
"Once or twice," he records, "I met persons whom I had
known, and narrowly escaped discovery. Sometimes I had
nothing to eat, and had nowhere to rest at night,—but notwithstanding, I kept steady to my purpose, and pursued my
journey. Before, however, I reached the borders of England, I would gladly have returned, but I could not : the
die was cast. My pride would have impelled me to suffer
death, I think, rather than to have exposed my folly,—and
I pressed forward."

—"I kept steady to my purpose," "the die was cast," "my
pride would have compelled me to suffer death rather
than to have exposed my folly," "I pressed forward,"—
these are the watchwords of this youth of enterprise, of
pride, and self-reliance, and they read off his character.

He might be homeless, breadless, and friendless. He might discover his folly and lament it till it stung him to the quick, but he would not yield. From sheer obstinacy—if not from aught that deserves as yet a higher name—he pursued his wayward course, but we shall see at last that God was leading this blind though decided youth, as He has led many besides, by a way which he did not know. He emerged from his waywardness by a terrible ordeal; but he *did* emerge. God had work for him to do.

Claudius Buchanan was thus taught that the way which seems right to men, especially to young men, is generally far from being right in itself. His self-confidence might be great, and his pride indomitable,—at least by mere grief,— but he was compelled by suffering to change his mode of travelling in spite of his pride. It was hard, he confesses thus early, to live upon the benevolence of others; and he accordingly proceeded from the north of England to London by sea, soothing his fallen greatness with the thought that it was not in his own country, but on the Continent of Europe, that he wished to travel as a pedestrian. The dangers of that brief voyage were somewhat like those of Jonah's flight, and led at the time to wholesome resolutions, which were soon forgotten when the peril was past.—However decided man's nature may be in acting according to self-will, no man by nature ever became decided in obeying the will of his God. Every prepossession and every bias fights against *that* consummation.

Poverty and distress were Buchanan's lot in London, and his visionary project now appeared to him in its true light. He had to sell his clothes and his books to meet the pressure of want, and was soon reduced to the lowest depths of wretchedness. Sometimes he had not even bread to eat, —so that the story of the prodigal became a reality in one case more. He saw his folly, as he confesses, but he did not feel his sin; his determined resolution to follow his own devices was still unshaken; and though he abandoned the day-dream of a continental tour on foot, he was constantly anticipating other scenes of future grandeur, and indulging in the baseless pleasures which fancy presented, to lure him onward or sink him into darker depths. He was relieved at last from his penury by being employed as clerk to an attorney in London, and, utopian as ever, he began to entertain some hopes of following the law as his profession.

The persistency of Buchanan's nature was manifested in another way. He continued occasionally to correspond with his relatives in Scotland, but he contrived to write to them as if he were really travelling on the Continent, and thus perpetuated the deception by which he obtained their consent to leave his native land. His life was still so chequered that he might have been prompted to reflect, could trial by itself have done so. But "bray a fool in a mortar, and his folly will not depart from him;" and though Claudius Buchanan lived in London often on the verge of starvation, or was sometimes obliged to pledge his clothes, and other articles, to secure a bit of bread, none of these things moved him from his steadfast purpose; he had chosen his path, and he persisted in it. As resolutely as if he had been upholding high and holy principle did he adhere to his own ways; and neither his father's death, nor a fever which assailed the wanderer about the same time, could turn him from his singular career. He might vow—and break his vow on behalf of what is good and true. When conscience smote him for such things, he might indicate at once the wickedness and the energy of his character by exclaiming, "I swear I shall do so no more." But the strong man armed was not to be subdued by such means, and Buchanan went on frowardly, the pride of his heart preparing him more and more for a fall.

When this youth, so decided for evil, began to reflect on the life which he had led, his character still appeared with the same energy, but was turned in a different direction. He had been resolute in sinning. He would brook no restraint upon his will. He would deceive, and continue his deception for years rather than be turned aside from his chosen path, or even confess that he had chosen amiss. He had been thus betrayed into sins not a few; but after the lapse of what he calls three tedious years, he was to be arrested by One yet more resistless and decided than he. In his fourteenth year, and at other times, young Buchanan had felt some concern about religion and eternity, but as he was ignorant of the divine plan of escaping from sin to safety, he continued still to "drink up iniquity."

A casual visit, however, from a religious friend, and a casual conversation with him, bent Buchanan's mind in a new direction. He was too prompt and too energetic to halt or to hesitate, and instantly resolved to reform his life. He did not know what was implied in that resolution, or what power was needed to enable him to keep it; but with little delay and great self-reliance he locked himself up in his chamber; he fell upon his knees; he endeavoured to pray—he failed; he tried again, and again he failed. He reflected on his sins with horror now. Sabbath began to be longed for as the day on which he could appeal to the Physician, for he now felt that he was diseased. At one time, listlessness and languor—the collapse after strong feeling; at another, earnestness and hope, signalized him; and to escape from such alternations, with his usual decision, he separated himself from all his former Sabbath-day associates, and wholly withdrew from pleasure and amusement such as he had once zealously pursued. For seven months he thus strove to reach a quiet resting-place, not yet enlightened to know the plain and heavenly path--but seeking, and therefore sure to find; diligent, and therefore sure to make rich; decided, and therefore escaping at length from the woe of those who are neither cold not hot.

But the freedom of Buchanan's soul from that bond of iniquity which his own hand had both forged and rivetted, was to be accomplished by other means than his own energetic purpose. He communicated his state of mind to his surviving parent; and in her reply she counselled him, if possible, to cultivate the acquaintance of John Newton. That was the pivot of Buchanan's life. The prodigal, as he came to himself, became first a hearer, and then a friend of that remarkable man, himself a brand plucked from the burning. Buchanan's sorrows and anxieties were at first anonymously communicated to Newton, who referred to the letter in the pulpit, and invited an interview. It was as eagerly sought upon the other side; and that was the occasion employed by God to set the prisoner free. A man whom God had made wise to win many souls won this one also; and all the energies of young Buchanan's nature now became as cordially enlisted on the side of what is good and true as they had before been zealous to earn the wages of iniquity.

And the hour had now come when this wayward son must undeceive his long deceived parent. By Mr. Newton's advice, he communicated to her the history of the past sinful years, confessing while he did so, that he once thought he would rather suffer torture than betray his secret. Pride, acting in concert with a strong will, made that step appear too humbling to be ever taken. But the "sinews of iron" in his nature had become like those of a little child. The lion was tamed into a lamb; and Claudius Buchanan not merely became another proof of the power of truth as uttered by John Newton, and blessed by God, but a defender of that truth himself—ever steadfast, unmovable, and abounding in the work of the Lord.

It is well known that in the Holy Land, and other oriental countries, the earth is at seasons burned up and parched. Vegetation droops and dies; the herbs are turned into fuel by the fervour of the sun; and man, and beast, and bird are forced to seek what shelter they can find, probably that of some "great rock." But the rains return; the arid earth drinks in the copious moisture, and in a single day some verdure may begin to reappear. All nature seems to be suddenly revived. It is a kind of resurrection; or it is in some degree like what occurred when God at first created herb, and flower, and tree. Now that change may illustrate what takes place alike while the soul is dead, and when the mighty power of God bids it live once more. From that moment, all that is eternally noble dates. The drooping soul revives. The weary soul is refreshed. The polluted soul is made pure. The soul which seemed withered and dead is restored to activity and real joy. It was thus at length with Claudius Buchanan.

And with him, as we have said, to will and to attempt were nearly the same. He now entered on a course of training for the Christian ministry, and was introduced by Newton to Henry Thornton—one of the men who know that they are only stewards, while God is the Proprietor of all—and who furnished his new friend with the means of proceeding as a student to Cambridge. In his zeal, now so decided as to be self-sacrificing, he had thought of proceeding at once to Sierra Leone, to tell God's message to the perishing; but there was other work in store for him, and he became a student of Queen's College, Cambridge.

At the University, Buchanan was as decided as before, and he needed all his decision. From the first, he selected the godly for his companions and friends. Divine things were now uppermost in his soul, and if they were ever displaced by other studies, it was with a grudge and a complaint. Whether he was contemplating the interests of this life, or the still more cogent claims of the life to come, his language was ever firm and unfaltering; he gave no uncertain sound. "By the grace of God he was what he was;" and if ever any man calmly but resolutely strove to live for the one thing needful, it was Buchanan now—the man who, as a lad, had left his father's home with a lie for his only reason, and a phantom for his only guide.

It was about this time that his attention was first turned to his future sphere of labour and of triumph—our Eastern possessions. About the year 1790, they had begun to assume a magnitude which foreshadowed what they have now become—and when Buchanan's mind was turned to that vast and dark-souled land, as a scene of Christian labour, he never afterwards lost sight of it till his dying day. While taking his place in the front ranks of the students at Cambridge, he tried to cultivate brokenness of heart and conformity to Christ yet more than the studies of the University; he avowed humility as the first object of his aim, humility as the second, and humility as the third. He had already learned in the school of Christ that whosoever would be great must begin by being little—and with great decision, young Buchanan practised the lesson—while all that he did or thought began to be associated with "the regions beyond," lying in the shadow of a threefold death.

In directing his mind to India, he did not rely merely on the firmness of his own decisions, or "walk in the light of his own eyes" (Eccles. xi. 9). His great anxiety now was to learn the will of God, and in simple faith to do it. While afraid to tarnish the honour of such a momentous embassy by an ungraceful or unskilful negociation, he was yet ready to go if sent to that land, well assured that if God did send him, he would not be sent in vain. His aim, in short, was avowed; namely, to devote himself—a martyr if need be—

to the Saviour of sinners; and that is the spirit which makes a man triumphant; the world is sure to feel his weight, and to weep, or else to exult, at his fall. In 1796 Buchanan was appointed to proceed to the East—and results which reached far into eternity hung upon that appointment. On the 11th of August he sailed for Bengal.

He was one of the men who knew that if we would succeed in our efforts to do good, labour in season and out of season must be employed; and scarcely had he embarked when his efforts to do good were commenced. All the appliances within his reach to promote the chief end of man were employed in that little world—the ship. But when he reached India, in the month of March 1797, he found much there to sadden and depress him. Europeans were deeply sunk in Oriental vices; and indifference reigned paramount, except as regards hostility to vital religion. Such a state of things, however, was overruled to develop and draw forth the energies of the new Chaplain, as persecution braces principle, and draws forth faith, and renders the tried more fit to work the works of God. He who a few years before had entertained the romantic notion of travelling afoot over Europe with a violin for his provider, and with visions of future felicity, as attractive but also as unsubstantial as the aurora, gleaming before him, is now to engage in the battle of life in far different conditions. He is to encounter the rude repulse, or what is sometimes worse to bear, he is to be tried by hope deferred. But to opposition in every form he learned to present the calm front of firm determination guided by Christian principle, and he triumphed in the end. The weight of his character was soon felt; and even when he was opposed, he was respected or feared.

It is not our purpose, however, to narrate the various incidents in this man's life further than shall suffice to

manifest his decision of character, and the results which
followed from his calm determination to do good. At one
time he became a professor in the College of Fort William,
in Bengal, combining the duties of that office with those
devolving on him as a religious teacher, but all with the
design of helping to win India to the Saviour; and if ever
there was a labourer of his class who was instant in season
and out of season, it was Claudius Buchanan. As Professor
of Greek, of Latin, and English—as a devoted pastor, and a
frequent preacher—as an able correspondent, administrator,
and counsellor, the care of a hundred things devolved upon
him. But he was ready, because he had a heart interested
in them all. And more: he now not merely repaid
what his own education had cost the generous man who
befriended him, but, in his turn, became himself such a
friend, and remitted £500 for the education of some hopeful
youth in England. The remittance was accompanied with
the following statement: "While it is in my power, I wish
to do some good for the gospel of my blessed Lord," and
that is the action, that the sentiment of a man who is
sure to be heard of. We may be as certain of that result
as we are that spring has come and that summer is coming,
when the singing of birds is heard in the land.

In June 1802 the Governor-General of India was
instructed by the Court of Directors immediately to abolish
the college of Fort William, where Buchanan was a professor. All was proceeding with zeal and proportionate success in that Institution; but under pretext of expense,
though in reality because it was feared that the natives
might be alarmed by the use of Christian agencies, the order
to abolish was issued. Lord Wellesley ventured to ask the
Directors to revise their decision, but that only postponed
the evil day. It became more and more manifest that the
Christian religion and Christian morality were to be care-

fully excluded from the College—and the students at least
were quick enough to detect, and witty enough to expose
the sinister evasion. In a parody on Henry IV.'s speech to
his son, they said,—

> " Pluck down my officers; break my decrees;
> For now a time is come to mock at form;
> Have you a Writer that will swear, drink, dance?
> The Court shall double gild his treble guilt,"

and these were the fruits of man's zeal for gold and power
—of his indifference or hostility to the truth of God.

Buchanan was one of the officers thus plucked down;
and while the enemies of revelation were "grinning their
ghastly exultation," religion fell in the streets, and the
symptoms of a return to sound morals which had begun
to appear vanished away. But he was not to be daunted.
He knew that in spite of ten thousand enemies who might
be pitted against the truth, it was still the winning cause;
and to reinforce it in India, he despatched letters to
the Universities of Oxford, Cambridge, Edinburgh, Glasgow, St. Andrews, and Aberdeen, to enlist the most eminent
men at these seats of learning in measures for promoting the welfare of Buchanan's adopted country. To the
universities he added Trinity College, Dublin, with Eton,
Westminster, and Winchester schools; and proposed Prize
Essays to each on the best means of evangelizing the sixty
millions of Hindus who were then subject to the British
authority. He saw that before much good could be
done a deep foundation must be laid : a sound public
opinion must be created—and tedious as the process might
appear, in no other way did he expect to rouse the
British people to consider the highest interests of India.
English essays and poems, and Latin and Greek odes
were thus drawn forth, and Buchanan, on this occasion, devoted no less a sum than £1650 to rouse British

thinkers to think of India, or shed light upon that ignorance which made men fear the ascendency of the Prince of Peace. All this was done exclusively by Buchanan's own liberality. He formed the plan with wisdom: he carried it out with an almost impassioned decision which shrank from no sacrifice, and though his triumph was tardy, it was also great. He had chosen his part in life: he was steadfast and immovable in working it out, and his deeds praise him in the gate. By fixing his thoughts, and concentrating his efforts upon that one object—Indian renovation —he was honoured to commence a brilliant revolution which affected the destinies of uncounted millions.—When Prince Henry of Portugal, toward the close of the fifteenth century, resolved to push forward his maritime discoveries beyond what the mariners of his day could contemplate or achieve, he had to establish a Naval College and erect an Observatory for educating seamen. Only thus could he train men to realize his own conceptions; but thus he did it—and Buchanan acted on the same principle in a still nobler sphere.

But more was needed ere the way to victory could be opened. The former appeals to the Universities were made in 1803. In 1805 they were renewed to the English Institutions, and five hundred pounds were allotted by Buchanan to each University to draw forth essays on the design of Providence in placing India under Britain; on the best means of securing translations of the Scriptures into Indian dialects, and spreading Christianity in the East; along with illustrations from history of the luminous track left by truth as it journeyed from nation to nation.

Whatever was the moving cause, the Court of Directors had for a time modified their orders to shut up the college of Fort William. It was to be continued for the present on its original footing, and our devoted friend of India laboured with renewed zeal in its cause. He had fixed his eye upon a certain point, and towards that point he pressed whoever might appear to impede his progress. At one time he had to contend with a strong tide of Hindu and Mohammedan prejudice against translating the Scriptures, augmented by all the encouragement which the old Civil servants of the Company could impart—semi-Hinduized as many of them were. But Buchanan was not to be daunted. He laboured without ceasing at what he called hewing wood and drawing water for the future sanctuaries of India, and he was not left to labour in vain. The Essays which his munificence called forth now began to influence and to mould public opinion. It became apparent that our Oriental empire would, in time, share the benefits of sound learning, and of what is yet more precious, sound religion—and cheered by such symptoms, our devoted labourer continued his efforts, now frowned, now smiled upon—at one time caressed and helped even by the Governor-General of India; but at other times scorned and opposed by the men whose vices Buchanan's measures did so much to unmask—for what is it to gross and godless men though millions perish, if only they may sin undisturbed?

After adopting some steps for securing more ample means for meeting the religious wants of Europeans in India, Buchanan proposed to proceed upon a tour of inquiry among the Syrian Christians on the coast of Malabar. Though prevented by sickness which brought him to the verge of the grave, from accomplishing his object at that time, he lived to carry it into full effect. Neither his own debility, nor the intelligence of the death of his wife near St. Helena, on her way to England, could repress the single-eyed aim of the man. His heart felt and bled, as few could have done; but the more and not the less was he stirred up to work while it was day. He acted like one in a boat ascending

the rapids, where success depends not merely on the
strength, but yet more on the persistency of the rower; and
he rowed with all his heart, for he felt that the eternal life
of myriads was concerned.

Buchanan's next appeal was to the Archbishop of Canterbury, to enlist his aid in the cause of India—the cause for
which the Chaplain was willing to spend and be spent. It
was the year 1805, and Napoleon Buonaparte had about
that time occasioned great anxiety by his attempts or his
designs against our Eastern empire. Buchanan knew the
sure defence. He wished to take religious possession of
Hindustan, and consistently argued that five hundred
ministers of religion planted there would do more for its
real welfare than fifty thousand British soldiers. Even now,
after the lapse of more than half a century, there are only
about four hundred missionaries in India: but had
Buchanan's proposals been adopted when he made them,
many a heart which has ached in anguish, and many a soul
which has perished for ever, would have been spared their
agony. Yet though he did not accomplish all that he
aimed at for his own Church, he did achieve not a little.
Degraded as Hindustan still is by its hoary superstitions,
it would have been worse, and darker, had he not concentrated his energies upon it, and lived, laboured, died, in
seeking to place it under the sceptre of Him whose right it
is to rule. It required, no doubt, as Buchanan once said,
the heart of a lion and a countenance of brass to contend as
he had often to do. But his armour was on. The victory
was promised; and though he had times of dark forebodings,
like other zealous men, when the clouds returned after the
rain, he held on his way like the swallow in its migration,
or like some animals in their strong instincts, true to the
one point, and the one achievement—Christianizing India.
Dark, hopeless, or impossible as that result might then

appear to the eye of sense, he was convinced, and held his conviction against all comers. Not even death—and he was put to the proof more than once—not even *death* could shake his heaven-born purpose. His one decision was life-long, and had he been less firm he would have been less honoured.

It will readily be believed that Buchanan's guide for the present, aud his hopes for the future, were sought and found exclusively in the Scriptures. His next enterprise, accordingly, was to adopt measures for their translation into fifteen of the languages of India; and he pushed his proposal with characteristic ardour among all classes from Delhi to Travancore in India—from the Court of Directors and the Bench of Bishops down to many private individuals in Britain. In this cause also sermons were to be preached and published at the Universities. Rewards were given by this friend of India to those who engaged in the work of promoting its welfare. He even hoped to enlist the aid or the countenance of the Governor-General, Sir George Barlow; but that timid, equivocal man declined officially to identify himself with the measure, and Buchanan was left, without aid from that quarter, to harmonize conflicting interests, or, in plain language, to make a little room for God's word in God's own world.

He was now prepared to proceed on his visitation to the Syrian Churches in Southern India. It was in quest of information to guide him in his life-work that he went, and Hindu and Romish temples, as well as Syrian and Protestant churches were all visited to discover what might promote the object in view. His conduct there has been compared to that of Howard, who travelled far and wide to remember the forgotten, to tend the neglected, and visit the forsaken—and there is justice in the comparison. At his own expense, borne up and borne onward by his devotion to the highest interests of the land of his adoption, Dr. Buchanan (for that was now his title), proceeded on this lengthened tour, and at each successive stage made it more and more manifest how man can achieve grand results— by utter consecration to what God has given us to do. Far up among the passes of the Himalayas, there are rivers struggling to find their way through gorges which threaten, at a hundred points, to render the escape of the waters impossible. Yet on they press, and either find or form a channel. It is an attribute of genius to do likewise in regard to moral results, when consecrated to God, and cheered by his light. A thousand obstacles may obstruct it, but they only render it more resolute—and while some men are toiling for that bread which is only like the apples of Sodom, or seeking that safety which is found under gourds, others, like Buchanan, choose the better part—they do good; they get good; they are blessed and made blessings. He was all this, because one of his deep convictions was that he might "seek for no resting-place here but in a close walk with God."

True, the horrors of Juggernath, as described by Dr. Buchanan while on this tour, appalled and agonized him. Two or three hundred thousand devotees assembled at that loathsome and revolting shrine—the dogs devouring the dead—the vultures disputing with the dogs—the indescribable odours that made the air fœtid and stifling— the bones partially gnawed—the skulls rolling about in ghastly mockery, with the hideous spectacle of the car and the self-murdering devotees, all drove him in horror from the spot: but they also nerved him to more eager resolution to seek the welfare of India ; for if it is ever to be well, Juggernath must fall. And neither did impenetrable forests, where jungle fever and prowling tigers competed for the destruction of men, daunt this intrepid Christian. On he pressed, cheered by not a little that was encouraging, as well as saddened by many sights which he saw. He visited in succession no fewer than seventeen Syrian Churches, and did what he could to reclaim them to the simple truth by circulating God's word among them. In short, he hastened his own departure from this world by his devoted and exhausting endeavours to lead others in the way to glory in the next.

On returning to Calcutta, Dr. Buchanan was not allowed to publish the results of his Researches in the Government Gazette; the "traditional policy" was too rampant then to tolerate such a step. But he was not to be turned from his purpose, and other channels were soon found for fixing men's thoughts on the necessity of spreading Christianity among the Asiatic tribes. He was, however, obliged to contemplate a formal opposition to the Government plans, under Lord Minto, for checking the gospel; and though he felt sometimes as if he were leading a forlorn hope, with few, few to follow him, he was determined not to surrender. The threatened rupture accordingly came. Dr. Buchanan *would* preach the whole truth of God. The Government would not tolerate such conduct. The MS. of some sermons on the propagation of the gospel, which he had preached, and was requested to publish, was demanded on behalf of the government. Of that request he took no immediate notice, but, on the contrary, memorialized the Government on the subject of its recent measures with the temperate firmness of a man who knew that the gospel is the power of God unto salvation, and was "neither ashamed to profess, nor afraid to defend it." In that spirit, he could bear, even while he deplored, the neglect with which Lord Minto treated the memorial. Buchanan believed, and did not make haste.

He was now, however, on the eve of returning to his

native land, and had deserved, as he received, the encomium
that he was worthy to be the Metropolitan of the East.
He had encountered much to test him there. From the
horrors of the Inquisition at Goa, and the loathsome scenes
of Juggernath, up to the coldness of Governors-General,
he had much to endure; but he bore it with as much love
to India as any European that ever left our shores; and on
his arrival in England his labours on behalf of Hindustan
began anew: they even increased till the time when missionary men could be driven from its borders was past for
ever.

Some would pursue a bolder policy or more catholic
plans than Buchanan adopted; but when we remember the
trammels which impeded him, or the Imperial, and Direc-
torial obstructions with which he was forced to contend,
what he attempted seems wise, and what he accomplished,
wonderful. He did more than lay the foundation; he
largely helped to rear the structure of India's spiritual
emancipation. He was one of the chief promoters of that
measure which opened India to Christian influences in the
year 1813; and for some time after that event, he continued to labour in the same cause. With still concentrated though waning zeal, he sought the good of Hindustan till he died in the month of February 1815, at the
early age of forty-eight; and even his Will indicated the
precision of his views, as well as the energy with which
he performed all that his hands found to do. A monu-
mental inscription in the church in Yorkshire where he
is interred, declares that he roused Britain to a sense
of her duty to send forth labourers to the East—that
he was bold and intrepid in his work of faith—and his
whole life, from the day when he heard John Newton
preach, till the day when he died at Broxbourne, in
Herefordshire, attests the truth of the encomium. "He

gave himself wholly to his life work "—he did it with all his might—and he is shining now among the starry lights.

This, then, is another model. Would men stamp themselves upon their day, or their neighbourhood—would they make themselves felt in their age, or their country—would they, in lowly or in lofty spheres, do what will make them loved while they live, and missed when they die? These things will not be accomplished by random efforts, or ill-directed aims; by mere wishes, or mere schemes. There must be a path selected; there must be energy, decision, and persistency manifested there. First desire—then resolution—then enthusiasm to pursue—must ever precede pre-eminence. Painstaking and continued effort—urgency, to tears and prayers, if need be—caution at the basis, but resolute determination further up—*these* must signalize us, or we are self-doomed to insignificance; we are like a dead fish swept down by the current, not a living one, shooting the very rapids. In Dr. Buchanan there was little that was remarkable, excepting his calm persistency. No brilliant genius—no flashing oratory—no ancestral prestige. But he was not to be moved; neither was he to be precipitated—and the secret of his strength was this: he had chosen aright; he had chosen for ever; and he could say to the God who guided him—

> " More tranquil than the hush of summer noon,
> More peaceful than the calm of midnight hour,
> More bless'd than mortals are, my spirit lies
> Beneath Thy power."

Were we to act like Buchanan, we might say the same, and take rank like him among the bright souls whose track through the world is light—for was not he a safety lamp to many? Is not his radiance flickering still?

Have the arms of our island, its diplomacy, its administrative power, or its national resources won an empire

more rich and ample than the parent state? That is only
the harbinger of a far more glorious subjugation to a far
more glorious king. The achievements of the past century
in India are only dim-foreshadowings of far grander events
when the myriads of its people shall learn to honour the
name of Jesus. Our representatives in the East have sometimes complained that annexation was forced upon them
by the rigour of an uncontrollable law; it was a necessity
of which the formula was—Annex or abdicate. Now one
boundary and then another and another was set to our
empire there. But God on high had other limits than ours,
and He has done all his pleasure. River after river was
therefore crossed; battle after battle was fought; kingdom
after kingdom was annexed—now the country of the two
rivers, or the Doab; anon the country of the five rivers, or
the Punjab; this year Rajpootana, next year Oude—until
the Himalayas became the only barrier that could arrest
our progress, as they are the grand boundary of our empire.

Now, Dr. Buchanan was among the first to realize the
operation of this law of annexation in reference to the
higher kingdom. In this respect, the law is still more
pressing, or still more inevitable, for it is the revealed
decree of God. He whose kingdom is never to be moved,
and of whose dominion there shall be no end, will yet see
those kingdoms all subdued, and all annexed to His. It
may be slowly—or he may come quickly. But one thing is
certain. Those "regions beyond" must be annexed in this
sense. Their hundreds of millions of down-trodden men
must be lifted up, and Dr. Buchanan was among the first to
take up that conviction in its grandeur.

CHAPTER III.

𝕻𝖍𝖎𝖑𝖆𝖓𝖙𝖍𝖗𝖔𝖕𝖎𝖘𝖙𝖘.

" Love thyself last: cherish those hearts that hate thee;
* * *
Still in thy right hand carry gentle peace,
To silence envious tongues."

SHAKESPEARE.

HE proofs that our world is a distempered one meet us on every side,—behind, and before. But among them all, none seems more cogent than the fact that even the efforts which are made to cure that distemper are keenly resisted,—nay, resented, as if they implied an insult or an injury. It would be difficult to recall a single effort thus made which did not provoke an amount of hostility, which would have been unwarranted even though the endeavour had been malignant in its aim.

John Howard, for example, arose about a century ago, and after a peculiar training, entered on his great life-work —the mitigation of misery, or, if possible, its extermination, in some of its most wasting forms. Surely, then, such endeavours will be hailed with instant acclamations ; surely open arms, and loving hearts will welcome this friend of man ; surely not even a dog will bay against him or his enterprise. But far from that : he had to repel many malevolent attacks, for a time, at least, till he had borne down opposition by goodness, and silenced slander by the glories which gathered round his character. He was, in truth, the object of ungenerous imputations; and even to this day the friends of his memory have sometimes to defend him against slanders. A monument in St. Paul's Cathedral attests the admiration of many of his countrymen; but the echoes of the attacks made upon him while alive, may still be heard by those who revere his name.

And Wilberforce woke up, when he felt the power of that truth which liberates the soul, and began to seek the liberty of others—their liberty in every sense. His grand aims were to break *every* yoke, and let *every* captive go free. And yet, in that labour of love, what hostility did he not encounter! What rancour did not assail him! From year to year, till a quarter of a century rolled away, he had to do battle with selfishness, cupidity, oppression—in short, with every form of opposition which enmity the most intense could occasion. The philanthropist was treated by many as the filth and off-scourings of all the earth; and minds less buoyant than that of Wilberforce and his coadjutors, or less upheld by that strength which is not of earth, would have abandoned the struggle as hopeless. Scarcely less could the opposition have been though Wilberforce had tried to rivet chains upon men, instead of attempting to break them in every land.

Again: a humble missionary, in a colony of slaveholders, ventures to take measures cautiously, yet scripturally, against the crushing abomination. But he is assailed and maltreated by the brutal men who bought and sold their brother man as if he were a brute. He was cast into prison, where he died—all because he had tried to make some of the troubles to which man is born, less galling and less fatal. The thunders of the British Senate might be evoked—as they were—by that and similar outrages. But no interposition could prevent the martyrdom of some whose sole offence was benevolence, and sympathy for the down-trodden children of Africa.

Now, these and a thousand other examples enable us to see more vividly the horrible distemper which prevails on earth—where a love and a pity like those of God have been too often repaid by buffetings, by imprisonments, or death. And such things are not drawn forth from that oblivion, into which it were well if they could sink, from any desire to rail at the delinquents of the past. They are quoted now to furnish another reason for that manly energy which is needed to cope with the evils which riot in our world. A sarcastic philosopher has justly sneered at rose-water revolutions—a true revolution—that is, a change from evil to good, is not to be effected without stanch, stern, and sturdy determination. Before they can reach a point where they can do good to their fellow-men, philanthropists need the spirit of him who said, "With me it is a very small thing that I should be judged of you or of man's judgment." They must even be content, like the same great friend of man, to fight with men as if they were wild beasts, if misery is to be diminished, or if man's moral disorders are ever to cease to make our world a moral chaos.

When we look, indeed, at the overmastering aggregate of guilt and subsequent misery which surrounds us on every side, we may well be appalled. Had we only the human arm to lean on, or human wisdom to guide, we might indeed despair. But it is not so. There is a bright future before our distempered world yet. "At evening time it shall be light"—and he is the truest philanthropist who, first, most firmly grasps that truth; and secondly, tries with greatest energy and decision to usher in the promised day, by withstanding all forms of evil, and promoting all forms of good. Some have devotedly done so: let us now trace their steps, and endeavour to catch their spirit.

I.—GRANVILLE SHARP.

A.D. 1735–1813.

"Patron of else the most despised of men,
Accept the tribute of a stranger's pen!
Verse, like the laurel, its immortal meed,
Should be the guerdon of a noble deed. . . . .

O that the voice of clamour and debate
That pleads for peace till it disturbs the State
Were hushed in favour of thy generous plea,
The poor thy clients, Heaven's smile thy fee."

COWPER.

His birth—Studies—Undertakes the cause of a slave—Takes up another—
Establishes the maxim, "No man can be a slave in Britain"—Resigns his
office under Government for conscience' sake—His poverty—And difficulties—
Renewed efforts to do good—Is bequeathed an estate—His labours in founding Sierra Leone—Anti-slavery Society—British and Foreign Bible Society—
Protestant Union—Sharp's religious habits—His illness—Death, and character.

IT has often been noticed that neither great men nor
great occasions are needed in order to do good.
The humblest instrument may produce the
mightiest result—it always does so, when God works with
it. He does not usually work by means of our strength,
for that is too often the rival of the Holy One, but by
our weakness, and that becomes His glory. Who slew
Goliath—and what was the instrument employed? Who
overthrew the paganism of ancient Rome, and made a Roman emperor either a Christian indeed, or politically a pre-
tender to that character, because he saw that it would fix
him on the throne of the world? Who was the chief instrument in producing the Reformation—was it a king or any
potentate? What was the power that first originated those

measures which are now helping so largely to win the world to Christ? In all these cases, and in a thousand more, the Eternal accomplished great results by feeble instrumentalities, and has therefore all the glory of evil overthrown, or of good promoted. Conspicuous powers are not needed to produce great effects in regard to eternity—the blessing of God is enough when his truth is the guide and the counsellor of man.

These remarks are exemplified in the case of GRANVILLE SHARP, who was born at Durham on the 10th of November 1735. In the year 1750, and before he was fifteen years of age, he was sent to London, and apprenticed to a linen draper. Soon after his apprenticeship, however, he relinquished trade, for his tastes as a scholar had turned his attention to other pursuits. One of the earliest recorded evidences of his decision, and of that energy which made him what he afterwards became, was occasioned by a controversy with a companion who was a Socinian. The divinity and atonement of the Saviour were challenged by him as not warranted by the Greek Scriptures. At that time Sharp did not know Greek; but he was neither to be baffled in argument, nor driven from the strongholds of truth by a mere assertion. He therefore set himself resolutely to study that language, and did not pause till he could read it and meet the assailant of the sinner's only hope by arguments deduced from the very source to which that assailant had appealed. In the same way, Sharp learned the Hebrew language, that he might be able to answer a Jew, who alleged that he misinterpreted the prophets through ignorance of the language in which they wrote, and through all his life he continued mighty in the original Scriptures.

But though these and similar things indicate how strenuous Granville Sharp could be in prosecuting what his hands found to do, they do not bring him before us in the character in which he was best known. In the year 1765, his attention was turned to the sufferings of slaves, and their condition drew forth alike the tenderness and the energy of his character. He had a brother, a medical practitioner in London, who devoted his morning hours to the gratuitous relief of the poor. Among those who sought advice there, Granville met a slave named Strong. Pain and disease, the result of brutal treatment, had led him to the place where the hopes of relief were held out. To behold such a spectacle of suffering, the result of dire oppression, was enough to enlist the deepest sympathy of Sharp, and he soon learned that Strong's owner, a lawyer from Barbadoes, had first reduced him to weakness by barbarous treatment, and then turned him out of doors. But by tender care the slave was restored to health, after which he entered the service of an apothecary in London. Two years after that period, however, he was recognised by his former owner; and as the slave was now well-conditioned, and fit for labour, his oppressor instantly formed the design of recovering his property.

It was not difficult to discover the residence of Strong, and Lisle, his owner, sent a message which brought the slave to a meeting-place which was indicated. Thither the wily captor was accompanied by two of the Lord Mayor's officers; and as soon as Strong arrived, he was seized and placed in custody as part of his owner's goods. The man to whom Strong was then a servant interfered, but was easily scared by Lisle, who threatened a prosecution against him for fraudulently retaining what was the property of another. But the poor slave, who was now in a London prison, found means of communicating with Granville Sharp, who forthwith proceeded with great earnestness to investigate the matter. It was at first denied by the jailer that

he had any such person as Strong in his keeping; but Sharp
was not to be foiled. With characteristic ardour he threw
himself into the cause of the poor slave—took measure after
measure to secure his discharge, and baffled at last the owner
of his brother man.

But this was not to be accomplished without a struggle—
indeed without many a struggle. Sharp was even accused
of having robbed Lisle, the original proprietor of the slave
—a law-suit was commenced against the philanthropist and
his brother—but annoyances in other forms were employed,
and Sharp was actually challenged by the slave-holder to
fight a duel, on account of the part which his benevolence
had taken on behalf of the victim. This was characteristic
—for why should not the barbarous oppressor of a slave
manifest his ire against any man who crossed his path or
dared to challenge his usurpation of power?

But though Sharp, as a Christian man, could easily dispose of the challenge, he could not so easily accomplish his
benevolent purpose among lawyers and the labyrinths of
law. Decision after decision had declared that merely because a slave had landed in Britain, he was not, therefore,
free; and Sharp was now obliged to devote himself to the
legal view of the matter in order to unravel the intricacies
of the case. For nearly two years he gave himself up to the
intense study of the laws upon the subject of liberty, so
much was he bent upon securing the freedom of this poor
slave, or of others who were like him. He applied to
lawyer after lawyer for aid, though scarcely ever with success, and did all that philanthropic ingenuity could devise to
accomplish his object. He circulated the results of his
studies wherever he thought they could be of service to the
cause; and before Lisle's law-suit was finally disposed of,
the lawyers who were to have pled against the slave, had
become emancipationists. The claimant of property in the

flesh and blood of a brother mortal was thus vanquished by
the indomitable perseverance of Sharp.

But another case of a similar nature soon arose, and into
the inquiries which it occasioned Granville Sharp once more
threw himself with even augmented ardour. The question
now raised was, "Whether a slave, by coming to England,
becomes free?" and America and Africa were ransacked
for helps to decide it. The common rights of man were
asserted to prove that in Britain there could be no property
in human flesh and blood—and after full discussion, where
the verdict long hung in doubt, the decision of the judges
was in substance, that "as soon as a slave sets foot on
British ground, he is free." Sharp was thus amply repaid
for all the trouble which he had taken, and all the sacrifice
of time and of personal ease which he had made. It was a
befitting reward of endeavours put forth in the cause of
injured humanity, and upheld by indomitable perseverance
—a perseverance which would yield to no difficulty, or be
daunted by no foe.

He had now become known, then, as the advocate and
friend of the slave, and was encouraged from various quarters to persevere in his selected work. It was in connection
with these proceedings that the wish utterly to abolish
slavery and the slave-trade first gathered strength in Britain
—and Sharp may be regarded as the father or the founder
of those societies which ended in the abolition of that bloody
traffic on the part of Britons. From small beginnings in the
bosom of Sharp, humanity grew strong, and triumphed at
the last.

His position now became one of difficulty in consequence
of the war which had broken out between Britain and her
American Colonies. He was then a functionary in the
Ordnance office, and was obliged, in the course of duty, to
send forth stores to be employed against our brethren in

America. Disapproving as he did of the war and its causes, he could take no part in such matters, and resolved to resign his office for conscience' sake, though, in doing so, he virtually gave up his only means of support. He had expended all his private patrimony in befriending the helpless ; and as numerous acts of bounty had exhausted both his paternal inheritance and the salary which he derived from his office, he who had hitherto been the helper of many now stood in need of help himself; he was in truth "without the means of sustenance." But amid all this, he was not left unfriended. He who had yielded to the impulse of a generous nature, and declined no sacrifice if only he could do good, was not forsaken amid the difficulties into which he had been led. A less decided or less loving nature might have kept him free from all such embarrassments as those which had now come upon him. But then, the decision would never have been recorded, that as soon as a slave touches the British soil, he is a slave no more ! A foundation would not have been laid, at least by Sharp, for sweeping away the shame and the guilt of slavery and the slave-trade from our land. He was only the pioneer, no doubt, but his unquenchable zeal made him an admirable pioneer, and multitudes have learned to call him blessed.

But this zealous philanthropist was soon engaged in other enterprises for alleviating distress, or rescuing the oppressed. Indeed his was a mind which could not be at rest while he knew of a grievance to be redressed, or a sorrow to be soothed. The case of impressed seamen, and various proposals for improving the condition of the country, now called forth his strenuous advocacy; but his loving nature evermore recurred with tender solicitude to the case of the down-trodden slave. In the year 1783 his efforts in that cause were renewed, in connection with a case of atrocity transcending the ordinary doings even of that abomi-

nable traffic. The master of a slave ship which traded
between Africa and Jamaica, had taken in a cargo of four
hundred and forty slaves. During the voyage he dreaded a
scarcity of water; and under that pretext threw one hundred
and thirty-two of the most sickly of his unhappy victims
into the sea. This brutality might have passed unnoticed,
or at least escaped detection and exposure, had not the
owners of the ship and of its living load claimed from an
insurance office the full value of the drowned negroes, pleading necessity for throwing them overboard. The plea was
resisted, and hence the disclosure. Sharp rushed to the
rescue again, and turned the revolting circumstance into
one means more of awakening the dormant sympathies
of the nation on behalf of the injured negro. It helped to
rally others to the aid of that mercy which slave-dealers
trample in the dust.

But Sharp attempted far more than these insulated cases
imply on behalf of the descendants of Ham. He was a
chief means of founding the Colony of Sierra Leone, in the
hope of creating a check upon the obnoxious trade in slaves
—to operate against the cruel cupidity of the slave-dealer,
as the breakwater at Plymouth does against the Channel
wave. He roused the government by his solicitations, and
large sums of money were in consequence expended by
them. He advanced other sums collected from private
sources; but amid these labours of love, and these sacri-
ficings of self-interest in the cause of humanity, Sharp succeeded to the manor of Fairsted in Essex, bequeathed by a
friend who admired his philanthropy, and took that mode
of rewarding it. The income derived from that property,
it is believed, was mainly employed in founding the colony
of Sierra Leone. A self-denial which has been called parsi-
monious, and an energy which could be broken by no difficulty, bore Sharp through what was to him a mighty under-

taking. It was about the year 1785 that this philanthro·
pist accomplished this work—at once giving one Colony
more to Britain, and providing, as he hoped, some antidote
to slavery.

But such employment grew upon his hands. The subject
of slavery had now taken a deep hold upon the minds of
many. Friends in America then co-operated with others in
Britain to limit or suppress the nefarious traffic, and Sharp,
who was becoming a veteran in that service, engaged in
the work with heart and soul. In the year 1787 a few men
were brought together to devise some combined efforts to
check the evil, and wipe away the ignominy which was
connected with it—and Granville Sharp was one of those
who were first elected to commence a holy war against the
accursed trade. A proposal which had been made in the
British parliament eleven years before, to declare that trade
contrary to the laws of God and the rights of man, was now
renewed; and the devoted Sharp began to see the probable
reward of his studies, his lawsuits, his poverty, and his
struggles—all continued through years where only the deep
conviction that his cause was a righteous one could have
borne him up. That cause was now smiled upon by many
in Britain, in America, and France. They who knew not
the deep moral degradation into which the practice of slave-
holding, slave-buying, or slave-selling has sunk many thousands, might have begun to hope that the days of slavery
were numbered, or soon to close. Little could they think
that forty-seven years at least must yet pass away ere the
foul blot of slavery was wholly removed from the statute
book of Britain and all her dependencies.

Sharp, however, did not confine his enterprises for the
moral good of man merely to one channel, however wide or
important. When the British and Foreign Bible Society
was formed in the year 1801, he was called to preside over

the first General Meeting, and could hail that Institution as
one that was sure to prove an ally to himself and other
philanthropists in every land.   Some time subsequently,
he helped to form a Protestant Union to defend the sacred
cause of religious freedom, for through life he bore a heart-
hatred to Popery, as the antagonist of all that is good and
true ; at once the corrupter of God's truth, and the en-
slaver of man's soul.   Sharp was the author of most of the
documents emitted by the Union, and did much by his
intrepidity to rouse the dormant energy of Protestants to
resist a system whose wily encroachments even he could
scarcely have anticipated at the period to which we refer.
He assailed it as utterly subversive of the principles of
genuine liberty, and as having enslaved every nation in
which it has been dominant ; and holding that belief, this
man of deep convictions and enlightened vision, for the time,
threw all the energies of his nature into that enterprise.

And here we may glance at the habits of this earnest man
in regard to religion and his soul.   No doubt, God over all
may employ men of great powers but little love, to accomplish his designs on the earth.   "The wicked man is God's
sword."   But in promoting the moral improvement of man,
the God-fearing have mainly been the instruments employed.
This at least was true of Granville Sharp.   Profoundly
reverent in spirit, he bowed like childhood before the
authority of truth.   He rose early, and his first employment
was the reading of the Scriptures, or chanting a portion of the
Hebrew psalms to his harp.   His day was closed in a similar manner ; and his whole deportment was that of a man
whose soul was pervaded by deep convictions, prompting to
high and holy aims.   Wherever he resided, he was careful
that God should have an altar from which the morning and
evening sacrifice regularly arose.   Nor only that.   Even on
ordinary occasions, Truth, in its highest form—the hea-

venly—presided over the thoughts, words, and deeds of
Sharp. "Nothing was more remarkable," it has been said,
"than the firmness with which he delivered his most serious
opinions on many ordinary occasions, and the unembarrassed
simplicity with which he uttered them, blending religion
with almost every topic, both in conversation and in
writing." He might carry some of his convictions to the
verge of singularity, but still they were the moving power
in a mind of no great vigour, perhaps, but yet of determined
tenseness. If ever there was a man whose eye was single,
that man was Granville Sharp; and by his indomitable zeal,
based upon a profound conviction of truth, he achieved
results which would have seemed utopian to a more profound but less concentrated mind.

It was in the year 1813 that the death of this honoured
man took place. He was arranging his temporal affairs,
and designed to make a present of some books to the
library of the Temple, where he had for some time resided.
He was anxious to make the presentation in person, but
as his strength was not deemed sufficient for the effort,
he was strongly dissuaded. He proceeded, however, by
a public conveyance, and while in the metropolis stupor
crept over him — the forerunner of his close. This was
in the month of June, and on the 6th day of July he
died. On the 13th of that month his remains were deposited in the family vault at Fulham, where his tomb bears
an inscription which tells that "at the age of seventy-eight,
the venerable philanthropist terminated his career of almost
unparalleled activity and usefulness." The same authority
anticipates that "his name will be cherished with affection
and gratitude as long as any homage shall be paid to those
principles of justice, humanity, and religion, which for
nearly half a century he promoted by his exertions, and
adorned by his example." These sentiments will be re-

echoed by all who study the character, or trace the footprints of Sharp through the world of tribulation to the
home of the sinless.

We have dwelt chiefly on the public conduct of this
friend of the oppressed, based and built up as it was upon
all-sustaining truth. But amid the agitations and contendings of his public career, it would be wrong to lose sight of
his more quiet pursuits. With infinite difficulty, and at great
price, he established the right of the negro to freedom, at
least in Britain. He founded the society which at last
quashed the slave-trade; and in various ways left his impress deep upon his age. But not less determined was he
in other pursuits. He was, as we have seen, critically
skilled both in the Greek and the Hebrew tongue. His
work on the Greek Article, directed against the assailants
of the Redeemer's divinity, gave him an eminent place
among scholars; and altogether he was one of the men
raised up by the Supreme for advancing the purposes of
mercy, by making our world by some shades less guilty,
and men by some shades less wretched.

These things, then, indicate in one case more how a resolute and loving man can mitigate misery, and help on its
final overthrow. Sharp was one of those men who throw
their whole soul into whatever they undertake, and he was
honoured to stimulate others to finish what he could only
commence. The promptitude and the heartiness with which
he faced the evils which he assailed render him a model.
Indeed, he was "zealously affected" in every good thing,—
and for that reason he takes his place among the world's
benefactors,—a pioneer, perhaps, or a pilot, rather than one
who had powers of surpassing greatness; but withal a resolute and dauntless friend of the oppressed. His history
tells with deep significance that wherever man's powers are
religiously devoted to his God, He will bless us and make

us a blessing. The humblest, we repeat, become the mightiest when the hand which wields them is divine.

Could we picture the case of some youth just entering upon life, and seeking a guide to well-doing during his career, few could be pointed out more suitable or more encouraging than Granville Sharp. When he began the study of Greek, to enable him to cope with a Socinian, little did that student think that he was to throw up a new bulwark between the truth and error. Yet he was honoured to do so. When he took a poor, buffetted, and apparently dying slave by the hand, little did that philanthropist think that he was soon to establish the maxim that the British soil held such a charm, that whoever touched it was from that moment free. Yet Granville Sharp did that. When he helped to found a Society against slavery and the slave trade, little did he think that he was adopting a measure which would end, after a thousand struggles, in the emancipation of eight hundred thousand slaves, or lead Britain to expend twenty millions of her gold in procuring their freedom. Yet Sharp did that. And when he helped to found the British and Foreign Bible Society, little did he think that in half a century from that date the word of God, in whole or in part, would be read in one hundred and twenty dialects at least. Yet Sharp helped to accomplish that. In short, his deeds were seminal. They embodied great principles; they were therefore the germs of events which are to be reckoned great, even when tested by the standard of eternity, and that mind which tries to do likewise has in it a spark which was kindled in heaven.

II.—ROBERT RAIKES.

A.D. 1735—1811.

"O day most calm, most bright,
The fruit of this—the next world's bud;
The indorsement of supreme delight,
Writ by a Friend, and by His blood;
The couch of time; care's balm and bay;
The week were dark but for thy light;
    Thy torch doth show the way.
     *   *   *   *

Man had straightforward gone
To endless death; but thou dost pull
And turn us round to look on One,
Whom, if we were not very dull,
We would not choose but look on still,
Since there is no place so alone
    The which He doth not fill."
                         HERBERT.

Present state of Great Britain—Its past—Robert Raikes—His birth—And first labours—Previous attempts to train the young on the Sabbath—The Reformers—Puritans—And others—City of Gloucester—Prisons—Sunday schools—The results—Progress—The means employed—His motives—And principles—Triumphs—The system spreads—Indirect blessings—Death of Raikes—His character—Conclusion.

IT has been ascertained that in thirty-four of the great towns of England, which contain a population of three millions nine hundred and eighty-seven thousand souls, considerably more than the half, or two millions one hundred and ninety-seven thousand, never worship God, at least in public: they never enter a house dedicated to His service. In this island, as some compute, there are between five and six millions, out of about twenty millions of a population, who have lapsed into the same condition. Darkness, gross darkness has covered them,—

and all this in spite of educational and religious appliances such as no former age could boast of possessing.

From these facts it is easy to infer what must have been the condition of this country anterior to the recent moral and philanthropic activities. Multitudes were steeped in ignorance, and though many of the large towns, the centres towards which all that is debasing gravitates, had not yet sprung into existence, the population, both rural and civic, were far gone in all that can debase and enslave the mind. The life of the Reformation was spent, and death reigned over thousands.

But from time to time, friends of man and of that truth which elevates and saves, arose to shed light upon the darkness. Whitfield, Wesley, Charles of Bala, and other burning lights, helped to awaken many to a sense of that degradation into which multitudes had sunk. They plied the nation with truth, and arrested thousands on the way to ruin. But means were needed to take possession of the young before they were hardened in crime, or familiar with the way of their fathers; and one prepared to meet the emergency appeared when ROBERT RAIKES, the founder of Sabbath-schools, the friend of the poor, the benefactor of mankind, was born. He accomplished a bloodless revolution, and deserves a place among the great and the honoured as the author of blessings to uncounted millions.

Raikes was born at Gloucester on the 14th of September, in the year 1735. He was the son of a printer in that city, who published and owned a Journal which exerted great influence in those parts. We have scarcely any information regarding the early years of young Raikes. Nearly all that is known of him is, that he was well educated, and in due time became his father's assistant in conducting their Journal. He appears to have been its editor, or at least to have contributed largely to its columns,—and it was through that channel that he first unconsciously began his life-work, —calmly as all his future proceedings were conducted, but energetically, and with a degree of earnestness which was sure either to provoke eager hostility, or enlist as eager friendship.

Prior to the days of Raikes, many insulated attempts had been made to turn the Sabbath to account in arresting the spread of ignorance, and its offspring, crime. Among the great Reformers of the sixteenth century, among the Puritans and Nonconformists of the succeeding ages, as well as by the Church of England, and even by private individuals, some efforts had been put forth to reclaim the wandering, and train up the young in knowledge. In Scotland, in England, and even in Italy such endeavours had been employed. But it was reserved for Robert Raikes to be the first who should systematically and permanently introduce the method of Sabbath-school instruction. As printer, editor, and publisher of a Journal, he had space and time at command. Along with these, he had the heart of a generous philanthropist, and a genial, loving man,—and when the occasion arose, he was ready to embrace it. His heart, it has been said, was "one of Mercy's earthly temples," and all its charities soon found a befitting outlet through his endeavours.

The first thing that attracted his notice was the miserable state of the Bridewell-prison in the city of Gloucester. Criminals of all ages and all degrees of guilt were there immured together, without classification or distinction, as was then customary in this country. The youthful delinquent was schooled in crime by the mature felon; and that prison, like many more, was in consequence a very nursery of iniquity. Scarcely any allowance was made to the prisoners for their support: they were largely dependent on the charity of casual visitors for dragging out their sad existence; and all these things combined to render the Bridewell-jail of Gloucester a focus of misery. Its inmates had no work, and scarcely any food.

Now, Robert Raikes saw all this, and pitied the unhappy criminals. But he was a man of action as well as of sentiment, and forthwith employed his pen, his influence, and his means to secure some measure of relief. Finding that ignorance was often the source of crime, for men violated law because they did not know it, he resolved not merely to meet their bodily wants, but to let in the light of knowledge upon their moral darkness. When he found a prisoner who was able to read, he hired him to become the teacher of others. He furnished books adapted to such students,—and the progress was such as amply to encourage this experiment in transmuting vice into virtue. To these appliances he added work, believing that if he could succeed in curing their idleness, he would go far to cut the tap-roots of iniquity,—and Raikes has now fully entered on his high vocation. As a philanthropist of the right spirit, and a patriot of the highest type, he has plunged into the dark recesses of a county prison. He is mingling with the outcast and the profane that he may rescue them from the depths into which they have sunk: he has quietly and unflinchingly determined to do good; and he does it.

Still, however, his efforts in that prison were but the commencement of what he was to do. It is well known that Gloucester is the seat of an extensive manufactory of pins; and those who have visited that venerable city have no doubt examined the process with care. Multitudes of children were employed in the fabrication. For six days of the week they were kept busy, but on the seventh they were turned loose, often to live by plunder, or at least to be sources of trouble and discomfort to all around them.

Raikes saw some of these ragged children thus employed
on the Christian Sabbath, and with him to see a sight
of misery, moral or physical, was felt to be a call to remove it if he could. He accordingly instituted inquiries
regarding the moral condition of the young pin-makers, and
the result was the discovery, that certain of the streets and
suburbs of Gloucester were crowded on the Lord's day with
multitudes of these children. They spent their time in noise
and riot, such as indicated great pre-maturity in crime,
and unspeakable peril to their interests here and for ever.
Boisterous games, gambling, blasphemy, and other accom-
paniments of ignorance were rife, till the scenes "suggested
an idea of hell rather than of any other place." Neglected
by their parents, who were themselves steeped in ignorance, many of them in guilt, those youthful criminals were
ripening fast to be the pests of society—nay, they were
already all that, in cases not a few.

It was a conversation with one of the citizens regarding
these waifs, that suggested to Raikes the idea of training
them to decency on the day which they were abusing to
increase their guilt. It occurred to him, he says, that it
would at least be a harmless attempt should some little plan
be formed to check the prevailing profanation of the Sabbath. To carry out his idea, he inquired for teachers who
might be willing to attend to the neglected crowds, and soon
discovered four. These he engaged for the reward of one
shilling each Sabbath-day, to educate as many children as
he could induce to attend. The clergyman of the parish
entered into the plan with great cordiality, and undertook
to be inspector of the schools thus opened—and such was
the formal commencement of the system of Sabbath-school
instruction—such the feeble fountain from which myriads
of blessings have flowed.

This took place about the close of the year 1780, or the

commencement of 1781.* The effects were soon visible in the city. One of the lanes which was formerly the scene of boisterous doings, and in which Raikes planted a school, became a model of order, and "the place was quite a heaven on Sundays compared to what it used to be." The children were marched to church on the afternoon of every Sabbath-day; and by the wholesome effects of the truth, the blacka-moor was washed; in some cases he was far more—his skin was changed. The numbers who learned to read were so great as at once to astonish and reward their generous and self-denying friend; and he speaks with obvious glee of his " little ragamuffins" who spontaneously attended the early morning prayers in the cathedral of Gloucester. They assembled at the house of one of the school-mistresses, and went in procession to church. Raikes was careful to meet them there—they marched past and saluted him, and often seized the opportunity of carrying their appeal to him, when any animosity had arisen—seasons which he readily embraced to enforce his other lessons.

In addition to kind and judicious counsel alike regarding God and man, Raikes now printed a little book for his Sabbath scholars. Presents of Bibles were sent to him for distribution—the system, in short, is now fairly in operation, and such was the success attending his experiment, that other schools were opened in Gloucester. A whole parish, he says, entered upon the work, and the philanthropist began to hope that the plan would soon be adopted far and wide in the nation. In a brief period, between two and three hundred children were in attendance; and Raikes cordially dwells upon the pleasure which he derived from the discovery of latent good qualities in those who, but for him,

---

* In a letter dated 25th November 1783, Raikes says, " It is now about three years since we began," and this seems the nearest approach to the exact date that can now be made.

would have grown up the Ishmaelites of society. He calls his work in that respect a "botanizing in human nature;" and that pleasure, increased by the joy of parents over children reclaimed, and homes made happy, was his first reward for all that he had done. To hear some of the prisoners among whom he laboured thanking God that they had been detected in crime, and imprisoned, that they might meet with him who taught them to love what was good and true, was a joy such as no mere wealth could purchase.

But we should not fail to notice other means which this calm but resolute friend of the outcast adopted to compass his object. He roused the public attention through the channel of his Journal. He made personal application to his friends for funds and for help. He sent memorials and remonstrances to those who had the power of remedying the evil which he was combating. He gave of his means to help forward the labour of love; and by calm persistency directed by Christian principle, at last succeeded in rooting the tree, of whose salutary fruit we shall forthwith hear. He had found the key to the human heart—the key of kindness—he opened it, and was blessed to introduce into many a dark soul much of that knowledge which enlightens and makes glad. The lion was transformed into a lamb; moral order took the place of moral chaos.

Nor should we overlook the principle on which Raikes acted—the motives which stirred his soul. Calm and untroubled as he was while seeking to do good to some of the most unpromising among the sons of men, we are to find the secret both of his serenity and his success in the maxims which guided him.—No truth but that which came from heaven will ever renovate the whole man. Science may enlarge the understanding, and widen the field of view. Civilization may whitewash the sepulchre, or wipe the outside of the cup; but the interior cannot be cleansed by any mortal power. Now Raikes knew that truth; he acted upon his knowledge, and was therefore successful. A man who held only some fragments of truth might have been daunted and repelled amid the crowding abominations with which he had to struggle, or the mountains which he had to remove. But not so this intrepid man. Applying the divine antidote to mortal ill, he found that health was the result. He avowedly aimed at the glory of God —does philanthropy always aim so high? He avowedly sought to plant the good seed of heavenly truth early in the soul—has benevolence always kept that end in view? He anticipated a plentiful harvest, and his expectations were more than fulfilled—"Our Saviour," this philanthropist wrote, " our Saviour has taken particular pains to make it manifest that whatever tends to promote the health and happiness of our fellow-creatures were sacrifices peculiarly acceptable on his own day;" and guided by that maxim, Raikes took hold of the ox and the ass which had fallen into the pit to rescue them from peril imminent and deadly.

It will be noticed that the Sabbath-school system, as it was first adopted by this calm and resolute man, was not in all respects what it has since become. Secular knowledge was imparted on the Lord's day, as well as spiritual instruction. From the alphabet upwards, such an education was given as is now commonly confined to ordinary schools, and Raikes could not easily be induced to change this method. At first, moreover, the teachers were all paid, and he and his friends had to meet the pecuniary demands with which the system was at first encumbered.* But with these draw-backs, which it is well known are now entirely removed, the system grew and prospered.

* Rev. T. Charles is regarded by some as the first gratuitous Sabbath-school teacher, having begun that system in 1785. Hannah More and her sister followed in 1789.

Bishops lent it their sanction. Men like Cowper, Newton, and Scott encouraged it. The melancholy poet just named was specially captivated by the method which Raikes had struck out, and said that "he knew not, while the spread of the gospel continues so limited as it is, how else a reformation of manners, in the lower class of mankind, could be brought to pass, or by what other means the utter abolition of all principle among them, moral as well as religious, could be prevented." In Gloucester, at least, his hopes were realized to the full. That city soon began to wear a new aspect. Tranquillity took the place of riot; religion of blasphemy; and the worship of God, in numerous cases, superseded the revolting scenes which were before so common. Activity prevailed instead of idleness; moral beauty supplanted lawlessness,—and all this as the result of a happy but simple idea which took possession of a thoroughly practical mind, guided by Christian principle, and actuated by Christian love.

Honours now began to be conferred on the founder of Sabbath schools. His zeal in the cause, and his liberality in promoting it were widely recognised. Indeed his life appears to have been eminently happy—tranquil, yet active, and full of the bliss of doing good,—

> "His ways were strewed with flowers and happiness;
> There was no month but May."

Amid his honours, however, his zeal did not flag. He longed and laboured for the time when "the knowledge of the Lord shall cover the earth as the waters cover the sea." He regarded the crowds of children who everywhere flocked to Sabbath schools as scarcely less miraculous than the draught of fishes. Some French *savans* who visited Raikes rejoiced in his joy, and encouraged him in his labours. Adam Smith, the author of "The Wealth of Nations," was as much captivated by the method of Raikes as Cowper had been, and remarked that "no man had promised to effect a change of manners with so much ease and simplicity since the days of the apostles."

Attracted by the soundness and the simplicity of the system thus happily commenced, nations hastened to adopt it. Scotland, Wales, Ireland, America, all felt the impulse, and walked in the path struck out by the printer of Gloucester. Sabbath schools for adults began to be opened, and it seemed as if the countries of Christendom were to be swept and garnished from many of their reigning abominations. As early as the year 1826, it was computed that at least 90,000 teachers were gratuitously labouring among the otherwise neglected young. The expense of maintaining such an army for only a single year, has been estimated at £351,000, while some raise it as high as two millions sterling and more. But take the lowest sum, and that represents, in a material form, the benefits conferred by one man upon his own and succeeding ages. No wonder though philanthropists like Wilberforce, and devout minds like Hannah More's, co-operated in the system with heart and soul.

But where goodness has a fair field, it is indefinitely expansive. It is self-propagative, and this was extensively the case with the system of Raikes. Not merely did it sweep many a street, and many a lane, and many a hamlet of those who disfigured and disturbed it—that system led to results which were not at first anticipated. It trained up crowds of readers, and so called forth a literature adapted to itself. It necessitated the rapid multiplication of the Scriptures. It improved the physical condition of the poor. In 1833, the schools in England and Wales were 16,827 in number; the scholars 1,548,890, or one in every seven of the population at that period. In 1846, the scholars in England and Wales alone, were estimated at not less than 2,000,000; the teachers at 300,000; and the school-houses at more than

20,000; while the cost of these erections was valued, perhaps extravagantly, at five millions sterling.

Now, we cannot too often repeat that all this originated in the suggestion of one solitary but noble-minded man. The most enlarged philanthropy never struck out a grander device; it has even been said that "angelic wisdom could not have originated the plan—it was the suggestion of the Spirit of God." When we add to the other effects, the blessings and the benefits reaped by the teachers, the pulpits filled by many of them, and the mission-fields occupied by many more, there will be no difficulty in reaching the conclusion that "all the wealth of either Ind" could not have purchased such benefits for man. Raikes was the honoured instrument—but it was because he was guided by the wisdom which comes from above, alike majestic in its simplicity and mighty in its effects, that he achieved such results. It was because he felt the heavenly love, and reflected the heavenly light.

Among the other honours bestowed on Robert Raikes, it was one to stand before princes. He was visiting in the neighbourhood of one of the abodes of royalty, and when Queen Charlotte learned that he was there, she sought an interview. It was, of course, granted, and the origin and success of the Sabbath-day revolution were set forth to a queen, who, in the case of Raikes as of Caroline Fry, honoured herself by encouraging and cheering the good.

But the labours of this "Father of the poor" drew to a close. On the 5th of April 1811, he passed away, in his native city of Gloucester, in the seventy-fifth year of his age. He was interred in the church of St. Mary de Crypt, and the narrative now given, brief as it is, may, perhaps, supersede the necessity of any further comment. The accounts which have reached us of Raikes and his labours are singularly meagre and disjointed. The hero of war and bloodshed is lauded by a thousand voices: the hero of peace, in the present instance at least, has been too long overlooked, or known only by name. Enough, however, remains to show that he did not possess any remarkable gifts. There was nothing transcendant about him, but his gentle, genial love; no flash or outbreak of genius, none of the qualities which take men captive at pleasure. On the contrary, his powers, though well balanced, were not commanding. It was not by any strong, impulsive power that he did his life-work, but by the calm, unwavering, and persistent pursuit of his selected object. He saw a need, and determined to supply it. The misery of multitudes pained his generous spirit, and decided him to try to remove it. The streets of Gloucester rang with the sounds of riot, and the voices of young blasphemers. The environs of the city were overrun and infested by youthful depredators. Raikes longed to tame them; he employed the heavenly weapon, and accomplished more than he dreamed of; and as the result, he is now enrolled among the friends of the outcast and the degraded for ever. No idle wailing; no dreamy sentiment; no saying, Go, be warmed and clad, when there was neither fuel nor clothing. He supplied both—and in doing so stood forth among the men who are born to dry tears, to give beauty for ashes, and the oil of joy for mourning, by the blessing of Heaven on the means which they lovingly and persistently employ.

But with parts and powers like those of Raikes, any man may become a benefactor, if he have love, earnestness, and perseverance. These, and not brilliant gifts, were the attributes of this honoured man; and with his example of calm energy and invincible decision before us, no counsel is more appropriate, or can emerge more readily from the life of Robert Raikes, than "go thou and do likewise."

III.—EDWARD JENNER.

1749—1823.

> " Here see, acquitted of all vain pretence,
> The reign of genuine Charity commence,
> Though scorn repay her sympathetic tears,
> She still is kind, and still she perseveres. . . .
> The danger men discern not they deny;
> Laugh at their own remedy, and die."
>
> COWPER.

His birth—Early pursuits—His apprenticeship at Sodbury—Proceeds to London —Employments there—Sir Joseph Banks—Jenner's work—First hints of cow- pox—His decision—His restless activity for good—Illustrations of the single eye—The hint—His first vaccination, 1796—His "Inquiry"—Hostility—The Royal Society—Jenner's caution—Continued opposition—James Phipps— Jenner's position—Resorts to London—Opposition still—Invited to settle in London—Declines—Inoculation for small-pox prior to vaccination—What did he expect to accomplish?—False friends—Crowding assailants—Friends arise—Vaccination spreads—Incipient triumphs—Parliamentary grant of £10,000—Jennerian Institution founded—Jenner removes to London—Re- tires again—Second national grant—Progress—Family afflictions—Successes abroad—His honours—His death—His monuments.

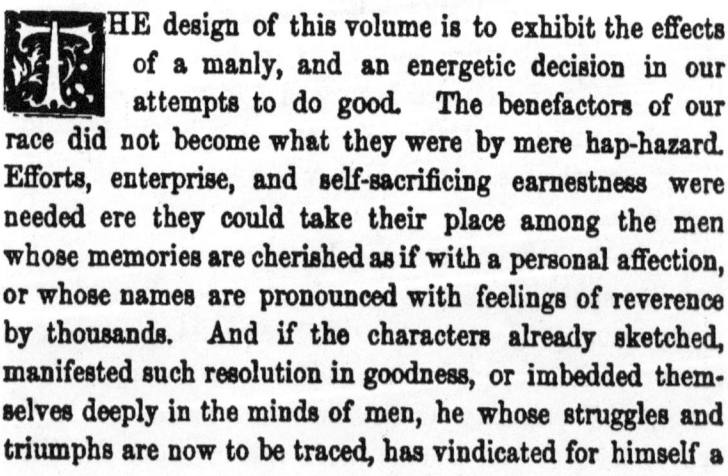

THE design of this volume is to exhibit the effects of a manly, and an energetic decision in our attempts to do good. The benefactors of our race did not become what they were by mere hap-hazard. Efforts, enterprise, and self-sacrificing earnestness were needed ere they could take their place among the men whose memories are cherished as if with a personal affection, or whose names are pronounced with feelings of reverence by thousands. And if the characters already sketched, manifested such resolution in goodness, or imbedded them- selves deeply in the minds of men, he whose struggles and triumphs are now to be traced, has vindicated for himself a position at least as high as the highest. He is one of whom posterity must often hear.

EDWARD JENNER, the discoverer of the virtues of Vaccination, the benefactor, or the preserver of millions, was a man of inextinguishable ardour, and of a calm but resolute will, which sometimes invested him with the grandeur of a hero. He was born in the vicarage of Berkeley in Gloucestershire on the 17th of May, in the year 1749. His father was vicar of that parish, as well as rector of Rockhampton, and possessed landed property in Gloucestershire to a considerable extent. From his earliest years, Edward manifested a love for the study of natural history. To some men, and Jenner was one of them, everything in nature speaks of a present God. Voices come murmuring to them from the brooks, or pealing from the thunder. The rain, the dew, the sunshine, and the storm are all eloquent, when man has ears to hear, and a heart to understand. They can tell us nothing of the new creation—the new heavens or the new earth. Of these we read only in the Book of Revelation, that book of which Jenner used to say, " The Sacred Scriptures form the only pillow on which the soul can find repose and refreshment." But nature is vocal about *its* God, though silent about the God of grace, and Jenner was a reverent listener. He had made a collection of the nests of the dormouse before he was nine years old; when at school at Cirencester, his play-hours were spent in searching for fossils in the oolitic formation of that neighbourhood; and when the period arrived for entering on the business of life, he was articled to an eminent surgeon at Sodbury near Bristol, to be instructed in the elements of surgery and pharmacy. From Sodbury he proceeded, when in his twenty-first year, to London to prosecute his studies; and lived for two years in the house of the celebrated John Hunter, whom Jenner ever afterwards delighted to honour.

His progress in natural science had already begun to attract the attention of learned men, and he was employed to classify the objects brought home by Sir Joseph Banks, when Cook returned from his first voyage round the world. So well was that duty discharged, that it was proposed to appoint the young naturalist successor to Banks, to proceed with the second expedition which sailed in 1772. Home, however, had stronger attractions for Jenner. Perhaps we should say, He who sees the end from the beginning had other work in reserve for him—and the offer was declined. He entered on a different career.

And what was it—what was Jenner's life-work? How was he to become one of the most signal benefactors of the human race? He was a man of firm purpose and strong will; though mild and genial in nature, he was neither to be scared nor allured from his chosen path,—and what was that path? That question is now to be answered.

It was known in a few districts of England that cows were subject to a disease which infected the hands of those who milked them; and those who had been thus infected were reckoned safe from the attacks of small-pox. But no exact inquirer had ever turned his attention to that subject; it floated about in uninquiring minds, till one arose who could investigate the rumour, to ascertain the truth. That was the career upon which Jenner entered. While still a youth, his mind was turned to it; and as that mind belonged to the order which refuses to be checked by difficulties, he never more let go the master idea which henceforth possessed him; which not merely gave a tinge to his whole life, but decided the character of his thoughts, words, and deeds till his dying day.

Reflection on the subject of what was afterwards called Vaccination had been no stranger to Jenner when studying under John Hunter. After returning from London to

Gloucestershire, the future discoverer began the active life of
a country practitioner, but continued to take an interest in
pursuits not always attended to in such a sphere. Natural
history and kindred subjects attracted not a little of his
attention; and an incident is mentioned as having happened
at this period which illustrates both the character and the
pursuits of the man. A discussion arose where Jenner was
present, as to whether the heat was greater in the centre of
the flame of a candle or at a small distance from the apex
of the flame, and Jenner settled the dispute by a decisive
experiment. He inserted his finger in the flame, and held
it there for a short time uninjured. He then placed it just
above the flame, but was compelled by pain instantly to
withdraw it. "There," he observed, "the question is
settled." It was like Columbus placing the egg erect—and
a person of political influence who was present, and admired
the tact and decision of Jenner, made offer next day of an
important appointment in the East Indies. He carried the
same promptitude into every sphere, and as he added a
kind and gentle nature to his energy and decision, the
friendships which he formed were not seldom passions, as
his pursuits were enthusiasm.

Jenner's active mind soon found both outlets and expansion in all that could improve the condition of his native
district. He formed more than one society with that
design; but the time was fast drawing on when the one
definite and absorbing pursuit of his life was to take the
command of his soul. If hitherto he had been much employed with secondary objects, such as registering the
habits of hedge-hogs, or determining the incubation of the
cuckoo, such things are now to take their subordinate place
—the great life-work has begun.

Or rather it has already made some progress. At one of
the societies which he helped to form, Jenner had made fre-

quent attempts to fix the thoughts of his associates on the subject which he could not long banish from his mind—the antidote, as he believed, to perhaps the greatest scourge of the human race—the small-pox. But so distasteful was the topic, or so wearisome did his re-iterations appear, that he was threatened with expulsion from the society unless he became silent on Vaccination. Already had he, with earnest perseverance, explained some difficult problems in ornithology ; made considerable advances in geology; improved some processes employed in the healing art, and investigated or explained some of the most extensive evils to which animals are subject. But all are now to be made subordinate to the one great pursuit which dominates like a law over the whole future course of Jenner.

It was while pursuing his professional studies at Sodbury that the subject of Vaccination was first brought under his notice. A young countrywoman had come to seek advice, and the subject of small-pox was mentioned in her presence. She immediately observed, " I cannot take that disease, for I have had cow-pox." The idea took possession of Jenner's mind, and was never again dislodged—he obtained a glimpse, though only a glimpse, of what was involved in the fact intimated by a peasant girl. Many things combined to fasten his thoughts upon the disease for which she at least knew a remedy. The ravages of small-pox, and the treatment which preceded inoculation in the manner practised prior to Jenner's time, all helped to fix the subject in his mind like a nail in a sure place. He resolved to let no opportunity escape of acquiring knowledge on so important a subject. Perseveringly, successfully,—nay, even triumphantly, he held on his way, although he had to encounter a host of enemies, and obstructions which were literally incalculable in number and in force. But his master, John Hunter, had a maxim on which the pupil now resolved to

act. It was, " Do not think, but try." Now Jenner tried
—that is, he experimented, like Newton, Bacon, and other
great thinkers, and thus early began that revolution which
is certainly second to none in the history of our race. In
the spring of 1796 he performed his first Vaccination, but
from that day he became the object of scorn and of ridicule
to many. Harsh and groundless aspersions were uttered
against him. Deep wounds were inflicted on his feelings as
he strove to mitigate misery. Bitterness and reproach were
the weapons with which he was assaulted. But in spite of
them all, the gentle yet intrepid man held on his way, and a
new epoch in the physical history of man was the result.

In aiming at that, it was requisite for Jenner to lay his
views before the public, and he did it in an " Inquiry" published in 1798. The remark of the peasant girl had been
the starting-point of the whole. It was to him what the
fall of the apple was to Newton (unless that tradition be a
myth), or what the steam of a tea-kettle was to Watt; and
Jenner set himself with irrepressible zeal to wring one of
its scourges from the hands of death. Evil omens were
not slow to appear. His fellow-practitioners in his own
district continued, for the most part, hostile or indifferent.
Predictions of failure were rife. Vaccination had been a
subject of meditation with him at least as early as the year
1770, when he mentioned it in London; but many would
not make it a subject of meditation at all. When brought
under the notice of the Royal Society at an early period of
Jenner's inquiries, it was coldly received; and the President,
Sir Joseph Banks, sagely advised the discoverer to be
cautious and prudent, and not to risk his reputation by presenting to the learned body anything which appeared so
much at variance with established knowledge, or indeed so
incredible as Vaccination.

Amid these things, however, Jenner had glimpses of the

future for his encouragement, and they proved to be prophetic. He seemed to feel that, in God's good providence,
he might yet stand between the living and the dead, with
his discovery in his hand, dispensing health to myriads, or
even banishing small-pox from the world. While on the
one hand he had to say, "I am the mark my medical
brethren all shoot at," he was, on the other, just the more
careful in his experiments. In every way he could devise
he tested his conclusions. He questioned and cross-ques-
tioned disease. He investigated every aspect of it that bore
on his great pursuit, and though some of his experiments
seem revolting to non-professional observers, they helped
to correct, to modify, or confirm the conclusions of one
whose zeal amounted to intrepidity, and whose battlings
with ignorance or prejudice proved him to be a hero.

Having once reached a full conviction regarding the
virtues of Vaccination, Jenner was no longer to be disturbed
or deterred either by prejudice or hostility. His friends
treated his enterprise as chimerical, but when he could pit
experiment against ignorance, and thorough investigation
against superficial impressions, why should he be dismayed?
Nay, he boldly went to the conclusion, as induction led
him, that it was possible to propagate cow-pox from one
human being to another, as he had already seen it spread
from the lower animal to man. His first case was that of
James Phipps, a healthy boy, about eight years of age. He
was vaccinated with matter taken from the hand of Sarah
Nelmes, who had been infected by her master's cows. That
boy was found to be proof against infection from small-pox,
and till his dying day, Jenner cherished Phipps with a care
like that of a parent.

This much being ascertained, then, beyond the reach of
cavil, if men really knew the facts, all the rest followed
without difficulty, and Jenner never more had need to waver.

The position in which he now stood, perhaps, never had a parallel in the history of man. In his benevolent heart there was enjoyed the blissful anticipation of misery lessened, pain, disfiguration, and death warded off from uncounted millions; and these things did not rest on the fancies of a sanguine dreamer. They were based upon experiment, and to himself, at least, were as certain and infallible as that water seeks a level. Prudence, caution, and singular modesty presided over his mind at this stage, as ever; and though he had been disposed to be elated, the antagonism which he encountered would certainly have quelled his pride. Of man in such a position, it is gratifying to know the precise state of his soul, and Jenner thus describes himself: " While the vaccine discovery was progressive, the joy I felt at the prospect before me of being the instrument destined to take away from the world one of its greatest calamities .... was often so excessive, that in pursuing my favourite subject among the meadows, I have sometimes found myself in a kind of reverie. It is pleasant to me to recollect that these reflections always ended in devout acknowledgments to that Being from whom this and all other mercies flow." The results which are traced to that resolute man's discovery are the fitting product of such a mind. Whence could the most important contribution ever made by science to human happiness and life be derived but from the Author of every good and every perfect gift? If it be true that Jenner seemed to hold in his hand one of " the gates of death," who but the Lord of life could have given him the key?

It was in the year 1798 that Jenner's " Inquiry" was published. He professed to prove, and did prove, " that the cow-pox protects the human constitution from the infection of small-pox." In spite of all the bitterness with which he was assailed, all the scorn, all the scurrility, all the fraud and oppression with which he had to contend, that discovery

places him side by side with Columbus—shall we say, with
Newton? Less brilliant than the marvellous disclosures of
that sage of the skies, those of Jenner have not been less
beneficial; they have been more.

It is no part of our design to furnish even an abstract of
the scientific bearings of Vaccination. Enough to know that
Jenner regarded cow-pox and small-pox as modifications of
the same distemper—the former being the milder of the two.
When he employed vaccine inoculation, therefore, as an
antidote to the virulence of the deadly scourge, he was just
improving on a hint from nature, or he used a ready-made
antidote for an appalling bane. Yet when he resorted to London, he could not, during a stay of three months, procure a
single person on whom he could exhibit the vaccine disease.
At first suspicion, and then hostility arose; and though
some one or two, or at most a few, learned to regard the
discovery as " promising to be one of the greatest improvements that have ever been made in medicine," the
discoverer's labours were just those of Sisyphus—up the
high hill he had to heave a huge round stone, which evermore rebounded and threatened to crush him. The subject grew, however, and the Faculty were divided. Indeed
Vaccination, for a time, became the arena of many a struggle.
Some did justice to the discovery, and examined the facts.
Others repudiated the whole. They did not adopt Hunter's
maxim, " Do not think, but try." They just reversed it,
and banter, derision, keen antagonism, and all the fixity of
foregone conclusions, were what Jenner had to meet. From
day to day, from month to month, from year to year, he had
these things to endure; and unless he had been one of the
most resolute as well as most humane of all the sons of men,
he would have succumbed amid the strife.

But his friends were sanguine of his success. Jenner was
advised to remove to London, and assured by their par-

tiality of an income of £10,000 per annum. But such predictions could not move him. "Shall I," he writes, " when my evening is fast approaching, hold myself up as an object for fortune or for fame? Admitting it as a certainty that I obtain both, what stock should I add to my little fund of happiness?" It was a proof at once of his caution, his wisdom, and his humility. Indeed, few discoverers have been so little dazzled as Jenner was. He was not callous; nay, he was sensitive as few men have been, and watched over his discovery with a parent's fond anxiety. He predicted danger or abuse in its application, and these accordingly befell. But when we find his judgment so calm amid all that tended to agitate, we just rely the more on his sagacity—he becomes the more conspicuously another model man. It was one of his sayings that "man is just a puppet moved by wires which reach the skies," and was not *he*, at least, God-guided?

Long prior to Jenner's time, inoculation was practised in many lands. In the East, in the South, indeed in numerous regions, the practice was observed. But it was inoculation for small-pox with small-pox matter, and it was far from being successful. Lady Mary Wortley Montague, in the year 1722; the king and prince of Wales of that day, and many others, encouraged the practice, and it did good; it saved the lives of many; but the contagion was often spread by the very means employed to check the disease. In England, in Scotland, and Ireland, as well as in many places of Germany, inoculation was either never tried, or soon ceased to be employed. Jenner's discovery, however, supplied the antidote in the mildest form; infection ceased, or all but ceased; and had men calmly contemplated the results, the discovery would have had fewer assaults to encounter, while his opponents would have been spared many a rancorous and virulent feeling.

But next, and more exactly, what were the benefits which Jenner expected to bestow on man? Have we the means of judging of the extent of the evil which he tried to remedy? The details are ample, and at hand.

—It was proved before the British House of Commons, that no fewer than 45,000 died annually of small-pox in the British Isles. Jenner professed to save all these. He held that Vaccination, rightly and skilfully performed, would banish that pestilence from the island.

In spite of the most approved methods of inoculation, it has been established that, previous to the adoption of Vaccination, every seventh child born in Russia died of small-pox, and the annual aggregate it is appalling even to record.

Taking all countries into account, it was computed that that fatal disorder carried off one in fourteen of all that were born. From Greenland to Asia and Africa, from the temperate regions of Europe to the countries under a vertical sun, these effects prevailed.

In Thibet, the capital was on one occasion deserted, on account of small-pox. In Ceylon, its appearance caused whole villages to be forsaken. In Constantinople, the disease has cut off every second person affected. Its annual victims in Europe have been estimated at 210,000, while others compute that its ravages amounted to 600,000 every year. Three-fourths of the blind in some asylums have been found to have lost their eye-sight by the hideous destroyer.

Now these are only specimens of the havoc caused by this enemy of man. But Jenner proposed to grapple with it; he thought that its power might be exterminated, and in support of his convictions, he advanced no crude theory, but substantial facts—the results of experiments cautiously, or even sceptically conducted. And what was the result? Opposition the most determined—it was even rude and imperious. Dr. Ingenhousz, a foreigner of eminence, then in this country, assailed the discovery, and eventually the discoverer. He was physician to a despotic emperor, and forgot that here such despotism as he seemed disposed to display is ignored. He became offensively violent, resisted every explanation, contended for the accuracy of his own assertions, and tried rather to overbear than to convince his opponent. And this case was not singular. Here, as elsewhere, the world's benefactor had to contend with crowds of assailants. "Not the least assistance," were his words, "from a quarter where I had the most right to expect it!" At the same time, his means were straitened, for this noble man, like many more, impoverished himself to do good. He was trying to bestow an unwelcome benefit, and one of incalculable value to mankind; yet had he to confess to "impecuniosity." How marvellous that he persisted in doing good, even to those who were neglecting him!

So intense did the hostility grow, that some refused to listen to any plea in vindication of Jenner's discovery. The accuracy of his details was questioned; the conclusiveness of his reasonings was denied, and derision, distrust, and suspicion, were still his chief reward. While some utterly denied the facts, others argued that they had long been known. Open enemies were joined by insidious assailants, who continued to act as if they were friends; and the ordeal to which the discoverer's firmness was exposed was perfect —had he not possessed the patience of a martyr to science, as well as the composure produced by unchallengeable facts, he must have yielded in the strife. One of his apparent friends wrote—"Your name will live in the memory of mankind, as long as men possess gratitude for services and respect for benefactors;" yet that friend became at last one of Jenner's most relentless antagonists.

True, some experiments began to be made, but it was in circumstances which were sure to mislead; the discovery was not fairly tested. All Jenner's remonstrances were unheeded; attempts were even made to rob him entirely of the merit of the discovery, and substitute one of his keenest enemies in his stead. Evidence of his claims was systematically set aside, and he was compelled, contrary to his gentle nature, to exclaim, " I am beset on all sides with snarling fellows, and so ignorant withal, that they know no more of the disease they write about than the animals which generate it." " It is impossible for me, single-handed, to combat all my adversaries." They rushed into print against him, and by distorted facts retarded his day of triumph.

But friends at last arose. Jenner's enemies had only done what Satan is understood to do at the canonization of a papal saint—namely, bring forward all possible objections against the new object of worship. The discovery was just the more scrutinized, till men gradually grew more assured of its importance. The nobility of Britain began to encourage it. At Geneva, at Hanover, and Vienna, advocates arose. Vaccination was recommended to parents by physicians who had no petty jealousies to warp them. From city to city it was practised, and he who before stood erect and undoubting against opposing prejudice, was cheered and encouraged now by the ardour of friends. Vaccine Institutions arose, and it appeared as if one of the plagues of mortality was about to be removed. Royalty lent its countenance to Vaccination. Prussia, Russia, and other countries, solicited a share in the blessing. Thousands were vaccinated without a single failure. Converts in high places became numerous. The Duke of York ordered it to be introduced into the army; and though a miserable jealousy still attempted to insulate vaccination from Jenner, that only recoiled upon the jealous. He suppressed his indignation, for he now saw that victory was only a question of time; but his friends were indignant, and the contention became more and more keen.

Meanwhile Jenner is getting his rightful place. Two royal dukes—York and Clarence—take him by the hand; the Earl of Egremont becomes his fast friend; after many annoyances, a Royal Jennerian Society is formed; Jenner himself is summoned to visit the king and the queen; he frequents drawing-rooms at St. James's—and now Vaccination is triumphant; its discoverer is standing at the right hand of royalty. America receives the gift with some incredulity and not a little ridicule; yet some of its most zealous friends are there. President Jefferson vaccinates with his own hands. France, in spite of war; Spain, in spite of its political death; the British army and navy; India, both British and native; even decrepid Turkey, all admit the mercy, and rejoice in it. Medals are presented to the discoverer; he is consulted even by a Secretary of State; epic poems begin to be written in his praise; and surely Jenner has triumphed now—surely his enemies are silenced —surely malignity dies!

Nay; Jenner's position as a benefactor to our world was not to be so easily established; his firmness was to be further tested, and his fair fame still further marred. Erhmann of Frankfort tried to prove from Scripture that Jenner with his Vaccination was Antichrist. He began, indeed, to be addressed as "the benefactor of mankind," or "that immortal benefactor of mankind." The Empress-Dowager of Russia desired that the first child that was vaccinated might be named Vaccinoff, and a provision was settled on her for life. But, benefactor as he was, he was still compelled to struggle with a too narrow income; and when it was proposed that Parliament should aid him by a grant from the public money, an attempt the most resolute was made to deprive him of both the honour and the reward. Rival claims were conjured up; efforts were even made to prove that he was ignorant of the whole matter. But when it was testified that " two millions have been already vaccinated in the world, and that of these two millions not an individual is known to have died in consequence of the infection," even malice was abashed for a time, and £10,000 were voted to Dr. Jenner by the British House of Commons.* Some murmured because the grant was so small; others murmured for a different reason, and continued to slander and traduce.

We have reached a point, then, where this discoverer may be supposed to be beyond the reach of malice. All lands have agreed to honour him. He is admitted into many foreign Societies; but some in his own land still continued to exclude him—and, moreover, rival claims began to be lodged. France befriended Rabout, a Protestant minister at Montpelier. Some claimed for the Hindus, resting that claim upon documents which had been forged to induce them to vaccinate, by pretending that the practice was ancient. Half-thoughts and hints were paraded against Jenner's full, explicit, and clearly proved title—and still these forgeries found supporters. He had, in short, to fight every inch of his way; and had he not been formed of the stuff of which heroes are made, he would have quitted the field, and left man to perish, since so many would have it so. But he had chosen his position: he would maintain it—and he did.

When a Jennerian Institution was founded in London in 1803—when the King and the Queen patronized it—and when Jenner was elected its President, it might be hoped that he had at length reached a haven of rest. But in a

---

* Pity that he had to wait for many months ere the money was paid, and to pay about £1000 of fees for his honour.

few years the Institution melted away, and clamours were renewed with a rancour which seemed only to increase with time. Again and again, one is prompted to inquire— Why is this man so hunted and harassed? What evil has he done? Is he provoking hostility by selfishness? Is he an upstart empiric, with no credentials but impudence to support his claim? And when we discover that he is a humble, unpretending man—of rare simplicity, and over-flowing benevolence—the wonder grows that such an one should have been so vexed and assailed. But it was his price for greatness and for fame. He was both tested and refined in the furnace, while he displayed a calmness in devising, and a decision in prosecuting his plans, such as have rarely been witnessed—were they common, the trade of defamation would be less prosperous. Bitter and rancorous as is the hostility of ignoble minds to the lofty and the pure, it is really astonishing to notice the persistency with which Jenner was harassed.

And the wonder deepens when we know that geographical boundaries were overleapt—that the hostility of nations at war was disarmed—that even religious animosity was calmed, in order to welcome Vaccination. The red men of America, the devotees of Brahma, the worshippers of Mohammed, the disciples of Confucius, combined to rejoice in what some British physicians resolutely opposed. The discovery was voted a true one by the world, and Jenner's enemies were left to carry their opposition to the grave. In little more than six years after it was made known, Vaccination journeyed round the globe; and it is computed that in a brief space of time 20,000,000 profited by the discovery.

In an evil hour, Jenner was over persuaded to begin practice in London, but it failed. When the parliamentary grant was voted, the Chancellor of the Exchequer sanctioned £10,000, instead of £20,000, because he believed that Dr.

Jenner might realize the former of these sums every year in practice. " Elated and allured," he confesses, by such words, he tried without success. Vaccination, in Britain at least, was still too precariously accepted to admit of such hopes being fulfilled, and Jenner soon returned to Gloucestershire. At length, another parliamentary grant was voted, and it was now £20,000, without any deduction for fees. Though one of the Universities frowned on him, the other made him one of its doctors, and though malignity traduced him at home, his birthday became a high festival in other lands. The Marquis of Lansdowne said to him : " You have conquered more in the field of science than Buonaparte has conquered in the field of battle ; and I congratulate you on so glorious a testimony of your success as that which the Spanish Narrative affords." *

It now appears, then, as if Jenner and his discovery had gained the ascendency so far as to be beyond the reach of injury. Twice had Parliament considered and conceded his claims. India had sent him from Bengal £4000, from Bombay £2000, and from Madras £1300. From Greenland to the Cape—from the Mississipi to the Ganges, Vaccination was common.† The children of the Wilderness—the Red men of the West—sent their felicitations to him as their benefactor, and besought "the Great Spirit to take care of him in this world and in the land of spirits." They saw and felt the blessings which Jenner had been the instrument of imparting; and as they had no theories to uphold—no malignity to indulge—out of the fulness of the heart the mouth spoke. Then, at the other extremity of society, he was made a member of the National Institute of France

---

* The Narrative of an Expedition sent out to carry Vaccination to the New World.

† A Pole, Dr. Reyss, presented Jenner with an embossed silver cup; asked his portrait, and a small piece of the cloth which he generally wore, that Reyss and his friends might wear the same coloured garb on Jenner's birthday, 17th May.

—and yet, amid such varied tributes to his success, he continued to be assailed by some in this land with a venom which seemed to grow with what it fed on. "The persecutors of Galileo," one says, "would, I believe, have been eclipsed in their monstrous and outrageous hostility to the splendid discoveries of this illustrious man. . . . ." The question was publicly discussed—"Which has proved a more striking instance of the public credulity—the gaslights of Mr. Winsor, or the cow-pox inoculation?" So rabid, indeed, was this persecution, that one man who tried to write Vaccination down but failed, actually shot himself when maddened by chagrin. Amid all this, however, Jenner moved calmly and resolutely forward—sometimes he could even make merry at the expense of his assailants. By the instinct peculiar to genius, he fixed his mind on the work given him to do. He refused to swerve from its pursuit; and while the antagonism which he encountered is almost without a parallel, his firmness—calm, dignified, and unflinching—is not less signal.

The encouragements by which Jenner was cheered amid his trials deserve to be recorded. One disciple, Dr. Sacco, an Italian physician, vaccinated, we read, 600,000 with his own hand, and about 700,000 by assistants. Napoleon, when war between France and England was at the hottest, liberated several British prisoners at Jenner's request; and the Emperor of Germany and the King of Spain did the same. Moreover, Jenner was allowed to grant passports to those who travelled on the Continent for scientific purposes, and they were not molested. But amid these honours in foreign parts—while medals were struck to commemorate his achievements, attempts were still made to degrade him in his own land, and in consoling him, one of the wisest of his friends had to say that " the promulgation of every discovery by which mankind has been benefited, has

always been attended with such circumstances; it is a general
condition, and must be submitted to." Jenner knew it by
the experience of many years.

The ailments of age now began to be added to his other
annoyances. Death after death, in his family and among
his friends, touched his tender nature; and all the while he
continued to be libelled and lampooned till some of his
friends counselled legal prosecution. He wisely declined to
adopt such a course; but the mere suggestion of it is a
marvel in the history of such a man. He saved more lives
than were destroyed in the wars which raged during a
great part of his career. In Russia alone, in eight years,
1,235,597 persons were vaccinated, and in two years, 305,676
in the presidency of Madras alone. Similar things were
done in every land, and yet that is the man whom some
would have persecuted to death, had the spirit of their age
permitted. It is really a phenomenon—and yet, with unswerving decision, he held fast by all his conclusions. "My
opinion of Vaccination," he said when near his close, "is
precisely as it was when I first promulgated the discovery.
It is not in the least strengthened by any event that has
happened, for it could gain no strength; it is not in the
least weakened; for if the failures you speak of had not
happened, the truth of my assertions respecting those coin-
cidences which occasioned them would not have been made
out." Against a man so firmly posted, and so unflinching,
what can vulgar hostility do, but confirm him more and
more? To the last, therefore, he was resolute, and the moral
grandeur of his character shone out more and more.* He
might be stung by the assaults of his enemies, but it was
only for a little; for the gentleness, the simplicity, and the

---

* At a levee, Jenner once heard a minister of the crown detailing some of the
current slanders against him, not knowing that he was near. He introduced
himself to the nobleman, who speedily retreated from the truth.

artlessness of his manners speedily supplied an antidote to the venom. With a peculiar buoyancy of nature, he knew how to render all things tributary to his great pursuit. He resolutely declined every dishonourable or unworthy course, exclaiming, " I would not do it for a diadem;" and if he advised his friends to write in his defence with an eagle's quill, promising to " find a hard one, and to sharpen the nib," it was in jest and not in hostility.* It was his prayer—found after his death among his papers—" that those sacred truths revealed by Him who condescended to assume a human form, and appear among men on the earth, might be engrafted upon his mind "—and in no small measure the prayer was answered. Indeed, so gentle was he amid all provocations, that he might have worn among physicians a title similar to that bestowed on Milton at Cambridge, when he was called " the lady " of his college. The fixedness of his moral purposes nothing could shake; yet was he, as near as possible, " gentle unto all men,"— kingly, but humble—firm, yet not less calm.

The honours heaped upon Jenner are such as few men have ever received during their lifetime; they were his compensation for detraction and spite. Diplomas, addresses, and various communications from public bodies and distinguished individuals are recorded to the number of about forty-five, and the language of most of them is that of unmeasured encomium. Nine medals were struck to commemorate his great discovery, or himself as the discoverer. In the year 1814, he had interviews with some of the allied sovereigns in London, and takes credit for having been probably the first to contradict the Emperor Alexander. He had mentioned that Jenner was happy in the gratitude

* ..... "Think no more of these wasps who hum and buzz about you," wrote one of his friends, "and whom your indifference and silence will freeze into utter oblivion, ... The great business is accomplished, and the blessing is ready for those who choose to avail themselves of it ....."

of all the world; but the great discoverer was obliged to
qualify the eulogy. He had received, as the Emperor said,
"the thanks and the applause of the world," but not its
gratitude.

Jenner died at his residence, The Chantry, in the month
of January 1823, and in the seventy-fourth year of his age.
He was interred at Berkeley on the third day of the following
month; and we know not that a better estimate can be
formed of his greatness than is conveyed by his biographer.
The most remarkable events of our age, he records, are not
that we have subdued the elements to our use—not that we
can multiply at will the products of ingenuity—not that we
have brought mechanical agents to take the place of active
and intelligent beings—but that we have been enabled to
stay the power of death, to keep him for a season from his
victims, and to say that the day of grace and preparation
has been lengthened.

"Dear to the human race" was a record to Jenner's
honour at Berlin, and he deserved it. We may desire,
indeed, some more vigorous displays of the religious element
in his character, and are not sure that the truth from
heaven always got its proper place. It was there—but
rather latent than developed. The fuel was collected, but
the match was not fully applied. With that truth more as-
cendent, Jenner would have been altogether one of the
grandest of the sons of men.

And such is a sketch of one who lived with the generosity of a good man, and the simplicity which becomes a
great one. From his first Vaccination in 1796* to the last
day of his existence here, he laboured for the good of man,
and spurned away every impediment which would have

* The day on which this experiment was made was long kept as an annual
festival at Berlin, where Vaccination found early and devoted friends—at once in
palaces and among the learned.

hindered his work.   Amid such swarms of assailants as
rose up against him, we are not to suppose that his life was
an unhappy one.   On the contrary, Dr. Jenner enjoyed a
still small pleasure of which he could not be deprived.   In
himself—in his home—in his success—in the ample field of
nature—he had a thousand sources of joy.   Swift's "uncon-
trolled truth," that "no man ever made an ill figure who
understood his own talents, nor a good one who mistook
them," was verified to the letter in Jenner's history, and
that man must have been ill-deserving of happiness who
could not find it in the world-wide triumphs of Vaccination.   Like the truth which came from heaven to guide
us thither, that discovery was opposed, maligned,—nay,
hated!   Just as the facts of Scripture are often doubted,
merely because they are there, Jenner's word was often
challenged, merely because he pled for Vaccination.   At
length, however, his enemies, not himself, had to succumb,*
and while his life is a study alike for the resolution of the
discoverer and the pertinacity of his opponents, few such
spectacles can be seen in the history of the past as the
decision, the perseverance, the heroic benevolence of Edward
Jenner.   No better summation of the subject than the
following could perhaps be submitted : "In the whole course
of our censorial labours,† we have never had occasion to
contemplate a scene so disgusting and humiliating as is
presented by the greater part of this controversy (regarding
Vaccination); nor do we believe that the virulence of political
animosity, or personal rivalry, or revenge, ever gave rise,
among the lowest and most prostituted scribblers, to so
much coarseness, illiberality, violence, and absurdity as is
here exhibited by gentlemen of sense and education, dis-

* Singular causes sometimes promoted his objects.   At one place the cost of
coffins for the poor compelled their guardians to try Vaccination in the hope of
diminishing the number of deaths.
† Edinburgh Review, Vol. IX.

cussing a point of professional science with a view to the good of mankind." All this Jenner suffered, just as Harvey did after his great discovery as to the circulation of the blood, and as hundreds have done, both before and since. We may, perhaps, add that there are methods of healing struggling into a scientific place in our day, though frowned upon by the Faculty and traduced, as Vaccination was half a century ago.

In Gloucester Cathedral there is a Memorial of Jenner. Westminster Abbey or St. Paul's has none; but Trafalgar Square contains his monument where it ought to be—among the heroes who guarded, or won renown for our land. His place among philanthropists is far up in that region of serenity which the agitation produced by puny things never can disturb.

IV.—ARCTIC EXPLORERS.

1853-55.

—" Cimmerian darkness shades the deep around,
Save when the lightnings in terrific blaze
Deluge the cheerless gloom with horrid rays;
Above, all ether, fraught with scenes of woe,
With grim destruction threatens all below;
Beneath, the storm-lashed surges furious rise,
And wave uprolled on wave assails the skies;
With ever-floating bulwarks they surround
The ship, half swallowed in the black profound."

FALCONER.

Sir John Franklin—His expedition—Public anxiety—Searching expeditions
fitted out—Results—American expeditions of Henry Grinnell—The second of
these, Kane's—Their perils—Escapes—Icebergs—Winter, August 24—Daylight disappears—Searching—Midnight of the year—Sledge dogs—Scurvy—
Discomforts thickening—Sources of strength—The sun's return—Chaos come
again—Misery—Frost-bites—Amputation—A funeral—Esquimaux—Explorations continue—Strength returning—Hopes of finding Franklin revive—
Arctic botany—Bears—A hunt—First thought of abandoning the brig—
Another winter on the ice contemplated—Disease prevalent—Renewed
dangers—Starvation—" Sunday thoughts "—Return of the sun—Preparations
for leaving the *Advance*—Difficulties and toils—The start—Homeward bound
—Perils—Reach Upernavik—The close.

E are now to glance at one of the most remarkable chapters in the history of man.

It is too well known that Sir John Franklin sailed from England in the year 1845, in command of the *Erebus* and *Terror*, which had been fitted out to explore the north-west passage, in the remotest northern regions, and that he never returned. It was on the 19th of May that he set sail with crews picked for the special and arduous service, and, after touching at some points in his outward voyage, the little squadron was last seen by a whaler in Baffin's Bay on the 26th of July. The letters of Franklin at that time indicated bright hopes of success,

as the expedition had till then been perfectly prosperous.
He was previously well known as one of the most adventurous explorers, and had pushed his way far to the north
amid sufferings greater than even those of Cook in his
voyages round the world. When he sailed, Franklin was in
the sixtieth year of his age, but as intrepid and adventurous
as he had been in early youth, and high hopes were entertained of the result of his expedition.

But in the year 1847, when nothing had been heard of it
for more than two years, anxiety began to be felt, and from
1848 to 1854, one searching party after another was sent
out, regardless of expense, and of every consideration but
one—the hope of recovering the missing commander and his
crews. Lady Franklin, with a devotedness and an energy
which cannot be eulogized—they are beyond the reach of
eulogy—roused public attention, contributed funds, and
enlisted the resolute and adventurous in her cause. France
sent Bellot, an officer of singular intrepidity and bravery.
Henry Grinnell, a citizen of America, generously fitted out
two expeditions from that country at his own expense. In
the month of August 1850, traces of the missing ships were
discovered, and it was ascertained that their first winter
had been passed at Beechy Island, where they remained till
at least the month of April 1846. But it was not till the spring
of 1854 that further traces were discovered. It was then
ascertained, through some Esquimaux, that in 1850 about
forty white men were seen dragging a boat over the ice near
the north shore of King William's Island—and later in the
same season, the bodies of the whole party were found by
the natives of those wild regions, at a short distance north-
west from Back's Great Fish River, where they had perished
from the effects of famine and cold. Some continued still
to cherish slight shades of hope, but to the most it became too certain that the whole had perished.

Some of the expeditions sent out in quest of the missing voyagers led to exhibitions of philanthropy which are actually chivalrous. Never, perhaps, in the annals of our race were greater daring, and greater self-sacrifice displayed. Undertaken at the bidding of science, such expeditions would have been noble—but begun and conducted, as they were supremely, for the sake of the suffering, or in the hope of rescuing the imperiled, they became sublime. In comparison with the deeds and endurance of at least some of the searching vessels, nearly all that is recorded of human suffering appears like the small dust of the balance. Human achievement amid nameless privations culminated there; and were it desired to exhibit man as the brother of man, in his highest, noblest aspect, we might point to some of these searching parties.

In the year 1850, the First Grinnell Expedition, under the command of Lieutenant De Haven, sailed from the United States. That expedition failed. Dr. Elisha Kent Kane or the United States Navy was a member of it, and in 1852, he was named to take charge of the Second Expedition. He sailed from New York in the *Advance*, a brig of one hundred and twenty tons burden, on the 30th of May 1853. The vessel was equipped for the arduous service with all that the experience of the former voyage could suggest; and in due course, reached the northern regions where the work of search was to begin; and we single out the darings, the sufferings, the heroisms, the anguish, and the deaths of that little expedition as one of the best illustrations which history affords of the persistent power of right principle, the noble deeds which man is enabled to perform, when he has selected a right sphere for his energies, and resolved wisely and perseveringly to pursue it.*

* It seemed one token for good in this expedition, that when the seamen were engaged, one of the laws to which obedience was exacted was that there should be no profane language used on board the brig.

In othei circumstances than the present, it might be
interesting to notice the Moravian Missions, for example, at
Lichtenfels in Greenland, and trace their doings and results
among the Esquimaux. Glimpses of these may meet us as
we proceed ; at present, it is determined intrepidity, and a
perseverance which sets all selfishness at defiance, that are to
be studied.—Scarcely had the enterprising crew of the
Advance entered on the peculiar scene of their labours
when peril and disaster began. They were moored, for
instance, to an iceberg on the 29th of July, to avoid one
danger, but only rushed upon another; for scarcely was the
vessel made fast when the crew were startled by a loud
crackling sound above them. Fragments of ice began to fall
from the iceberg, and they had just time to cast off the
brig, when portions of the mass fell into the sea, resound-
ing like artillery. It was the commencement of perils
which lasted for two years and more, or through the whole
extent of the enterprise. Yet those generous men found
some reward even amid their dangers. When the sun, at midnight, shone over the crest of the berg which had so lately
threatened disaster, the whole became a vast resplendency
of gem-work. It blazed as if with rubies and molten gold—
a sight such as southern climes never can exhibit.

Yet to cut their way through ice-floes, to crunch through
ice-drift, where their little bark would have been crushed to
pieces had it not been constructed for the service ; to anchor
to icebergs only to find danger augmented, all tested the
power of endurance of those friends of Franklin. On they
pressed, however, in spite of every danger, eager to reach
the field of search—wind, tide, icebergs, currents, and all
that is deemed formidable, were encountered from time to
time; but the determination of those hardy men to rescue
the explorers if possible, bore them up amid all their exhausting trials; and though they were at times excited to

enthusiasm, as when they unfurled the flag of America on the west cape of Littleton Island, their life was, for the most part, one of calm, sober, and resolute perseverance in their painful path. They were not to be turned aside, though the unpacked drift-ice and chaotic upheavals impeded their way and threatened utterly to thwart their purpose. But the thought of relinquishing their object was not once suggested, and the fact that those seamen persevered in the face of every peril, proved how resolute a thing right principle is—how indomitable, how sustaining.

At times, and these quite early in the expedition, Kane and his party had to crowd all sail, and try to force their way through the drift. On one occasion, four of the party were inevitably left upon the ice, where they must have perished, had it not been for the adventurous spirit of the commander, but still they were undaunted. Three-quarters of a mile sometimes formed the extent of their progress northward in the course of a day. It was solid pack before, solid pack behind, solid pack all around, and amid such struggles, if ever on earth, principle was put to the test— the strain was such as might have snapt it. It may be remarked, however, that stern as was the ordeal to which those heroes of humanity were at first exposed, they were only in training for more searching trials which lay before them, when some of them were kept awake by disease, danger, and toil, for eighty-one hours out of eighty-four; or had to weigh their food by ounces, or devour it reeking and raw, as it was cut from some animal in the agonies of death. They lived with their lives in their hand, as the price of the life of others.

But let Dr. Kane tell his own tale, at this early stage. A storm was dreaded; it came on heavier and heavier, and the ice began to be drifted wildly by the tempest. The commander, who had just sought rest and warmth after long exposure, had scarcely laid himself down when the sharp twang of a cord was heard—it was a six inch hawser snapt like a thread. Half a minute more and twang, twang, came a second report: it was another cable snapt. A third speedily rang out in the storm, like the cords of an Eolian harp that thundered—but it was the death-song! The shrouds gave way with the noise of a shotted gun, and the little vessel, formerly anchored by three cables, was now tossed at the mercy of tempest, drift-ice, and bergs.

Even this, however, was only the beginning of sorrows. The brig had lost her best bow-anchor in attempting to baffle the storm, aud now drove along a lee of ice, seldom less than thirty feet thick—at one place it was forty by measurement. An upturned mass rose above the gunwale; the bulwarks were smashed by it, and a block, half-a-ton in weight, was deposited on the deck. The vessel, we are told, seemed to have a charmed life; but so apparently had her crew. They might have been at ease amid the comforts of home; but in the cause of humanity, they chose to battle with the wildest of the elements in their own stronghold, and that battle has shown man to be, by some degrees, more noble than he was deemed before. "We passed clear," it is said concerning some impending bergs, "but it was a close shave. . . . Never did heart-tried men acknowledge with more gratitude their merciful deliverance from a wretched death."

On their way to the North Pole, as these intrepid men were, they had reason to anticipate an early winter, and it came. On the 26th of August, they began to doubt whether they could reach a higher latitude during their first summer. Even then some dark forebodings arose; yet on they pressed, stimulated by the hope of carrying relief to those whose condition had roused the anxieties of the civilized world. At one time the brig was driven by the ice up the slope of a berg as if some huge steam-propeller were forcing her into a dry-dock; and then she would glide back into the icy rubbish, a mere plaything for such agents. Amid all this, the commander had to admire the calm and manly demeanour of his comrades. It was, indeed, a time either to concentrate every effort upon one single object, or else to paralyse all minds but the strongest. On this occasion, officers and men all struggled alike, though some of them were carried adrift on floating ice, and rescued with difficulty. Shock after shock impelled their ship up the berg, and when she was free, the crew had to drag her as if along a canal. After some amazing efforts, she suddenly struck the ground, and within three days, she struck it five times. Exploring parties were now sent out to select the best spot in which to winter, but in truth, tempest and the season took that under their own care. After some hopeful explorings, the harbour of Rensselaer was chosen for their purpose. " We found seven fathom soundings and a perfect shelter from the outside ice, and thus laid our little brig in the harbour which we were fated never to leave together— a long resting-place to her indeed, for the same ice is round her still." *

The winter now came rapidly on. In the month of October, or about four weeks after they were laid up, the night without a day would commence, and for four or five months they would never see the sun. They had sailed into a day which had lasted for two months; but the scene is changing now; and if those friends of the wretched have felt the perpetual glare to be offensive, they are now to be tried with the opposite extreme of perpetual gloom. Yet those hardy men calmly persisted in duty—they continued their accustomed morning and evening prayers. The Sabbath was observed as a day of rest, as long as the

* Kane's " Arctic Explorations," p. 103.

terrible scenes which environed them allowed; and now,
after a hundred struggles, they are to pay one instalment
more for the privilege of doing or attempting good—they
are to have a night of several months' duration, relieved by
scarcely a glimmering of twilight.

But now began, as long as that twilight would allow, such
searching as they could, or rather preparations for a search.
It was not long that these could be continued, for in truth
the life of Dr. Kane and his crew soon became a battle hand
to hand with death : instead of doing much to rescue others,
they had to contend with the last enemy in appalling forms,
on their own behalf. During the intervening time, however, they did what they could. They deposited provisions
at selected spots; but only to find them afterwards dug up
and destroyed by the polar bears. They made excursions upon
sledges to investigate the condition of those wild regions.
At first, on these excursions, they carried with them quanti-
ties of provisions from the ship; but they lived long enough
in the brig, and toiled long enough in Arctic service, to
adopt the Esquimaux ultimatum of simplicity—raw meat to
eat, and a fur-bag to sleep in.

When parties left the vessel on any of the expeditions,
whether for depositing food in some *cache*, for facilitating
explorations, or for any other purpose, the friends separated
with the solemnity or the sadness of men who might never
meet again. The ice-floes, the ice-pack, the icebergs of their
appalling region, made such sadness natural, and the crashing collisions and frequent mishaps would have forced
reflection on the most thoughtless. On one of these excursions, Kane drove a sledge, which was drawn by a team
of Newfoundland dogs, and had one of his companions with
him on the vehicle. The rents in the ice over which he
skimmed made it often dangerous, for the dogs had to leap
across them, so that the sledge was dragged by sudden

twitches over the chasms. In one of these flying leaps his companion was tossed from the sledge. He caught hold of it as he fell, and but for that would have been swept away by the rapid tide. The dogs were whipt up: he held on; and was thus hauled from the sea. Though he was then twenty miles from the brig, he did not suffer from the bath; and it was well, for even that was only the beginning of troubles. The most wasting were ahead.

In spite of all such mishaps the labour of love went on. Food was concealed wherever it was likely to be of use. At one place no less than six hundred and seventy pounds' weight of pemmican, besides other articles, were deposited —for the most part only to reward the bears. On such expeditions, the escapes were sometimes hair-breadth. Fatigued, nay, exhausted till sleep was instantaneous when they halted, a party on one occasion turned in to rest upon the ice. About one o'clock in the morning a sound like the snap of a gigantic whip was heard, and the ice opened directly beneath them. Repeated detonations told them that it was breaking up; and, with the thermometer at ten degrees below zero, the poor wayfarers had to gather up their tent and their furs and leave the inhospitable spot.

Such discomforts of course grew more numerous as the winter wore on. Lanterns were kept continually burning at the brig. The lard-lamps were never extinguished below decks, and stars even of the sixth magnitude were seen at noon. On December 15th what we call noonday and midnight were alike; and, except a vague glimmer, there was nothing to tell that the Arctic world had a sun—it was the midnight of the year. The death of dogs, far more precious than rubies, had incommoded the voyagers beyond what can be told; but where all was discomfort it was fruitless to complain, and the continued buoyancy of most of the party is one of the wonders of the expedition. There

was one generous feeling which seemed to guide them all—
they were seeking to rescue fellow-creatures from woe; and
even though they lost the last vestige of day in their search,
the hope of aiding Franklin was to them for light.

The dogs of the Arctic regions have been called more
precious than rubies.   But during the terrible darkness
of the winter months, even they were so affected, though
natives of the Arctic circle, that several of them died.
Some of them had to be nursed like babies, and their
disease was as clearly mental as in the case of their masters
when they began to sink.   Epilepsy supervened; symptoms
similar to some of those which are common in hydrophobia
appeared.   Lockjaw came on, and some dogs died of brain
disease, after passing through violent paroxysms ending in
lethargy and stupor.   How priceless such poor animals were
may be understood from the fact that Dr. Kane travelled
about three thousand miles by sledge, and of these fourteen
hundred were with one team of dogs.

About the 21st of February the sun returned, and brought
promise of relief and restoration.   But one of the first
things which his light enabled the explorers to descry was
the scurvy spots which mottled their faces.   These were
the sad precursors of other trials, and unfitted not a few
of those who had wintered in the brig for doing more
than repel, and that with feebleness, the approaches of
death.   Indeed, each member of the party had now become
a Franklin, needing a deliverer,—while some, like him, were
not destined to be delivered by the hand of man.   Still,
however, the work did not stagnate.   They did what they
could, and that while the chief of the corps had to record,—
"Not a man now (March 1854), except Pierre and Morton,
is exempt from scurvy, and as I look around upon the pale
faces and haggard looks of my comrades, I feel that we are
fighting the battle of life at a disadvantage, and that an

Arctic night and an Arctic day age a man more rapidly and harshly than a year anywhere else in all this weary world." After such mournful sights, it is needless even to glance at the minor discomforts, although the words sound like a dirge, "We have not a pound of fresh meat, and only a barrel of potatoes left." How heroic these men long continued to be may be inferred from the fact that their heavy griefs only made common troubles seem light and insignificant.

Again and again one is prompted to pause and inquire, Why all these sorrows? Whence this exposure to life-long woe, to a night that lasts for months, and, after all, to days of disease, starvation, and all-sapping death? The master reason was that these men *would* do good, and sorrow was the path to it. These men *would* rescue some poor children of humanity from misery if they could, but the alternative was that they themselves should suffer! Oh, how mysteriously distempered our world is! How dark or dismal ten thousand scenes there, had not God in mercy placed in our hands the golden key which opens up the secrets of the woe! The whole creation groans and travails together in pain, and few ever felt the force of that truth like Dr. Kane and his companions.

At this stage, the temperature was often 45° below zero, while in the course of the expedition it was sometimes as low as 50° or even 60°, and it were superfluous to tell how such a temperature augmented the trials of the explorers. Amid all this, the crunching and grinding of the ice, the dashing and gurgling of eddies, and the toppling over of nicely poised ice-tables at the time of spring tide, rendered the whole scene indescribably chaotic. Yet efforts were still made, in spite of the elemental war, to carry out the purposes of the search, and wide ranges of the dreary region were examined,—but who will wonder if the men

became less hopeful? Yet toiling amid such scenes, swollen, haggard, and scarcely able to speak as some of them
now were, they exhibit, beyond all question, one of the most
signal proofs of indomitable perseverance ever given on
earth. On one occasion, three out of seven returned from
an expedition : but where were the others? They were
lying upon the ice at some distance, frozen, drifted up, and
unable to proceed. The return party were themselves sinking with fatigue and hunger, and could scarcely even tell
the party at the brig in what direction their comrades had
been left. One of those who had returned, though stupid
from exhaustion, was instantly strapped to a sledge and
taken as a guide to the party who hastened to the rescue
—such were the men who attempted to discover Sir John
Franklin and his companions.

Kane's missing seamen had to be sought for over a region
" within a radius of forty miles," and in that terrible search,
some of the stanchest of the men were seized with trembling
fits, while the leader himself, cool and intrepid as he always
was, fainted twice on the snow. After a search of eighteen
hours, they found some traces of the lost men, and in three
more they were discovered. Fifteen in all were now assembled
in a small tent. The thermometer was 75° below the freez-
ing point, yet on their return with the sick, they had to cast
everything away except the veriest necessaries. They expected the journey to occupy fifty hours; frost-bitten fingers
and feet were the result, and some of the sufferers will
carry the traces of those appalling hours to the tomb. The
homeward march to the brig was begun with a prayer.
Nearly a mile an hour was their progress. Sleep, sleep was
the cry of the exhausted heroes, although to sleep in such
circumstances was to die. Nine miles were struggled over
for the most part in a stupor, and the vigilant chief had to
wrestle, box, jeer, or reprimand, to keep the party in motion

at all. "I recall these hours," he records, "as among the most wretched I have ever gone through,"—and, considering the occasion which called them forth, they are enough by themselves to immortalize the men who left what was tame and domestic, to enter on such scenes. It was a noble offering laid on the altar of humanity.

When the party fell asleep at their halting place, they soon became environed in ice, and Dr. Kane had to be cut out with a jack-knife. Necessity obliged him at last to concede three minutes for sleep to each of the party in their turn. They grew quite delirious, and had ceased to entertain a sane apprehension of their circumstances when they returned to the brig. They moved onward like men in a dream,—dragging the lame,—and reaching their asylum after being absent on the rescue for seventy-two hours. One of them suffered long from blindness; two underwent amputations of part of the foot; and two died in spite of all efforts to save them. Who can wonder, when they tell us that they travelled between eighty and ninety miles, dragging a heavy sledge for most of the way? And these, we repeat, are the noble men who went forth with chivalrous humanity to rescue Franklin, and whose endurance and achievements place them high up among the heroes of our race.

Anxieties and sorrows thickened. The frost-bitten, those who had undergone amputations, and those threatened with a kind of epilepsy, were all huddled together in the vessel. Lockjaw seized one; on the 8th of April he died, and that funeral procession was perhaps the saddest that ever approached a grave. It was not dust to dust,—it was to snow: the burial-service was read, the Lord's Prayer was repeated, and the explorers returned from the dreary resting-place of their companion to their scarcely less dreary abode. When the summer thaw came, and when stones could be gathered, a grave was built—not dug,—a cairn was raised, and there Jefferson Baker awaits the peal which is to summon our race to the tribunal.

Of course this did not end the difficulties of the party: it was only one step more towards their full development. The explorers had had trouble from the visits of some Esquimaux, yet the explorations went on. But now one, and then another was put on the sick list. Scurvy re-appeared, or rather became more virulent; their depots of food were found to be entirely rifled by the bears; and while taking an observation for an altitude in one of those excursions, Dr. Kane again fainted from sheer debility. He had to be strapped in utter feebleness to his sledge, and that under what he calls "the otherwise comfortable temperature of 5° below zero." Epilepsy, dropsy, and other symptoms appeared in his case, and as he became delirious, and fainted as often as he was moved from the tent to the sledge, the physician of the party thus reported concerning him: "You were carried to the brig, nearly insensible, by the more able men of the party, and so swollen from scurvy as to be hardly recognisable. I believe that a few hours' more exposure would have terminated your life, and at the time, regarded your ultimate recovery as nearly hopeless."

Yet, amid their own sorrows, "these ice-leagured exiles" had time to think of Franklin. By the use of seal-flesh and other productions of that region, the worst aspects of their disease began to disappear; and Dr. Kane records, "They are fast curing our scurvy. With all these resources, ... how can my thoughts turn despairingly to poor Franklin and his crew? . . . . Can they have survived? No man can answer with certainty; but no man without presumption can answer in the negative." A few months before that time, when want and disease were pressing upon him, he might have answered otherwise; but when food—the food of such a region—became more plenty, he became more hopeful. The seal, the walrus, and clouds of aquatic birds, then flocked to every speck of open water, and food could thus be procured; and buoyed up by such hopes, Dr. Kane strove and struggled on. Of the hundred and thirty-six Orkney men who accompanied Franklin, the American explorer could not doubt, even in the year 1854, some would have survived. Meat, he saw, could be procured; acclimating was not impossible. Again, therefore, he hoped, and strained every energy, not merely to carry relief to the lost, but to show to others the grounds of hope in continuing his efforts. "My mind," he says, "never realizes the complete catastrophe—the destruction of all Franklin's crews. I picture them to myself broken into detachments; and my mind fixes itself on one little group of some thirty, who.... have set bravely to work, and trapped the fox, and speared the bear, and killed the seal, and walrus, and whale. I think of them ever with hope. I sicken not to be able to reach them." Such were the aspirations which sustained the party while they were themselves living from day to day next door to death. True, they had now been a year absent from New York, and Dr. Kane confessed that he had become less sanguine with time. His enthusiasm was checked and his hopes were moderated by sad experience; but still he *did* hope, and bravely strove to accomplish his grand mission, although it lay through a thousand perils, each of them enough to end in death.

Little incidents, however, still occurred from time to time, to re-animate the drooping. The discovery of a little flower blooming in beauty in some quiet nook, formed well-nigh an era in their dreary existence. But the sight of such flower-life could do little to keep the explorers safe from the attacks of bears, which now began to infest them. Those tigers of the ice could with difficulty be repelled by men

wading knee-deep in snow; and again, again, and once
again, the question occurs to those who accompany them in
thought amid their wanderings, How could men so circum-
stanced, any longer hope to be the means of aiding others?
Yet they even continued their scientific inquiries and astronomical observations, and the results of these are not the least
remarkable part of their achievements. But when the needle
began to perplex them by its variations, their movements
became more and more precarious or harassing. At times
they had to grope their way out of some maze like a blind
man in the streets of a strange city. At other places
they had to build ice-bridges over huge chasms, ere they
could proceed a step on their journeys. The very sledge
dogs, noble animals as they were, would cower, and whine,
and tremble, and crawl along, awe-struck by the surrounding terrors. In short, if ever the indulgence of humane
feeling could be called a martyrdom, the indomitable men
of the Second Grinnell Expedition were martyrs. They had
set their hearts on an achievement which they pursued with
the whole soul, till it led them every day nearer to the verge
of the grave.

Reference has just been made to the annoyance occasioned
by bears; but they were sometimes also the means of miti-
gating the monotony of life, and the following is Dr. Kane's
account of a hunt: A bear and her cub were started, and
fled. The cub, however, was not able to keep ahead of the
dogs, and the dam's instinct prompted her to drag it forward
to some distance, that she might meanwhile face the dogs,
and drive them away. That done, she pitched the young
one forward another stage, for it would not run without
her, as she obviously wished it to do; and when the dogs
returned, she was prepared to give battle again. By
pushing the cub, by coaxing it, or by tossing it forward,
she did what she could to rescue it, and was as devoted

in her way as the Second Grinnell Expedition in its search for Franklin.

For a time the retreat was rapid, so that the two men of the party were left far in the rear. But after fleeing for about a mile and a half, the bear and the cub both became jaded by their toil, and the fight now became desperate. When the dogs rushed on, the dam defended her young with maternal determination, roaring the while, so that she could have been heard a mile off. She tossed her paws like the arms of a windmill; and when she durst not pursue the dogs, lest the cub should be attacked in her absence, she would utter a roar of baffled rage, pawing, snapping with her shining teeth, facing all her assailants in turn, and grinning in the intensity of her passion.

That dam could baffle the dogs, but not the rifle, and a bullet laid her dead. The cub sprang upon the carcase, and seemed determined to defend it to the last; but the same weapon was more than a match for its affection, and when the savage beast was finally despatched, the fresh provision thus obtained was a boon alike to dogs and men.

At last, and after innumerable dangers, the thought of abandoning the brig occurred to Dr. Kane, and began to take shape in his mind. He repelled it as long as possible, for he felt bound by honour and many other ties, to abide by her while one ray of hope remained. But when the thought did occur amid the discomforts of the party—for example, after a journey of sixty miles on the ice, with only three hours of sleep,—one cannot wonder that the hopelessness of their position became more and more clear. The coolness with which every kind of danger had been faced, placed their heroism beyond a doubt. The icebound condition of the brig, and the utter despair of ever getting her to sea—for large portions had been used for firewood, at the bidding of dire necessity—compelled

them to look the worst in the face ; and the thought of
dragging the remaining boats to the sea, and trying to
escape in them, did at length take definite form in their
minds.   Did a sledge break down?   They had "a fatiguing
walk of thirty-six miles to get another."   When in open
water in their boat, did a storm arise?   The same man, for
twenty-two unbroken hours, had to stick to his post as
steersman, for no other could take his place.   Now, surely
men in such a condition are ripe for retreat, if a way such
as brought no dishonour be open.

The brig had now been imprisoned in ice for eleven months,
and had not moved an inch from her wintry site in all that
time.   But the probabilities of removing her gradually diminished, and at length to abandon her became a necessity.
Pile after pile of ice was heaped up between her and the
sea, and what had been her berth so long must continue to
be so for a longer time still.

Yet, as matters stood, that vessel must be the abode of
those men for another winter.   They had so long cherished
the hope of getting her off, that the season was too far advanced to admit of an escape till next season.   "I must look
another winter in the face," recorded Dr. Kane..... "It
is *horrible*—yes, that is the word—to look forward to another
year of disease and darkness, to be met without fresh food
and without fuel.... *August* 20, *Sunday*—Rest for all
hands.   The daily prayer is no longer, 'Lord, accept our
gratitude, and bless our undertaking;' but 'Lord, accept
our gratitude, and restore us to our homes.'   The ice shows
no change.   After a boat and foot journey around the entire
south-eastern curve of the bay, no signs."   All was ice, ice,
ice; and now the question of return is settled by Him to
whose will all must bend.

Dr. Kane, in a former expedition, had visited the place
where Sir John Franklin passed his first winter, but could

find no record of him there. He was now determined that it should not be so with his own little crew. On a conspicuous cliff, the words, "ADVANCE, A.D. 1853–4," were painted. A pyramid of heavy stones was reared; the dead of the party were placed below it; and Kane remarks, "It was our beacon and their grave-stone." A narrative of their explorings was also deposited in the cairn.

, And now, their chief effort was to meet the coming winter as they best could. Scurvy was general; food was scarce already; fuel was not more plentiful—it was weighed out by the pound; and yet these broken-down men had all the horrors of an Arctic winter before them. Appalled at the thought, about half the crew at last resolved to brave the desolation, rather than face the future. One of them returned in a few days, but months rolled away before the rest were seen again; and when they left the brig, the sad position of those who remained behind pressed upon them anew, and with fresh force. Their reduced numbers; the helplessness of some; the waning efficiency of all; the cold, dark night of the approaching winter; the scarcity, and ills present or dreaded, were causes of wasting anxiety. For a time, Franklin and his friends, who had been the daily topic of the men on board the *Advance*, gave place to the question, How are we to escape? how to live? Dr. Kane mournfully adds, "The summer has gone, the harvest is ended, and—We did not care to finish the sentence."

Yet with zeal still undiminished, though with weakened strength, the intrepid men expended their remaining energies. The details of duty—food-gathering, fuel-gathering, the religious exercises, astronomical observations, in short, the whole appointed routine—still received attention; and though, as trials increased, the tale of work was diminished, it shows what manner of spirit those men were of, to say that they entered with ardour upon their months of darkness and of hope deferred. Every precaution was taken against the cold. All the available timber of the vessel was stripped for firewood; and toiling thus for life or death, they had to forego the Sabbath rest, though not its religious exercises.

To provide some fresh food, a party now proceeded on a seal-hunt, and in their eagerness got upon unsafe ice with the sledge. In such circumstances, the dogs commonly became paralysed by fear. In the present instance, they rushed furiously along, so that the sledge had not time to sink. As soon as they paused, however, the ice gave way. But by struggling, scrambling, and pulling on the part of the other dogs, one which had fallen in was dragged from the water, and the party reached the land. An Esquimaux attendant, a Moravian, was the first to land, and he hastened to pray for the safety of the rest. The escape was a marvel, and it seems inexplicable how the team and all it bore were not lost for ever. All the dogs were saved; but the sledge, the kayack, the tent, the guns, the snow-shoes, and all besides, were lost. Such is another example of what it cost to attempt the rescue of Franklin; and those who know the power of truth to brace and sustain, will not be indisposed to ascribe part of this heroism to that cause. The Scriptures were daily read by those men; prayers were daily offered; the protecting power of the Supreme was habitually recognised, by those bold but now forlorn adventurers, and wonder grows as we follow them step by step amid such " deaths oft."

During the second winter, active disease raged in the little band, aggravated by want of food. Everything that was eatable was greedily consumed, measured out sometimes by ounces. Walrus steaks, seals, bears' flesh, blubber, entrails, foxes, hares, rabbits, birds, blood when it could be found, all uncooked, were indiscriminately devoured. The limbs of the men became rigid. In the case of some, the joints would not move. The gums were diseased; the ankles swollen; lumbago supervened, and misery seemed now to culminate in the little band. At one time they had to travel forty-five miles for fresh food for the dying members of the party, and were driven back without success, by the violence of the tempest which raged. Those who went on that expedition tried to press on the dogs; but the poor broken-down animals could not surmount the hummocks of ice; and to save the lives of dogs and men, the former were driven and the latter walked back to the brig, a distance of forty-four miles in sixteen hours. Rats, dog-flesh, bears' heads preserved in better days as specimens, were now devoured. Raw blubber, walrus-beef, and liver, became necessaries of life to those scorbutic sufferers. They even learned to swallow their rations as the Esquimaux do; and the vitality which was extracted from the uncooked juices of the meat was spoken of by the sufferers with a kind of Epicurean glee. The walrus fat was pronounced " the best fuel a man can swallow;" and there is wit latent in the description of the supply which that animal yields: " The outside fat of your walrus sustains your little moss fire; its frozen slices give you bread; its frozen blubber gives you butter; its scrag ends make the soup." *

But " Sunday thoughts" occurring, helped to buoy up the sufferers. " A pint of raw blood," obtained from some rabbits, was hailed as a cordial by the invalids. The gale

---

* On one occasion these noble men had to feed on intestines, not commonly given to the dogs. Thin chips of raw frozen meat, not exceeding four ounces in weight, were the ration of a man per day. The nearest point for supply was seventy-five miles distant. In one of these straits, they divided impartial bites of the raw hind leg of a fox, to give zest to their biscuits, spread with frozen tallow. Amid such scenes, the generous leader of that band has said, " Sick, worn out, strength gone, dogs fast and floundering, I am not ashamed to admit that as I thought of the sick then on board, my own equanimity was at fault."

might often sing in wild discord through the cordage of the
brig; they might have no human agent or human influence
whose sympathy was on their side nearer than eighteen
hundred miles; still some of them had gleams of peace;
and, though the hope of rescuing Franklin was gone, they
were cheered by the thought that what they could do they
had done.

Dr. Kane, then, has given up all hope of rescuing his
vessel. She had been the safeguard and the home of the
party amid many perils; but her time has come—she could
never float above the waves again; and one of her occupants
solemnly asked, "How many of us are to be more fortunate?" Now, what kept these sufferers still alert, at least in
mind? Whence the light which illumined their horror of
great darkness? Dr. Kane's own words should tell: "A
trust," he says, "based on experience as well as promise,
buoyed him up at the worst of times. Call it fatalism, as
you ignorantly may,—there is that in the story of every
eventful life which teaches the inefficiency of human means,
and the present control of a Supreme Agency. See how
often relief has come at the moment of extremity, in forms
strangely unsought, almost at the time unwelcome. See,
still more, how the back has been strengthened to its increasing burden, and the heart cheered by some conscious
influence of an unseen Power."

Such were Dr. Kane's convictions amid trials which have
never been surpassed. He and his party had three months
of intense cold still before them. They had all their outfit
for a return of more than thirteen hundred miles to arrange.
The ravages of disease were already extreme. When the
party moved, four at least would require to be carried—
three in consequence of amputation, and one from frost
wounds. To crown all, these debilitated men must sledge
the boats which were to bear them homewards, over sixty, or

perhaps ninety miles of ice, before they could be launched in open water. With all this, a section of the party was needed to guard the property from the pilfering Esquimaux; so that when meditating on their return, all these things had to be faced, provided for, nay, actually *fought.* Those gallant men, however, determined to try. They were to live or die together; and their chief recorded on the spot, "There is comfort in this view; and, please God, in his beneficent providence to spare us for the work, I will yet give one more manly tug to search the shores of Kennedy Channel for memorials of the lost, and then, our duties over here, and the brig still prison bound, enter trustingly on the task of our escape." Now, is not this loving our neighbour as ourselves? Is not this fulfilling the precept, "Be not weary in well-doing?" Is not this, in short, one of the noblest attitudes in which man was ever placed?

But trials still thickened. The moral and material world sometimes seemed equally dark. One after another of the crew was prostrated by sickness, till at last none but Dr. Kane remained to do all menial drudgery—to cook, to scullionize, to nurse, to purvey, and be physician, all in one. On a Sunday he sadly wrote, "The day of rest for those to whom rest may be; the day of grateful recognition for all."

But the sun returned at length, and the jubilee which that occasioned among the emaciated invalids drew forth feelings akin to those of the fire-worshippers of the East. As the adjoining icebergs now flashed out in sun-birth, it prompted a "Sunday act of worship." But the men still fainted under the least exertion; the best and the stanchest had given in. It was now becoming more and more certain every hour that unless their supply of fresh meat were renewed, the days of the party were numbered; and though wonder-

fully borne up, some of them looked back upon those hor-
rific days with recollections like those of nightmare.

Slowly, however, their health improved with the advancing season. In the chamber fitted up in the brig for all
purposes, against the Arctic winter, gloomy silence had
often reigned ; but a degree of cheerfulness now began
to supplant it, though that was counterbalanced by the
desertion of one of the crew, who would bear no longer
the terrors of such a life. "The grasshopper had become
a burden" to each man of the party : how crushing, therefore, the load which they had every moment to carry!
The daily prayer, "Accept our gratitude, and restore us to
our homes," was now uttered with ever deepening earnestness; and it was not unheard. Some supplies were provided
which the sufferers could not but acknowledge as coming
from Him who opens his hand and satisfies the wants of all.
An Esquimaux, Hans Christian, a devout Moravian, had
often been of service to the party, but he was laid up at the
distance of seventy miles from the brig, and to rescue him,
there was none strong enough but Dr. Kane. He drove a
dog-sledge over that terrible distance, though he had to
walk all the way returning. It seemed a funeral march,
seventy miles in length ; but it was in the cause of humanity,
and strength was given.

Before starting homeward, these heroic men resolved to
make one search more for Franklin, and struggled manfully to force their way through all opposing rigours. Days
and nights of adventurous exposure, ending in reiterated
disaster, were the chief result; and the little exploring party
found its way back to the brig more completely worn down
than ever—in one significant sentence, which sounds like
the tones of a funeral bell, "*The operations of the search
were closed.*" It is now, Homeward if we can! On the 20th
of May 1855, the flags were hoisted, and hauled down again;

the party walked mournfully round their little vessel. They felt, recorded, and left it on the spot, that they had done all they could to prove their tenacity of purpose, and their devotion to the cause which they had undertaken. They read prayers and a chapter of the Bible. Dr. Kane removed Franklin's portrait from the spot which it had occupied in the desolate little den of refuge—and thus they abandoned for ever the abode which had been to them a home both of safety and of peril. Their instruments were left behind; many specimens and other scientific collections shared the same fate; the library perished; and it is scarcely too much to say that they escaped with only the skin of their teeth. "I admonished them all," Dr. Kane says, in referring to that parting scene, "to place reliance on Him who could not change;" and under the impulse of his closing address, and with the recorded conviction that a longer sojourn would in no degree advance the search after Sir John Franklin, they slowly moved away, like men who had been entombed escaping from the grave.

But where was Sir John Franklin at that hour? . . . .

The retreat was admirably conducted, but it is not to be here described. The perils of the boats; the arrangements made for morning and evening prayer, wherever it was practicable; the scientific observations, which continued to be made; the march overland to the sea, when a team of dogs carried Dr. Kane between seven hundred and eight hundred miles during the first fortnight after leaving the brig, or about fifty-seven miles each day; with a hundred other things, all help to enhance our wonder at the trials endured by those philanthropists. They knew the secret place of strength; and while danger crowded upon danger, so that on one occasion no less than fifty-two hours were spent in forcing a single passage through the ice, they persevered, and they triumphed. One of their companions perished by the way. But at length the adventurers reached the Danish settlement of Upernavik, where they learned, among other strange tidings, that Franklin's party, or traces of the dead who represented it, had been found nearly a thousand miles to the south of where the Second Grinnell Expedition had been searching for them. First Europe, and then America, welcomed these wanderers; and it is surely no overstrained encomium to say, that if ever defeated men triumphed—if ever the baffled were the victors—it was in the case of that expedition.

Such is a sketch—and scarcely even that—of the adventures of these men. They are referred to here for a twofold purpose: First, to show what is the energy of right principle ; and, secondly, to manifest the perseverance or the ardour with which high-souled men will pursue the object of their devotedness.

There have been martyrs in the cause of religion. The history of the world is crowded with the terrible details. The lurid light of such sacrifices glares on the pages of the past.

There have been martyrs in the cause of science. Men like Galileo, and others, have endured unto bonds and imprisonment, rather than forego their pursuits; while secrets have been wrung from nature at the cost of eyesight, of health, nay, of life.

There have been martyrs to the thirst for gold. The gold fields in other lands, and the temples of Mammon in our own, display them in thousands—miserable, haggard, and offensive self-destroyers, often in most ignoble ways.

There have been martyrs in the cause of ambition. They are to be counted by myriads, nay, by millions. But never in the world's history was it made more manifest than in the case of Dr. Kane and his companions, that humanity has its martyrs also. For what was it that led them far within the Arctic Circle, away from home and its peace, its comfort, and its joys? There might be scientific aims in view; national rivalry might enter into the motives which stirred their minds; the love of enterprise, and the ardour which signalizes our age, might add their propelling influence; but, these things all conceded, there is still a noble residue of intrepid humanity underlying the Grinnell Expedition. That dominated in the mind of him who furnished the chief means—it was like a passion in the mind of Dr. Kane. It bore him through trials unutterable, and amid them all, it kept him from ever hinting at regret. He did feel for the sufferings of others, and spoke of that as "the fox which gnawed his energies away," amid the struggles, mental and bodily, which were needed to keep the adventurers from desponding. Yet, undaunted amid a hundred deaths, he and his companions persevered in their search from day to day, from month to month, and from year to year. When they emerged from their Arctic seclusion, it was like a return from the dead—and now, the sum of the whole matter is this: Never was a nobler tribute paid to the cause of humanity—never a clearer indication given of the power of principle, stanch, resolute, and unflinching.

CHAPTER IV.

Patriots.

"We give in charge
Their names to the sweet lyre. The historic Muse,
Proud of the treasure, marches with it down
To latest times; and Sculpture in her turn
Gives bond in stone and everlasting brass
To guard them and immortalize her trust."

COWPER.

THERE is nothing more remarkable—we are induced to say it once more—in all God's world, than the agony which it often costs to accomplish any good. No great invention was ever allowed to go abroad till it was tested by an opposition which threatened to crush it in its cradle; no new principle ever was developed into practical application without encountering a hostility which seemed likely to defraud the world of the whole.

For example, Sir Isaac Newton read off the theory of the skies. He thrid his way through the labyrinth of the stars; and though he left much for subsequent philosophers to fill up, he at least showed them how to guide their way through inquiries which had baffled the previous ages. But he was checked, thwarted, assailed, and his own college was the last to adopt his system.

And Luther re-revealed a grand central truth, one of the stars of the spiritual firmament, and bade it shine once more upon the sons of men, but the world knows with what result. He was dragged from place to place for that truth's sake; he had to stand before princes on its behalf; a pope excommunicated him; an emperor would have put him to death if he could; and in the person of that solitary monk, truth had to struggle heroically on its way to daylight. Both he and it would have been buried out of sight, had he been given up to the power of man.

And Galileo proved to the nations that the sun is the centre of our system—that the earth and other worlds roll around it. But that also must involve persecution. Priestly intolerance must deny the demonstrations of science; and the philosopher who had discovered a fact which was to give consistency to the magnificent investigations of astronomy, must go down upon his knees before Inquisitors, to confess that he had erred in adopting a truth.

But why mention merely mortal examples of the fact that it is by pangs and throes that truth is born into the world? He who was the Truth itself had the same enmity to encounter, the same persecution to face. He offered men pardon; they hastened to consummate their guilt by putting him to death. He offered them life; "Away with him, away with him; crucify him, crucify him," was their reply. He was to "give his life a ransom for many;" but the answer of his countrymen was, "His blood be on us and on our children;" so that in His case, as in all besides, good enters the world by means of throes and agonies. Evil is indigenous to earth. It is self-propagated, and seems to grow like those plants which spring up in some places, and in a way, for which no mortal can fully account; but truth, even God's, must be propagated in dungeons, at stakes, on crosses and scaffolds.

In no respect is all this more remarkable than as regards the love of country. Has a man stood forth the champion of freedom? Has he come to free groaning millions from the heel of the oppressor? Has some one tried to assert the rights of that deep conviction which dwells in every soul not brutified or blind—that man was created to be free?

Then despotism tries to crush, and has too often succeeded: it endeavours to perpetuate the ascendency of chains and bondage by the murder of the friends of freedom. What a tale could the Bastile have unfolded? What says the Bass Rock? What is the story of Neapolitan dungeons or papal Inquisitions, but a horrible comment on the efforts of tyranny to suppress the true and the free?

But while all this seems to possess the force of a general law, men have been raised up, in all ages, to dare the worst that tyranny could attempt. If it be true that the death of the martyrs is new life to the Church, it is no less true that the death of the patriot has become the life of freedom. It may have appeared, at times, as if oppression had triumphed, and its power become established by the slaughter or the exile of those who challenged its power. But there is a God that judges in the earth, and sooner or later oppression recoils upon itself; it just stimulates into vigour the energy which breaks the arm of the oppressor, and recalls the exile to his home. What would be the condition of Italy in a single quarter of a century, were all its tyrants put down, and were that truth which proclaims liberty to the captive in *all* respects allowed to have free course there? "Italy free from the Adriatic to the Alps," would no longer be the watchword of Imperial egotists—truth and freedom would soon walk hand in hand through the lovely but down-trodden land.

In the following sections the lives of some are sketched who have contended to the death, because they could not brook the bondage of their country. We know that the wrath of man worketh not the righteousness of God. There is a sense and a sphere in which it is true that they who take the sword shall perish by the sword; but on the other hand, the conduct of Gideon and his conquering band, not to mention Joshua, that prince among generals, makes it plain that oppression may be resisted, and that unto the death. And what do we not owe in these last times to those who went down to the grave, rather than bow before the oppressor? Who wrought out the civil and religious liberties of Scotland when they were trodden in the dust by superstition and despotism in league? The Covenanters, in dungeons, on lonely moors, on the scaffold, or in exile. Who secured the British constitution as it has existed since the year 1688? The men who could face death, but would not stoop to oppression; who could forfeit all that is cherished here, but who would be no parties to the ascendency of a dark superstition. The memory of such men is dear to all who have inherited aught of their spirit—and though, no doubt, some strove only for freedom in time, without caring for that which is for ever, God most high had so bound them up together, that the one led in the other. We sit under our own vines because our fathers did battle on the scaffold for the liberties of their children.

Now, is it desirable that these liberties should be prized aright? Is it desirable to hand them down unimpaired? These ends may be promoted by studying the lives of those who were willing to die, if such were the appointment of their God, but were not willing to be enslaved. Some such lives are here sketched—the lives, for example, of Russel and of Sydney, who died on the scaffold, and of Hampden, who bled in the field. Superstition in their day strove for the mastery; it is doing the same in ours—and would we walk in the footsteps of the fathers of British liberty? Then let us study their example.

I.—ALFRED THE GREAT.

A.D. 849–900.

"Tender plants must bend;
But when a government is grown to strength,
Like some old oak rough with its armed bark,
It yields not to the tug, but only nods
And turns to lofty state."

DRYDEN.

THERE is a marked tendency among men to dignify the objects of their idolatry with the epithet of great. Let us select three examples—Alexander the Great, Herod the Great, and Frederick the Great—to illustrate the wisdom or the folly of that custom.

As to Alexander, we know what marvellous achievements he performed, and how he over-ran the world as it was known in his day, almost with the velocity or the violence of a tornado. But amid his military doings what of his character as a moral being? Where does he stand in rela-tion to the Judge of all? What was Alexander's conduct in regard to self-government, or self-sacrifice—the latter the true mark of moral grandeur? In *that* respect, Alexander the Great was really an object of pity—instead of the great soul of a hero, he could manifest the ferocity of a fiendish and malignant spirit. It is well known that Gaza withstood for some months the besieging army of the haughty conqueror, and the deeds of heroism which were then displayed might have commanded his admiration, had he been truly great. But far from that, when he got possession of the man who had fought so bravely for his home and his country, Alexander dragged the dead body twice round the city walls, in imitation of Achilles, his model.—It was the doing of a brutal and ferocious nature, however it may be deified by men.

Again, the same idolized hero, in a drunken brawl, killed his friend Clitus—the man who had saved his murderer's life at the battle of the Granicus. Alexander was inconsolable for this loss, but the man who is dignified as great could not command his own fierce passions: he was both a drunkard and a murderer.

Further, he is known to have hastened his own death by the quantity of wine which he drank at a banquet. He sickened, fevered, and died in a few days thereafter.

But next, if we were to hear concerning any king that he had first put his queen to death, then one of his sons, then another, and then a third, the last just before his own demise, would our verdict upon such a man be high or very favourable?

Or if we learned that the same monarch was so incensed when he knew that his people were rejoicing in the prospect of his death, that he caused the chief men of his kingdom to be imprisoned, with orders that they should be butchered the instant that he died, in order, as he said, to make sure of mourning for him, could our encomiums on one so brutal be high? He not merely waded through blood to a throne on earth, but even to take his place before the great white throne—and that was the Herod whom men called the great!

As to Frederick the Great, a single incident may suffice.

He had issued an order, on a certain occasion, that all the lights in his camp should be extinguished by a certain hour at night, and watched in person the fulfilment of his law. Perceiving a light in the tent of an officer, the king entered, and found him in the act of closing a letter. Recognising the monarch, the subject immediately implored forgiveness, and in answer to a question, said that it was a letter written on the eve of battle to his wife. The king calmly desired him to re-open it, and add a sentence such as he should dictate. It was done, and that sentence intimated that next day, at a certain hour, the writer would be no more ;—the letter was despatched, and the death which it announced was inflicted. Now, such an incident, which is in entire harmony with the character of Frederick, is one which proclaims him to have been the brutal rather than the great. The death might be due by the terrible laws of war ; but such barbarous trampling on affection could be the dictate of no mind but one that was steeled against the generous and the kindly in man. Yet Frederick also was called the great !

There are cases, however, in which the epithet is merited, —and we are now to consider the life of one who earned and deserved the title. It was the saying of one of old— " The good does not consist in the great ; but the great in the good," * and it is verified in the case of ALFRED THE GREAT. He was born at Wantage, in Berkshire, in the year 849, and was the youngest son of Ethelwolf, king of the West Saxons. Alfred succeeded his brother in the year 871, but the crown descended to him stained by the blood of that brother, who was slain in battle by the Danes. For a time Alfred hesitated to accept of such a crown, and the cares which wearing it implied. The times, however,

* Οὐκ ἐν τῷ μεγάλῳ τὸ εὖ,
'Αλλ' ἐν τῷ εὖ τὸ μέγα, κεῖται.

brooked no delay, and the future lawgiver of England—the founder, perhaps, of the British Constitution—entered on a career which obliged him to fight no fewer than eight pitched battles during the first year of his reign.

But before proceeding further, it may be right definitely to fix what appeared to be the master aim of Alfred's life. That he was prompt, energetic, far-seeing, and sagacious, cannot be questioned; upon what, then, did he concentrate his energies ? To what terminus did his aims and aspirations tend ? It was to the improvement of the people whom he ruled. Plan after plan was adopted, battle after battle was fought, institution after institution was founded, all having that end distinctly and prominently in view, and from it he never swerved. He gave himself wholly to that one thing, and hence the influence of Alfred is still felt in our island, after the lapse of nearly a thousand years. His activity, and his leisure; his learning, and his very ignorance ; his royal influence, and his personal endeavours, were all bent towards the one object, so that he was as sure to stamp his character upon his times and country, as rivers are sure to wear their channels deeper. The schools which Alfred established for his nobles, the masters whom he provided, the learned men whom he invited from foreign countries to his court or kingdom, his patronage of all who were skilful as artizans, or ripe as scholars, bespeak this master object; and though his purposes, like those of other men who are in advance of their times, were often thwarted by ignorance or prejudice, that only blazons more vividly the grandeur at once of Alfred's mind, and of Alfred's aims as a king.

And yet he was twelve years of age ere a tutor could be found capable of instructing him even in the alphabet. His times have been fixed upon by some as the central point —the very midnight of the dark ages, though Alfred himself gleams like a star amid the darkness. His brothers cared little for what delighted him. The bloody days in which his lines were cast seemed likely to perpetuate his ignorance —and the future lawgiver might thus have been mentally stifled in his youth : he whom Voltaire regarded as perhaps most deserving of the respect of posterity of all that ever lived, and whom Herder held up as a pattern to kings, and a star in the history of mankind, seemed doomed to mental darkness. The kingdom was then a camp, or rather a battle-field, and learning had little chance of successful culture there. His mother, however, ingeniously devised means for developing the mind of her son. The musicians and rude poets of the age helped to stir his youthful spirit. The strong bent made way for its own increase, as plants vegetating in darkness expand their energies in pushing towards the light and air, and at length Alfred was able to read. It is, no doubt, a meagre attainment now; but a thousand years ago, he who had made it was chief among a thousand ; and the knowledge even of the alphabet was to Alfred what it has been called, the possession of a fairy wand.

Amid all this, we are to bear in mind that the future king was his own stimulant, for nearly all around him helped rather to repress. The nobles were ignorant; ministers of religion were the same, and Alfred himself records that he knew few of them who understood their daily prayers: darkness covered the land, and even he, with the resources of royalty at command, had to complain, that "when he had the age, permission, and ability to learn, he could find no masters."

But did these things repress this royal youth? They would have lulled many into the all-prevailing torpor. How did they influence Alfred? He persevered in spite of them. He was determined to advance, and he advanced;

his mind craved knowledge, and he sought it far and near. In spite of a disease which haunted him through life, he continued to gather learning from youth to manhood, from manhood till he died; and few spectacles are more noble than this royal man's devotion to his pursuit. At various times he sent to foreign parts in quest of instructors: he invited them to his court; he invested them with dignities, and did all that he could to spread the light which he almost alone in the land cared to diffuse. As ever happens, the acquisition of a little created a desire for more, and Alfred thus advanced, impeded by the nation which he had to drag along, and yet determined to drag it. France, Ireland, and Wales furnished tutors, and England at last became a little learned.

When the king succeeded to the throne, some events took place which are rather darkly hinted than fully described in the chronicles of the times; for a while, Alfred was under some eclipse. Whether kingly power had made him falter in the path on which he had entered, or whether he was only thwarted and disliked by an embruted and oppressed people, amid his attempts to elevate them, cannot now be decided. But between the incursions of the Danes, and the inner difficulties of his rule, Alfred's popularity was for some time obscured: he thought rather of purchasing peace than of conquering it, but that only occasioned new difficulties. For a time he withdrew from public notice, and neither his friends nor his enemies knew the place of his retreat. Some of his instructors had remonstrated with him in terms which it is not easy to understand; and either these remonstrances, or the resistless power of the Danes, drove him into a hiding-place—an islet formed by the waters of the Thone and the Parret, in Somersetshire. It is not needful to record at length the incidents which befell him there—to tell, for example, how he was scolded by the wife

of the peasant who gave him a shelter, because he allowed
her cakes to be burned, instead of toasted—or how he penetrated into the camp of the Danes in the garb of a harper,
studied their position, and then attacked and routed them.
Enough to say that he left his hiding-place a wiser man
than he appears to have been when he fled. He gradually
gathered round him those who were best able to defend his
kingdom, or rid it of its enemies; and one of his most admiring biographers records, that henceforth " his reign was one
unvaried stream of virtue and intelligence, so as to attest
that his fortunate humiliation had disciplined his temper,
purified his heart, and enlightened his understanding."
Alfred was eager to be learned before: he is now bent on
goodness, and he had to pursue it amid all but ceaseless
struggles against powerful enemies for a period of nearly
twenty years.

Scarcely yet, however, have we discovered the reasons of
Alfred's power in his kingdom, or explained why he is the
best known of all the English rulers previous to the times of
Elizabeth. Let us next endeavour this.

Bent as this king was upon his people's improvement, he
adopted measure after measure to promote that end. A
mere catalogue of these must here suffice, and it will display
both his decision and his wisdom.

1. For the sake of good and easy government, he divided
his kingdom into shires. Each shire was subdivided into
trythings, or third parts. Then a trything was divided into
hundreds—meaning a hundred households; and each hundred into tythings, or dwellings of ten families. Each
householder was pledged for the good behaviour of his
house, and all the ten were pledges for each other. This
mode of promoting good order, called frank-pledge, rose
through all the divisions up to the shire, which was presided
over by an earl; and though such a system be radically

erroneous in some respects, it tended to reduce an ill-ordered community to order. So far, it met the aspirations of Alfred; for such was the safety of property, that gold bracelets could be exposed, and yet no thief dared to touch them.*

2. Alfred is regarded as the founder of the British Constitution, and the words embodied in his will, " It is just that the English should for ever remain free as their own thoughts," indicate how justly he judged regarding national rights. Such a sentiment held at such a time, and so distinctly announced, seems to entitle him to the encomium pronounced upon him, as "the wisest, the best, and the greatest of kings."

3. It was Alfred who established trial by jury, or at least adopted its distinctive principle ; and in defending that institution he is known to have condemned some judges to death because they decided in criminal cases by an arbitrary violation of the rights of juries.

4. The king's attention to the administration of justice was so great, that many of the most important cases were decided by himself in person, and judge after judge was condemned to die because their sentences were unjust—one, for example, because an insane person was adjudged to death ; and another, because he pronounced a similar sentence upon one whom, in mere caprice, he found guilty. The retributions of the king were stern ; but they proceeded on the fundamental maxim, " Whoso sheddeth man's blood, by man shall his blood be shed," and the age demanded severity, for the only alternative was that or lawlessness.

5. In his zeal for his country's safety, this earnest king laid the foundation of the British navy. The Danes, who infested the island, were defeated by Alfred in many battles on shore ; but it was better still to prevent them from land-

* It is right to observe that the fact of these arrangements being first made by Alfred, and some other points, are questioned by Hallam.—*History of Middle Ages.*

ing. "Long ships and galleys" were therefore built, which
were more than a match for those of the invaders, and which
largely contributed to crush the power of the sea-kings, who
so often and so fiercely ravaged the shores and the kingdoms
of this island.

6. There seems no reason to doubt that Alfred was the
first founder of the schools at Oxford. Seeking the welfare
of his subjects along every open channel, and deploring as
he often did the ignorance of England, he adopted the wise
device of planting public seminaries. The struggle for
seniority and precedence between the two English universities may have thrown some doubt upon the subject—but
partizanship aside, Oxford appears to be the elder sister.

7. Moreover, the genius of Alfred sought, with characteristic earnestness, to foster the Arts in his kingdom. Ship-
building, we have just seen, he patronized. Architecture
was also encouraged. Workmanship in gold and silver
reached very considerable perfection, and relics of it remain
to this day, bearing the name of Alfred, which attest his
interest in such branches. The accounts handed down are
full of interest, as at once indicating the far-seeing zeal of
the king, and the difficulties with which he had to cope, in
seeking to civilize a still savage people. From many lands
artificers were brought, and he annually set apart a sixth
part of his revenues to remunerate their skill and labour.
The designs of his palaces were his own; the towns which
he caused to be constructed were skilfully selected as to position, and considering the age, were elegant and substantial
—the whole indicating the mind and influence of a man who
was raised up to help his country centuries forward in the
course of a single life-time. His furniture in some respects
may be called sumptuous, as his inventions for comfort were
ingenious.

8. Along with all these civilizing influences, Alfred

sedulously employed that of literature, if such a name may be applied to the meagre productions of his age. Devoted as he was to learning, and feeling its benefits in himself, he was eager to see it extended to others; and assiduously strove by means of translations and otherwise, to spread the humanizing influence. The king himself translated some works as a stimulus, or example to others—"sometimes word for word, sometimes sense for sense," as his instructors Plegmund, Asser, Grimbold, and above all, John Erigena, the most noted man of his age, had taught him. It is indeed a spectacle which explains the influence of Alfred's age upon those which followed, to see the king, amid the turmoil of frequent wars, the distractions of business, and the anguish of disease, thus labouring for his people's welfare, and seeking to hasten their progress. When we read that he translated Orosius's "Summary of Ancient History;" Bede's "Ecclesiastical History;" Boethius's book, on the "Consolations of Philosophy," and "The Pastorals of Gregory," a work designed to stimulate the ministers of religion at once to cultivate learning, and to prosecute their peculiar duties, we may understand how appropriately Alfred might have used the language of Augustus, who boasted that he had found Rome built of bricks, and left it of marble.

9. Nor should we forget the prominence which the Saxon king gave to religion amid all his endeavours to elevate his little kingdom. The Romish superstition had now got possession of the land, and the shepherd on the banks of the Tiber claimed the fleece of the flocks in England. Alfred had adopted the creed of Rome; he was surrounded by its ministers, and his conduct in some degree partook of its spirit. Still we must do homage to the zeal of him who sought to rise superior to the slavery of passion, by employing the means at his command. It was his custom, as Asser

his friend and biographer records, to rise at day dawn and resort to various shrines, there to pour out his soul in prayer for the guidance of Heaven. So intent was he upon his great work, and so bent on advancing it fast and far, that he even implored that some affliction might be sent, if it did not, like blindness or leprosy, unfit him for doing good. When paroxysms of pain did come, he welcomed them as designed to promote high ends; and however questionable that zeal might be in some of its aspects, no one will doubt that the self-sacrificing earnestness of this man deserves the eulogy pronounced upon it: "It was noble beyond applause;" it was "Such as no praise can exaggerate."

But, further to evince the devotion of Alfred—he not merely translated the works already mentioned: one notice of him says, "that he made many books;" another, "that he put into English a great part of the Roman composi- tions," and a third tells that the number of his translations cannot be known, while he wrote parables of "great edifica- tion, beauty, pleasantry, and nobleness." His proverbial say- ings were collected and admired: his manual, or note-book, was stored with information gathered from every available source. But his most remarkable translation was his last, and an ancient historian records that "Alfred began to translate the hymns of David, but had hardly finished the first part when he died." "A youthful prince," writes one well able to instruct us, "thirsting for intellectual enjoy- ments, for domestic happiness, and for the word of God, and who sought by frequent prayer for deliverance from the bondage of sin, had ascended the throne of Wessex in the year 871. Alfred being convinced that Christianity alone could rightly mould a nation, assembled round him the most learned men from all parts of Europe, and was anxious that the English, like the Hebrews, Greeks, and Latins, should possess the Holy Scriptures in their own language. He is the real patron of the Biblical work—a title far more glorious than that of founder of the university of Oxford. After having fought more than fifty battles by land and sea, he died while translating the Psalms of David for his subjects." *

To illustrate the deep interest of Alfred in religion, we may mention an embassy which he sent to India. He had learned that there were Churches and Christians there who traced their descent from Thomas, the reputed apostle of the East. Whether to fulfil some vow, or with some other design, cannot now be decided, but the voyage is mentioned by author after author, some of whom describe the Indian curiosities brought to England by the messengers of Alfred. Events these which make us wonder more and more at the boldness and the ardour of this king.—There is a precocity in nations, as well as individuals, and such proceedings on the part of Alfred evince the precocious development of British enterprise. It was still but "the morning twilight of mind" in the land, and yet there was light enough for one, at least, to see across the great waters, and sympathize with fellow-believers who were there. Alfred might even then have asked,—

"What is royalty's short flower?
What the triumph of an hour?
What fleet pleasure's fading bower
And control?
God's own presence is the dower
Of the soul."

But we have still more explicit evidence of the devoutness of this sovereign's mind. Many of his recorded prayers might be quoted, but a single specimen will suffice: "Oh, how Thy goodness is to be admired, for it is unlike all other good. My desire is to Thee; and this most chiefly, because without Thee I cannot come to Thee. If Thou abandonest

* M. D'Aubigné.

me, then I shall be removed from Thee; but I know that Thou wilt not forsake me, unless I forsake Thee. But I will not forsake Thee, because Thou art the highest good. There are none of those who seek Thee rightly, that may not find Thee. But they only will seek Thee rightly whom Thou instructest to seek Thee, and teachest how to find Thee. . . ." Altogether there is a depth and a grandeur about the religion of this man which too few have equalled.

10. After statements like these, it will readily be believed that the king was zealous in seeking to impress his own family for good. His sons and daughters were trained with all the care that royal resources could command, and appear to have imbibed not a little of their father's spirit. As a specimen of Alfred's earnestness and devotion in his family, we quote what is recorded as his last words to his son and successor, Edward: "My dear son," he said, with a kind of patriarchal simplicity, "set thee now beside me, and I will deliver thee true instructions. My son, I feel that my hour is coming. My countenance is wan. My days are almost done. We must now part. I shall to another world, and thou shalt be left alone in all my wealth. I pray thee (for thou art my dear child), strive to be a father and a lord to thy people. Be thou the children's father, and the widows' friend. Comfort thou the poor, and shelter the weak, and with all thy might, right that which is wrong. And, son, govern thyself by law; then shall the Lord love thee, and God above all things shall be thy reward. Call thou upon him to advise thee in all thy need, and so shall he help thee the better to compass that which thou wouldst." It is pleasing to know that such instructions were not ignored.

We need scarcely dwell now upon the private life of Alfred, or tell how gentle it was—how considerate—how his time was regulated with scrupulous care, and his resources husbanded only that they might be well spent; for one of his maxims was, that "gold does not differ from a stone, but by discreet using of it." In regard to his time, Asser, who was one of Alfred's clergy, tells, that in order to divide it aright, the king caused six wax candles to be made, each twelve inches long, and as many ounces in weight. On the candle the inches were carefully marked, and having found that one of them burned just four hours, he made that the basis of his arrangements as to time.—It was a small matter, and a slight effort of ingenuity was enough to devise such a plan; but the king who acted upon it was one who, beyond a doubt, would achieve much in little space. His was not "the wit which trembles at labour, nor the genius which pants to create," but ends in doing nothing. He was attentive to the minute as well as the majestic, the homely as well as the national; and is undoubtedly one of the most remarkable and most honoured men of all the past.

Historians love to dilate on the deeds and the pre-eminence of Alfred. His merit, it is said, may "be set in opposition to that of any monarch or citizen in which the annals of any age or any nation can present to us." Hume calls him, moreover, "the model of a perfect character," the embodiment of what was rather a fiction of the imagination than anything that could be expected to be actually realized. An enterprising spirit, tempered by coolness and moderation; resolute perseverance along with easy flexibility; severe justice side by side with gentle mercy; deep love of knowledge and study, along with equal aptitude for action; the utmost grace of person, combined with the most winning deportment, are all enumerated as helping to constitute the personal greatness of the king. The energies of such a man, or such a monarch, all converging upon a single point—his people's welfare—necessarily made him great; and hence he has long taken his place among those who shall be held in everlasting remembrance. In any age such a prince would be a wonder. Between the year 849, the date of Alfred's birth, and the year 900, the period of his death, his existence and acquirements were a prodigy.

Such, then, is a mere glimpse of the character of King Alfred. Early in life, when he lurked as a dethroned monarch in the isle of Athelney, he chose his part—he resolved to live for the good of his people, and from that period till his death, his purposes were followed out with a decision which could not be curbed, and a perseverance which refused to be repressed. We wonder at his multifarious achievements. More than fifty battles were fought; many books were translated, among which, according to an old history, were the Old and New Testaments; cities were built; a university was founded, and a navy begun. Judges were appointed; the kingdom was divided for safety, and that as we have seen so successfully, that golden ornaments could be exposed without being stolen; and all these by a man whose life was one long disease, or who, though generally calm and cheerful, was rarely free from pain, often excruciating to torture. "Such was the dreadful anguish which his disease perpetually produced, that if for one short hour it happened to intermit, the dread and horror of its inevitable return poisoned the little interval of ease." It was such an agony that it "would have disabled a common man from the least exertion;" but though thus racked, Alfred advanced with all his schemes for improving his people. Like the first Pitt, he "trampled upon impossibilities," and though he reigned only eight-and-twenty years, and died at the age of fifty-two, he accomplished far more than many who survive the allotted limit of three-score years and ten. When this imperial man passed away, there fell a great warrior, and a greater statesman; the protector of the weak, the deliverer of the oppressed, a father to freedom, and a friend to the people; a devotee to learning, and a patron of the learned; a model of industry, one alike capable of devising and of executing plans which stretched into the remotest future. Upon his memory were lavished not merely the encomiums of admiration, but the endearments of love, and the climax of their eulogy ever is, "In servitio Dei vigilantissimus et devotissimus—in the service of God most vigilant and most devout." It was devotion that surmounted the whole, like a gilded dome upon a princely palace.

And on the review of such a character, and after the study of Alfred's determination to do good—a determination which never could be shaken, one cannot help feeling that God's world is full of glorious sights had we eyes to see them. It is with us as with the prophet's attendant when his eyes were opened, and he saw chariots and horsemen of fire surrounding him as a body-guard where he thought that all was appalling danger. We may conclude that our sin-laden earth is all marred, and that its moral beauties perished when Eden withered; but Alfred's life says no. Much remains to show the primal dignity or goodliness of man, for when that mighty power which creates the soul anew is put forth, the wilderness begins to blossom like the rose. It was thus with Alfred—a man who has established his claim to be called Great, if ever mortal might wear the title. But it was not the greatness of mere brute force: it was based upon goodness; it was pervaded by affection, and hence his name is still like a household word; his mark is seen upon the laws, the privileges, and the customs of the English, nearly a thousand years after his death. That one sentiment already quoted, "It is just that the English should for ever remain free as their own thoughts," ranks him among the men who have contributed by *their* thoughts to elevate mankind—and were Alfred's choice of the good and true, his rejection of the vicious and the false, more generally copied, our true liberty would be greater; our country would then be blessed indeed, as "Alfred the Truth-teller" longed, and laboured, and prayed that it might be.

The grand moral of this monarch's life is plain. He chose a right path—one worthy even of Alfred's energies, and he pursued it with unwavering steadfastness. That path might be steep and toilsome, but he knew where to obtain strength—not spasmodic, but persistent: not the caprice of an hour, but the energy of an age. He sought it —he found it; and his track through life is therefore radiant still. This true man became the benefactor of thousands: he would have been a king even though he had never been crowned.

II.—DANTE ALIGHIERI.

A.D. 1261–1321.

" Tuscan, that wanderest through the realms of gloom,
With thoughtful pace, and sad, majestic eyes,
Stern thoughts and awful from thy soul arise,
Like Farinata from his fiery tomb.
Thy sacred song is like the trump of doom;
Yet in thy heart what human sympathies,
What soft compassion glows, as in the skies
The tender stars their clouded lamps relume."

LONGFELLOW.

His birth and studies—Bologna—Padua—Paris—Reference to his battles—Civic honours—Is driven into exile—His wanderings—The cause of his exile—His love of freedom, and hatred of Papal abuses, and tyranny—Proposal to re-admit him to Florence—Rejected—His death—And honours—Persecuted by the Pope even in the grave—His place in history—And power for good.

DANTE, or DURANTE ALIGHIERI, was born at Florence, in May 1261, and as he ranks, by universal consent, among those who have suffered unjustly for their country, and for struggling to uphold its freedom, a study of his life may help to impart some portion of his spirit.

He lost his father in childhood, but by the assistance of an able teacher, he was carefully trained in the scholarship of his times, and applied himself closely to literature and other studies. He omitted no pursuit, we are told, that tended to the formation of a manly character, and took part in the athletic exercises which formed a part of the training of youth in his day. His powers were in some respects precociously developed, and this fact is believed to have exerted no little influence upon the whole of his subsequent career. The ascendency of deep affection signalized him even as a boy, and all that he did, he did intensely.

As Dante was of honourable lineage, he was soon called to take a prominent part in the rough doings of his age. Florence was then divided into factions, which warred against each other with singular ferocity, and in a battle fought at Arezzo, the young poet distinguished himself by his bravery. "At the memorable battle of Campaldino," writes Carey, his translator, "Dante was present, served in the foremost troop of cavalry, and was exposed to imminent danger." It was a partizan struggle, and Dante then fought upon the side which he subsequently abandoned as hostile to the freedom of his native state. He was present at another engagement between his countrymen and the Pisans, where the Florentines took the castle of Caprona.

But it does not appear that these raids interfered with his studies. At Bologna, and Padua, as well as at Florence, he had pursued them with ardour, and natural and moral philosophy were his favourite pursuits. It is believed that he even proceeded to Paris in his zeal to gather knowledge, and Carey is not indisposed to credit the statement that Dante was for some time a student at Oxford. But be these things as they may, he was soon involved in the troubles of the period, and sorrows, both domestic and public, became the lot of him whom Florence was soon to cast out, but whom all Italy was at last to regard as a glory. At the age of twenty-five he had been raised by the suffrages of the Florentines to the rank of one of the chief rulers of Florence. It was towards the year 1300, and Prior was the title which his office conferred upon him; but in his case, as in many besides, elevation was but the prelude to sorrow. The complications of the period made eminence hazardous, or a kind of protracted death.

The Florentine city and state were at that period distracted by the opposing factions of the Guelphs and Gibelines, already referred to. The latter were subdivided into two parties, the Neri and the Bianchi; these Dante attempted to reconcile, but only shared the common lot of peacemakers,—he became an object of hatred and persecution to those whom he strove to befriend. The Neri secretly resolved to apply to the Pope of the day to send Charles of Valois to pacify and reform the city. The Bianchi took alarm at this proposal, as involving danger or exile to them. They rushed to arms, and repaired to the Priors, demanding the punishment of the other faction as enemies to the liberty of their country. Mutual criminations followed; wild misrule prevailed, and Dante advised his colleagues to call in the people to protect and aid their rulers. That step was followed up by the banishment of the chief men of the two factions. The future poet is believed to have conducted himself with impartiality; but he was soon assailed with a rancour which deepened into settled enmity, when the Bianchi chiefs, as the less guilty, were permitted to return from their exile, while the Neri continued in their banishment. The recall of the former, however, took place after Dante had quitted office, so that he seems not to have been further implicated in the matter.

The Pope, as ever, was prompt to seize the opportunity which these events afforded for extending his power by means of the puppet princes, whom he could then make and unmake at his pleasure. Charles of Valois was accordingly despatched by him to Florence, where he reversed all the former proceedings, recalling the proscribed, and banishing their opponents. Dante was at that time at Rome, as ambassador to the Pope, to propose a voluntary return to peace on the part of the Florentines; and during his absence on this pacific mission, his enemies took their revenge. They passed a decree of banishment against him, and confiscated all the property which remained to him after his goods had been given up to pillage. On the 27th of January 1302 he was fined 800 lire, and condemned to two years of banishment. But on the 16th of March, the rage of the party who persecuted Dante became more violent. He and his associates were then sentenced to be burned alive, should they fall into the hands of the faction which was dominant in the state. The shameless document which embodies this sentence still exists.

When Dante learned the full extent and nature of these proceedings, which he did at Sienna, on his return from Rome, he proceeded to join the Gibelines at Gorgonza. In the year 1304 an attack was made upon Florence, in the hope of rescuing it from foreign rule, but Dante and his friends were compelled to retreat, and from this time he became a wanderer from place to place. He had loved his country, and hazarded his life again and again that it might be free; but in the heat of faction it had been decreed that he should be burned; and though he continued to love his native city, and lament his exile till his dying day, Florence was never again the home of her greatest son. In 1306 Dante was at Padua. In 1307 he was at Nugello, and in the course of that year he found an asylum with one who had formerly been his opponent. At a subsequent period he removed to Verona, where he resided with the Signore della Scala. In his own words, he was learning "the way for man to win eternity;" and the discipline was, as usual, severe —it tested to the uttermost both his decision and his affection. His resolution, however, was unflinching: he could face exile, but he shrank from baseness.

Dante's mortifications in exile were profound, for he looked back to his country with deep, Italian passion. He felt, moreover, that he suffered unjustly. Exile and poverty had become his lot, since Florence, he says, " has cast me forth out of her sweet bosom, in which I had my birth and nourishment even to the ripeness of my age, and in which, with her good will, I desire with all my heart to rest this wearied spirit of mine, and to terminate the time allotted to me on earth." But instead of that, he was compelled to wander from place to place, he records, "as a mendicant," "a vessel without sail, and without steerage," "carried about to divers ports, and roads, and shores by the dry wind that springs out of sad poverty." He had formed the plan of teaching the Church and the States of Italy that the impudence of the Popes, and the civil wars between the cities, with the introduction of foreign arms to which these led, must end in bondage to the Italians. He took his place " among the reformers of morals, the avengers of crimes, and the assertors of orthodoxy in religion;" but his reward was exile, poverty, and life-long grief. The real cause of his exile, we have seen, was his refusal to receive Charles of Valois, whom the Pope had sent to Florence, in pretence to restore peace, but in reality to enslave; and Dante himself proved at last that the wars of Italy sprang from the doctrine that the Pope had a right to interfere in temporal affairs. Strange that six centuries, or nearly so, after Dante's time, the same baneful doctrine, and the same pretence, should press like an incubus upon millions, crushing liberty where it exists, and keeping it down where it has been suppressed!

Some gleams of hope dawned upon this gifted wanderer in the year 1308, when it seemed not unlikely that he might be restored to Florence; but they ended in deeper darkness than before. He had been employed, during the course of his life, in fourteen different embassies, and succeeded in most of them; but his country would admit of no mediation in his case, and his chief solace was his own sentiment—

"That so my conscience have no plea against me,
Do fortune as she list, I stand prepared."

Here, then, is one whose patriotism was a passion, and who could surrender everything but conscience and freedom for his country's sake. He was on all occasions a fearless assertor of civil and religious liberty. His poetry, his prose, and his private intercourse, all, and all alike, manifest the same ardent love for these rights of men. That love dwelt deep in his soul, side by side with reverence for his country —and yet that man was compelled to roam from place to place an unhappy, sometimes a homeless, exile. In addition to those places already mentioned, Casentino, Urbino, the territory of Gubbio, the castle of Colmallaro, Udine, Tolmino, Paratico, and others, are pointed out as the temporary homes or shelters of this outcast—the man who felt towards Florence as the Jew does toward the Holy Land, the home of his fathers, his heart, and his hopes.

But what was the origin of all this? How did it happen that one so devoted to his country was cast scornfully out by her? Why was evil made his good, in return for all that he tried to do for Florence? That question deserves a more ample answer than we have yet given, and those who have investigated the matter with greatest care do not scruple to regard him as the victim of ecclesiastical oppression. His great Poem shows that he was the earnest opponent of the usurpations of Rome, and hence he was hated by those who loved her. He and his fellow-labourers prepared the way for the redemption of Christendom from spiritual bondage. He tried to convince men of their vassalage, and at the same time to show them their rights. He was in hourly conflict with that power which caused the bones of a noble Italian, Manfredi, to be dug up, that they "might be washed by the rains and scattered by the wind;" and as the result, the hatred of the friends of Rome was long concentrated against Dante. Petrarch, in succession to him as the poet of Italy, ·dared to call Rome "the hell of the living;" but to utter such a sentiment near that city was what it would not endure, and Dante must suffer because he and his friends dared to proclaim the truth. All this is manifest from many portions of his "Divine Comedy," where pope after pope, cardinal after cardinal, priest after priest, are represented among the spirits of the lost—and he was bold of spirit who dared to send holiness and infallibility thither. But his deep convictions "bade him do and fear not;" and he obeyed their bidding to the letter, for Dante was not the man to quail when the rights of conscience urged him on. For example, he places Saint Celestine among those whom Justice cared not to punish, and whom Mercy would not welcome, because of his meanness and pusillanimity. In other words, Popery made that pope a saint; Dante deemed him an idiot, and had the poet concealed his convictions, or been false to them, he would have felt himself deserving of being sent to the region where, he says, "the traitor is eternally consumed," as well as

"The souls of tyrants who were given
To blood and rapine."

—Sentiments such as these sufficiently explain the exile of Dante, and the hatred of Rome to his name. To unmask her vileness is always to incur her wrath.

It is believed that one opportunity of returning to his native state was offered to the poet, but it was upon ignoble conditions. He was to pay a fine, and, in a church, confess himself guilty, at the same time imploring the pardon of the republic. He rejected the proposals as implying what was false, and called them ridiculous and impertinent. This noble man had now been an exile for fifteen years, though guilty of no crime against the republic, unless seeking its freedom were one; and he would not, therefore, offer himself up in chains even for the sake of returning to his beloved city, but cried aloud for justice, while he would not compro-

mise his conscience to appease his persecutors. "I will return with hasty steps," he wrote, "if a way can be found
that shall not derogate from the honour of Dante; but if by
no such way Florence can be entered, then Florence I shall
never enter." Everywhere, he added, he could contemplate
consoling and delightful truth, but nowhere could he accept
of the terms proposed, without rendering himself inglorious,
nay, infamous to the people and republic of Florence.
"Bread, I hope, will not fail me," were his touching words.

It has been said, however, that bread *did* fail him, and
that the picture which he drew of a man stripping his
visage of shame, trembling in his very heart, placing himself
in the public way, and stretching out his hand for charity,
was not a fancy picture. Yet though that word-painter, so
vivid and so true, thus endured to the uttermost, he never
parades his own griefs, never tells of a father without a home
for his children, or bread with which to feed them. They
shared his exile; but he does not buy our sympathy by
telling us their woes.

And Dante accordingly died in exile. He had been sent
on an embassy to Venice on behalf of friends—or of one who
had given him an asylum—and his object was to make peace
with that State. So rancorous, however, were the feelings
of the Venetians against the man who sent him on the embassy, that Dante could not even obtain an audience at
Venice; and he returned to Ravenna, the abode of his
patron, and, for the time, of himself, only to die. That event
took place in July, according to some, in September, according to others, in the year 1321.

And thus passed away one of the greatest of the sons of
men—the Michael Angelo of poetry—if we should not rather
say, the Michael Angelo and the Raphael combined. He
had been ignominiously banished by his countrymen, yet he
loved them to the last with all the force of his strong

nature; and though he refused to bend his lofty mind to any degrading compromise, the yearnings of his great soul were still over Florence and the Florentines. The patron, in whose palace he died, gave the poet most sumptuous obsequies. A prince delivered his funeral oration. Monument after monument was raised to his name. Too late for him or themselves, the Florentines relented, and instituted lectureships to expound his poetry, in which Bologna, Pisa, Venice, and other places, followed their example; and after the lapse of years, they implored that his remains might be granted to them to be laid beside the ashes of his fathers. Leo X., and Michael Angelo renewed the attempt, but in vain. The Ravennese would not surrender the sad memorials of their own honourable hospitality; and Dante sleeps on the shores of the Adriatic, not in Santa Croce, beside others of the illustrious dead.

Judging from the strain of Dante's "Inferno," no doubt can remain but that at least the prolongation of his exile was owing to papal hatred. In that work he boldly names the crimes of the papacy, and pours scalding words on some of the pontiffs. He likens them to a she-bear, "eager to feed her whelps." He denounces their simony and crimes in terms which, if used in Italy even now, at least where the Pope has power, would lead to exile or a dungeon. Hatred on that account was rampant. The Jesuits often attacked his memory as if he had been a Luther, a Calvin, or a Zuingli. The successors of his last patron, Guido Novello da Polenta, had even to defend the ashes of the poet from the sacrilege meditated by Pope John XXII., when he sent a cardinal to Ravenna to drag the bones from the sepulchre, consume them, and scatter the whole to the winds as those of Wickliff had been. Now, all these things distinctly tell what was the origin or the main cause of the great Florentine's sorrows. He would not yield to a corrupt power, and must suffer for his boldness. He would not patiently see his country enthralled by priestly usurpation; and by the priesthood he was persecuted to the death. In truth, Dante lived five centuries too soon for Italy—the land which sorely needs some Dantes *now*.

Such, then, is one of the most signal illustrations of heroic and suffering patriotism of which history tells. Little reference has been made to the poetry of Dante—its pictorial power, its weeping gentleness at one time, its judge-like severity or its grandeur at another. Our sole object has been to show the power of iron will, based upon truth and conscience, to surmount every obstacle, to resist temptation, and to triumph even while it seems defeated. Dante is not to be held up as a model man, but he is a representative one; and the grandeur of his views, supported by the firmness of his purpose, enables us to see what is needed to secure the rule of God, of truth, and of conscience among the sons of men. The indignation which he felt against corruption in all its forms, proclaims how much he was needed, and how much he is needed still in all the states of Italy. The liberty which he sought, but might not enjoy, is now in a measure conceded; and in his spirit we may pray that it may more and more brighten the land which has "the fatal gift of beauty."

III.—JOHN HAMPDEN.

A.D. 1594–1643.

"Let laurels drenched in pure Parnassian dews
Reward his memory, dear to every muse,
Who, with a courage of unshaken root,
In honour's field advancing his firm foot,
Plants it upon the line that Justice draws,
And will prevail or perish in the cause.
'Tis to the virtues of such men man owes
His portion of the good that heaven bestows."

Cowper.

A king's duties—Charles II.—Hampden's birth and youth—His times—His life-work—Abuses unmasked—Collisions—Parliaments dissolved—Members sent to the Tower—Hampden imprisoned—Ship-money—Hampden retires into private life—The atrocities of the times—Leighton—Prynne—Hampden's deportment at this crisis—At last purposes to emigrate—Hindered by Charles—A new parliament—Speedily dissolved—Another convened—Lord Wentworth—The "Grand Remonstrance"—The king visits the House of Commons to seize Hampden and others—Their escape and concealment—Struggles—War—Hampden's death.

 GREAT preacher of France, in addressing Louis XIV. from the pulpit, once boldly and clearly defined the end and object for which kings reign. "A prince," he exclaimed, "is not born for himself alone. He owes himself to his subjects. The people, in exalting him, entrusted him with power and authority, and reserved to themselves, in exchange, his cares, his time, and his vigilance. . . . . It is the people, who, by the appointment of God, make kings all that they are; and it is their duty to be what they are only for the people. Yes, it was the choice of the nation that placed the sceptre at first in the hands of your ancestors. It was the nation that elevated them by the bucklers of the soldiery, and that proclaimed them sove-

reigns. After that, the kingdom became the heritage of your
ancestors, their successors. But they owed it originally to
the free consent of the subjects. Afterwards, it was their
birth alone that put them in possession of the throne. But
it was the public voice that at first attached that right and
that prerogative to their birth. In a word, as the primary
source of their authority comes from us, kings ought to use
it only for us."

—It is not often that sentiments so noble find their
way to the ears of monarchs surrounded by sycophants,
flattered by courtiers, or victimized by the countless
corrupting influences which hover near a court — and
kings have too often used their people as if they were
born only for the aggrandisement of the creature whom they
had exalted to power. Grinding oppression has been carried
on under the pretext of a divine prerogative; and millions
have suffered, or pined, and died, that the one might riot,
and waste, and crush. "The King of England is an absolute monarch. . . . . He can do no wrong. He is the sole
judge, and we ought not to question him;" was language once
officially used in this land. "The right divine of kings to
govern wrong," has thus become a proverb; but it was also
an offence to all who understand how kings rule, why they
wield their power, and who made them what they are.

When Pere Masillon addressed the words which have
been quoted to the youthful Louis XIV., the preacher had
before him one who lived to become a despot among despots
—an arch-oppressor among crowned tyrants. But we are
now to endeavour to gather some lessons of practical wisdom from events which happened in the times of one
who has been called a more unprincipled tyrant than
even Louis XIV. It is Charles I. of England—a man
who acted as if this island and its people had been created
only for him—who attempted to rule the nation not merely

without law, but in spite of it, and by trampling on its ruins.
At present we give but a single example. Contrary to the
law of England, the king just named, received nuncio after
nuncio from the Pope of Rome, and contrary to the law of
England, that king had an envoy and agent at the court of
Rome. But in a hundred ways besides these, he strove to
make his will supreme in all things. Parliament must bend
before the royal prerogative. Taxes must be imposed according to the monarch's dictation, and paid in some of the
harshest forms of exaction. Or if parliament will not bend
to that man's wishes, it shall cease to exist; and five
times, in a few brief years, did that haughty ruler try to
govern his kingdom without a parliament at all. But five
times also, during those years, a man was raised up to
challenge and checkmate the king; and the study of that
man's life will shed a brighter light upon the blessings made good to many by unbending decision—by that
heroism which will not yield to oppression, as it will not
infringe upon the right—that stern and fearless determination which grows pale at no danger and shrinks from no
sacrifice.

JOHN HAMPDEN was born, probably in London, in the
year 1594. His father died while the son was only a child,
and he then succeeded to very large estates in Buckinghamshire, some of which had been in the possession of his ancestors for hundreds of years. Young Hampden was cousin to
Oliver Cromwell, as the father of the former had married
Elizabeth, daughter of Sir Henry Cromwell of Hinchin-
brooke, the aunt of the great Protector. John Hampden was
educated first at Thame in Oxfordshire, and then at Madga-
lene College, Oxford, which he entered in the year 1609.
Four years thereafter, he was admitted a student of the
Inner Temple, with a view to the law as a profession, and
about the year 1620, began to take some subordinate part

in the management of public affairs. Little is known, however, concerning his early training, and nothing that would signalize him. He was one of the men whose latent powers are developed by the force of circumstances, and whose character becomes best known amid difficulties, as gold is tested in the crucible.

When Hampden entered upon his public duties as a citizen of England, the country was fast drifting into that state of anarchy which ended in the execution of a king, and the change of a dynasty. The royal prerogative, pushed to extravagant lengths, was slowly coming into collision with the liberty of the subject, goaded sometimes, perhaps, to a corresponding extreme. The question was gradually put into shape, and prepared for a dread solution, Whether shall one man live for the millions of England, or the millions of England for one man? James I. said in as many words, "All is for one." Utterly destitute of all that could command respect or win affection, that silliest of kings had acted as if the souls and the bodies of his subjects existed only for him. He was as insincere as Charles I., as profligate and unprincipled as Charles II., and as bigoted as James II. He could, with his own hand, write down instructions for the torture of a criminal, and close them with the prayer "God prosper you in your good work;" and *that* was the man who claimed to hold sovereignty directly from God, by a divine and an indefeasible right. In public he engaged in controversy with Cardinal Bellarmine; in private he corresponded confidentially with that dignitary regarding his Church; and, to crown the whole, he protested that " if he thought his son and heir could give any toleration to popery, he would wish him fairly buried before his eyes." Such was the man who began the dire collision which resulted in driving his family from the British throne. Scarcely was the first year of his reign in England brought to a close when his unconstitutional assumptions began. Arbitrary taxation, king-made laws, money extorted from his subjects to be lavished upon his minions, or wasted on debauchery and riot, all helped to precipitate matters till parliament was dissolved; and when any of the members dared to act contrary to the royal despotism, that was the signal for dissolution. One parliament was dissolved after it had sat for only two months.

But men were rising up to meet the emergency, and John Hampden was one of them. In the year 1620-1, he took his seat for the first time, as a member of the House of Commons. Delinquencies were so rife that common honesty demanded their exposure, and Hampden allied himself to those who sought to correct abuses. He was always diligent, and sometimes eager in the discharge of his duties; and here we may ask, as in other cases, What was the life-work of this man? He did not press himself into notice; on the contrary, he was driven, by a sense of oppression, from a privacy which he loved; and when he walked out into public life he was mature, as well as calm, in judgment. His was a character which must make itself felt,—how then did he begin, and how did he continue?

All the boldness, all the calm decision, all the discretion, and all the wisdom which Hampden possessed were needed in his peculiar position. It was a dire necessity that was laid upon such a man to oppose his sovereign, instead of deferring, as he would have wished, to all that sovereign's pleasure. But Hampden must either face that necessity, or let his country be robbed in detail of many of its constitutional rights; and he gave himself with characteristic decision to the correction of abuses which the royal prerogative would have screened. Culprit after culprit was unmasked, and even Lord Bacon himself was detected and punished for the bribes which he had taken. No royal frown could deter

a man like Hampden from exposing and reforming such
disreputable doings: and Bacon's abject sense of his own
degradation, as expressed in his own words, furnishes a
melancholy comment on the painful doings of Hampden.
The great chancellor, when detected, confessed; and his
humble submission, "My lords, it is my act, my hand and
my heart. I beseech your lordships to be merciful to a
broken reed," forms, perhaps, one of the most humbling
incidents in British history.

Having entered on his life-work, then, John Hampden is
soon to discover that it is not a sinecure. The House of
Commons resolved that its members were free from all impeachment, imprisonment, and molestation for any speech,
or matter touching the parliament and its duties. But that
was not to be tolerated by self-willed royalty. Shall it
forego its cherished prerogative of silencing or sending to
the Tower those who dare to stand up for the laws of England? Nay, rather shall parliament be dissolved and dispensed with; and having dissolved it, King James, with his
own hand, blotted out the obnoxious declaration from the
journals of Parliament. Nor did matters improve when
James died and Charles succeeded. Along with his throne
he inherited his father's pride, his scorn of the people's
rights, and his insolent self-assertion. The war of opinion
became more and more concentrated, and all the calm energy
of such a man as Hampden was needed to contrive and
to execute the measures which liberty now demanded. If
he will have liberty, he must zealously contend for it. If
grievances must be redressed, the redress must be extorted
from an incensed and unbending king. If illegal imposts
be resisted, it must be by a parliament which that king is
determined either to coerce or dissolve. A parliament could
refuse supplies; but it could not, at least not yet, perpetuate
itself; the king will therefore sweep it away. He will raise

funds by monoplies and other means, without consulting parliament at all. He will issue orders under the privy seal, requiring loans from private parties, taking care that the exaction shall fall most heavily on the friends of those who defended liberty against absolute prerogative.

But if the king was oppressive, Hampden was stanch. In parliament after parliament it was resolved that supplies should not be granted unless abuses were corrected : but parliament after parliament was dissolved by the king, who wished to get the supplies and yet retain the abuses. Some of Hampden's friends were sent to the Tower; outrage after outrage was perpetrated, and at length came Hampden's turn to suffer in person. The king required a general loan, but Hampden refused to contribute his share. As one of the richest commoners in England, he was willing to contribute to all the necessities of the state in legal ways; but he took his stand upon Magna Charta, and would neither compromise his own liberty, nor be a party to compromise that of others. For his refusal he was committed to close and rigorous imprisonment. When he was brought a second time before the Council he still declined to lend money to the king by force, and was again remanded to prison.

But Charles employed other means for raising money, and it was in regard to one of these that he and Hampden came into still more violent collision. The sea-ports and maritime towns had often been required to furnish ships duly manned and equipped, but the order was now extended to inland places, and all lands were assessed for that purpose. One of Hampden's estates was taxed to the amount of a guinea and a half, and another to the extent of twenty shillings. He resisted the trifling impost as arbitrary and unjust, and that with inflexible resolution because of the principle involved, and an eager contest began to be waged. On the one side the king and the upholders of prerogative, on the other the Commons battling for freedom, were standing face to face, and all the heroic firmness of Hampden was needed to carry him through the contest. But he persisted, unlike unawed by imprisonment and by royal threats. In regard to the privileges of parliament, to measures affecting religion, or to supplies of money, he has now taken his place among the foremost men of the kingdom, though the affectionate feelings of his heart suffered not a little amid the scenes through which he was passing. Some of his friends were dying in prison because they would not submit to the dictates of despotism; and when Hampden saw these things, without any apparent remedy for the time, he retired to his estate in Buckinghamshire, there to await better times, or rather the approach of a rupture between the king and the parliament, which could not be much longer avoided. In retirement his mind was braced for yet more stirring scenes than any through which he had passed.

But for a time the king was triumphant. Personal liberty was extensively infringed. Many of the gentry were ordered home to their country seats, and forbidden to return to the capital. Large portions of their land were confiscated. Families were impoverished and ruined. The Puritans, who were now becoming powerful, were visited with heavy penalties, and the oppression which drives a wise man mad was wasting the best energies of the nation. Men like Hampden, calm yet resolute, determined yet wise, were needed much when cannibal cruelties were practised on some of the most devout men of the age. The father of Archbishop Leighton was sentenced to be publicly whipped, to have his ears cut off, his nostrils slit, his tongue bored, his cheeks burned, and afterwards to be banished. Prynne, a lawyer, suffered yet more harrowing atrocities. Once mutilated, he was not thereby deterred from publishing his convictions, and his original punishment was repeated.

The remaining stumps of his ears were dug out with a knife, his cheeks were branded with a red-hot iron, and he was sentenced to an imprisonment which was meant to be life-long. Amid such agonies, inflicted not in the cause of order but of despotism, the need of some strong arm and resolute will was becoming more and more apparent. The arena is in course of being cleared for a conflict, where blood will touch blood. The determination of Charles or his advisers is to have a government without a parliament, or by the sword, if that be needful, to maintain the prerogatives of royalty; and the question now to be practically settled is, will the people of England consent? A terrible tyranny is in course of preparation for them. Taxes imposed by the king, and collected by the military, were by no means dubious events, they had begun—will they be perpetuated?

The affair of the ship-money, already referred to, became the cause or the occasion of augmented violence ; it led to the misery of eleven years of almost uninterrupted civil war. The dispute at first gathered its main force around Hampden, whom Lord Nugent calls " the most able, and resolute, and popular person in the country." A nature already inflamed and distempered by oppression, gradually became fiercer still. In the course of the first year of the impost £200,000 and more found their way into the royal treasury, all levied without the sanction of law or of parliament. But against this violation John Hampden resolved to make a vigorous stand, and he did it in the spring of 1636. Those who refused to pay the impost were numerous; some of them acted boldly and openly in declining to contribute, but the eyes of the court and of the people were alike fixed on the recusant Hampden. He was to the one a victim, on whom they gladly seized, to the other a champion, in whom they learned to glory, and he did not decline the struggle. Though aware of the issues that hung upon the measure, he resolutely

proceeded to oppose for himself, for his country and posterity, the arbitrary taxation of Charles I. Shall the word
of a single man give law to Britain, or can it be made manifest that the majesty of law is yet more august than that of
any single mortal? The judges have decided against Hampden; but are they venal, or have they rightly interpreted the
law? Tyranny might exult as if its victory were secure, but
has it learned to count what that victory will cost? These
were some of the questions raised when John Hampden
threw himself on the Constitution of England as his rock,
resolved to do battle with royalty rather than let liberty
be trampled in the dust. He boldly demurred to the
whole charge of ship-money, as well as other imposts, as
unjust and grievous; and now Charles I. and John Hampden are in the arena: what will the end be? We can scarcely
doubt, when we hear even the royalist Clarendon confess
that Hampden now "grew the argument of all tongues, every
man inquiring who and what he was that durst, at his own
charge, support the liberty and prosperity of the kingdom."

Meanwhile men grew more earnest in this matter, microscopic in its commencement, to become vast in its results.
It was believed by many that the dearest rights of all were
placed in jeopardy. Hampden daily rose in public admiration and honour. The eyes of all were turned on him as
the champion in the crisis, the pilot in the storm. The
firmness of his purpose had been tested. Every induce-
ment that could operate on a mind less resolute operated
upon him. But the calm courage which he displayed, and
the firmness without violence which he maintained, marked
him out as the man for the emergency which had arisen.
Even his enemies confessed that he acted with a temper
and a modesty which won the hearts of men. Lord Wentworth, himself a renegade, might write, indeed, to Archbishop Laud, and express the desire that Hampden and

others were " whipt into their right senses ;" but with the exception of such eager partisans, the man who declined to pay
an unjust impost had become the idol of thousands. Even
the men who were retained to prosecute him could not but
admire his unflinching resolution—his determination at all
hazards to stand by what is now confessed to have been the
constitution and the law of England.

The atrocities which abounded at this period, under the
dark reign of Laud as primate, suggested to many the thought
of emigration, and Hampden and his cousin Oliver Cromwell
were among the number who prepared to seek freedom in
New England. But the king would regulate even such
movements ; and by an order in Council, dated April 6, 1638,
he prohibited shipmasters from conveying passengers to
America " without special license." Eight emigrant vessels
lay at that time in the Thames. On board of one of these
were Hampden and Cromwell. They disembarked, however,
and never perhaps did any of the sons of men unconsciously
plan their own ruin so surely as did Charles I. at the period
now referred to.

But another parliament was at length summoned. Men
would not be longer trifled with. Ten thousand Hampdens
were beginning to lift up their heads, and something must
be done. There had been no parliament for nearly twelve
years ; and as soon as the members had assembled, some
troublesome inquiries began to be made, though, as a whole,
that parliament was dutifully submissive. But Hampden's
case was taken up. Past proceedings were scrutinized. The
fair speeches of the king could deceive no longer ; and a
request was made by the House of Commons for information
to enable them to proceed against those who had pushed
the prosecution against Hampden. He had now withdrawn
from his much-loved private pursuits, and devoted all his
energies to the Commonwealth; and though, like other bene-

factors of mankind, he must suffer if he would do good, he is prepared. He will suffer.

Yet once more the king dissolved the parliament. It was bent on the redress of grievances. He wished nothing but supplies, and again there was collision. And not merely did he dissolve the parliament,—he imprisoned some of the members, and determined to govern without a parliament, or even in spite of it. Soon, however, did it become apparent that the struggle was hopeless, and another parliament must be convened. It was the Long Parliament, and some of its earliest measures were to make compensation for past atrocities, in as far as that was possible. Leighton, Prynne, and others, were freed from their dungeons, though their mutilated members could not be replaced. Pressed by want, the king was obliged to make some concessions; but proposals were now made by the court to impeach Hampden and others of high treason, while the accused in their turn as boldly and at once arraigned Lord Wentworth by a sudden resolution of the House of Commons. That bold and able man attempted to frown down the charges, and scare those who accused him. But John Hampden had confronted royalty when it was pursuing unlawful ends, and did not blanch before the scowl of Wentworth. He knew the inherent weakness of all that is false, the strength of all that is true; and, buoyed up by deep convictions, Hampden and his friends addressed themselves to what they reckoned a great retribution with a manliness equal to the occasion. His industry could not be wearied; his vigilance could not be surprised; his penetration could not be eluded by the most subtle. These and all his gifts he laid with devoted ardour on the altar of his country; and thus did he strive, with a noble decision, to establish in England the security of person and of property, that freedom, in short, which, next to the truth of God, is the glory of our land.

Amid all these things, the struggles between the king and the representatives of the people were waxing more and more eager. In the month of December, 1641, a grand Remonstrance was presented to the king, embodying all the grievances under which the parliament and people had suffered during the reign of Charles. That document was adopted amid an indescribable scene in the House of Commons, and only the calm firmness of Hampden prevented violence, perhaps bloodshed. Measures were speedily adopted by the Court against some of the Commons. The lodgings and repositories of Hampden and four others were sealed up by the king's command. The House resolved that their serjeant-at-arms should break the seal. Then a messenger came requesting the persons of five of the members, Hampden being one of them. They were accused of treason—in short, the coming collision, to end in ruin, is hastening on ; and while Hampden declared his readiness to yield a dutiful obedience to a lawful sovereign and his privy council, it is manifest that a violent disruption is at hand.

Charles now went in person to the House of Commons, accompanied by a band of armed men, with the design of seizing the offensive members. Being forewarned, however, they escaped ; and from that hour we may date the commencement of a civil war. Hampden and his four friends lurked in the city of London, where they were sheltered and kept in safety. He continued to influence from his hiding-place the counsels of the Commons. The quarrel between Charles and Hampden now appears to have assumed not a little of the keenness of personal hostility. At all events, it was Hampden that now urged the adoption of the most decided measures. He argued that the time for compromise was past. Lord Nugent says—" Henceforward we shall always find him foremost to urge the strongest and most decisive measures." . . . . . "In the Council of War and

Committee of Public Safety" " he was the most in favour of bold and rapid enterprises;" so that, for a time, the destiny of a royal house seemed dependent on the movements of this strong-willed man. He was prompt, resolute, and unwearied in all that his hands found to do. He rose with the occasion; and even amid the amenities of a tender nature, he was iron-willed and indomitable.

As a result, brother now rushed against brother, and citizen against citizen, in the favoured kingdom of England. Where the flowing tide meets a full river rushing seaward, the surge occasioned by the collision is often dangerous. Shipwrecks have happened amid such scenes, and that found a parallel in the case before us. Royal prerogative pushed to excess, chafed, and, as many believed, pillaged and oppressed the people of England. The spirit of freedom resented the aggression, and a monarch lost his life and his crown ere the struggle was ended. In entering on that struggle, Hampden characteristically counselled his associates to terminate it by a few bold and decided actions. For his own part, it was with prodigious activity that he discharged what he deemed a solemn duty.

But he fell in discharging it. In an attack which he hastily made with a small detachment against a body of Prince Rupert's troops, Hampden was mortally wounded. His head drooping, and his hands resting on his horse's mane, he was seen slowly withdrawing from the fight, and reached the village of Thame, where he had been educated. His wounds were dressed; but, after about six days of agony, he died, praying for his king, and exclaiming, "Lord Jesu, receive my soul. O Lord, save my country. O Lord, be merciful to"——; but the sentence never was completed. John Hampden fell back in his bed and expired.

Such were some of the efforts of one of the most conspicuous men of all this nation's past. Calm, self-contained, and resolute, rapid and determined when quick decision was needed, and not to be daunted by danger, any more than he could be bribed by interest, he became the foremost man of his party, at a time when great minds were developed by a great occasion. The British constitution was then receiving some of its finishing touches. Many excrescences required to be cleared away, and much that hindered its growth had to be removed. The sagacity and the energy of Hampden were well fitted to promote these results, and even Hume, with all his favour for the Stuarts, was compelled to confess, that in profound capacity, undaunted courage, and great enterprises, Hampden and his associates were not much inferior to Cato, to Brutus, or to Cassius. But without attempting any decision in such a case, it is enough to say, that by firm purpose and unflinching zeal, this man wrought out an amount of good for this island for which the latest ages may hold his memory sacred. True, he secured that good at an appalling cost. To be compelled to withstand that king for whom he prayed in the very act of dying,—to be obliged to urge measures so far that civil war became inevitable—or, more precisely, to take his stand for a great principle in an affair which cost him only twenty shillings—implied a trial, or a strain, which few would have had nerve to face. But Hampden had nerve : he faced the whole ; and, as a result, we can now rejoice in blessings which, but for that indomitable man, might have been swept utterly away.

It is known that Richard Baxter placed Hampden far up among the excellent of the earth. The author of the "Saints' Rest" actually declared that one of the pleasures which he hoped to enjoy in heaven was the society of Hampden ; and an eulogy so peculiar requires to be well supported—but it is so. In regard to secular things, the great Puritan managed

the House of Commons by his easy courtesy, by his calm
sagacity, and his unflinching firmness. He could direct a
campaign, or rule a family. He could confront royalty in its
error, and yet devoutly pray that that royalty might be put
right. In a word, Hampden was one of the men whom
partizans may attempt to entomb in obloquy—but that
resurrection of character which may take place long anterior
to that of the body, has placed him far up among the beacon
lights which guide men in the path which all the worthies
trod : the path of suffering and sorrow—of struggle and
tears, to glory, honour, and immortality. Like the Hebrew
heroes at the border of the Holy Land, John Hampden
dared to follow wherever Truth and its Author led, and his
name has been for six generations and more a synonyme
for freedom.

IV.—ALGERNON SYDNEY.

A.D. 1622—1683.

" Mortals that would follow me,
Love Virtue : She alone is free.
She can teach ye how to climb
Higher than the sphery clime ;
Or if Virtue feeble were,
Heaven itself would stoop to her."

COMUS.

His birth—And early training—His first appointments—Principles adopted—Wounded at Marston Moor—The king's trial—Sydney's part in that transaction—His public life—Expelled from parliament by Cromwell—The Restoration—Sydney an exile—Germany—Italy—A plot to assassinate him—Returns to England—Is sent to parliament—His principles—The Rye-house plot—Sydney seized—Sent to the Tower—Tried—Condemned—Executed.

N the Arts, proficiency is attained by the study of exquisite models. The galleries of Venice are crowded with students of Titian and Canova. Florence is preferred by those who would study Raphael for painting, and Michael Angelo for sculpture; while Rome concentrates many of the works of all the masters, at whose feet thousands sit to appreciate high beauty, and to learn to imitate its charms. It is well to have similar models in the domain of morals, and, in some respects, ALGERNON SYDNEY was one. He is often spoken of as an example of pure and disinterested patriotism, and has been called the champion and the martyr of freedom. Milton has praised him ; all except the friends of despotism have heaped high encomiums on his name. The love of liberty and his country was literally a passion in his soul. The cause for which " Sydney bled upon the scaffold" has been cherished by ten

thousand times ten thousand ; and lessons of wisdom may surely be learned from the life of such a man.

ALGERNON SYDNEY was born in the year 1622. He was the second son of the second Earl of Leicester, and his mother was a Percy of the house of Northumberland. At an early age he indicated extraordinary talents ; and his father, who was British ambassador at various Courts, carried Algernon with him, that his education might be conducted under his parent's eye. The progress of the youth was such as to repay the care which was bestowed upon him. Denmark, France, and Italy thus became, in succession, the countries where the future martyr to freedom was trained ; and though he was destined for the army, his education was so comprehensive that affairs of state were familiar to him from his youth. He early became the favourite of some high dignifaries who bestowed their favour upon few.

Charles I. was then precipitating his kingdom into trouble by his arbitrary measures, and, at the same time, unconsciously rearing his own scaffold, with a dogged infatuation of which there are few examples upon record. Amid these scenes, young Sydney grew familiar with the measures which were employed by those who tried to guard the liberties of their country from extinction ; and his aversion to tyranny, and his love of freedom, were fostered by what he saw and heard. In his nineteenth year he was appointed to the command of a troop of horse, and displayed on all occasions an extraordinary spirit and resolution ; even thus early, he appears as one of the most intrepid of men in following the path which he deemed the right one. When Charles, urged onwards to ruin by his own dark spirit, seized on five members of the House of Commons because they dared to oppose his arbitrary measures, matters hastened to a crisis, and Sydney was early among those who were compelled to provide for the defence of freedom. He and his brother were at one time taken into custody in the interest of the king; and their affections, hitherto loyal, now became estranged from one who wielded power chiefly to abuse it, or tried to aggrandize himself by the ruin of others.

Sydney's promotion was now rapid, and the parliament passed vote after vote to aid him in various enterprises on his country's behalf. He was severely wounded at the battle of Marston Moor, and in danger of falling into the hands of the Royalists; but, after his recovery, he was attached to that division of the army which Cromwell commanded, and bore upon his banner the motto which guided him through life—"The sacred love of country makes a hero." Disaster after disaster pursued the royal cause. Charles was soon the prisoner of his own injured subjects; and no prophet's eye was needed to foresee that calamities of no common kind were coming. Sydney was now a lieutenant-general of horse, and zealously employed in the cause he had espoused; but as he was deprived of his position as Governor of Dublin, by some who secretly favoured the king, that and similar things just helped to render him more resolute in preventing the ascendency of what would have crushed the people of these islands as if they had existed only for the sake of one despotic man. He was, in truth, inseparably united now with men who felt that the defence of freedom was a duty which they owed at once to their country and their God.

Algernon Sydney, then, has resolutely chosen his part in the eventful times in which he lived; and without following him through all the stages of his career, it must be enough to fix attention upon those great leading events which helped to make him what he was, and hand down his name to all time as one of the most unflinching friends of freedom in his own or any age. The king's duplicity had now wrought its natural effects—few could trust his word; and his trial was not distant. Sydney was appointed one of the commissioners to sit on that memorable trial; and during some of the preliminary steps, he occasionally attended the court. He withdrew, however, from the solemn scenes in their more advanced stages, though he was one of those who reckoned a king morally responsible for his guilty actions, just like other men.

According to the British Constitution, as it is now adjusted, the monarch cannot be tried: the ministers are responsible for crimes committed against the nation, and can be impeached for their offences. But Charles had tried to rule as if he had a divine right for despotism; and hence the troubles and the sorrows of his life—hence his trial, his condemnation, and his death. Sydney was at Penshurst, the family residence, from the 22d of January till the 29th of that month; and during that period the sentence was pronounced, and the warrant for the execution signed. It is alleged that he disliked Cromwell's growing influence; that he foresaw the purpose of that bold man to become king himself, and that that discovery was one cause of Sydney's absence from public life at this critical juncture. He thought, however, that the terrible example of the monarch's death would be a lesson to all future tyrants. Hating oppression as Sydney did, and believing that Charles was incurable in his obstinacy, or his determination to rule unchallenged, as he was unquestionably criminal against his kingdom, our patriot acquiesced in the sentence against the king as deserved—deserved, because he had usurped a power above all law, had acted as if the millions of his subjects lived for him alone, and had added treachery to all his other crimes. They are blessed who are freed from the dire necessity of ever repeating such an act; but those who adopt the maxim that the king is raised up for the people, as Sydney did, and not the people for the king, approved of that deed—all solemn and startling as it was.

Sydney henceforth continued to take an active interest in all the proceedings of his times. In 1651, he became assiduous in attending to his duty in parliament; and when Cromwell dismissed that body in 1653, because he reckoned it incompetent, Sydney, who sat at the right hand of the Speaker, refused to obey the Protector's command. Not till hands were laid on him to force him from his place, did he consent to withdraw; and Cromwell had to issue repeated orders ere that was effected, for Sydney then as ever was steadfast and unmoveable in what he deemed the path of duty; he did not fear the face of man, whether it was that of a king or a protector. He again retired, however, to Penshurst, the residence of his father, and sought to console himself amid rural beauties for political discomfiture. But his steadfast adherence to the cause of liberty was not to be shaken by any deed of man. During his retirement, he stored his mind with knowledge for future use; he studied the history at once of free and of despotic states, and thus deepened the foundations on which he was afterwards to build. Keeping always aloof from Cromwell, he was determined to own no authority but that which was deemed constitutional, that is, authority originating in the choice of the ruled, and employed for their highest good.

It was in the year 1659 that he returned to public duty, and soon thereafter he was sent as a commissioner to mediate between Denmark and Sweden, where his large views and his firm conduct successfully promoted the object of his mission. But when Charles II. was restored to his father's throne, Sydney felt that his occupation for the time was gone. Powerful inducements were held out to him to enter the service of royalty; but he could not belie his con-

victions, or imitate those who had meanly trampled on their
former principles: the reward of iniquity he would not
touch, and he therefore remained abroad, a wanderer for
many years, all but disowned by his father, and often in
pecuniary straits.

But at this point it may be well to glance at some of this
man's peculiar opinions. He was hereafter to prove his
steadfastness by dying rather than surrender his convictions.
What, then, were the tenets of Sydney at the period now
referred to? What were the opinions which he afterwards
wrought out into a system, and which he held till they
brought him to the scaffold as an arch-martyr for liberty?

He had given some evidence of the love which he bore to
his native land; but even that love was not so strong as his
love of freedom and of truth. He would willingly have
redeemed himself from exile, (he writes) " with the loss of a
great deal of his blood;" but when he saw that country
which he once esteemed a paradise, steeped and soaked in
debasing crimes, it was no place for him. Luxury and vice,
he continues, had taken the place of piety and virtue; the
best of the nation were made a prey to the worst; the people
were enslaved; none but the mean were safe; none but the
panderer to iniquity honoured; and he boldly asks, " Is it a
pleasure to see all that I love sold and destroyed?" He
deemed life among strangers preferable to the ignominy
which reigned at home; and determined that while he lived
he would endeavour to preserve his liberty, or, at least, not
consent to its destruction. With noble firmness this exile
half prophetically proclaimed, " I hope I will die in the same
principles in which I have lived, and will live no longer than
they can preserve me . . . . . I have ever had in my mind
that when God should cast me into such a condition as that
I cannot save my life but by doing a dishonourable thing,
he shows me that the time is come wherein I should resign

it." And this man, at once undaunted and unbribed, was taken at his word: he had at last to resign his life, because he would not succumb to oppression, or smile upon royal crime. Sydney felt that the glory of the king was the shame of the people. He declared that the guilt of the land was akin to that of Judas, and that where the friends of freedom could not live in safety, he would not live at all. Where the souls of millions were bowed down and enslaved to gratify the passions of one bad man, Sydney would not willingly dwell: and though he felt, and said he was assured that God would avenge the blood of those who perished, our patriot could find an asylum only in the thought, that if he lived to see the day when right should reign once more, he would be ready at the sight to say, "Lord, now lettest thou thy servant depart in peace."

Amid all this, Sydney always declared from his place of exile, that if Charles did what was right, no man should be a more faithful servant than he; and his constancy in upholding these determinations makes him a model of intrepidity indeed. His maxim ever was, "Not millions for one man, but one man for millions;" and steadily and boldly did he move through life guided by that maxim—the pole-star of his voyage—ashamed of nothing but meanness and crime. Acting with strict honour and stern consistency, he rose superior to the ills which now entered into his lot. All, indeed, may not subscribe to his imperious words, when he said that the execution of Charles I. "was the justest and bravest action ever done in England or anywhere else;" but if the sentiment was extreme, he suffered for his boldness. He durst not visit his native land even to adjust his private affairs, and was rather like a pelican in the wilderness than one of the noblest sons of England.

It was the saying of Burke that Charles II. was a man without any sense of duty as a prince; without any regard to the dignity of the crown; without any love to his people; dissolute, false, venal ... ;" and the effects of his example were soon apparent in the land which he misruled. Profligacy came in like a flood; corruption ate into the heart of England, and while Sydney's sad forebodings were thus realized to the full, he was wandering over Germany an exile for his love to his down-trodden country. His father had all but cast him off. The wanderer was sometimes without the means of immediate support; but after long troubles he reached Rome by way of Venice, and for a time found rest in that capital. Some of his friends who had returned to England, safe, as they thought, under a deed of amnesty, were taken, tried, condemned for treason, and put to death with all the barbarity attendant upon punishment for that crime. With intrepidity, indeed, some of them suffered in that cause for which they had hazarded all; but Sydney was made still more wretched by their deaths. His mind, however, was still unshaken, and the love of freedom which he cherished buoyed him up amid all his trials, at the instigation of the king of whom it has been said, "I doubt whether a single instance can be produced of his having spared the life of any one whom motives either of policy or revenge prompted him to destroy." "If we can honestly put him out of the way," was, as we shall immediately see, the avowed maxim of Charles regarding those whom he feared or disliked; and such a maxim gives too much appearance of truth to the saying of a statesman of our day, that "no murder which history has recorded of Cæsar Borgia exceeds in violence or in fraud that by which Charles took away the life of the gallant and patriotic Sydney."

In the year 1660, while settled in Rome, our exile studied with great care the conduct of the pope, the cardinals, and the priesthood. His verdict upon some of the most noted Romans was that "pride, laziness, and sensuality" had

eaten away the former spirit of Italy. Though never a bigot
where there was common ground to stand upon, Sydney
recoiled from the selfish policy of a See called holy, and from
the absurdities of a creed even then in its dotage. It was
at Rome, too, that his mental anguish became the deepest,
both on account of his country and his own position. Defrauded, disowned, and deserted, the keen sensibilities of
Sydney's nature were deeply wounded. It seemed as if his
friends deemed it enough if he had only bread to eat, and
left him long without suitable resources. To speak the
truth, he refers to himself as having nothing to subsist on
in a place far from home, where his rank, as well as his
principles, made shameful compliances detestable. All this
because his steadfast soul could not be driven from its steadfastness; because he was too earnest, or too much of a true
man to veer and change as if principle were a shifting sand-
bank, not a solid rock. Shut out as he thus was from the
world, he had nothing to solace him but a pure conscience,
and that form of truth which he loved. But he continued
his studies, and though he had to say, "I wander as a vaga-
bond through the world," that neither shook his confidence,
nor unmanned his soul, nor modified the principles for which
he had imperiled life itself. His "half burial," he said,
was "a preparative to an entire one," and he bore up under
the consciousness that there *would* come a rest for the
weary, and a triumph for the truth.

While Sydney's friends were slaughtered in England under
various pretences, and while the king, in a letter which
is still extant, was writing to a judge concerning one
whom he disliked, that "certaynly he is too dangerous a
man to lett live, if we can honestly put him out of the way,"
our patriot was forming a plan for raising a corps from
among his former associates to be employed in the service
of a foreign prince. He hoped by these means to provide

an escape. That plan, however, was never carried into effect; and Sydney was now obliged to move from place to place to avoid the plots and persecutions of his enemies. He narrowly escaped assassination at Augsburg; and all this, be it remembered, because he refused to become the partizan of a king who flooded our island with grossest crimes; who trampled on all the rights which he durst assail, and who is now undisguisedly known, as Sydney knew him, to be one of the most unprincipled men that ever caused a kingdom to groan. Driven to desperation, there can be little doubt that the exile meditated an invasion of England, for the same purpose as that which was happily effected a few years thereafter by William of Orange, to free our forefathers from the grinding bondage of the Stuarts. Indeed, in several respects Algernon Sydney antedated the Revolution in England. He asserted principles which were only then embodied in practice; but he did it before the time, and, amid the sufferings and the hardships of an exile, had to pay the penalty of his boldness. He made the selfish tyrant who reigned in England uneasy by coming so near to London, even as Paris, where Sydney sojourned for a time; and it has been truly said that few things can show more clearly the ascendency of the good, the meanness of the vile, than to know that a king of England trembled at the name of an exile who was in solitude and in want. His lofty tone of independence made him the terror of the voluptuous despot.

At length, however, the Earl of Leicester, Sydney's father, when far advanced in years, wished to see his son before he died; and at the interest of the court of France, an assurance of safety was conceded to Sydney. With the king's passport in his possession he returned to England in the autumn of 1677. He designed to remain only for a short period; but a suit in chancery, arising out of his father's affairs, detained him for years in the island. He soon began to take a part in public matters, and was, after some time, returned as a member to parliament. But the Court still watched him with an evil eye; and to verify the truth that "uneasy lies the head that wears a crown," the nearness of Sydney made Charles restless indeed. He was accused to the king of being engaged in a plot against him, but obtained an audience to disabuse the royal mind. That, however, and similar incidents showed him that he was not safe in his native land, and he resolved to retire to France, by whose ambassador his enemies allege that he was bribed.

This persecuted man was now occupied in maturing his great work on Government, announcing the principles which should guide both the ruler and the ruled. His fundamental maxim was that the consent of the governed was an essential part of all rule over men; not brute force, nor proud and egotistic despotism, but a rule founded on the common will, and guided by the grand maxim, the highest good of all. That was a compend of Sydney's politics, and because he held such opinions, he was hunted as an outlaw; he was proscribed by despotism because he was the friend of man. But a few of his principles, as they became more mature, may indicate how he thought, and how he was likely to act:—

"Man," he contends, "is naturally free and cannot justly be deprived of his liberty without a cause. . . . This liberty, however, is not licentiousness of conduct, but an exemption from all to which he has not given his assent."

"Magistrates are distinguished from other men by the power with which the law invests them for the public good, and the people may proportion, regulate, and terminate that power as seems most convenient to themselves."

"As to popular government, in the strictest sense, that is pure democracy, where the people perform all that belongs to government, I know of no such thing, and if it be in the world, have nothing to say to it."

"There is no mortal creature that deserves so well from mankind as a wise, valiant, diligent, and just king, who, as a father, cherishes his people; as a shepherd, feeds, defends, and is ready to lay down his life for his flock—who is a terror to evil-doers, and a praise to those that do well."

"He who is set up for the public good, can have no contest with the whole people whose good he is to procure, unless he deflect from the end of his institution, and set up an interest of his own in opposition to it."

—Nor were such opinions the result merely of an iron or an obstinate will. They were held by men of his times whose love of truth has made them models. An archbishop, whose praise for gentleness is in all the Churches, has said, " . . . . . Kings and rulers too often consider not for what they are exalted; they think it is for themselves, to honour and please themselves, and not to honour God and benefit their people—to encourage and reward the good, and to punish the wicked. They are set on high for the good of those that are below them, that they may be refreshed with their light and influence, as the lights of heaven are set there, in the highest parts of the world, for the use and benefit of the very lowest. . . . . And the mountains are raised above the rest of the earth, not to be places of prey and robbery, as sometimes they are turned to be, but to send forth streams into the valleys, and make them fertile." *

By these and similar maxims, then, Sydney unfolded a system of government wise in itself, and sure to be beneficial in its results, if not thwarted by the selfishness and corruption so ascendant in all men—so rampant, too often, where power is possessed. But whether wise or not, the author of this system was soon to be crushed by the arm of power.

* "Leighton on 1 Peter ii. 13, 14. '

He was now much mixed up with public affairs, and sus-pected in them all. A plot was alleged to have been formed to assassinate the king and his brother, called the Rye-house Plot. Sydney was artfully implicated in that transaction ; and it became the occasion of his death. He was siezed by an order from the Privy Council. His papers were sealed up. He was examined by the Council, and committed a close prisoner to the Tower of London, on a charge of high treason. Conscious of his innocence, he sought to possess his soul in patience.

—Conscious of his innocence. There can be no doubt that the corruptions of those times prompted many hard speeches against the arch-corrupter, the monarch, and his minions. Much was done, and still more was said, which no other ruler would ever have provoked. But no evidence has ever been produced to show that Sydney was a party to any plot such as that of the Rye-house was said to be. His durance in the Tower, however, was as strait as if he had been a convicted criminal. His money and his property were seized. His friends were denied access to him ; his servants were even prevented from conveying to him a change of linen. " For conspiring and compassing the death of the king," was the crime laid to his charge ; and attempts to draw evidence against him from his own mouth, were made at an examination to which he was subjected in the Tower. But he nobly baffled those who were compassing his life, and kept them at bay with a skill, a tact, a power, and a calm self-possession, which form a presumptive proof of his innocence.

But that he should die was a foregone conclusion. Jeffries was one of his judges—and that was enough. Sydney was denied a copy of his indictment, yet had to plead his own cause. Indecent haste at one time, and vexatious delays at another, wore out the man. Law and common

decency were outraged upon the trial. He took advantage
of every point where he could make a stand, but was
driven from position to position by men determined that he
should perish. The violence both of the bench and the bar,
was directed against him; and a mind less heroic than his
might have succumbed under the tyranny with which he
was hunted to death. The prisoner's innocence was manifest to all but the creatures of the king. With an effrontery
never surpassed, the Lord Chief-Justice left the court, and
went to the jury while they were consulting, instructing
them as to the verdict which was expected from them. Is
it wonderful that, with a packed jury, and with a venal
judge, Sydney was condemned to die? He was, of course,
found guilty, and no subsequent appeal could save him.
The Duke of York interfered to make death more certain;
and Jeffries, in his own furious way, declared that either
Sydney or he must die. When receiving sentence, he was
assailed and browbeat by one of the judges, who appeared
to be drunk; and when the martyr to freedom could not gain
a hearing amid this perversion of justice, he only exclaimed,
"I must appeal to God and the world; I am not heard."

Sentence of death was pronounced, and Sydney, with
unaltered mien, exclaimed, "Then, O God, O God, I beseech
thee to sanctify these sufferings, and impute not my blood
to the country, nor to the city through which I am to be
drawn....." He felt that he was persecuted for righteousness' sake, and yet maintained his calmness amid what
might have goaded him to madness. He once held out his
hand to his judge, and said, "My lord, feel my pulse, and
see if I am disordered. I bless God, I never was in better
temper than now." While the inhuman Jeffries acted the
chief part in these outrages, it is said that the king rewarded
him with the present of a costly ring.

As truth and decency had been so outraged at his trial,

Sydney drew up a narrative and an appeal to posterity; and in concluding it he said, with the calm sublimity of a martyr, "I know that my Redeemer lives; and as he hath, in a great measure, upheld me in the day of my calamity, hope that he will still hold me by his Spirit in this last moment; and, giving me grace to glorify him in my death, receive me into the glory prepared for those that fear him, when my body shall be dissolved." He had expressed to some ministers of religion his deep contrition for his sins, and prepared to die like a believer indeed. When he saw his death-warrant he expressed no concern, but rather astonished those around him by his calm demeanour. One of the sheriffs even wept before him, when the dying man reproved that official for the part which he had taken in procuring the condemnation of the innocent. But the world, he said, was now nothing to him. He had long been familiar with death, and was ready to die—not in the spirit of bravado, but calmly, hopefully, like a hero and a martyr.

On the 7th of December 1683, five years before the Revolution was to enshrine Sydney's deepest convictions in a great national act and constitution, he was led to the place of execution on Towerhill; for the king, in consideration of his victim's noble descent, had remitted those parts of the sentence which doomed the patriot to be murdered and mangled at Tyburn. He ascended the scaffold with a firm step, and submitted without delay or formality to the executioner, to whom he gave three guineas; but as that functionary deemed the sum too little, the dying man ordered him to receive a guinea or two more. He then kneeled down, and after a brief silence, having calmly unrobed, he placed his head upon the block. The executioner, for some reason, asked Sydney if he would rise again, and his reply was, "Not till the general resurrection—strike on." One blow severed the head from the body.

But though Sydney was thus judicially murdered, his maxims lived, and sank deep into the minds of thoughtful men who would not barter freedom and be slaves. The oppression and the corruptions of those in power drove all independent minds back upon the principles which he had so firmly maintained, and ratified at last in his blood. His name was soon enrolled among his country's martyrs, and became to thousands the very watchword or synonyme of freedom. Then the Revolution came. Sydney's attainder was reversed, and all records of the proceedings were ordered to be torn from the public registers. All was done, in short, that could efface the recollection of a deed so unprincipled; but the memory of it had sunk deep into many hearts, and the man who took his life in his hand to resist the encroachments of arbitrary power, is still embalmed in many a memory as one of the firmest friends of freedom, of England, and of man. We are far from defending every action of his life. There are moral charges against him which, if they be proved, are to be unequivocally condemned. But it cannot be questioned that the great aim of his life was to restore his native land to freedom, when honour and virtue were banished from the palace and the throne. He did not entirely succeed—nay, he fell like a warrior in the breach—but the foundations of our liberty were cemented by his blood. One of the legal lights of the past has said, "There was some little colour of law in Lord Russell's trial, but Algernon Sydney was absolutely murdered;" and that fact, of course, made his death a power. He lived in an age when truth passed for treason, but he dared to speak it, though in speaking it he died; and which now is the most honoured—Charles the tyrant, Jeffries the butcher, or Sydney the murdered?

Here, then, is another example of the pains and throes which are needed ere any great truth can be born into our world. But here also is a glimpse of one who could endure these throes even unto death, that truth might be born. Undaunted by the hatred of a king, and not quailing even before Jeffries and his coadjutors, Sydney stood by the convictions which he had espoused, though a grave, which was meant to be one of ignominy, was his reward. Firm conviction taught him to take his stand. Firm conviction enabled him to maintain his position; and that country is guarded by something better than a wall of fire which has men of his maxims and his intrepidity to uphold its cause. It is not needful, we repeat, to defend every deed of his life. Enough to know that his aims for his country were not less lofty than they were good and true; and merely to sympathize with aspirations such as his is itself a kind of nobility. It was a fable that the waters of Castalia made him who drank of them a poet; it is a truth that he who catches the spirit of Sydney is a patriot.

V.—LORD WILLIAM RUSSELL.

A.D. 1639—1683.

> ".... A crown,
> Golden in show, is but a wreath of thorns—
> Brings dangers, troubles, cares, and sleepless nights,
> To him who wears the regal diadem,
> When on his shoulders each man's burden lies;
> For therein stands the office of a king,
> His honour, virtue, merit, and chief praise,
> That for the public all this weight he bears.
> Yet he who reigns within himself, and rules
> Passions, desires, and fears, is more a king."
>
> *Paradise Regained.*

Contrasts in history—Russell's birth and education—Travels—Returns to Britain—Enters parliament—The corruption of the times—Charles II.—The Duke of York—Russell at variance with the royal policy—His first speech—Plots of Romanists—Counteraction—Russell proposes a bold measure to parliament—Attacks Popery afresh—Meal-tub plot—Rye-house plot—Russell seized—Sent to the Tower—Tried—Condemned to die as a traitor—Endeavours made to obtain a pardon—They fail—His demeanour in the Tower—His religious views—Last interview with Lady Russell—His demeanour on the scaffold—His dying testimony—His attainder reversed—Conclusion.

THERE are many beacons shining in history to warn us as to whom we praise. There are few men or few kings whose character is more distinctly settled now than that of James I. He is rarely spoken of without some measure of ridicule, or even of deeper feelings —those of resentment and contempt. Yet an archbishop whom he had raised to dignity, thus spoke of that king as being " zealous as a David ; learned and wise, the Solomon of our age ; religious as Josias ; careful of spreading Christ's faith as Constantine the Great ; just as Moses ; undefiled in all his ways as a Jehoshaphat and Hezekiah ; full of clemency as another Theodosius." That was the man who could rarely speak without uttering impiety, and who scarcely ever was trusted without betraying the trust, when it suited his own sinister ends.

But other men there are whose characters rise from generation to generation, till at last they are embalmed among the objects of a nation's reverence—the founders of their liberty, the defenders of their rights, the authors of blessings manifold. LORD WILLIAM RUSSELL, the third son of the fifth Earl of Bedford, belonged to this latter class. He was born on the 23d of September 1639, and received his education at Cambridge. He subsequently visited the continent of Europe, and sojourned some time at Augsburg. During his journeys, he appears to have paid much attention to the Romish ceremonies, and wrote to one of his friends in England that Romanists seemed to him to "take more paines in going to hell than a good Christian doth in going to heaven." In giving attention to such things, he was treasuring up knowledge or receiving impressions which swayed him all through life with the power of master motives.

In the winter of 1658 young Russell was at Paris, and in the following year returned to England. Previous to this date he had been visited by a severe illness, which appears to have been the means of rousing him to some serious thought; and he tells us that his prayers were that God would give him not health alone, but grace to employ it in his service; yet there is reason to fear that these impressions were only like the morning cloud. At a subsequent period, the dissolute court of Charles II. for some time caught Russell in its meshes, or swept him along in its vortex; but he escaped, and became, as we shall see, in many respects a model for sobriety of judgment, and unflinching adherence to truth. He most probably owed that change to his wife.

Upon the Restoration of Charles II., Lord William

Russell was chosen member of parliament for Tavistock, and subsequently represented the county of Bedford in four successive parliaments; but for more than twelve years he was a "silent member," and might have continued to be the same through life, had not the stirring events of his day dragged or driven him into publicity. A mind like his could not remain in obscurity when great deeds were to be done. When Russell entered upon that career in which he never more found rest till he mounted the scaffold, Great Britain was reduced to the lowest condition, both morally and politically. One of the most unprincipled monarchs that ever occupied a throne then ruled or misruled these lands. Maxims the most flagitious, and conduct the most abandoned at once in king, courtiers, and subjects, made that period one of deepest national disgrace. To enable him to become a despot and reign without a parliament, Charles had formed a secret alliance with the king of France. He had adopted the religion of Rome yet disguised it, like an unprincipled hypocrite, even while subscribing a treaty with the French king, of which the following is a part:—"The king of Great Britain (it says) is convinced of the truth of the Catholic religion, and resolved to make his declaration of it, and to reconcile himself with the Church of Rome, as soon as the affairs of his kingdom shall be sufficiently established to permit him." In truth, unprincipled ambition, shameless venality, and cool hypocrisy signalized the king, and that treaty, one competent to judge has said, will for ever remain a monument of ingratitude, perjury, and treason. "His perfidy was as spontaneous as it was unexampled."*

At the same time, the king's brother, the dark-souled Duke of York, was plotting for the restoration of Popery, and its twin power, despotism, with even more determined

* Earl Russell.

intrigues than the king's; and it was to oppose these schemes against his country that Lord William Russell left the tranquillity of private life to be involved in turmoils which ended only with his days. He saw what was in preparation, what bonds and miseries were in store for Britain; and threw himself with manly calmness, yet with unwavering zeal, into the task of preventing such results. The conduct of the king, when in straits for money, to enable him to reign without a parliament, was such as would disgrace a professional impostor. On a certain day, he adopted a measure which was equivalent to seizing a million-and-a-half of other men's property, and that shameless step Russell deeply deplored. Further, the king attacked the Dutch fleet as it returned richly laden from the east, though peace still existed between Great Britain and Holland. By these means he hoped to replenish his exchequer, so that fraud and violence were the means at first employed to suppress the liberties of our island.

Such doings needed a check; such times demanded patriots, and patriots appeared. Lord William Russell, as a lover of his country, stood in the front rank of those who thus came to the rescue of our liberties, although he seemed unfit for a popular leader. He was a man of undaunted courage and unshaken firmness, but yet slow of mind, and sparing of discourse. His judgment was sound when he had leisure to consider what was proposed, but there was nothing impulsive in his temperament; and he seemed altogether unlikely ever to become prominent in times like those in which he lived. Yet such was his firmness, such his unfaltering decision, and such his high-toned morality, that his ascendency was everywhere acknowledged; and they who had loved oppression soon learned to hate Russell. Perhaps no man ever possessed greater influence among his friends.

In the year 1674, when parliament met on the 7th of
January, it was obvious that the plots against the laws and
liberties of this empire could not be much longer endured.
Russell then made his first speech, in which the perfidious
measures of government were plainly commented upon.
Some of the king's advisers, among others the notorious
Duke of Lauderdale, were assailed as the enemies of their
country; and a struggle as determined as ever shook a kingdom now began. The devices of tyranny were manifold:
the boldness of Russell and his friends in confronting them
were proportionate, and he was soon obliged to face royalty
itself, to prevent it from becoming despotism of the worst
type—and we must remember it was a royalty then

> " Whose smile was rapture, and whose frown despair."

It is well known, and has been already noticed, that the
Duke of York, next heir to the throne, was bent on restor-
ing Popery in Britain.   He was as bigoted to the full as
the bloody Mary.   At the same time, his influence over the
king was great, and always used for evil.   It became requisite, therefore, to counteract this influence, and Russell undertook to lead in the attempt. Not because he
possessed extraordinary powers : not that he was endowed
with the gift of eloquence : not that he was able to rouse
the popular mind, or grapple with the accomplished in-
triguers on the throne, beside it, or behind it ; but because
he was a man of unswerving firmness, and temperate love
of liberty, was Russell chosen to move regarding the royal
brother ; and it is not difficult to picture the effort which
it must have cost one constituted like him to confront
those whom he would rather have honoured and revered
—for whom he may be said to have died praying, as he
cherished all rightful love and homage.

The history of those times, as it can now be calmly reviewed, does not leave the shadow of a doubt that a deep plot was laid to restore Popery in Britain. England and Scotland alike were to become its victims once more. Coleman, who was at one time secretary to the Duke of York, wrote to one of the creatures of Charles in France, and said concerning England, " We have here a mighty work upon our hands, no less than the conversion of three kingdoms, and by that perhaps the utter subduing of a pestilent heresy which has domineered over great part of this northern world a long time." That was, in truth, the guiding aim of king, prince, and tool in those times. Deep and sinister plans were laid for the purpose, and nothing but measures the most energetic could ward off the woe. The question which patriots had then to ponder—a dire and a painful one, no doubt, but forced upon them by necessity, was this : Shall we tamely lose both our religion and our liberty, or shall we meet and repel the aggression ? and Russell, at least, was ready with an answer.

At this stage men were compelled to act in a manner which all loyal subjects would gladly have avoided. A proposal was made to set aside the title of the Duke of York to succeed to the throne, and to ask the parliament to arrange regarding a successor to Charles. It was a bold measure, a painful one, and could be adopted only under the guidance of profound convictions, or a solemn sense of duty to the country. But Russell, though most temperate, was resolute. Amid such discussions, the Duke of York might appear before the Commons, as he did, with tears in his eyes. Others might attempt the same womanish form of appeal ; but tears could neither melt the chains nor wash out the disgrace which were in preparation for the three kingdoms, and Russell would not be moved. The struggle between power and liberty, accordingly, grew more keen. He was strongly backed by the approbation of his country, as appears from the fact that he was chosen member for two counties at the same time. But the plot thickened, and Lord Russell had need of all his self-possession to hold his own. On one occasion he heroically moved for a committee of the Commons to "draw up a bill to secure our religion and our properties in case of a Popish successor"—such was his conviction of the threatening danger, and his means of providing against it.

Following up this movement, it was next resolved that a Bill should be brought in "to disable the Duke of York to inherit the imperial crown of these realms." Men then knew the real nature and tendencies of Popery. They saw it preparing to extinguish the light and crush the freedom of their country, and could not passively submit to its usurpations. On the contrary, they strove to secure the succession to the throne to the next in line after the Duke of York, "in the same manner as if the Duke was dead," and may we not pause here and ponder over this grave and unparalleled proceeding? How terrible must the bondage of Popery have appeared, when the prospect of its ascendency dictated such a measure! How profound the pity we should feel for the men who so loved their country that they were compelled to oppose their prince rather than see that country trodden down, sold to France, and enthralled! How infinite the obligations under which posterity lies to Russell and his friends, who forgot self and who sacrificed their very life rather than compromise what their country had entrusted to their keeping! With a great price they had to secure our freedom, and deserve all the honours which still cluster round their memory.

Such measures dragged their slow length along, at one time thwarted by the prorogation of parliament, at another by adverse decisions in the House of Lords. Once more, however, in the year 1680, Lord William Russell stood forth to say, in his place in parliament : "I am of opinion that the life of our king, the safety of our country and the Protestant religion are in great danger from Popery, and that either this parliament must suppress the power and growth of Popery, or else that Popery will soon destroy not only parliament, but all that is near and dear to us. . . . . ." Nothing daunted by delay, he persisted in pressing the subject on his fellow senators. He thoroughly knew the power and the wiles of Romanism. He had seen it rampant abroad, and tracked its sinister influence at home; and to him it was a matter of life or death to have the system so fettered as to be unable to injure his native land. The glorious Revolution of 1688 set its seal to his far-sighted wisdom and resolute persistency.

Zealously attached as Russell was to the monarchy of Britain, he could not calmly see its liberties trampled on, and was therefore willing to adopt measures for "disabling James Duke of York from inheriting the imperial crown of this realm." The king was actually the pensioner of France, and that was ignominious. He was, moreover, a Romanist at heart, and that roused all the patriot's alarms. Money could not be voted to Charles, lest it should be employed to subvert the Protestant faith ; and while Russell declared that he was "ready to give all he had in the world" to get the abettors of Romanism removed from places of trust, he would vote no public money, for that "would only have the effect of destroying themselves with their own hands." His zeal in some cases urged him, perhaps, to extremes, but it was a zeal which the experience of ages has proved to be right in the main. He clung to his object with the vitality of a deep passion, and went to the scaffold and the grave rooted and grounded in the conviction that Rome was the master enemy of Britain. Yet what success could such a man expect in an age so profligate that Sir John Denham and Lord Chesterfield were both accused of poisoning their wives, while the latter is said to have added deeper horror to his crime by administering death in the cup of communion.* One stands appalled at the tale of such villany, and yet it was but a sand grain to the mountain of the crimes of that age.

But our present object does not require us to enter further into the details of this man's calm but resolute life. A time had come when good and evil, liberty and bondage were struggling face to face for the mastery in the land. The darkest evil was Popery, and against it Russell strove with all the energy of a nature which feared nothing but falsehood. Whether the parliament met at Oxford—where the king could cherish the hope of packing it—or in London, this patriot was at his post confronting the wrong with the right, and thraldom with freedom. His patriotism was fearless; his will indomitable; his ardour unceasing, and he enjoyed some gleams of hope for his beloved country when he saw the Prince of Orange not unwilling to befriend the liberties for which our patriot had struggled so earnestly and so long.

He was not, however, to be allowed to struggle much longer. In his own words, he had long "been sensible he would fall a sacrifice; arbitrary power could not be set up in England without wading through his blood," and his foreboding was to be verified. The Meal-tub Plot—a pretended conspiracy against the Duke of York—had agitated not a few. It was contrived by a miscreant, who secreted a bundle of seditious letters in such a way that their discovery implicated some of the most prominent men of those times. But he was apprehended as the forger of those documents, and this led to the discovery of others concealed in a *Meal-*

* See Earl Russell's " Life of Lord W. Russell." chap. iii.

tub, and hence the name of the fictitious conspiracy. The author of it died of the punishment which was inflicted upon him for his crime. This took place in the year 1679, but in the spring of 1683, another and more formidable scheme was detected—namely, the Rye-house Plot, by which, it is alleged, a plan was formed to murder the king and his brother on their return from the races at Newmarket. This plot is by many deemed as purely fictitious as the former; but without entering into the controversy, it is enough to say here that Lord William Russell was arrested as a party to the design, and not a few of the noblest patriots of the day were seized in the same manner.

He was examined before the King and Council, and forthwith committed a close prisoner to the Tower. He was able to deny all knowledge of the matters with which he was charged, though there can be no doubt that during those times of keen contention, when passion ran high, for danger was rife, he had allowed remarks or proposals to be made in his hearing which he should have indignantly put down. And he did recoil from them; he abhorred them, whether as involving insurrection, or any attack upon the king; but when brought against him by informers and others, they gave a colour of truth to the charges. Upon his entering the Tower, he assured his servant that his enemies would have his life, and from that moment deemed himself a dying man. He accordingly turned his thoughts wholly to another world. The Scriptures, especially the Psalms, became his frequent study, and he behaved with all the serenity of a man preparing or prepared to die.

It will easily be believed that everything was done that could blacken or malign such a man as Russell; but nothing was ever found to implicate him further than has been mentioned. On his trial at the Old Bailey, he was assisted by his wife, one of the most admirable and heroic women of

any age; but his condemnation was pre-determined, and no
efforts could save him. Some of the usual forms of justice
were outraged in his case. He had to challenge no fewer
than thirty-one of the jurymen who were to try him;
and though he resisted, like some of his contemporaries
in the same condition, at every point and upon every principle where he could repel the charges falsely brought
against him, all was unavailing. It was well understood to
be the will of the Court that he should die. Lawyers were
obsequious; judges were subservient; a jury was packed as
far as possible, and the sentence was death. Witness after
witness spoke in his favour. Dr. Burnet, Dr. Tillotson, and
others, all upheld his integrity, and one of the witnesses at-
tested as follows:—"I have been acquainted with Lord
Russell for several years, and conversed much with him. I
took him to be one of the best sons, one of the best fathers,
and one of the best masters, one of the best husbands, one
of the best friends, and one of the best Christians we had."
But in spite of all these testimonies he must die. He declared that he had " ever a heart sincerely affectionate to the
king and government," and that he was always for preserv-
ing it "upon the due basis and ancient foundation." He
explained the different things laid to his charge in a manner which completely freed him, and history has accepted of
his explanations as the truth. All thoughts of rebellion he
disclaimed as abhorent to his nature, though parliamentary
freedom he asserted to the last; but the hearts of those
who tried him were not to be moved, and on Friday the
13th of July 1683, Lord William Russell was pronounced
guilty of high treason. He had contended for freedom alike
for soul and for body, at once against superstition and despotism, and must pay the penalty of his boldness by meeting death at the hands of men who perpretrated a fragrant
violation both of law and of justice.

After his sentence, many attempts were made to save Lord Russell's life. It is said that £50,000, or even £100,000, were offered by the Earl of Bedford for his pardon; but the king durst not yield for fear of incensing the Duke of York. Lady Russell applied to Charles, and proposals were made to accomplish Russell's deliverance in other ways. The king of France is said by some to have tried to obtain a pardon for him. He was himself over-persuaded to appeal to his king for mercy—but all was vain; and from the first, he believed and declared that it would be so. He knew how deadly is the venom of Popery when it takes possession of man's nature, and expected nothing at its hands but relentless persecution.

Amid all this, however, his steadfastness never forsook him; it increased as the scene darkened around him. Tillotson and Burnet attempted, but in vain, to modify his views of civil liberty; and while the axe was in course of being whetted to do execution upon him, Russell was steadfast still. During the week which intervened between his trial and his death, his patience, his fortitude, his affection to his family, his love of country, and his trust in God, became more and more signal. Of his own death he spoke with calmness, and a kind of dignity which awed those who were about him. He thanked God that, as a man, he had never feared death, and did not consider it with so much attention as the drawing of a tooth. His courage, he declared as death drew near, was of the kind which is sustained by peace of conscience, and assurance of the mercy of God; and his chief agitation in regard to death arose from the thought of being gazed at by his friends and enemies. He dreaded also his separation from Lady Russell; indeed, the thought of that was *the only thing* that seemed at all to unman him. Steadfast as he had been in the discharge of duty, he was no less so in facing the last enemy, and though he fully confessed his sins, he had such repose in the Saviour's mercy that he passed on to death with greater tranquillity than those who accompanied him in that sad procession. He could not pretend, he said, to the high joys and longings of some on the verge of eternity; but he felt entire resignation to the will of God, and a perfect serenity of soul, while he died in the hope that his death would do more service than his life could have done.

Lord Russell's last interview with Lady Russell has in it a certain moral grandeur. He took her by the hand, remarking that the flesh and blood which she felt would soon be cold. At the last, she so controlled her sorrows as not to aggravate his distress by the sight of hers; and they parted, not with sobs and tears, but with composed silence, the wife wishing to spare the feelings of the husband, and the husband those of the wife. In truth, their grief was too great for utterance, and was subdued by a certain moral heroism peculiar to each. When she had left him, he observed that the bitterness of death was past—and so it was. He slept calmly through the hours which intervened between that separation and his final moment. His composure and equanimity were actually sublime, and even when the executioner approached to do his last duty to the martyr of freedom, not a muscle quivered; the cheek grew not pale. "I once looked at him," says Bishop Burnet, who was present on the scaffold, "and saw no change in his looks; and though he was still lifting up his hands, there was no trembling, though in the moment in which I looked, the executioner happened to be laying his axe to the neck to direct him to take aim; I thought it touched him, but am sure he seemed not to mind it."

The executioner at two strokes severed the head of Lord Russell from his body; and so perished in the forty-fourth year of his age, one of the noblest of the sons of Britain, for

Russell was more noble by the grace of God than by his lordly birth. While dying to vindicate our liberties, he evinced a heroism far above that which can confront kings, and suborned judges, and men blindly abetting tyranny. "In the words of a dying man," he said, " I know of no plot either against the king's life or government. But I have now done with the world, and am going to a better. I forgive all the world heartily, and I thank God I die in charity with all men, and I wish all sincere Protestants may love one another, and not make way for Popery by their animosities. . . . . I am now more satisfied to die than ever I have been."

Nor did his love for men leave him even on the way to the scaffold. Just before leaving his prison he wound up his watch and said, " I have done with time; now eternity comes ;" but when he afterwards met Lord Cavendish, and took leave of him, he turned for an instant to press that nobleman to apply himself more to religion than he had hitherto done. He took care, moreover, that even when his body should be mouldering in the grave, truth should still circulate in his words among men. He had carefully prepared a document embodying his opinions, which he delivered to the sheriffs at his execution, and the following extracts will show how he lived, how he died, and how he may speak to us still :—

" . . . I bless God heartily," he says, " for those many blessings which he, in his infinite mercy, hath bestowed upon me through the whole course of my life; that I was born of worthy and good parents, and had the advantage of religious education, which are invaluable blessings; for even when I minded it least, it hung about me and gave me checks, and has now for many years so influenced and possessed me, that I feel the happy effects of it in this my extremity, in which I have been so wonderfully (I thank God) supported, that neither my imprisonment nor fear of death has been able to discompose me in any degree; but on the contrary, I have found the assurances of the love and mercy of God in and through my blessed Redeemer, in whom only I trust; and I do not question but I am going to partake of the fulness of joy which is in his presence. These hopes, therefore, do so wonderfully delight me, that I think this is the happiest time of my life, though others may look upon it as the saddest. . . . .

"For Popery," he proceeds, "I look on it as an idolatrous and a bloody religion, and therefore thought myself bound in my station to do all I could against it; and by that I foresaw I should procure such great enemies to myself, and so powerful ones, that I have been now for some time expecting the worst, and, blessed be God! I fall by the axe, and not by the fiery trial. Yet whatever apprehensions I had of Popery and of my own severe and heavy share I was like to have under it, when it should prevail, I never had a thought of doing anything against it, basely or inhumanely, but what would consist with the Christian religion, and the laws and liberties of the kingdom."

Such, then, was the man who could not be tolerated by royalty in this land about two hundred years ago; his blood must flow upon the scaffold because he would not let tyranny trample on the laws of man, nor Popery upon the truth of God. Never did a calmer mind mingle in the strifes of men. Never did a more self-contained soul address itself to duty, heedless of personal suffering, bent only on the right and the just. Never was man more decided and unflinching wherever conscience bound, or truth led the way—firm in the senate—firm before his judges—firmest on the scaffold. What was death to him when the Saviour in whom he resolutely confided was ever at his right hand? That truth which imparts a certain majesty even to the humblest, when it is enthroned in the heart, made Russell more than noble ; and thus upheld, his convictions,—

" O'erswept
All pain, all time, all fears, and pealed
Like the eternal thunders of the deep,
Into his ears this truth—' Thou liv'st for ever.' "

And the memory of the just is blessed. When William of Orange sat upon the throne of these realms, the second Act to which he affixed his signature was one for reversing the attainder of Russell, and in which his execution was called a murder. In 1694, the Earl of Bedford was created a duke, and one reason assigned was that "he was the father of Lord Russell, the ornament of his age." So completely had Lord William Russell now found his right place in the minds of men, that the king and queen wished their royal patent to "remain in the family as a monument consecrated to his consummate virtue, whose name could never be forgot, so long as men preserved any esteem for sanctity of manners, greatness of mind, and a love of their country, constant even to death." In brief, every stigma which had been attached to the name of the Martyr was now effaced as far as royalty could do so. His honours were more than restored, and were it our object here to trace the history of the family which he left behind him, it would appear that honour after honour was heaped also upon them; the calm, intrepid man left them a rich legacy when he submitted to death, rather than be a party to the destruction of British liberty.

VI.—EDMUND BURKE.

1730—1797.

> " Unmoved,
> Unshaken, unseduced, unterrified,
> His loyalty he kept, his love, his zeal;
> Nor number, nor example with him wrought
> To swerve from truth, or change his constant mind
> Though single.   From amidst them forth he passed
> Long way through hostile scorn, which he sustained
> Superior, nor of violence feared aught;
> And with retorted scorn his back he turned
> On those proud towers to swift destruction doomed."
>
> MILTON.

His Birth—Boyhood—Training at Trinity College—Goes to London—Enters Middle Temple—His Literary Pursuits—Pecuniary Difficulties—Struggles—Dr. Johnson—Becomes a Politician—Receives a Pension—Rejects it—Becomes Secretary to Prime Minister—Enters Parliament—His Success—Changes—Buys an Estate—His Labours in Parliament—The American Revolution—The French Revolution—Trial of Warren Hastings—Burke's General Character—His Trials—Decline—Death.

THAT must have been a remarkable man of whom it could be said, "He not merely excelled all his contemporaries in the number of his powers, but some in the peculiar excellence belonging to each: a tolerable poet even while a boy; a penetrating philosopher; an acute critic; and a judicious historian when a very young man; a judge of the fine arts whose opinions even Reynolds valued; a political economist when the science was scarcely known, or known to very few; a statesman often pronounced the wisest that ever adorned our country; an orator second to none of any age; a writer of extraordinary powers on every subject; and in politics the first for depth and eloquence in our language; and, in addition to these, possessed of a vast and multifarious store of knowledge of which all who had any intercourse with him, whether friend or opponent, have spoken in terms of strong admiration and surprise."

Such was EDMUND BURKE, a man who has been called "a vast storehouse of knowledge," "a mighty mind," "a wonderful man," "an illustrious man," "an unequalled man," "an all-knowing mind," "a boundless mind," "an exhaustless mind," "the most consummate orator of the age," "the greatest orator and wisest statesman of modern times." From the life of such a man, his rise, progress, and ascendency, some deep lessons may be learned, especially as he had difficulties to surmount, and obstacles to encounter, such as might have repressed a less imperial mind. He was literally the architect of his own fortune. By sheer power he took possession of the lofty position to which he mounted; and what were the stages, what was the spirit, the energy, or the means by which he reached it? Let us trace them.

This distinguished man was born in Dublin, on the 1st of January 1730, O. S., but little is remembered concerning his early years. His constitution was deemed consumptive, and he was thus prevented, in very early youth, from profiting by public instructions. His first instructor was an elderly woman who was partial to the boy, and found amusement in training his mind. His father was an attorney in the Irish capital, and though the accounts of his resources are somewhat conflicting, his position was respectable as his lineage was honourable. In youth Edmund Burke was often removed from place to place on account of his health; and so many parts of Ireland became associated with his name, that no fewer than seven compete for the honour of his birthplace. In his twelfth year he was placed at a school in Ballitore, in the county of Kildare, and there he became remarkable rather for solidity than for aught that promised brilliance; rather for steady application and perseverance than for powers that could indicate his future greatness. He was then, as he always continued, of a deeply sensitive nature; fond of being alone; less lively than other boys, but always willing to teach what he knew or learn what he did not. Even then it appeared that the hatred of oppression, and of the exercise of might against right was to form a prominent feature in his character. He was always on the side of the weak.

As Edmund Burke was one of those who have to work their own way to eminence, his profession was a matter of great importance. In 1744, he entered Trinity College, Dublin, as a student; but while there, his talents do not appear to have rendered him more than respectable. He was not, indeed, wholly undistinguished; but nothing as yet betokened the man who was to "control the destinies of the world," as some of his admirers boast that he did. He pursued his studies, however, with not a little zeal. Shakespeare, Bacon, Addison, and others were his favouites among our authors. Demosthenes was his favourite orator; and other classics of antiquity he studied with assiduity, making their beauties his own, and quietly clearing out, if not actually laying, the foundation of mental power.

As soon as he had taken his degree at Trinity College, young Burke hastened to London—it was in 1750—with a view to qualify for admission to the English bar. When he left Ireland, his sensitive nature, he tells us, sought relief in tears. The attractions of home and kindred which endeared "the family burying-ground," even to his young nature, appeared then in great vigour, and clung to him beautifully all through life. London, after a short survey, he described as containing just two classes—the undoers and the undone—and though the distribution was unjust, it is not altogether inapplicable.

It appears that either he did not find the study of law congenial to his taste, or that his health was not equal to the drudgery; and he soon abandoned it for the more fascinating though often profitless pursuits of general literature. He was never called to the bar; and from this period, the year 1752, we may date some of the struggles through which he had to pass, on his way to his place in the great arena of life. Instead of devoting his time to Littleton and Coke, and other lights of the law, he was forced, by his straitened circumstances, to support himself by literary labour. The exhausted state of his finances demanded some immediate means of recruiting them, and essays, letters, and paragraphs for the periodical publications of the day became his means of support. Either his father was unable to assist him, or Edmund's change of pursuit had displeased him; and, judging from some accounts, the life of the future statesman was, at this date, one of make-shifts to secure a competence.

He was not, however, to be daunted by such difficulties; nay, he manfully faced them, like one determined not to be repressed. He became a candidate for a chair of philosophy in the University of Glasgow, but failed; he planned various literary works; he published pamphlets; and imitated some of the distinguished writers of the times so expertly that his publications were sold as theirs. Amid all this his conduct at this time has somewhat the appearance of a struggle for existence in the sphere which he had selected; his habits, from necessity or choice, were those of an assiduous plodder. His application was unwearied, for whatever of genius might be stirring within him, he knew that all depended upon persistence; and he did not trust for a day to chance, but moved forward amid the difficulties which surrounded him, acquiring knowledge, storing it up, and unconsciously preparing for the time when he was to

astonish the empire by his powers. He had no excesses, it
has been said, but those of study. His first essays at
oratory were made at a debating club, where his chief
opponent was a baker, a man so stringent in his logic, and
so powerful in discussion, that it was said of him he should
have been made Lord Chancellor of England. It was
against that champion who, for some time, held the lists
against all comers, that Burke first whetted his lance; and
though victory was often on the side of the baker, the
future orator was just the better trained for a higher sphere
of action.

Burke had now secured admission into the high literary
circles in London. He published a treatise on the Sublime
and Beautiful, which, among other effects, restored him to
friendly terms with his father, who sent him a gift of one
hundred pounds. Withal, however, his pecuniary straits at
this period were great, and might have damped the ardour
of one less resolute than Edmund Burke. So great was his
embarrassment at one period that he had actually to sell
his library—a measure, doubtless, to which nothing but the
extremity of distress could have driven him. Some of his
friends have attempted to throw doubt upon this fact; but it
is too well established to be denied; and it shows us, in one
example more, what obstacles Burke had to surmount, and
through what difficulties he had to force his way, ere he
reached the level which made him the marked of all
observers. Translations from the Latin, Biography, an
Essay on the Drama, a "Vindication of Natural Society,"
were the means of gratifying his literary tastes, or of earn-
ing his daily bread; and through these labyrinths he worked
his way, till at the age of twenty-five he published the book
just mentioned—his Essay on the Sublime and the Beautiful.
In solitude, amid irksome toils, he continued to write for
pay. For one work he received fifty guineas; for another

one hundred; and it was thus that the future lawgiver was trained for his allotted work. "He who writes otherwise than for money is a fool," was a dogma of Dr. Johnson's; from necessity, Burke made it his own, and lived by what he earned.

Such were his prospects at this period, so unpromising and dubious, that he thought of emigrating to America. The motive for this is unknown, but his plans were changed; and he struggled on under the pressure of providing for the wants of an increasing family. One of his firmest friends tells us of his indigent circumstances, but assures us also that no bribe, however magnificent, could tempt Burke to be untrue to his own convictions. Goldsmith, his countryman and associate, might jocularly describe him as,—

> " For a patriot too cool, for a drudge disobedient,
> And too fond of the right to pursue the expedient,
> In short, 'twas his fate, unemployed, or in place, sir,
> To eat mutton cold, and cut blocks with a razor."

But, the wit of the words apart, even thus early, Burke was resolutely firm in upholding what he deemed the good and the right. He had been early trained in the knowledge of the sacred Scriptures, and their power over him was never disowned. Even when he had reached his highest eminence, his income is described by his admirers as a poor pittance compared with his expenditure; and there is evidence that he had to struggle against the pressure of debt, not merely at the commencement of his career, but at various subsequent stages.

About this period, Burke became acquainted with Dr. Johnson; and even that colossus of literature was constrained to defer to the wondrous acquirements of the struggling Irishman. Johnson's praise of him was cordial, constant, and deep; indeed Burke was from the first his special favourite, and admiration of the orator's genius drew

forth eulogies which were precious because they were rare.
"Burke is an extraordinary man," he said, "his stream of
mind is perpetual." "No man of sense could meet Burke
by accident under a gateway, to avoid a shower, without
being convinced that he was the first man in England,"—and
the prediction was speedily verified to the full. Whatever
impediments might hamper Burke at first, and though he,
like many more, might find that literature as a profession
was poor and pinching, he was soon to surmount all difficulties, and claim his place among the men whose names
and influence are more than European.

He had been early drawn, as if by some latent instinct,
to frequent the House of Commons, and listen to the debates,
and this enticed him more and more into the region of politics. Some allege that he was then living in obscurity and
distress; but whether that be true or only a slander, he
now enters on the path where he is to leave his mark upon
thousands. This, however, was not reached without many
a struggle more. "I was not," he said, "swaddled, rocked,
and dandled into a legislator—*Nitor in adversum*, I struggle
against opposition, is the motto for a man like me;" and
Nitor in adversum might be inscribed upon every page that
describes his career. The culture of his mind was elaborate
and comprehensive. The ancients and the moderns, law,
morals, politics, science, poetry, history, criticism, all had
been laid under contribution to furnish his mind. Perhaps no man who ever entered the House of Commons had
laboured so diligently to qualify himself for that sphere as
Burke had done, and in this respect he is a model of eager
and successful endeavour. He began to move forward at
first slowly, and amid numerous entanglements ; but it was
the procession of an avalanche, it was the swoop of an eagle,
and nothing could stand against its onward movement.
All this, be it remembered, was accomplished, not amid the

quietude of affluence, but in the bustle of struggling for an adequate provision in life.

When Burke entered parliament he was about thirty-six years of age. In the month of March 1761, he had been appointed private secretary to the Secretary-in-chief of the Irish Lord-Lieutenant of the day, and proceeded in that capacity to his native island. His literary pursuits were not, however, abandoned, as he frequently visited London regarding them. In the spirit of those times, his services in Ireland were requited by a pension of £300 per annum; but in less than eighteen months he, with characteristic decision, renounced it, because he found that he was expected, in return, to stoop to things which his generous soul abhorred. Upon that pecuniary allowance, claims for future servitude were founded, to which he was not the man calmly to submit : he had struggled for bread, and he could struggle again, but he could not bow down to be base. The impression still exists, in some minds, that by that pension Burke was to be rescued from the pressure of poverty; but be that as it may, he would not let good offices become snares : he would suffer no man to transform his reward for long and laborious services into a chain with which to bind him; and with some degree of indignation he spurned both the proposal and the pension away. His honest independence here appears for the first time in the higher spheres of public life.

Though Burke was still in pursuit of employment, and though necessarily straitened in circumstances, he began, with true Irish generosity, to foster genius, and to find assistance for some who were struggling like himself along the rugged, upward way. He continued, however, to cultivate his powers by all available methods. Such solitary drudgery as literary men often have to perform was enlivened by the debates at the "Robin Hood" society,

already mentioned; and now he is carefully adding to his
stores by intercourse with the leading minds of London and
the empire.   At all times, however, he was open, decided,
and bold.   He chose his path without fear when he believed it was the path of duty, and walked in it in the
same spirit.   He was avaricious of excellence, though the
poor celebrity of *shining* was never coveted by Burke.
His earlier career, in short, is a model of persistency, of
devoted struggles, and aims so well directed as certainly to
lead to success in life.

At length the time arrived when he who was already
reckoned by some the foremost man in England, was to
reach his proper sphere—he entered the House of Commons.
On the way thither he had met with many assailants.
The zealots of corruption hated his patriotism, and again
and again was he checkmated in his path.   But his favourite
maxim, "*Nitor in adversum*,"·continued his watchword, and
he became one of the most remarkable men that ever climbed
from middle life to influence an empire, or take a place at
the right hand of royalty itself.   It was one of those
changes in the rulers of this land so common in stormy
times that introduced Burke into parliament.   In the year
1765 he had become Secretary to a nobleman who was for
some time prime minister of Britain, and was by him advanced to the position for which he was in providence so
wonderfully fitted.   But his office of Secretary, and the
honours which it opened up, were not to be enjoyed without a struggle; nay, he must fight every inch of his way,
and if the conflict with indigence, or something akin to it,
be over now, another contest must immediately take its
place.   To his chief, the Marquis of Rockingham, Burke
was accused as a man of dangerous principles, and a Papist.
One of his first acts, therefore, was to defend himself against
that charge, and disabuse the mind of the premier.   His

frankness accomplished that at once; but he proposed to surrender his appointment, as the confidence of the marquis might be impaired. Such manly independence and such delicate feeling vanquished every scruple; and the result was a mutual attachment which lasted through life. In consequence of this connection, Burke was brought into parliament as member for Wendover.

Having thus battled his way, then, up to that place of power, it soon became apparent that Edmund Burke would make himself felt. Even Johnson, though unaccustomed to praise, and, least of all, to praise one who opposed him, as Burke did, in politics, confessed that the member for Wendover had gained more reputation by his first appearance in parliament than perhaps any man had ever done before. His speeches "filled the town with wonder;" "all at once he darted into fame," while he seemed as intent on doing good to his country as if he had been to receive a premium from the commerce of the empire which he tried to extend. Before invincible perseverance, and manly independence, directed by the lights of all ages concentrated upon his own pursuits, this man is henceforth the property of the nation : indeed, as we proceed, it will be seen that he became, in some respects, the world's benefactor, though he had largely to pay the price which malignity exacts from worth, or envy from success.

A change in the government left Burke again unemployed. He refused to be a party to some political arrangements which were then made, and, indeed, was regarded by some as an intruder, if not an usurper of the place of power. He had neither commanding wealth nor high connections ; and men who had both, looked askance upon one who had, by the mastery which mind asserts, taken his place beside those who reckoned themselves born to rule this empire, or even threatened to mount above them. Some of that

class felt themselves overshadowed by his nearness, or
dwarfed by his greatness—for, to paltry minds, one who
vaults from private life, not to say obscurity, into the high
offices of the state, is scarcely to be endured. Some of the
loftiest, however, were constrained to do homage to his
powers, and offer him a new position in the government.
But to the stipulations which were proposed to him he
refused to accede.

About this period, the year 1768, Burke was returned
again for Wendover. He now purchased an estate, for
which he paid upwards of £20,000, where he chiefly resided till his death. It has always been one of the mysteries of his life where such a sum could be found by one
who, a few years before, had been obliged to sell his library
to meet the claims of the passing day; and those who have
attempted to solve the mystery have done so rather by alle-
gations and assumptions than by established facts. He had
now succeeded to his father's property, by the death of his
elder brother; but that was a pittance compared with the
sum which was paid for his new abode, and the alternative
is that money was lent or gifted by a lordly patron. Some
of his admirers have wished that he had rather continued
to live by his literary labours, than become a grandee and a
senator by the help of such donations. More than once, however, Burke was indebted to such kindness. By his Will, Sir
Joshua Reynolds cancelled a bond on the great statesman
for £2000, and bequeathed to him a similar sum; while an
eminent physician and friend anticipated his own Will,
and paid to Burke £1000, because he had heard that the
great orator was pressed by pecuniary difficulties. It was
well that he had friends to proclaim abroad that he was
"proof against his own embarrassed circumstances" in all
that related to public measures, for these pecuniary wants
might have proved a snare.

The object of this sketch is nearly completed when Burke has been followed through his early difficuities and struggles to the front rank of the foremost in Britain. In all the great questions which agitated or engrossed the British Senate from this period till nearly the day of his death, he stood conspicuously forth. But without following him through all the windings of his political career, it must be enough to indicate some of the questions, in the discussion of which Edmund Burke made himself illustrious. This is not a biography in which to follow him year by year, and stage by stage, through the details of his life; it is only a lesson derived from biography, and designed to show how consistent conduct, decision of character, and perseverance directed by principle, may render a humble man useful, honourable, and honoured.

Burke, then, had early made up his mind as to the career he should pursue in public life. He resolutely repudiated the idea of siding with the rich and the powerful against the poor and the weak. He resolved to set his face against any act of pride or power, though countenanced even by the highest; and proclaimed in parliament that "if it should come to the last extremity, and to a contest of blood, his post was taken—he would take his fate with the poor, and low, and feeble." Animated by such principles, so sound, and so patriotic, he speedily had occasion to apply them in practice.

The first very great occasion in which his wonderful powers were exerted was the proposal to tax our American Colonies in a parliament where they were not represented. The result of these measures is now well known. First, an active and organized opposition on the part of America to all such proposals; then war and bloodshed; then Independence, made good at the cost of millions of treasure, and more in disgrace, to the empire of Britain. From the first Burke

boldly and resolutely opposed the taxation; he resisted
it at every stage as unconstitutional and oppressive.
He predicted what would be the result of the unnatural
struggle between the parent and the offspring states; and
by wit and argument, by constitutional pleading, and a
strain of eloquence, which placed him beside Demosthenes,
and above Cicero in terrible power, he strove to avert
the day of coming separation.   Upon that and kindred
subjects he poured forth pamphlets, speeches, disquisi-
tions in rapid succession; and even though he had not
announced it, his conduct would have showed that what he
called "that master vice of sloth," did not enter into his
composition as a statesman. Standing bravely up for the
subject's just rights, and disclaiming, like a high-souled
man, the monstrous dogma that the people live but for
the king—the self-complacent tenet of every despot—he
was the champion of freedom in every land, for the men
of every tongue and colour. He implored the British parliament not to tax America, but to leave America to tax herself: "When you drive him hard," he exclaimed, "the boar
will turn upon the hunters. If your sovereignty and American freedom cannot be reconciled, which will the Americans
take? They will cast your sovereignty in your face," and
they did it. The Declaration of Independence made on the
4th of July, 1776, amply verified the prophecies of Burke,
while it covered the British name with the disgrace which
attaches to impotent and baffled oppression.

   In consequence of this and similar displays of power,
Burke had become the leader of opposition—the first in
eloquence, high in fame, and admitted to the counsels of
the chief men of the nation. He who was lately dependent upon a precarious income for support now appears as
the champion of the oppressed, and he did it in a style which
left radiant streaks behind him in the path which he trod.

Philosophy and facts to illustrate it, politics, and the only principles on which they can be safely based, seemed to be all his own. Even Fox confessed that Burke was his master; that he had learned more from him than from all books, and all study, and wept like childhood in the British parliament, because the great orator declined to follow him in some of his measures. Amid all these things, the resolute man was still assailed by calumny in nearly every form. It was with him as with Wilberforce when he pled against slavery : rancourous hatred traduced him; names odious to his nature were applied to him; he was treated as the friend of rebels, and the abettor of rebellion; but on he moved undaunted—he had chosen his path and would not swerve. Those who stand on some elevated spot near the elephant's feeding ground, can trace his progress through the forest by the crashing and agitation of the trees on the line of his march, and it was even so with Burke in his contests for freedom. It often happened that all around was shaken by his power; even enemies were awed for a time by his grandeur, and it is not wonderful that amid such displays he was returned to parliament for two places at once, namely, Malton, and Bristol. His prophecies, indeed, like those of Cassandra, were often unheeded, till they were verified by melancholy facts; but we wonder just the more at the sagacity and comprehension of the prophet. His orations and his struggles to avert, if possible, the American Revolution, were enough to immortalize him. In the discussions he might sometimes announce his convictions with asperity, or press them imperiously, as the consciousness of power often prompts men to do. But whatever was the cause, parliament would not listen to his appeals; and the first blood shed at Lexington and Bunker's Hill, the raising of armies in America, and the nomination of Washington as commander-in-chief, made all hope of conciliation vain. Burke had implored the ministry

of the day not to consider those matters in the spirit of the
irritated porcupine with its spines set up ; but the result of
all was war prolonged, taxes increased in the vain attempt
to subdue the people of America, and other portions of the
empire heaving in the premonitory throes of revolution. We
do think that the sagacity of one man, had it been consulted, would have prevented all this. "For my own part,"
he once said at a period of dreaded revolt, and when retrenchment was loudly demanded, "I have very little to recom-
mend me for this, or for any task, but a kind of earnest and
anxious perseverance of mind, which, with all its good and
all its evil effects, is moulded into my constitution." The
disclaimer here is untrue, but the rest is one explanation of
his power.

And Burke did address himself to retrenchment with all
his heart. Were this a political history, the bare enumeration of his different proposals would startle us, unless we
had the courage of this great statesman. But here again he
had to persevere in his chosen path against an amount of
antagonism such as only he could resist. His measures were
contested inch by inch. They were pared away by various
counter plans, till they became comparatively insignificant ; for great as were the savings which he effected to the
nation, they formed but a fraction of what he had aimed at
in the face of sordid selfishness and hostile influence in every
form. It has been said that "statesmen are the most vilified of all the animals in the creation," and Burke in this
respect also, was among the foremost. He had to snatch
time for his parliamentary preparations, and make them in
ways which can scarcely be credited ; and yet with all his
grandeur, there were men in parliament who coughed or
brayed him into silence, when they could not otherwise
answer his appeals.

Another of the great questions to which Burke brought all

the energies of his nature, and where he evinced indomitable decision, was the French Revolution. It is well known that with that fiery and bloody outbreak in its earliest stages, thousands in this land sympathized. It was hailed as the harbinger of universal liberty—the emancipation of the nations from oppression—and many of the halls of the titled as well as the homes of the humble, were roused into a jubilee of joy by the event. But Burke had been recently in France. He had marked the symptoms of approaching convulsion; and far from sympathizing with the joy which was felt in Britain, he predicted the bloodshed and the woes which were sure to follow, and determined to warn his misguided country.

But he was in conflict here with some of his best friends, for example, Fox and others whom he loved, and who revered him. But that did not shake his steadfast mind. By oration after oration—by his work on the French Revolution—and by efforts of prodigious power in every direction, he strove to rouse men to a sense of the danger that was coming. Again was he vilified and defamed alike by populace and peer; but again he stood undaunted. In lampoon, in caricature, in pamphlets without number he was assailed, but he pitted his own convictions against them all. Slowly the tide of opinion began to turn—the rivers of blood which flowed —the millions spent in war—the appalling doctrines which were current—and the military despotism which crowned the whole were all foretold by Edmund Burke—and though he was summoned away to the world which we must die to see, long before the pacification, it is one of the most striking things in history that he sketched with some minuteness what would be the manner of the end. It was once more Athanasius against the world.

" The more one has to do, the more one is capable of doing," was one of Burke's maxims, and his life, especially at this

period, was an example. His next great enterprise—perhaps
his greatest—was the impeachment of Warren Hastings, the
Governor-general of India, for high crimes, misdemeanours,
and deeds of oppression in that marvellous portion of the
empire. But here again, he had a host of antagonists
to encounter, and labours Herculean to undergo. Through
several weary years that trial was protracted, and never did
mortal man, perhaps, appear in greater majesty of mind than
did Burke when asserting and proving the oppressions of
one whom he believed to be a cold-blooded tyrant, orien-
talized by habits which developed his in-born ferocity.
But whether these opinions be extreme, or truthful, that
trial formed an era in the history of oratory and of mind.
The illustrious culprit was acquitted, but as the statesman depicted the misdeeds of the oppressor, the agony
occasioned by the mere recital—the fainting of some among
his auditors — the tears shed by many long unused to
weep, all displayed his marvellous power over the mind of
man. He had noble coadjutors in that work, but he towers
far above them all: the impersonation of oratory, of
generous indignation, of sarcasm, of pathos—of all, in short,
that can render illustrious by the use of words, the most
amazing of all God's gifts to man. All that on the part of
one who had lately written books for a livelihood.

Burke, we have seen, was one of those who are born with
a detestation of everything like oppression: it reigned imperiously in his soul, and the entire energies of his mind were
directed against injustice wherever it appeared. In the case
of a parliament, as when ours would have taxed America; of
a nation, as amid the bloody scenes of the French Revolution, presided over by Danton, Murat, or Robespierre; or of
a man, as in the Governor-General of India, Burke launched
forth with an impetuosity which amounted to fury,
and suggested the idea of mania to minds which saw

less vividly or less comprehensively than he did. "Let who will shrink back," he once exclaimed, "I shall be found at my post. Baffled, discountenanced, subdued, discredited, as the cause of justice and humanity is, it will be only the dearer to me," and he kept his resolution. Through ten years—for the trial of Hastings through all its evolutions was spread over that period—he persisted in his efforts, to fail at last in one respect, but not till he had made some of the most remarkable displays of mental power that ever were made by man. In preparing an inscription for a mausoleum to the Marquis of Rockingham, Burke closed it with the words

"Remember—Resemble—Persevere."

and they might be inscribed upon his own tomb.

In some respects he had his reward. When he attempted to roll back the tide of blood, and mitigate the reign of anarchy, introduced by the French Revolution, an emperor, and an empress, the sovereigns of the continent, and many princes sent him their felicitations. Honours flowed in upon him from royalty downwards; and if that had been the object for which he lived, he was gratified to the full. He perhaps overdid his advocacy—there is rarely a middle path for minds of his order ; but his efforts gave the first serious check to a system which threatened to subvert all rule and all order—to trample alike on the laws of God and of man. The recoil from such a system led Burke, in some of his pleadings, to extreme views in which despotism is fain to lurk, and wait for a fit time to oppress the people. But that was not a day for half opinions, or hesitating verdicts ; a bold antagonism was required to arrest the surging desolation. He whose life was a continued struggle for the liberty of others was reviled, indeed, as the enemy of liberty. The attacks made against him in every form which virulence could dictate are computed to have amounted "to many thousands."

Like the breakwater at Plymouth, Burke had to withstand a terrific onset, but he did withstand it, and thousands were roused to a sense of their danger.

Amid all this, however, he was soon to experience the truth of his own words: " What shadows we are, and what shadows we pursue." His feelings and affections were all passions, and he clung to the objects of his regard with admirable tenacity. Even after he had risen to power, he could still spin the tops of his young visitors, as at an earlier period he had often romped with his children in their nursery. He could patronize poor artists, and poorer poets. He could pick up a fallen, forlorn woman in the street, conduct her to his own home, and restore her to virtue. He could resort to retreats for lunatics, there to study their malady and know its effects ; and in a hundred ways he could show how tender and how acute were his sympathies with the wretched. But just the more on that account, did he suffer when his own feelings were torn. He had an only son, an idol. He died,—and the deportment of the bereaved father was an agony that was unutterable. If he had great powers to wield, he had just the greater power of suffering, and he did suffer to the verge of madness—" truly terrific " are the words applied to that grief. " His bursts of affliction were of fearful force, so overwhelming as to frighten and almost paralyze those who were around him." Life from this time became all sadness—a sadness which tinctured all that he did. He referred to " the short and cheerless" residue of his pilgrimage. " For myself, or my family, (alas! I have none), I have nothing to hope or to fear in this world," was one of his sad confessions. " The sorrows of a desolate old man," he said were his lot. " The storm has gone over me," he wrote, "and I lie like one of those old oaks which the hurricane scatters around us. . . . I am torn up by the roots, and lie prostrate on the earth." " I am alone, I have none to meet my enemies in the gate...." These and similar utterances of grief tell how deeply the iron had entered his soul. The result was a somewhat premature decay, and Edmund Burke became before his time "a dejected old man, buried in the anticipated grave of a feeble old age."

But where was religion in this man's case? Was there nothing in *it* to point to peace, and explain the reason of the woe which shook him to weakness? Was it a failure in his case, or did he fail to profit by its lessons? The latter is the explanation of his undried tears. His friends, we have seen, are fond of asserting that he "controlled the destinies of the world" by his later writings—why, then, did he not control his own spirit? He had been early trained in the knowledge of Revelation. He was fond of quoting the sacred volume in his speeches, and some of his sentiments, as recorded, are in harmony with Truth; but it does not appear that he allowed it to hold that ascendency in his soul which would have made him, as a man, still nobler, grander, and more commanding than he was—hence his sorrows unsoothed, and his great spirit crushed. "I bequeath my soul to God, hoping for his mercy only through the merits of our Lord and Saviour Jesus Christ," were words employed in his Will—and when he said that none should ever hold any attitude but that of a penitent, because he could never have any character but that of a sinner, he spoke a deep truth. But, beyond all controversy, his life would have been still grander and more sublime than it was, had the truth as it is in Jesus been more consulted, more obeyed, and more prominent in his mind.

Burke died at Beaconsfield on the 8th of July 1797, and in the sixty-eighth year of his age. His departure was singularly serene, yet one of his last advices regarding public affairs was characteristic of his "wonted fire." "Never," he said, " succumb to the enemy : it is a struggle for your existence as a nation, and if you must die, die with the sword in your hand .... persevere till this tyranny (that of revolutionary France) be overpast." Amid all this ardour, however, he submitted with placid resignation, undisturbed by a murmur, to his growing debility, hoping, as he said, " to obtain the divine mercy through the intercession of a blessed Redeemer," which " he had long sought with unfeigned humiliation, and to which he looked with a trembling hope."

Such is the glimpse we have to present of this great man—great as an orator, a statesman, a patriot, and an author. He has been pronounced a man " of unspotted innocence, and firm integrity," and though we may not go so far, there need be no hesitation in declaring him one of the most remarkable men of a remarkable age. His rise from comparative indigence and obscurity to a leading position among British statesmen, where he was offered, but declined, a place among the peers, renders his life a profitable study for those who would so live as to be missed when they die. He chose his path wisely ; he walked in it with the decision and the energy of one who thought that he had truth for his guide, and the public good for his aim, and though Goldsmith's criticism may be true that—

" Burke gave up to party what was meant for mankind,"

it is no less true that, as a partizan, he was one of the grandest that our nation ever saw. Page after page might be filled with the eulogies which were heaped upon him. From his sovereign, down through all ranks, including Charles James Fox, Sheridan, Johnson, and nearly all that were illustrious in his day, our language was laid under tribute to describe the orator, his wisdom, his learning, and his powers.

VII.—HENRY GRATTAN.

1750–1820.

> " O Erin! O my mother, I will love thee,
> Whether upon thy free Atlantic throne
> Thou sitt'st august, majestic, and sublime,
> Or on thy empire's last remaining fragment
> Bendest forlorn, dejected, and forsaken.
> Thy smiles, thy tears, thy blessings, and thy woes,
> Thy glory and thy infamy be mine."
>
> WOLFE.

His birth—Education—Enters Parliament—Degradation of Ireland—Grattan's efforts and success—Granted £50,000 by Parliament—Opposed—Renews his struggles—In the British Parliament—His style of speaking—His death—And character—The lessons of his life.

PART from the Bible, there is no gift bestowed by God upon man to be compared with the use of words. The highest Authority calls the tongue both a fire and a world *—a fire because it penetrates and ignites—a world because in it or by means of it, all good or all evil may be produced. Words—nay, a single word †— may cause the heart to thrill with ecstasy or to throb with anguish—may spread peace or war among the nations—may lead to life or to death for ever—may elevate man to a throne, or even as a subject enable him to rule among the peoples. Words, in short, seem to make man more nearly creative than any other gift which he possesses. Without them, reason itself would be feeble, perhaps useless—with them, what might not even mere instinct achieve? Men who seemed contemptible in other respects have, by the ascendency of words, become the leaders, the dictators, the

---

* James iii. 6.   † See John xx. 16.

tyrants, or the benefactors of thousands. They have swayed the fierce democracy, or urged the soul nearer to God.

HENRY GRATTAN was able to wield this power in a manner which has rarely been surpassed. He was born in Dublin in the year 1750. His father was a barrister, and Recorder of the city, but not affluent; and the son had to depend on the exertion of his own powers for advancement in the world. He was educated at Trinity College, in his native city, and became distinguished there as a student. He subsequently went to London, and began the study of law in the Middle Temple; and it is said that while there, like his distinguished countryman, Burke, he was so straitened in his circumstances that, to obtain food for his mind, he had to stint the supply for his body. But a soul so resolute as that of young Grattan was not to be repressed by obstacles such as these. On the contrary, though his fare might be meagre or scanty, his industry was ceaseless. His desire to prosecute his studies was so great, and his wish to redeem time for that purpose so pressing, that he invented an alarum of a peculiar construction to awake him betimes for his work. He filled a small barrel with water and placed it over a basin on a shelf just above his pillow. The cock of the barrel was so far turned as to fill the basin in a given time, after which the water flowed over, fell upon the pillow, and awoke the sleeper.

After taking his degree at Trinity College, when he was about twenty-two years of age, Grattan was called to the Irish bar, where he attempted to get into practice without much success. Supposing that he could not rise there except by courses to which he would not stoop, he abandoned the law, and betook himself to politics, after acquiring some notoriety by his early publications. He was soon returned to the Irish parliament, and now he has reached his fit arena. He has had difficulties to contend with, but many of them are mastered, and he will soon be heard of as one of the most brilliant and resistless of Irishmen. In that great drama, which is so often a tragedy, Grattan is to be one of the prime actors.

When he thus entered upon public life, the condition of Ireland was abject. By numerous restrictions, and much unwise legislation, the English parliament had cramped the energies of the Irish nation. Disaffection was chronic, and not causeless. The Irish parliament could not originate laws for the country; the decisions of the judges there were not final; it was only like a province of England; and London was, in truth, in everything supreme. Now, in the eyes of an Irish patriot, this was not merely humiliation; it was bondage, and "discontent, bankruptcy, and wretchedness," one has said, "covered the face of the country."

It was in that crisis of affairs that Grattan passed up to the parliament of Ireland; and he entered it with a heart all a-flame to yield it some relief. He was, however, not merely a patriot, for the patriotism of many disappears in vapour of smoke; he was a statesman also, and saw the real remedy for his country's sufferings. He traced them up to the restrictions which pressed upon her commerce, and injured her in other ways; and, in the face of many obstacles, he boldly and wisely strove to rouse his countrymen to attempt to remove what cramped them. He had British ascendency to confront. He had crowds of place-men to oppose. He had the power of British gold to withstand; but he rose superior to them all, and so nobly pled for the Irish claims that they were conceded in spite of a hundred prejudices. He thus became the first man known in history to have freed a country from foreign domination, not by arms and bloodshed, but by wisdom, and energy; by ardour which would not be damped, and power which could not brook to be in bondage to the wrong. None of the illustrious men of Ireland, not even Wellington and Burke, have acquired a name so honoured, in this respect, as that of Henry Grattan. As already noticed, it is to be regretted that the name of hero is confined mainly to the battle-field, for there have been heroes greater far than kings and captains. There have been heroes in the dungeon. There have been heroes at the stake. There have been heroes on the bed of languishing —in the grasp of death. There have been heroes in the cottage, and heroes in the forum:—

> " The applause of list'ning senates to command,
> The threats of pain and ruin to despise;
> To scatter plenty o'er a smiling land,
> And read their history in a nation's eyes."

Grattan belonged to that class, and, with concentrated energy strove to do his life-work—to lift man up from degradation, and place him in a fairer field.

From this time, this bold and intrepid, but wise and far-seeing man, became the idol of Ireland. With indefatigable assiduity he wrought for her welfare, and though we may not approve of all his proposals, it is certain that no patriotism ever was more ardent, no energies ever were more concentrated, and no will more indomitable than those of Grattan in seeking his country's welfare. By efforts which surprise us, by an eloquence which was peculiarly his own, and by powers higher than fall to the lot of most men, he persuaded the Irish parliament to declare that " none but the king, lords, and commons of Ireland could make laws to bind her." It proved in the end to be an empty resolution; but the principle which it embodied had truth and wisdom in it, and Grattan's whole soul was thrown into that enterprise. He had so far achieved his country's independence by his individual exertions. He had no wealth to fascinate, no rank to dazzle ; it was the combination of love to his country with lofty powers which made him what he was ; and the legislature showed its estimate of his deeds by resolving that he should receive an estate worth £100,000 as his reward. At the express request of his friends, this sum was reduced to £50,000—and that was the price which a people struggling for a measure of freedom, spontaneously paid to him who secured it. The words of the grant declared that it was "a testimony of national gratitude for great national services;" and that was surely a lofty position to be held, in comparative youth, by one who recently before had been struggling with something akin to poverty.

But the tide turned. Encouraged by their success, the Irish people, or some of their friends, brought forward views with which Grattan could not sympathize; and after resisting till his popularity had waned, he retired for a short time from the fruitless strife, though what Lord Brougham calls Grattan's "awful energies" had been hurled, without being exhausted, against those who tried to push victory to excess. Yet in 1785, when new dangers appeared, he was once more all that he had ever been. Firmly, heroically, and successfully he resisted attempts to re-impose restrictions, or cripple his country. Hence his popularity returned; and though he was hated and calumniated by some, his influence as an orator, and his counsels as a statesman, did much to elevate Ireland from the depths into which it had sunk : he began a movement which had long been retarded, but which must sooner or later be matured. Fresh honours flowed in upon him. He was chosen member, first for Dublin, and subsequently for Wicklow—the latter, that he might oppose the union of England and Ireland, which was then projected, —an opposition which we, judging after the event, cannot but pronounce unworthy of one who has been called by high authority the founder of the liberties of his country, her emancipator from fetters which had cramped her for three centuries before. It was the error of his life, and showed, as patriotism has sometimes done, that he loved his

country not always wisely though always well. Referring
to his early efforts to elevate Ireland, and contrasting their
success with what he deemed the disaster of the Union, he
sorrowfully said of his country's independence, " I sat by its
cradle : I followed its hearse."

When the Union was consummated, a right measure
effected by iniquitous means—by bribery, by coronets, and
places—Grattan became a member of the British House of
Commons, and there his patriotism and his powers were as
signal as ever.   His genius was not local; it was for all
places; it was for man, and not merely for Irishmen : and
he rose to a position in England scarcely inferior to that
which he had held in Ireland.   And here we should not fail
to mark the personal as well as the public difficulties with
which he had to contend, ere he could command, and sway,
and fulmine as he did.   Somewhat in a tone of caricature,
he has been described as a little ungainly man, oddly com-
pacted, with a large head, and awkward gestures, rolling
like a mandarin, and sawing the air with his whole body from
head to foot as he spoke.   But in spite of these obstacles,
he took his place among the foremost, and he kept it.
It is one of the most signal triumphs of mind over body, to
hear it said of that ungainly man, that in his orations there
was a grandeur which both enforced reverence and elicited
admiration. He shed a light which irradiated without dazz-
ling—which both aided the judgment and delighted the
imagination.   At one time his argument was so concentrated
and pungent that it compelled conviction; at another, his
style was diffuse, lofty, and magnificent, bending the will,
working on the fancy, filling the understanding. His power
at times was irresistible; venality quailed before him, and
"place, pension, and peerage, had but a feeble hold even of
the most degenerate," when Grattan assailed them. He had
early difficulties to encounter and surmount; but what were

these compared with the obstacle to greatness which existed in Grattan's person, voice, and gesture? They were all forgotten, however, as soon as his pungent sayings, his alliterations, and epigrammatic point had taken possession of his hearers. Now pathos, anon sarcasm—at one time scathing invective, at another gentle persuasion—all characterized this gifted man.

Like his countryman Burke, Grattan took alarm at the ravages of the French Revolution, and became more and more cautious as he advanced in days. To the last, however, he maintained an indomitable ardour in regard to all that he deemed good and right; and near the close of his career once exclaimed, " I should be happy to die in the discharge of my duty." In private life, it is said, he was characterized by an exact discharge of all the domestic virtues, while there was a charm in his society which was, no doubt, one secret of his power. He was one of the few public men, one who knew him well has said, whose private virtues were followed by public fame, or could be cited as examples to those who would follow in his public steps. This hero of patriotism in public was a model of virtue in private, while the native grandeur of his soul shed an influence like sunshine upon those who dwelt near him.

Grattan's death took place on the 14th of May 1820, when he was seventy years of age. It was hastened, perhaps, by his anxiety to be in his place in parliament. His last words, we are told, were a prayer for the interests of Great Britain and Ireland—that they might be for ever united in the bonds of affection. There might be some extravagance in the lines which were quoted in parliament when his eulogy was pronounced :—

> " Ne'er to those chambers where the mighty rest,
> Since their foundation, came a nobler guest;
> Nor ever to the bowers of bliss conveyed
> A purer spirit, or a holier shade,"

but it is unquestionable, that among men who have given their days and their nights to the welfare of their country, few have gone down to the grave more sincerely honoured than Henry Grattan. It was a graceful thing when the great and the gifted of Britain united to solicit that his remains might be buried in Westminster Abbey, beside the dust of kindred greatness—"a place where he would not have been unwilling to lie—by the side of his illustrious fellow-labourers in the cause of freedom."

And such is an outline of the life of Grattan. It is introduced, like the rest, not to supply a narrative of incidents, but to illustrate a principle. And here is one who started in life with difficulty upon difficulty to block up his path. After surmounting the hindrances which beset him in his early years, he had to hover for three or four more about the courts of law unemployed, and, therefore, unfed. Then, when he actually entered upon public life, he saw injury heaped upon injury to the land of his birth, and the pride and power of the British people were sure to oppose the man who dared to assail a state of matters which was hoary with the growth of generations. But, undaunted by all, that youth—for he was still but a youth—launched his whole energies against the degradation of his country. He chose his path; he walked fearlessly there, and long ere he had reached the end, the pile which he assailed had melted away before his assaults. It was the triumph of a right choice consistently followed up, and leaving behind it streaks of light to guide those who follow in a path like that which Grattan trod.

Yet one thing regarding him is to be deplored. Those who have given us some account of his life have said little, nay nothing, of his religion. Was he one of those who bow before the crucified One, or was his country here so much the object of his engrossing regard, that the better country was not much regarded? Whether was it only the wisdom of earth or that of heaven which presided in his lofty soul? If the latter, then had he gifts before which even his other powers grow pale; if only the former, what were all his achievements but shadows and delusions in the high reckoning of eternity? The balance of the sanctuary—who can stand that test? Only they who have appealed to the Great Surety, or consulted the Great Counsellor, or sat down to learn the divine Wisdom.

VIII.—DANIEL WEBSTER.

1782-1852.

"He feared not in his flower of days,
　When strong to stem the torrent's force;
　When through the desert's pathless maze
　His way was like an eagle's course!
　When war was sunshine to his sight,
　And the wild hurricane delight."

HEMANS.

Encomiums—His birth—Education—His devotedness to study—His life-pursuit decided by a casualty—Difficulties—Studies—Becomes a lawyer—And member of Congress—His habits—His friendships—His deep sensibilities—Yet perfectly self-contained—His doings as a politician—Is a candidate for the American President's chair—Is rejected—His disappointment—Webster as an orator—His view of slavery—His religion—His death.

IF we heard of a man who was called at one place "The pride of his country, and the glory of human nature," and at another, "A mighty rock, our only defence against general corruption;" if we heard it said of him to-day that he is "worthy of the noblest homage which freemen can give or a freeman receive—the homage of the heart," and to-morrow, that "a section of America rejoiced in the promise of the youth, and America altogether in the performance of the man;" if it were proclaimed, amid the plaudits of thousands, that the state is "honoured in a citizen who is received with the acclamations of the world," and that "his country will never forget that his fame has extended her own among the nations of the world;" if we were, moreover, told concerning that man, that "his name was inseparable from that of his country in the records of time and eternity;" if it were assigned as a reason for that applause that "he had illustrated the glory of his country," and "had sown the seed of constitutional liberty broadcast over the world;" finally, if we heard it said of any man, he has "a heart large enough to comprehend his whole country, a head wise enough to discern her best interests"—with all this before us we could scarcely help desiring to know something more concerning a man so signally honoured. Who was he? What was his training? What were his gifts or his acquirements? How did he reach that position of eminence where millions awarded "the highest honours of the constitution to its ablest defender?" Such reasonable curiosity can be fully gratified in regard to the name now before us, and that gratification may help to augment the wisdom of men.

DANIEL WEBSTER, the American statesman, and the subject of the earnest encomiums which have just been quoted, was born in the town of Salisbury, in the county of Merrimack, New Hampshire, America, on the 18th of January 1782. His mother, as a woman of deep piety, was his first teacher; his father was a man of singular but quiet energy, and the training of the youthful statesman was well fitted to prepare him, at least in some respects, for the work which it fell to his lot to perform. From his mother's lips were first received the vital truths of the Bible; and the first copy of that book ever owned by Webster was her gift. Long subsequent to this period, and in the full blaze of his fame, he could say that he had never been able to recollect the time when he could not read the Bible, and supposed that his first schoolmistress began to teach him when he was three or four years of age. His first school-house was built of logs, and stood about half a mile from his father's house, not very far from the beautiful Merrimack. All was then humble enough with this great American statesman. He attended school only during the winter months, and assisted

his father in the business of his farm and his mill as soon as
he had strength for doing so. He was, however, the
brightest boy at school; and when the tempting reward of a
knife was promised to the scholar who committed to memory
the greatest number of verses from the Bible, Daniel came
with whole chapters, which the master could not find time
to hear him repeat in full. The boy secured the knife, and
his delighted teacher subsequently told the father of that
child that " he would do God's work injustice" if gifts so
promising were not nurtured at college.

But that consummation was not to be very soon realized.
For some time Daniel had to assist his father at a saw-
mill; but so resolute was he in acquiring knowledge and
training the mind while toiling with the body, that the
operations at the mill were systematically interspersed with
studies well fitted to form and to brace the embryo patriot
for his great life-work. The saw took about ten minutes to
cleave a log, and young Webster, after setting the mill in
motion, learned to fill up these ten minutes with reading.
As a patriot, a statesman, an orator, and a scholar, he became famous, and was called the greatest intellectual character of his country ; and we see where he laid the foundation
of his greatness—by persistent and invincible ardour even
in early boyhood. That magnanimous kindliness and tenderness of heart, which entered so largely into his character,
was fostered amid such scenes; and of all the men whose
memories we are fain to embalm, he ranks among the least
indebted to casualty, and the most to indefatigable earnestness, for the position to which he eventually rose. Amid the
forest wilds of America his perseverance laid the foundation
of power, of learning, of fame, and of goodness.

A simple incident which happened about this period decided his life-pursuit. He discovered a copy of the " Constitution of the United States," as drawn up by some of her

ablest statesmen. It was printed upon a cotton handker-
chief which he purchased in a country store with what was
then his all, and which amounted to twenty-five cents. He
was about eight years of age when that took place, and
learned then, for the first time, either that there were United
States, or that they had a Constitution.

From this date, or about the year 1790, his path through life
was decided, not formally, but really, not by any avowal, but
by a fostered predilection. Meanwhile other influences were
at work. The father of this New Hampshire boy was strict
in his religious opinions and observances, and the son had to
conform, sometimes with a grudge at the restraint, but with
effects of a vitally beneficial nature to the future patriot. His
father then kept a place of entertainment, where teamsters
halted to bait, and the attractions of the place were increased
by the fact that young Webster often regaled those visitors
by his readings. The Psalms of David were his favourite,
and there, when only about seven years of age, he first imparted that pleasure by his oratory which he afterwards
carried up to the highest level which an American citizen can
reach. To that humble abode Webster once returned in his
declining years, and with streaming eyes descanted on the
various events of the home of his youth.*

The school which he attended during the winter months,
was about three miles from his father's house, and he had
often to travel thither through deep snow. At the age of
fourteen he attended a somewhat more advanced academy

* Webster's own account of his father seems a photograph. "My father died
in April 1806. . . . I closed his eyes in this very house. He died at the age of
sixty-seven, after a life of exertion, toil and exposure ; a private soldier, an officer,
a legislator, a judge, everything that man could be to whom learning had never
disclosed her ample page. My first speech at the bar was made when he was
on the bench. He never heard me a second time. He had in him what I
collect to have been the character of some of the old Puritans. He was deeply
religious, but not sour ; on the contrary, good humoured and facetious, imparting, even in his age, a contagious laugh ; teeth all as white as alabaster;
gentle, soft, playful, and yet having a heart in him that he seemed to have borrowed from a lion."

for a few months, and his first effort at public speaking there
was a failure. He burst into tears : his antipathy to public
declamation appeared insurmountable, and neither frowns nor
smiles could overcome the reluctance. It *was* overcome, for
when young Webster felt the power which was in him, he
boldly employed it. At first, however, he was a failure as
a public speaker. With all this, he went forward in the acquisition of knowledge, and the bracing of his mind ; and in
his fifteenth year he once undertook to repeat five hundred
lines of Virgil, if his teacher would consent to listen.

About this time the elder Webster disclosed to his son
his purpose to send him to college. The talents of the boy,
and the counsels of friends pointed out that as a proper path,
and that son himself will describe the effects of his father's
information. "I could not speak," he says. "How could
my father, I thought, with so large a family, and in such
narrow circumstances, think of incurring so great an expense
for me, and I laid my head on his shoulder and wept." That
boy, however, had further difficulties to surmount. He had
to leave one of his schools to assist his father in the hay harvest ; he had, moreover, the hindrance of a slender and sickly
constitution ; but the Bible, side by side with some standard
authors, had now become his English classics, while Cicero,
Virgil, Horace, Demosthenes, and others, were his manuals
in ancient literature. It was knowledge pursued under unusual difficulties ; but in spite of all, acquired to an unusual
extent. So indomitable and persistent was the boy that in
a few months he mastered the difficulties of the Greek
tongue, and finally graduated at Dartmouth when he was
eighteen years of age. Incidents are recorded which show
that during his residence at college he was determined to
hold the first place or none.

It was at Dartmouth that Webster's patriotism first flashed
forth with true American ardour, a harbinger to his whole

future career. He had now mastered his boyish aversion to oratory, and on the 4th of July 1800, the twenty-fourth anniversary of American Independence, he delivered an oration full of patriotic sentiment, manifesting the decided bent of his mind, and deserving a place, in the opinion of some, among the works which he subsequently published. He was then only eighteen years of age.

To increase the straitened funds of the family, Daniel Webster for some time kept a school at Freyburg, in Maine. His income there, eked out by other means, which were the wages of indomitable industry, enabled him to send his brother, Ebenezer, to college—the grand object which he had in view in becoming a schoolmaster. He was, however, all the while prosecuting his studies in law, and in the year 1805, entered on the duties of a legal practitioner at Boston. His familiar title in the county where he resided was " All eyes," and he used them with singular advantage. In Boston, at Portsmouth, and elsewhere, he continued these pursuits, and he thus early adopted some of the maxims which guided him through life. "There are evils greater than poverty :" "What bread you eat, let it be the bread of independence :" " Live on no man's favour :" " Pursue your profession :" "Make yourself useful to the world. . . . . You will have nothing to fear." Such were his convictions, and he embodied them in deeds. One instance of his generosity is recorded at this period. His father had become embarrassed; the devoted son hastened to liquidate his father's debt, and he did it with a decision like that which signalized him all his days. He resided as a lawyer at Portsmouth for about nine years.

It was in the year 1812 that Webster was first elected a member of Congress, and he reached that elevation by his masterly ability in the affairs of his profession. By persistent patience first, and then by resistless power, he took up the foremost position in the sphere in which he moved. He

appeared in the majesty of intellectual grandeur, like one
who was all might and soul, and poured forth the stores of
an opulent mind in a manner which was entirely his own.
His words had both weight and fire ; and the contrast is
now great between the boy who broke down and wept
at his first declamation, and the man, bending opponents to
his will by his energy and indomitable zeal. The laurel of
victory, it has been fondly said, was proffered to him by all,
and bound his brow for one exploit till he went forth to
another. In his thirtieth year he entered the field of politics,
like one who had made up his mind to be decided, firm, and
straightforward ; and such was the serenity of this great soul,
amid wild commotions, that the enthusiast mistook it for
apathy, the fierce for lukewarmness. It was the great calm
of profound conviction, borne up by a thorough reliance
on the right—the right as to time, as to degree, and as to resources for the battle of life. From the day on which he threw
himself into the political arena, he belonged to the United
States, and not to his native county alone. Crowds soon
gathered round one who had mastered so many difficulties,
and taken his place among the kingly men who rule the
spirits whom they are born first to subdue, and then to bind
to themselves by the spell of genius.

While thus moving upward to a sphere of influence
beyond what falls to the lot of most men, we have seen that
Webster did not rise without effort, painstaking, and daily,
nightly labour. Dependent from the outset on his own
exertions, he was at all times a hard working man. And
even when he had reached his place of power, his habits of
persistent assiduity were not abandoned : they were cultivated perhaps more resolutely than ever. Among the first
at the post of duty from day to day, he left nothing undone,
from the destruction of all anonymous annoyances, such as
public men must often experience, to the answering or pre-

paration of the most important State Papers. He sometimes
kept two persons writing to his dictation in separate apart-
ments, he himself walking between them, and imparting his
portion to each. He excluded all topics of state from his
private intercourse with friends; but whether as lawyer, as
statesman, or diplomatist, Webster allowed nothing to interfere with the routine of his public duty. Though guided
by lofty genius, he sought no exemption from steadfast
system; but wrought as if he had been a mere man of
business apprenticed to toil, instead of a soaring and imperial spirit. Those who knew him best have put it upon
record that, " whatever of genius may be awarded to him,
it is certain that he was chiefly indebted to his own personal
exertions for his commanding position as an orator, a statesman, a jurist, and a man of letters." One of his maxims
was, " Nobody knows anything till he has learned it," and
he learned; another was, " Since I know nothing, and have
nothing, I must learn and earn," and his life was a comment
on his words. Nor can any one who has pondered the story
of his life decline to accede to the eulogy pronounced by a
friend who survived him : " The record of Daniel Webster's
life from the humble roof beneath which he was born, with
no inheritance but poverty and an honoured name, up
through the arduous path of manhood, which he trod with
lion heart and giant step, till they conducted him to the
helm of state . . . . . has been spread throughout the land.
Struggling poverty has been cheered afresh; honest ambition
has been kindled; patriotic resolve has been invigorated,
while all have mourned." Nor could it be otherwise; the
first man of his country had gained his position by the
energy of an iron will,—a will which once led him to earn
with weary fingers, and amid toils protracted till midnight,
the means of educating his brother, as Daniel himself had
been educated.

Another characteristic of this indefatigable patriot was the power with which he linked his friends to him—a power, indeed, which resembled fascination. They delight to speak of him as a man of a most noble heart. He was one of the most devoted of friends; and the result was that some of those who knew him best were ready to die on his behalf. "If I saw a bullet coming to his heart," said one with ardour, "I would jump in its way, and receive it myself." The explanation was his unstinted generosity, as well as his steadfast firmness in friendship. On one occasion he gave an aged man, a friend of his father's, money enough to buy a small farm; and by that and similar deeds, this man so resolute, yet so gentle, so determined to soar, yet so ready to be humble, earned the strong encomium, "I have yet to learn the name of man, woman, or child who ever knew Daniel Webster and did not love him." In short, some of his own lines were verified in his own history:—

> " We have a page all glowing and all bright,
> On which our friendships and our loves to write;
> That these may never from the soul depart
> We trust them to the memory of the heart.
> There is no dimming, no effacement here;
> Each new pulsation keeps the record clear;
> Warm, golden letters all the tablet fill,
> Nor lose their lustre till the heart stands still."

An old soldier of the Revolution once walked fifty miles to see and hear the great statesman, and on the same occasion another patriarch tottered towards him, threw his arms around him, and exclaimed, "God bless you; you are the greatest and the best man in the world!" His presence at his native farm was always a holiday; and there must have been some peculiar spell about the man whose neighbours in the country sometimes went in thousands to meet him on his return from the capital to his farm: without respect to party, they assembled to do him honour, and met him at a distance of ten miles from his home. The road was literally lined with women and children assembled to greet him, not merely as a great man, but as a good one. Garlands without number were strewed in his way, and more than once his return was a procession, an ovation, prolonged over miles. All this fell to the lot of one who some years before had been weeping, from deep sensibility, over the poverty of his lot; or struggling with all the energy of a noble mind to surmount the difficulties which crossed the path of himself and of those whom he loved so well. But, amid all this publicity and glare, Webster ever rejoiced in the solitude of his home and the amenities of its friendships, as if he had never known the excitement of one of the loftiest positions to which a subject can climb.

The foundation of all these cordial friendships was laid deep in the genial though decided nature of Daniel Webster. He was a man of strong emotion, and profound sensibility, so that—

> " The tear that flows
> Down Virtue's cheek for mortal woes,"

was often shed by him. It was his practice annually to carry his children to see their father's humble birth-place, where he loved to dwell on the touching incidents of his youth, and often wept in tenderness amid the well-known scenes. The river and the hills, he said, were as beautiful as ever; but the graves of his father, his mother, his brothers and sisters, and early friends gave to the whole something of the aspect of a city of the dead. We have seen how he wanted words to tell his father his joy at the intelligence that he was to go to college, and could only weep upon his father's breast; and that incident was one among many similar scenes which mark the life of this self-made man; self-made, at least, in as far as regards the smiles of greatness, or the props of affluence. When driving in the neighbourhood of his home, the great statesman would often rein up his horses, when he met a company of children going to school, that he might ask their names, and inquire about their parents. While he did so he thought, perhaps, of the time when he, like one of these children, went to school with his primer in one hand and his dinner in the other.

Webster's days and nights, however, were in reality given to his country. "Love your country, your whole country," was the appropriate counsel which he gave—appropriate, we mean, in an empire constituted like the United States; and as he counselled he acted. He was, no doubt, more cautious as a politician than many who had more fire and less foresight; one of his maxims was that "some questions will improve by keeping," and he kept not a few. He was one of those men who can afford to wait, because they have sagacity to forecaste with certainty what the course of events must be. Though bright and happy in the hours when he unbent, it was not difficult to trace in him the effects of the cares and responsibilities of governing the United States; but he was helped to bear up by his thorough independence, his self-possession, and self-reliance. Indeed, so far did he carry that tendency that he resolutely refused to read all reviews upon his works, or strictures upon himself, whether hostile or friendly. He declined even to know what had been said of him, assigning as his reasons that he had done his best through life, and that that consciousness was more consoling than any opinion however favourable, or applause however ardent. Whether he was advocating the integrity of the Union according to his own maxim, "Liberty first, and union afterwards," or both in one, "Liberty and union, now and for ever, one and inseparable," or upholding any of the great republican doctrines of which he was so zealous an advocate, Webster was alike independent, manly, and resolute,—it was a light matter to him to be judged of man's judgment. When he passed away it was said, that "the great luminary of the bar, the senate, and the council chamber was set for ever;" and we may add that that luminary was a sun, not a satellite—it shone in no borrowed lustre.

It is well known that this man, so humble in his origin, yet so masterly in his mind, passed through all the gradations of rank that are open to an American citizen, up to the right hand of the highest. We have seen when he entered Congress. In 1841 he became Secretary of State, and from that period bore the place in American politics which would be readily conceded, in that ardent country, to one who was deemed and called "the master mind of the world." In his love of freedom, Webster has been likened to Washington, or expressly called his equal in regard to patriotism and true greatness. It is not wonderful, therefore, that this patriot's friends proposed him as President of the United States. He failed, and felt the failure, but soothed his disappointment by the conviction that no man "could take away from him what he had done for his country." Those who loved and admired him thought that the word President would have dimmed the lustre of the name of Daniel Webster; and they add, in regard to his disappointment, "if we must sorrow that what men expected can never come to pass, let us not weep for him but for our country." Others, however, were of opinion that Webster was "rejected and lost;" while those who look deeper at the causes of events may see, in that disappointment, the needful antidote administered by the Supreme Wisdom to ward off the danger of too universal a success. This gifted and ambitious man was suffered to take an active part in the government of one of the greatest of the nations. By his bold and manly grasp of American interests, he did much to weld the different states more closely into one. He negotiated, on the part of his country, some of the most im-

portant treaties which promote the peace and the amity of
nations, for example, what is called the Ashburton treaty
with Great Britain ; and it would have seemed too much for
one mortal, successful as Webster had already been, to be
lifted to an official level with princes. That was denied him :
his empire was not countries—-it was minds. He was to be
trained for a nobler exaltation than a throne.

And that this check was needed is manifest from Webster's feelings. Some men, far below him in other respects,
have stood high above him in regard to their views of this
world's rewards. Mountstewart Elphinstone, for example,
was offered honour upon honour. He might have been
Governor-General of Canada. He was invited to take a
place among the peers of Britain. The vice-royalty of India
was pressed upon him ; but he smiled them all aside, and
acted like one who felt that what men deem the great prizes
of life are not worth the sacrifices which they entail. Webster's views were less lofty. He lived for action, and panted
for the widest possible arena on which to act.

Little has yet been said regarding Webster as an orator.
It was mainly in that respect, however, that he surpassed
his fellows, and mainly by that means was he enabled to
ascend to the high position which he held so long. The
versatility of his powers was very great, and the mode in
which he sometimes employed them was not a little remarkable. He had, on one occasion, spent several hours with his
colleagues in adjusting some important questions involving
the interests of kingdoms ; and on returning home he spor-
tively sallied forth and purchased some eggs, on the principle of seeing how extremes meet, in regard to occupation as well as in other respects. But there were serious
things mixed with his jests ; and as an orator Webster
stands in the first rank, if not foremost, in the New
World. When it was known that he was to speak, the ex-

citement sometimes amounted to a furor, and a hundred dollars have been paid for a ticket of admission to hear him. Two hours before his appearance, on that occasion, he was facetiously amusing his friends by wit somewhat at his own expense. Meanwhile the avenues that led to his arena were blocked up by the crowds pressing for admittance; and when he did appear, it was to rouse, to agitate, and convulse. He felt what he said in his inmost soul, and his words were winged with fire, even while they were massively powerful, and connected by a logic which tolerated no breaks in the chain. In some cases, his appeals were based upon Scriptural topics. One, for example, of a memorable kind, was fetched from the Saviour's injunction to let little children come to him, instead of repelling them from his presence. It was an argument for Christian education in the very highest sense. "Suffer little children to come unto me," the orator repeated, "*unto Me.* He did not send them first for lessons in morals to the schools of the Pharisees, or to the unbelieving Sadducees. . . . . He opened up at once to the youthful mind the everlasting fountain of living waters, the only source of eternal truth—'Suffer little children to come *unto Me.*' And that injunction is of perpetual obligation; it addresses itself to-day with the same earnestness and the same authority which attended its first utterance to the Christian world. It is of force everywhere, and at all times. It extends to the ends of the earth; it will reach to the end of time, always and everywhere sounding in the ears of men with an emphasis which nothing can weaken, and with an authority which nothing can supersede, 'Suffer little children to come *unto Me.*'" Such sentiments uttered, as Webster did, with trembling lips, with expanding nostrils, with brow wet with the starting perspiration, and with a voice varying every moment with the various emotion, easily explain not merely why the senate-chamber was

thronged when he spoke on great occasions, but why all the
passages leading to it, the Rotunda of the Capitol, and even
the avenues of the city were alive with crowds eager for
admittance, as long as admittance was possible.

At other times, however, this pupil of Cicero, and Demosthenes, for he had studied them both, though neither of
them was his model, was calm, logical, and incisive, but
never personal.* Earnest, thoughtful, weighty, wise, his
oratory was then signalized by massive truth rather than
by flashing brilliance; but still it was fitted to suggest the
figure which has been employed to describe him—that of a
Corinthian pillar, with its graceful shaft, and yet more
graceful capital. At all times, however, Daniel Webster
took full possession of his audience; he could "lift the soul
as with the swell of a pealing organ, or stir the blood with
the tones of a clarion in the inmost chambers of the heart."

His delight, it will readily be believed, was in grand
topics, such as could fill and more than fill, his own capacious
soul. The anniversary of American Independence was a
special favourite. The landing of the Pilgrim Fathers at
"The Rock" was another. The laying of the foundation
stone of a monument to commemorate the first victory
gained by the Americans in the war of the Revolution was
a third; and it has been said that the oration which Webster delivered on that occasion, as well as that which he
pronounced at the completion of the monument, will endure
long after the pile itself shall have crumbled into ruins.
The founders of American freedom, the Constitution of the
United States, and similar topics drew forth his mightiest
efforts, or gave occasion to his most signal displays of
oratorical power; and in tracing his triumphant march in

* "I wish your friendly advice," one friend remarked to another, "for I am
in trouble." "What is it?" was the inquiry; and the information was, "I have
a lawsuit, and Webster is opposed to me. What should I do?" The comfort
was American, "Send to Smyrna and import a young earthquake."

subjugating the minds of men, one is evermore recalled to
the difference between that result and his assisting his
father at the mill, or delighting the teamsters in the hostelry
by reciting the Psalms of David.   It is a noble illustration
of the effects of manly decision—a right choice early made,
and through life tenaciously followed out.   Yet amid all
this, we cannot but regret that he did not strike a bolder
note against the national blot of slavery.   His maxim was
that every state should be left to decide that question for
itself, and that was a corollary from his other life-long conviction that the Union was to be preserved by all means,
and at all hazards.   Had he, however, in his own majestic
way, moved in advance of his contemporaries, in regard to
an institution which must fall as surely as time rolls on,
Webster would have been yet more illustrious, and yet more
surely the glory of his country.

But one aspect of this man's character remains to be considered.   As an improver of his estates much might be said
concerning him.   For example, on one of these, he planted
one hundred thousand forest trees with his own hand.   His
liberality also might have deserved a notice.   While he
earned enough to have made a dozen men rich, he spent it
liberally, and gave to the poor by hundreds and thousands.
His last fee for a legal argument was eleven thousand
dollars; and that repeated from day to day might speedily
have made him a Crœsus, had he been a miser.   His intense
and glowing admiration of nature in all its moods and
aspects, from the rising of the sun down to the tiniest object,
was another peculiarity of his character.   But all pales
before what is said of his religion.*   He had two children,
Julia and Edward; he lost them both; and those who were
permitted to see him in his most retired and confiding
moments, tell us that from that date he was a changed man.

* See "The Private Life of Daniel Webster," *passim.*

But even in early life he had been impressed by the truth
—and it appears to have exercised a guiding power in
his great career.   He became a member of a Christian
Church in the early prime of his days. His mother's lessons
and his father's example never were forgotten—nay, habitually he bore about with him the thought of a world to come.
" When you look," he would write to a friend, "upon the
graves of my family, remember that he who is the author
of this letter must soon follow them to another world."   His
attachment to the Bible was very marked : he loved it ; he
read it in his family ; he made short extempore sermons of
great power and eloquence.   He never travelled without
the sacred volume as his companion ; and the story of the
Saviour, or the prophecies of Isaiah never seemed so
eloquent to his friends as when coming from his lips.   He
habitually spoke with admiring fervour regarding these
writings, and, without hearing him, it is said, it were difficult to comprehend " how much light he could throw upon
a difficult text, how much beauty lend to expressions that
would escape all but the eye of genius, what new vigour he
could give to the most earnest thought, and what elevation
even to sublimity."   " It would be impossible," one has said,
" for any one to listen for half an hour to one of his disserta-
tions on the Scriptures, and not believe either in their
inspiration or in his."   The eloquence and the sacredness of
the Bible were both deeply felt by Webster ; and so predomi-
nant was the latter that neither in public nor in private did
any irreverent allusion to the contents of the Book which
he deemed so holy ever escape from his lips.   The deep
low tones in which he sometimes repeated portions of the
word of God, amid the silence of the night or under the
shadow of the trees which surrounded his country abode,
evoked feelings of deep solemnity in the minds of his
friends, so that some of them do not hesitate to say that

no man whom they ever knew appeared to understand or appreciate the Scriptures so well. "This is *the* book," was the exclamation of one who had learning enough to compare it with the Iliad, the Odyssey, and other productions of the least mortal minds; and in that book he found not merely poetry to admire but theology to believe. "The plan of man's salvation through the atonement of Christ," was one of his great truths, and he used the appointed means for deepening and extending his knowledge. At one period of his life he spent his summer months in Dorchester; and when he first sojourned there, he waited on the minister to intimate that he had become one of his parishioners, adding that he was not to be one of the fashionable people who resorted to the place, but meant to be in his pew both in the morning and afternoon. Nor was such a proceeding strange in one who could say, "I have read through the entire Bible many times. I now make a practice to go through it once a year. It is the book of all others for lawyers as well as for divines, and I pity the man who cannot find in it a rich supply of thought, and of rules for his conduct. It fits man for life,—it prepares him for death."

But the incidents in Webster's life, which manifest his love and reverence for the Bible, are more than can be recounted here. His belief in the efficacy of prayer, in the great atonement, as already mentioned, and kindred doctrines, are specially described; and the influence which the truth exerted on his life was not less remarked. He never sat down to food with his family without imploring a blessing; and as he had become a professed member of the Christian Church while yet a lad at college, he continued a communicant till his closing day. The following sentiment is not altogether correct, but it at least shows the admiration in which Webster was held. "One of the most impres-

sive scenes I ever witnessed was to see him in full view of
the Capitol, the principal theatre of his exploits . . . . par-
taking of the sacrament of the Lord's Supper. That spectacle and the grandeur of his death are to me more eloquent
than a thousand sermons from mortal lips." " Neither in
his letters nor his conversation," said another, " have I ever
known him to express an impure thought, an immoral
sentiment, or use profane language." To say the least, the
one of these extracts is in beautiful consistency with the
other. Together, they tell what a Christian ought to be.

And is not this man's life another model—a model not
merely as to the irrepressible energy with which he pressed
on and up as regards this life, but, moreover, in his
view of the life to come? He had a vast and capacious
soul : he could grasp the most complicated of questions and
analyze them into simplicity,—and what was the most
befitting study for a mind so lofty? How could its aspirations best be met, its capacity filled and satisfied to the
uttermost? By what, if not with the Infinite, the Eternal,
the Omnipotent, the Omniscient ? By what, if not with
the wisdom which comes from above, and the truths which
inspiration has revealed to guide us back to God? Such
at least were the truths, and such was the One, with whom
Daniel Webster held daily communion; and were his example habitually followed by the rulers of nations, the
people would be rescued from the despotism or the blunders
of little men. The Eternal would get his place,—the first
and the highest,—and all else would fall into order the most
complete, as beauty arose out of chaos when Omnipotence
said " Be."

But Webster is now in his seventy-first year. He has
reached the allotted term of mortal existence, and must pass
away alike from the frowns and the applause of mortals.
On the morning of Sabbath, the 24th of October 1852, he

was summoned away. Though much enfeebled, his mind was calm, and he died with the confidence of a little child, reposing on the mercy of his God as revealed in the Saviour. Among his last utterances was this, "Heavenly Father, forgive my sins, and welcome me to thyself through Christ Jesus." His very last words were, "I still live," and his loving, weeping friends took them up as a prediction of that immortality on which he was about to enter. Through life he had hallowed the Sabbath, and he died upon it. The autumn was his favourite season, and he passed away amid its mellow glories, after affectionately and solemnly taking leave of his weeping wife, children, kindred, and friends, down to the humblest members of his household. His death, it is supposed, was hastened by injuries received by the breaking down of his carriage : but it did not find him unprepared. Long years before, he had erected his own tomb; and there, on a plain marble slab over the door, the visitor reads the simple inscription—

Daniel Webster.

Some ten thousand friends, countrymen, and lovers, helped to lay him there,—and one of the orations pronounced in connection with his departure was thus touchingly closed : " The clasped hands,— the dying prayers,— oh, my fellow-citizens, this is a consummation over which tears of pious sympathy will be shed, after the glories of the forum and the senate are forgotten."

The heart of America throbbed with grief at the tomb of Daniel Webster, but posterity has weighty lessons there to learn. When

> " He passed through glory's morning gate,
> And walked in paradise,"

he left behind him a thousand lights burning to guide those who shall come after. See how independent man is of posi-

tion; he can "make his life sublime" if his God be his
counsellor and truth his guide. Poverty need not repress:
the loftiest heights to which man's mind can soar may be
won, if only we follow where wisdom leads and act on
the maxim which even heathenism deemed sage, "The
gods grant nothing to mortals without labour." Most
assiduously did Daniel Webster labour all the days of his
life: his early decision was on the side of the good and the
pure, in one word, the Christian,—and he embodied that
decision in a life-long contest with evil,—a life-long pursuit of what he reckoned worthy of an immortal mind.
He had his faults: he was human; but his life is a lasting
protest against the grovelling grossness of many a statesman
in his own and other lands.

IX.—SILVIO PELLICO.

1789-1854.

> " A gentle knight was pricking on the plaine,
> Ycladd in mightie armes, and silver shielde,
> Wherein old dints of deepe woundes did remaine
> The cruel marks of many a bloody fielde;
> Yet armes till that time did he never wielde.
> His angry steede did chide his foming bitt,
> And much disdayning to the curbe to yielde;
> Full jolly knight he seemed, and faire did sitt,
> As one for knigbtly guists and fierce encounters fitt."
>
> SPENCER.

Italy—The first Bonaparte—Action and reaction—Results—Pellico's birth—Early training—His love of country—Arrested—Imprisoned—Milan—Venice—Spielberg—His sufferings there—And studies—Set free in 1830—Retires to Turin—His works—His death.

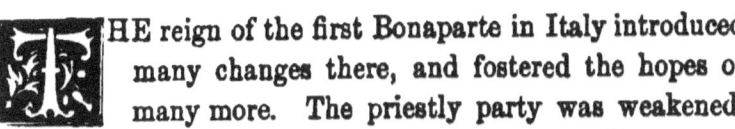

HE reign of the first Bonaparte in Italy introduced many changes there, and fostered the hopes of many more. The priestly party was weakened, and in some places suppressed. A measure of liberty was enjoyed, and the people felt their freedom reviving as the sunshine of spring and summer revive and beautify the earth.

But when Bonaparte fell, a reaction speedily began. Old despotisms were restored, and the Italians were trodden down as before. Many of them, however, could ill brook such treatment—accustomed as they had been to a measure of liberty, they could not silently submit to repression. The restoration of the priests, the inquisition, espionage, and all the adjuncts of a galling bondage, goaded men to cherish violent opinions, and some to do violent deeds. Dungeons, disease and death were the result to many, whose offence began in deep love to their native country,—that country which long centuries of dreary and crushing oppression has only rendered more dear to the hearts of millions.

These events and their attendant sufferings occasioned some of the most resolute displays of patriotism which the history of the world supplies. Never was unflinching decision on the one hand, or heroic endurance on the other, more signal than in the case of some of those who were immured in the dungeons of San Michele, of Venice, or of Spielberg,—and never was blood more freely shed than by those who died on the scaffold, because they loved Italy, not wisely, but too well.—We are now to contemplate some incidents in the life of one of these sufferers,—not in a detailed biography, but only to mark how bold was his decision, how nobly unbending his spirit, and how profound were his sorrows for his country's sake.

SILVIO PELLICO, to whom we refer, has said that "both religion and philosophy require calmness of judgment combined with energy of will, and that without such a union there can be no .... dignity of character, and no sound principles of human action." It will soon appear whether his life corresponded to his convictions.

He was born at Saluzzo in Piedmont in the year 1789. His father was in easy circumstances, and the training of the son was well fitted to develop the gifts which he possessed. In Turin, at Lyons, and at Milan, acquirements were made or pursuits engaged in which rendered Pellico an accomplished man, a devotee to literature, and passionately enamoured of the beautiful land of his birth. He associated with some of the most distinguished men of modern Italy, and became the author of some productions which rendered him an idol to many in that land. In the house of Count Porro of Milan, where the youth resided, he became acquainted with some of the most eminent men of his age.

Brougham, Hobhouse, Byron, Madame de Stael, Von Schlegel, and others were of the number,—and it was by associating with such personages that his love of country was developed and matured.

But Pellico could not look on the degradation of his country and the bondage of his countrymen without an effort to break their chains. He attempted it; but only to rivet chains upon himself. By his publications he strove to rouse and combine the Italians; and about the year 1820 became a member of a revolutionary society, from which date his manifold sorrows began. He conspired to improve the political condition of his country, when he saw it trodden down by an oppressive power,—and while we may not approve of the measures thus employed, we can at least explain how natural they were in a mind so devoted as Silvio Pellico to his native land, while it groaned beneath a yoke which patriotism could not brook.

On the 15th of October 1820 he was arrested for political offences, and confined in the cells of Santa Margherita at Milan. There his woes commenced. "Dungeons here, dungeons there," he says, dungeons to the right, and dungeons to the left, above, below, and opposite, everywhere met his eye. Moreover, the scaffold appeared in the gloomy distance, and, in the course of a few hours, he sank from the brightness of hope to the darkness of a solitary, uncheered cell. The remembrance of father, mother, brothers, and sisters, whom he loved with the vehemence of Italian passion, deepened the grief of the prisoner, and at the thought of them "he wept like a child." He knew, however, the real fountain of solace, and it is a touching record to hear him say that in his deep distress on account of those whom he loved, he hoped they would be consoled by Him who enabled a mother to follow her son to the Mount of Golgotha,—Him, the Friend of the unhappy, the Friend of man. It was then, he says, that the *power* of religion was first felt in the heart; and that, amid many changes, all of them saddening, bore him up with more than human strength.　He was permitted to retain his Bible in the house of his bondage, and it appears to have done its work in a soul which could not have rested satisfied with less than eternal truth.

Pellico was examined again and again at Milan, and again and again he needed all the fortitude which patriotism and the truth can supply.　He had written a note in his blood, for he had no other ink, to one of his fellow prisoners.　It was a mere salutation, but it was produced as an evidence of crime; and that is an early specimen of his galling treatment.　On other occasions, some of his judges treated him with ungenerous or malignant irony; but what could he expect when Count Porro himself—a devotee to all that was truly Italian—was obliged to flee, and was in absence twice condemned to death !

It is sickening to have to trace our accomplished sufferer from prison to prison, and from cell to cell.　Stronghold after stronghold became his abode; and yet, for the most part, he evinced a beautiful and consistent resignation.　From the first he felt assured that Austria would make some fearful examples among Pellico's friends, and that he himself must either die beneath her vengeance, or be subject to a long imprisonment.　His parting with his father, who visited him in prison after his seizure, was agony to his affectionate soul; but still the love of country was ascendant there, and though at times he could not enjoy even the sad relief of a tear, he bore up—the thought of Italy free was new life to the prisoner—and he prepared to face death on the scaffold, or any form of martyrdom, "with a blessing on his lips," even for those who sent him thither.　He strove to familiarize his mind with separation from those whom he loved— with the approach of the executioner, and all the dread insignia of a public death—meant to be one of shame—and by all this, to accustom his nerves to bear the sudden or fearful shocks which he foresaw before him. To crown his efforts, he from time to time quoted the model of Him who was "nobly pacific, both with regard to Himself and others, and whom we are all bound to imitate." In truth, the story of this man's prison woes, of his anguish, and yet of his strong consolations, constitutes one of the most remarkable narratives of our times. The blending of celestial truth with earthly woes is beautiful.

In the month of February 1821, Pellico was transferred from Milan to the prisons of Venice; and there new forms of trial awaited him. "The Leads," a portion of the prison attached to the palace of the Doge, in that city, became his dreary abode; and though he was able to mitigate the horrors of the place, as perhaps the gay and elastic mind of an Italian alone could do, it was still one of uttermost misery. Stifling heat, swarms of insects, disease, and annoyances which strained his endurance to the full, there rewarded his love for Italy. He had now, moreover, to confront the terrors of a state trial, where, for successive hours, and from day to day, he was harassed and excited far beyond mortal patience. The dread of undesignedly implicating others, or of being compromised by them; the conduct of one of his judges; and, in truth, his whole position, drove him to the verge of madness. He ingenuously says that he would have taken his own life, had not the voice of religion and the thought of his parents held back his hands. For a time he had neglected his Bible, amid the agitating scenes of his lot; but he resumed it now —he wiped away the dust—he read what the Saviour says about the offences which must come, and Pellico was soothed once more by the truth. "I placed the Bible upon a chair," he records, "and falling upon my knees, I burst into tears of remorse—I, who ever found it so difficult to shed even a tear. . . . . I rose with renewed confidence that God had not abandoned me. . . . . It was then that my misfortunes—the horror of my continued examinations, and the probable death which awaited me—appeared of little account . . . . ." And that is the secret of the power which nerved him to greatness, and fitted him to endure.

These ordeals were renewed every two or three days, by the Special Commission which tried Pellico at Venice. He bore up as best he could, and "left the rest to the will of God." But the stifling air of the place in which he was entombed depressed him to the verge of insanity, till at last he was tempted once more to think of self-destruction. It is one of the most melancholy records of human woe. A mind of a high order, and of exquisite culture, actuated by profound emotions and lofty principle, was goaded, chafed, harassed, till reason trembled on its throne. Besides his Bible, however, Pellico had other sources of solace. In one of his prisons, where he was allowed the use of paper and ink, he composed some of his works, all thoroughly Italian in their cast of thought, and pleasing rather than powerful in their tone. He also sketched several tragedies, and other productions, among which was a poem on the Lombard League, and another on Christopher Columbus. Standing, as he felt he stood, on the verge of death, with a fatal decree ready to sweep him into the grave, he had self-possession enough to persist in his studies—it was his antidote to madness : and amid employments such as these he could exclaim, "O blessed solitude! how much holier and better art thou than harsh and undignified association with the living!" In "The Leads" he had mitigated the monotony of his cell by feeding, and all but domesticating, some ants and a spider ; and when he was abruptly summoned to leave that abode, he felt his separation from these creatures of his care almost like a grief. A visit to these "Leads" has become a pilgrimage in our day.

In his new cell, this lonely, persecuted man had opportunities of once more holding communion with his fellow-men—at least, he could behold their countenances. Such, however, were the restrictions upon all personal intercourse that one of his keepers, who somewhat leniently indulged him, was bastinadoed for the crime; and his screams agonized Pellico more than his own personal endurance. At length his accumulated trials drove him to actual delirium. Phantoms haunted him. Sleep forsook him—he lost his reason, and in utter unconsciousness attempted self-destruction. In this horrible condition, he was only so lucid as to repeat the words, "My God, my God, why hast thou forsaken me?" and though such an application of the cry may startle us, that sentiment alone could fathom the depths of this agonized sufferer's woes. In his frenzy, he at other times challenged the justice of providence; and though he dismissed such thoughts as insane, and deplored them as a sin, they prove to the letter how surely oppression drives a wise man mad. In the whole range of human sufferings, few more affecting than those of Silvio Pellico at this juncture are on record. It was a crisis under which flesh and blood must have sunk.

Nor was he soothed when he learned that one of his companion patriots had been made to pass "the Bridge of Sighs," at Venice—the prelude to his death. Sentence had been pronounced on him and some others, so that the cause of Italian patriotism seemed likely to be quenched in the blood of the sons of Italy. The sentences of some who were condemned to die were commuted into long imprisonment; but even that was like a death-blow to their cause, as it added new miseries to former woe.

Amid these disasters the mind of Pellico, goaded first to unnatural effort, and then sinking into weakness, was agi-

tated beyond what calmer minds can comprehend. Again
and again did the thought of avoiding the scaffold by
suicide occur to him, but again and again did he spurn
it away as a base temptation; and his governing consideration, while death seemed near, was "how to die like
a Christian." Even when all hope of escaping the scaffold
had faded from his mind, he resolutely determined to "bear
his sentence with calm dignity, and to bless the name of
the Lord." He felt that the question of his country's freedom was only one of time. Though many dreary years of
bondage under a foreign yoke might be before it, the onward movement of providence, whose wheels are never
reversed, was sure to bring about the set time; and even
death upon the scaffold, for such a man as Pellico, would
only hasten the emancipation.

But his time had not yet arrived; and on the 11th of
February 1822, he was removed from the prison of Venice
to that of the island San Michele, in the immediate vicinity.
He had already been hurled from the summit of high hopes
into a deep abyss of wretchedness; but there was a lower
deep before him, as he was dragged from dungeon to dungeon, with death or chains apparently at hand. Scarcely
had he reached his new dungeon, when he received an
accession to his sorrow by hearing of the death of one of his
compatriots, who had sunk into the grave amid the agonies
of his imprisonment. On the 21st of February Pellico's own
doom was decided: the Special Commission found him
guilty. He was condemned to death, but the Emperor had
commuted the sentence into fifteen years of hard imprisonment in the fortress of Spielberg. * "The will of God be

---

* *Hard* imprisonment is a technical phrase. The *Carcere duro* implied that
the person condemned to it should have his legs ironed; be fed daily with warm
food, but no meat; his bed was bare boards; and he was forbidden to converse
with any but the officials. Such was the Austrian award to Italian patriotism—
the Austrian attempt to quench it.

done," was Pellico's reply when the inquisitor had finished his sentence. Some of the judges seemed compassionate, but one among them treated his victim with an insolence which stung and unmanned the sufferer. A tide of violent passion swept through his soul; and they who know the Italian temperament will understand what that implies. His head burned; his heart bled; he felt that political enmities had given additional severity to his sentence, and he was for a while like a deserted vessel drifting before the tempest, knowing of no harbour, and scarcely cherishing any hope.

But the trials which assailed Pellico at this stage were not nearly exhausted. It was part of his sentence that he should hear it upon the scaffold where he was to have died but for the clemency of the Emperor. That formality could not be dispensed with; and he was rowed back from San Michele to Venice, there in public, and surrounded by armed soldiers, and cannons ready to be discharged in the event of commotion, to hear the sentence read. Handcuffed like the vilest criminal, he and a companion passed through that ordeal of shame. As the words, " condemned to death," were pronounced, a general murmur of compassion ran through the crowd ; and a fresh murmur arose when the commutation into fifteen years of imprisonment was proclaimed. Have the bloody fields of Magenta and Solferino any connection with these and similar scenes? Who bears their shame—Austria, or the memory of Pellico? the most tyrannical of all the modern governments, or its victim so ruthlessly oppressed? Yet he clung to his country the more for its deep degradation. It haunted him by night and by day, and he was nerved calmly but resolutely to brave the utmost that despotism could do on that country's behalf. He spoke no word of reproach—he stifled his emotions, and tried to leave his cause before the Eternal.

In terms of his sentence, Pellico was now removed to Spielberg, near Brunn, the capital of Moravia, and not far from the field of Austerlitz. His journey thither was one of much bodily suffering, from his chains and disease; but an ovation as far as men durst manifest their feelings. Arrived at his destination, a gloomy and partially ruined castle, he and a companion in tribulation were confined in two dismal subterranean dungeons—he says, "entombed alive." He had travelled, we have just seen, in chains from Venice to Spielberg; and prison chains were now fastened on his limbs, and riveted on an anvil by a blacksmith retained for the purpose. In discharging that odious duty, the man dropped some words of commiseration in German, and when he discovered that the prisoner understood him, the smith stood aghast, lest he had been detected in showing sympathy. The jailer was sworn to treat all prisoners with equal severity. "I am bound," he said, "to treat all the prisoners alike . . . . . . no indulgence; no permission to relent, to soften the sternest orders, in particular as regards prisoners of state." And such was the new abode into which an odious system thrust this Italian.

Here, then, is the devotee of liberty imprisoned amid Austrian rigours, and in the hands of men sworn to be sternly severe. For fifteen years he was doomed to that treatment. Not even a straw bed could be conceded, until the doctor ordered it in the event of disease. The officials were "hard as steel" in the discharge of duty; and if we except the dungeons of the Inquisition, and the atrocities which were perpetrated there, no more signal display of cruelty could be made than in the case of this Austrian state prisoner. On his first night at Spielberg, he threw himself on his board-bed "less at enmity with mankind, and less alienated from God," than he had been during the chafings of his trial. But the reign of terror had begun, and Pellico, perhaps its noblest victim, was paying the penalty exacted by oppression. Down to the minutest arrangement, even to the changing of his linen and the colour of his dress, the oppressor's hand was on him; he had literally to work out freedom in sackcloth and chains.

Added to this sufferer's other sorrows was the pain of hunger. He could not swallow the prison fare, though he persisted long in the attempt; and was at times fain to partake of bread smuggled into his den by some official who felt touched by his woes, or who braved detection for proving that he was a man, and could feel. Disease at length began violently to prey upon the prisoner; but doctor after doctor was summoned to see him ere any real relief could be granted. So far had Pellico at one period sunk, that the last rites of the Church to which he belonged were administered to him as to a dying man. He recovered, however; but even the tender mercies of that prison were cruel. When allowed to walk out on a part of the castle to ward off death, he was guarded by two men with loaded muskets; and at a subsequent period, when his walk had drawn the eyes of some upon him, or procured some kindly greetings, it was hidden by palisades, so that no eye but that of his guards could see him; in short, cruelty was ingenious in torturing, or in reducing its victim to the minimum upon which a mortal could live without being driven to derangement or a voluntary death. When he begged that his chain might be removed from his legs, were it only for a day or two, that he might get some sleep during a fever which had seized him, the physician informed him "that the fever was not yet so bad as to require it." In other words, torture was administered according to the beatings of the pulse. It was something just short of murder, under the guise of a physician's prescription.

But there were refinements even upon this kind of cruelty,

for an attempt was made to bind him not to speak in prison.
It originated in the conversation which some of the patients
from Italy were enabled to hold with each other through
the walls or the grating of adjoining cells. Pellico was thus
to have been reduced to the level of the inarticulate beasts;
but he resented the attempt, and refused to be gagged by
anything but actual force. When he could catch a glimpse
of them, he enjoyed, with a poet's fervour, the brightness of
the sky, and the beauty of the earth. The voices of the city,
the very gambols of dumb animals—in short, all lovely
things were a joy, and amid his delight, he loved to speak
of them; it broke the dreary monotony of his cell. To be
silent, therefore, was a bondage to which he could not submit without ceasing to be a man; and the very proposal to
silence him seems the quintessence of cruelty.

The prison fare, we have seen, was disgusting, and when
Pellico, amid his sufferings, attempted to eat it, he swooned
under the effort. It was even supposed that he was dead;
and when he revived, his fetters were at length ordered to
be removed. An appeal was made to Vienna on his behalf;
but instead of being permitted to be placed in the infirmary,
he was ordered to be treated in his dungeon. There he became delirious again, and passed through a crisis which
seemed not unlikely to close his earthly career. As some
relief, he was now permitted to enjoy the society of a fellow-
prisoner, Maroncelli, in the same cell; but joyous as that
relaxation of rigour was at first, it added in the end to the
grief of Pellico. His friend grew ill. A scorbutic affection
seized upon both, and the limb of Maroncelli, after occasion-
ing much agony, had to be amputated. It was horror added
to horror; and if aught could have quenched the ardour of
Italian patriotism, such desolating woes might surely have
succeeded.

Application was next made by these two friends for the

use of pen and ink, and for permission to purchase books; but both requests were denied. Yet an antidote was found of which no tyranny could deprive them, except by driving them to madness. Pellico was enabled to compose extensive works, to retain them in his memory, and to correct and polish them there, insomuch that a whole tragedy was wrought off by that process. Maroncelli cultivated the same art, and was able to retain by heart many thousands of verses which he had composed. Rarely, we think, has such an asylum from oppression been found.*

The rigours of Spielbeig increased from year to year, and a dull monotony of woe had now become the lot of Pellico. The years 1824, 1825, 1826, and 1827, were thus endured, rather than lived; and during all that time he was forbidden the use of books. The prison, he says, was one vast tomb, without the peace and unconsciousness of death. He now learned to envy the happiness of some of the earlier periods of his bondage, and his dreary heart ached at the mental vassalage to which he was reduced. The Emperor sent him, indeed, some books on Ascetics—a most appropriate gift— and even such productions were the occasion of a merciful diversity amid the dulness of the dungeon. He resigned himself to the will of God, who hears the groaning of the prisoner; and instead of having his susceptibilities dulled by endurance—as would have been the case in less elastic spirits—Pellico's feelings grew more sensitive and acute. Morning, noon, and night, search was made through every corner of his dungeon; the links of his chain were tested, lest any attempt should be made to sever them, and a bondage, as petty and irksome as it was heavy and grind-ing, was from day to day and year to year inflicted. The

* At one period of his imprisonment, Pellico scratched his compositions upon his table, and after committing them to memory, erased them with fragments of glass.

very favours from the Emperor, announced with pretentious pomp, were a mockery. "I am commanded by his majesty," it was once said, "to communicate to you good tidings of your relations at Turin." The prisoner rejoiced, and begged for some details as to those whom he loved so well, for he knew not who were dead and who were alive; but the answer was, "I can show you nothing. You must be satisfied. It is a mark of the Emperor's clemency to let you know even so much. The same favour is not shown to every one." There also lacerated affection had to succumb to power.

Amid these rigours, and this mockery, friend after friend died at Spielberg, and the living envied the dead. The years 1828 and 1829 passed away like their predecessors, and it was now nearly nine years since Pellico was first imprisoned. Through a private channel he had learned that the Emperor would probably count the days of bondage by twelve hours instead of twenty-four, so that by a fiction of imperial clemency, fifteen years would be only seven and a half. But that period had past, and hope deferred was producing its usual effects—sickness and sinking of heart. At length, however, on the 1st of August 1830, and ten years after his seizure, it was announced to Pellico that he was free. "I have the pleasure," were the words employed, "the honour, I mean, of acquainting you that his majesty the Emperor has granted you a further favour. . . . . It is liberty." There were three included in the mercy, and no attempt need be made to tell their emotions. They were mute at first. The clemency was just not too late in reaching them; but their escape into the free air of heaven reinvigorated the bodily frame, restored their hope, and sent the man who had grown haggard and wan amid suffering back to some measure of joy. Some vexatious delays and hours of anxiety were still before Pellico, but they passed away. Italy was entered—Turin was reached—his parents were found alive, and he was restored to their affections like one who had long been dead. It was on the 17th day of September 1830. His own conclusion of the whole matter was, that "God renders all men, and all things, however opposite to the intentions of the agents, the wonderful instruments which he directs to the greatest and best of purposes." The words are prophetic, and the prophecy will be fulfilled: is it not in course of being so?

Such is a meagre abstract—scarcely even an index—of the sufferings of Silvio Pellico. As one who loved his country with a full heart, and grieved to see her trodden down by what he deemed a grinding oppression, he came into collision with one of the best organized despotisms of all time—one of the mightiest systems of repression which the world ever saw. But even that could not daunt his resolute mind, nor bend his will before the oppressor. Amid all that he endured, Pellico never uttered one word of regret that he had given himself to his country and its freedom. To the last, he endured with feelings of love as intense as ever actuated mortal man, and amid agonies which few ever passed through with their life. But though he was thus resolute and unswerving, his patriotism was calm and self-possessed; and of all the examples of energetic decision which the records of the past supply, few present a more extraordinary combination of moral forces than that of Silvio Pellico. He was impulsive, yet calm; he was passionate, yet self-contained; he was ardent, yet cautious; and looking at the powers of mind which underlie his whole history, we need not wonder either that he came into violent collision with a system which would hinder the onward march of man, or that he greatly, manfully, and for long endured, rather than succumb to what is, politically, self-destructive, and morally, a lie. No wonder, then, that the touching story of his "Prisons" has charmed the men of many lands. Of that

work there have been five translations into German, three
into Spanish, fourteen into French, and one into English.
It has thus helped to feed the flickering flame of patriotism,
always threatened but never extinguished, among the peoples; and here, as in a thousand other cases, sufferings and
agonies which even Pellico's words could not fully tell, have
promoted the object for which he lived, more, perhaps, than
the success of all his plans could have done. The cause for
which he died many deaths may be retarded in its triumph
—it can never be lost.

And no one can trace the history of his sufferings without
observing the important place which religion held in guiding and sustaining him.   From the period of his entering
prison to the close of his troubles, it was a power in his soul
presiding over all the rest. At times, indeed, the truth
which he held suffered an eclipse ; and his mind then sank
into weakness, or became the prey of passions which seemed
to constitute strength, but which were, in reality, exhaustion.
As soon, however, as the light which shines from heaven
illumined his soul again, he was himself and more—a match
for the griefs by which brute oppression strove to crush the
aspirations of a generous and most loving soul. If Italy
have many sons like-minded with Silvio Pellico, she will
yet be free ; free not merely from the oppressor's heel, but
better and higher far, from that mental bondage which has
for centuries wasted her noble people, and turned one of the
loveliest portions of the earth into a dreary desert by darkness and misrule.

Pellico lived four and twenty years after he was set at
liberty, and spent his time at Turin in literary pursuits. He
published some of the works which he had composed or
sketched in prison, and acted as librarian to the Marchesa
Barolo, at whose villa of Moncaglieri he died on the first of
January 1854.

CHAPTER V.

Men of Science and the Arts.

"..... And Science, eagle-eyed,
Soars on the lightning; dives into the deep;
Gages a dew-drop, or surveys a world;
Mounts Alpine summits, or an atom metes;
Thrids all the mazes mystic Nature hides, ...
Then points her sister, Art, to forms divine."

ALL forms of beauty exist at first in the divine mind. That is their architype. The majestic glory of the heavens, so full of grand repose like that of Godhead, especially when they are seen at midnight, is only a faint and shaded gleam of that glory which encircles the Eternal. The harmony which reigns among the heavenly bodies, "for ever singing as they shine," is only one portion of the anthem which all creation utters to the glory of the everlasting One.

Or, turning to other forms of beauty, when we stand face to face with the Venus at Florence, or the Apollo at Rome, we are awed by the wondrous display of gentle, timid loveliness in the one case, of imperial majesty in the other; and though we do not know that the trial was ever made, those forms of beauty would probably strike even a savage, at least with mute admiration.

Yet what are these but sparks, emanations, flashes from the Great Centre of all that is lovely—the mind of the Supreme? When this is overlooked, we lose far more than half the blessedness which might flow from the contemplation of the beautiful. "But my Father made them all," is a profound and gladdening sentiment; and if he *be* our Father (not merely our Judge), such beauteous objects become new bonds between the soul and Him who is "altogether lovely."

And the same holds true in science. What is the most wonderful discovery of Newton but a minute and microscopic fragment of the knowledge of the Everlasting? What were all the demonstrations of La Place, but hints to us concerning the wisdom of Him with whose power and presence the proud astronomer thought he could dispense, or whose works he supposed he could improve?

Or, to contemplate the matter in still another light, what are the inventions of Watt, with all the train of changes to which they have led throughout the world, but so many revelations of the powers which the eternal Mind has lodged in the work of His hands—hidden, no doubt, from the eyes of man, but waiting to reward his painstaking, and prove, as proofs are needed, how exhaustless are the works of God?

Or, further still, the philanthropy of this age is one of its glories. Men have plunged into the jungle, or climbed the Himalayas, of India, to learn what might be profitable to others. They have made the degraded children of Ham the objects of their care, and explored their rivers, or braved their terrors, or fathomed and mapped down their lakes —all with the purpose of bringing the savage within the pale of civilization and of truth. Or men have dived into dungeons, and been immured in Lazarettoes, or submitted to the scorn of unfeeling oppressors—all that the wretched might become more happy, the degraded be elevated, and the wandering reclaimed. Or missionaries have gone to far distant lands to spread the knowledge of a Redeemer. They have taken their lives in their hands, and hastened away to the ice of Labrador and Greenland, or the broiling suns of

India; they have made their home in the Red Indian's wigwam, or they have first tamed, and then Christianized, they have tamed by Christianizing, the man-eater, after he had banqueted on some of his very benefactors—and yet what was this, what were these but mere beams from Him who is the origin of all good, Himself God only good, God only wise?

Now, the following sketches will describe some of those who embodied in their life such gleams, such sparks, or such emanations from the Chief Good. They might or they might not recognise Him as the origin of all that they were, or did—but if He was overlooked by them, the wiser are we if we learn to trace all up to His open hand—to Him whose creative power is repeated every instant in prolonging the existence of all that He has made, and whose goodness finds an outlet in ten thousand times ten thousand channels, unnoticed, or often disowned by the children of men.

Let us see, then, how some of these instruments for diffusing the divine wisdom and goodness and power among their fellow men have succeeded in the enterprise, where consciously, or unconsciously they bore a commission from the King Eternal. When weakness is linked to the Almighty One, or when the wandering secure the guidance of Omniscience, what may they not accomplish, how far not climb, how much not enjoy? Nay, even though the Highest may lead them blindfold while they are working out his purposes, something *will* flash through to show that the Supreme Wisdom has been guiding; and that conviction may be deepened as we ponder the sections which follow.

I.—JOHANN GUTENBERG.

1397-1468.

" Those mighty masters of the earlier art,
 Those matchless wizards of the elder day,
From earthly things, and earthly thoughts apart,
 What grandeur their devisings all display !

Lofty conceptions their grand souls pervade,
 And take immortal shapes at their command,
With reverential feeling, moved and swayed,
 And silently inspire the cunning of their hand."

J. C. PRINCE.

Inventions and disputes—The art of printing—Chinese printing—Blocks
Stamps and seals—Moveable types—Gutenberg, Fust, and Shœffer — Their
respective shares in the invention—Gutenberg's troubles—Lawsuits—Charges
against him—Partnerships—·Vexations—His work—And death—His statue at
Mayence—Other printers—William Ged, the inventor of stereotyping—The
price of books.

WHO invented the Mariner's Compass ? The Chinese ?
or Marco Polo ? or Flavio Gioja ?

Who discovered the art of making gunpowder ?
The Chinese again ? or Friar Bacon ? or Michael Schwartz
of Goslar ?

Who invented the telescope ? Was it Baptista Porta ? or
Fracostaro ? or Roger Bacon ? or Jansen ? or Galileo ? or
who ?

Who founded the Infant School system ? Was it Pastor
Oberlin, in the Ban de la Roche ? or Wilderspin ? or some
other claimant ?

Who first discovered the virtues of Vaccination ? The
Arabians ? Fewster of Thornbury ? Jenner ? or some twenty
other claimants ?

Who first opened a Sabbath school? Was it Raikes? or did he only adopt and mature what had before been practised by many other friends of the young?

Whether was the Davy or the Geordy Safety-lamp first invented?

Whether was Arkwright or Wyatt the first who employed rollers in machinery for spinning?

Who was the first to decompose water into its two component parts? Watt, or Cavendish?

Who first detected the place of the new planet Neptune? Adams, or Le Verrier?

Who first decyphered the arrow-headed characters of Eastern inscriptions, and furnished a key to explain the excavations of Nineveh? Was it Rawlinson, or some other investigator of Oriental antiquities?

—Such are some of the questions suggested by a survey of the progress of discovery. Nearly every important invention has given rise to a keen controversy, and rival claims; it seems well-nigh an established law in all such cases that no progress can be made, none of the fruits of genius reaped, without contest and collision. It is part of the price which is paid for fame.

The greatest of all arts, the art of printing, is no exception to the remark. Nay here, if ever, disputes are eager and endless. Claimant after claimant has been named in the contest upon this subject, till no fewer than eight cities,—Mayence, Strasbourg, Haarlem, Venice, Rome, Florence, Basle, and Augsburg,—compete for the honour of the invention. Printing of a certain kind was known in China in the middle of the tenth century, and it is said to have been invented there by Foong-Taon, a minister of state. Even in times far more remote, for example in the palmy days of Babylon, traces are found of a mode of stamping impressible matter; and the seals and signet-rings, so often mentioned in the oldest records of man, are in principle just a mode of printing. In manufactures also, for instance, in the Low Countries there was a kind of stamping employed which might sometimes suggest to the weary copyists of ancient books a more expeditious mode of producing copies, and there are some evidences that it was so. But not till the first half of the fifteenth century, did the art of printing assume such a form as could give promise of what it has achieved. The chief claimants for the honour of the invention are, John Gutenberg, a man who ranked by birth among nobles, a native of Mayence, though often called of Strasbourg, owing to a long residence there; John Fust, of the same city as Gutenberg; Peter Shœffer, a scribe or copyist of Gersheim; and Laurence Coster of Haarlem. But the claims of Coster are so poorly supported that he may now be dropped from the list of competitors; we need attend only to the three first in tracing the origin or allotting the honour of the invention. It is well that we can assign his due share to each with tolerable exactness, but we confine attention chiefly to Gutenberg, for he was, beyond a question, the first of the three engaged in printing as the art is now practised; he alone had to encounter the main difficulties, delays, losses, and trials of an inventor.

JOHANN GUTENBERG, or GUTTENBERG, whose real name was Gensfleisch, was born at Sorgenloch near Mentz, in the year 1397, but not much is recorded regarding his early discipline. It was between the year 1436 and 1442, that he began to print; and there seems no reason to doubt that he was the first to use moveable types. Till his time, any printing that deserved the name was done with blocks, on which the contents of a page or some considerable space were engraved. The whole page was thus at once placed upon the paper, the letters on the block being, of course, cut reversed. But this was obviously a clumsy mode of proceeding; for example, only one side of a leaf was printed upon, and two leaves were then pasted together to form continuous reading. As far as can be ascertained, however, Gutenberg was the first to break up the blocks into separate letters, and print by moveable types in the manner still common in the art. This appears to be his pre-eminent merit.

At first, the types were of wood, being in effect just the wooden page-block cut into its minute parts, and for many years Gutenberg appears to have employed such types in his office at Strasbourg. All was then kept secret, as far as possible; and evidence led in one of his lawsuits indicates, in the case of witness after witness, how nervously anxious the inventor was that no one should see his types set up, so as to learn his plans : message after message, or order after order was given to prevent what would obviously have been regarded as a misfortune. But the same evidence completely proves that the types were *moveable.* In consequence of this secresy, the printer had to construct his own press, to cut his own types, and manufacture his own ink. In truth, the spirit of a martyr or a devotee was needed by the man who had often to write or translate the work he was to print, to compose his own types, and to act as his own pressman and corrector of the press. He required not less to be binder, editor, bookseller and publisher; and the man who could combine the functions of all these, even though not an inventor, was no ordinary mortal—he had to accomplish with his own hands what is now the work of hundreds, in various departments. The chafing impediments occasioned by all this may easily be supposed.

While at Strasbourg, and practising his art as secretly as possible, Gutenberg was induced, by urgent solicitations, to make it known to some of his friends. A contract was entered into. Money was paid to the inventor for his secret; and the friends, for some time, prosecuted their work in common. One of them died, however, during the currency of the contract. His heirs claimed a continued share in Gutenberg's operation, and though the claims were rejected by the judges in the case, in the year 1438, the lawsuit was one trouble more to one who was already sufficiently harassed.

In these circumstances it is not wonderful that Gutenberg did not increase his wealth by the invention which he had struck out. On the contrary, though he had done more for man than Egypt with all its lore, or Greece with all its eloquence, or Rome with all its legions, in addition to all the toils and annoyances to which he had been already exposed, his means failed. After struggling for some years at Strasbourg to establish his new art, he was compelled to leave that city and return to Mayence. It was with him as it has been with a thousand other benefactors of the human race—if he would do good, or work out an idea which was to become a power as influential in the moral world as that of the sun itself in the material, it must be, as ever, amid trouble, and crosses, and grief. He may have received from posterity the honour which his own age denied him. In spite of the charges brought against him of having pilfered the secret from Laurence Coster, and all that could harass a generous mind charged with such a fraud, he may have taken at length his right position in the minds of men. But it still remains true that Gutenberg had to fight his way through crowding obstacles, and though possessed of a secret destined, when fully made known, to revolutionize the world, he had to live amid trials, as he died, "after a life of much suffering and hardship," "in great poverty," * in some degree a victim to the

* Authorities differ as to this.

world's progress. Few who have done so much for man as
he did are allowed to sun themselves in prosperity; yet
is there a measure of reward in the conviction embodied in
the words, "Upright, self-relying toil! Who that knows
thy solid worth, would be ashamed of thy hard hands, and
thy soiled vestments, and thy obscure tasks, thy humble
cottage, and hard couch, and homely fare? Save for thee
and thy lessons, man in society would everywhere sink into
a sad compound of the fiend and the wild beast, and this
fallen world be as certainly a moral as a natural wilderness."

Gutenberg returned to Mayence, then, about the year 1445,
others say about 1450. As he had expended nearly all his
property on the invention, and in pressing it into use, he
was forced or tempted to think of abandoning the work
as hopeless. Difficulties thickened around him, and as his
efforts could not be renewed without money, he saw his hopes
fast vanishing away. At this crisis, however, he formed an
alliance with John Fust, or Faust, a goldsmith in Mentz,
and a man of considerable wealth, who advanced the large
sum of 2020 florins to enable the resolute, but hitherto
unfortunate Gutenberg, to prosecute his labours. Fust
was to be taught the secrets of the art, and to advance
the necessary funds, in return for which he was to be admitted to share the profits. But about five years after
his return to Mayence, this engagement led to a lawsuit
and abundant trouble to the inventor. It appears that the
gains were not sufficiently prompt or golden for the money-
lender, and the case became vexatious. As the result,
Gutenberg's materials, constructed at no little cost, at once
of means, of labour, and invention, fell into the hands of
Fust. This would seem to be proved by the fact that the
initials of Gutenberg and his partners, attached to works
known to have been printed prior to the lawsuit, continued
to be used by Fust and Shœffer after it. This mortifying

result, no doubt, galled the ardent inventor. Perhaps his own impetuosity helped to augment his troubles ; but, whatever was the cause, Gutenberg was now too far advanced to retreat. Nay, he appears to have started again with fresh vigour after all his crosses, not the least of which was the exclusion of his name from one of the works printed with his types, a Psalter dated 1457. He printed an edition of the Bible in 1450–5, which is described as a "superb book."

Previous to his engagement with Fust, the types used by Gutenberg had been made of wood. Now, however, these were superseded by metallic types. The letters of the alphabet were cast in copper or tin, and such is believed to have been Fust's contribution to the art. But even after the original inventor had been thus aided, the difficulties of the invention were by no means surmounted. Nay, debts to the amount of 4000 florins, equal, perhaps, to 60,000 in our day, were contracted before the new printers had proceeded far with the Bible which they had at press. This magnificent art, the patron of all others, had thus to fight its way amid impediments innumerable; and again and again it seemed on the verge of being crushed in the bud. Who would have ventured to predict that Gutenberg was working out an idea concerning a power capable of producing forty thousand copies of the *Times* in less than four hours, from one set of types, or of yielding, as "the annual returns of the publishing trade in all departments" about £5,000,000 sterling in Great Britain alone.

Once more, however, Gutenberg, and his partner Fust, were relieved by the co-operation of Shœffer, already mentioned, the son-in-law of Fust. He invented, or assisted in, a new mode of casting types in matrices, formed by a steel punch, which was the third stage in the discovery; and of which it has been said that the art was thus reduced to the condition in which it exists in our day. The details of these inventions were long kept a profound secret; indeed, an oath was administered to the workmen. The secret, however, was at last divulged; but to Shœffer the honour appears to belong of having invented the process of casting the types, instead of cutting each. The different shares of fame are to be allotted consequently somewhat as follows:—First, Gutenberg employed moveable types, but mainly or entirely in wood. Secondly, Fust introduced the use of metallic types, each letter being separately formed. And, thirdly, Shœffer added the plan of casting the types, instead of cutting each letter in detail.

But Gutenberg's trials were not yet surmounted. Even the metallic types were not sufficiently hard to withstand the power employed in pressing, and that also had to be remedied by the use of a hardening process. Then, as we have seen, he was involved in lawsuits of a vexatious nature in connection with his operations. As his private fortune, which was considerable, had been early swallowed up, he had become dependent on his more wealthy partner, Fust; and whether it was genius and enterprise smarting under such a state of matters, or the money-power asserting more than its rightful share of importance, it were difficult to decide, but new complications arose. New lawsuits were raised; and Gutenberg, the originator of the art, continued throughout his career beset with difficulties enough to repress any less ardent mind. He, however, was not to be daunted; though his work was a warfare, he faced it and triumphed. Again and again he had to recommence his enterprise, after being thwarted by causes which cannot now be explained. None of the books which he printed are now known for certain to exist, though some suppose that the *Biblia Sacra Latina*, without date, is the first product of the printing press, and appears to some to have been printed between 1450 and 1455, while Gutenberg and Fust were partners. Long before he ceased to be a practical printer, the art which he had invented had spread into many lands.

The partnership of the three ceased in the year 1458, and soon after that time the press had penetrated into many of the countries of Europe; for example, into Italy, in 1465; into France, in 1469; into England, in 1474; into Spain, in 1475; and in the year 1530, there were about two hundred printing presses in Europe. In 1465, Gutenberg entered the service of the Elector Adolphus of Nassau,—a fact which we cannot reconcile with the statement of those who tell that he died "in great poverty." It is certain, however, that after persevering for at least twenty years in maturing an art which has shed a light on mind similar to that of sunshine on the landscape, he did not find that it led to a recompense sufficient to smooth his way to the grave. Labour and sorrow were his lot; and he is to be ranked among the great benefactors of mankind who did good by self-sacrifice, who lived amid toil, and died, at last, in comparative neglect, after bestowing favours on our race, such as it never fell to the lot of any other mortal to bestow. His death took place at Mayence in the year 1468, and his epitaph could be read there so late as 1640, in the church of the Franciscans.

Posterity has tried to compensate for the neglect of contemporaries; and Gutenberg's memory is now deemed a household possession in Germany. A monument, executed by Thorwaldsen, was erected at Mayence in memory of the three—Gutenberg, Fust, and Shœffer. A Gutenberg society testifies men's tardy gratitude by an annual festival; and he who was left uncheered, or not seldom pressed by poverty, during his labours in perfecting the most noble invention of man, is at length recognised and lauded as

the benefactor of the globe. On the 14th day of August, in
the year 1837, fifteen thousand strangers resorted from
all countries to Mayence to inaugurate his statue, and do
honour to Gutenberg. It was uncovered amid the applause of myriads; and the monument reared by the subscriptions of many nations, now consummated by their
blended plaudits, told how much they revered the memory
of the great inventor. The processions—the imposing pomps
of Romanism — the great Bible of Gutenberg, Fust, and
Shœffer there exposed to view—the salutes of artillery—
the assembled representatives of the nations—the hymn
sung by a thousand voices—the orations, in short, the high
jubilee of those three days, proclaimed to the world, that
if honour was slowly paid to one who deserved it well, it
was paid with interest; and Gutenberg thenceforth became
a name of glory, as far as man could bestow it.

Most of the books which he is believed to have printed
were religious. It has already appeared that some of his
pecuniary difficulties were occasioned by efforts made in
printing the Bible; and Hallam did not assert too much,
when he said regarding the success of the partners in their
bold enterprise to print the whole Bible at first, and at
once, that "it was Minerva leaping on earth in her divine
strength, and radiant armour, ready at the moment of her
nativity to subdue and destroy her enemies." The other
products of that press and period are nearly all of a similar
class; and whether we attribute that to Gutenberg's own
predilection, or to the demands of the times, when men were
just awakening from a long religious stupor and darkness,
we are equally called to rejoice in that invention which now
enables us to produce, in this island alone, a complete copy
of the word of God, every five seconds in the working time
of a printer. It is wonderful in our eyes; and if Gutenberg
really loved the Bible, we can believe that all his toils

would have been cheerfully endured, and all his losses cheerfully borne could he have foreseen the measureless blessings he was bestowing upon millions of millions. But he had to work out his life-problem amid multiform trials. From the little we know of his domestic history, he appears to have been a liberal and generous man. He was surely a favoured one; and if he had to struggle and contend till his dying day, what is that but a repetition of the work done, or the woe endured by all the great since man's reason became distempered, and his affections estranged from the Chief Good?

Such, then, is another of those "starry lights" which help to irradiate the path of man. Ever since the decree went forth, that in the sweat of his brow they should wring their bread from the earth, we have seen the children of Adam walking in woe, till the mirth of the world has seemed to some like the laughter of the maniac. Yet amid the troubles which so often encompass the path of the gifted, we are not to forget their joys—the joy of triumph over difficulties— the consciousness that *at last*, if not *now*, others will see with their light. We know too little of the life of Gutenberg to be able to say how it was with him. But we do know that he persevered against a hundred obstacles; that he adds another to the list of decided and persistent heroes; and that the shout of many people, from many lands, at length and tardily called the inventor of printing to his lofty place among those whom the Supreme has made lights and blessings to mankind. In our poor world, the Great Giver dispenses his bounty by means of stewards of various degrees. Gutenberg was one of his high stewards; and in spite of the burden which he had to bear, he disbursed blessings in showers to the children of men. One of the orators of Mayence, on the day when the statue to the first printers was completed, summed up these blessings ; and we may let a German enthusiast speak the praises of his country's best benefactor, next to Martin Luther, for whom, as for thousands, Gutenberg opened the way. He says,* " If the mortal who invented that method of fixing the fugitive sounds of words which we call the alphabet, has operated on mankind like a divinity, so also has Gutenberg's genius brought together the once isolated inquirers, teachers, and learners, all the scattered and divided efforts for extending God's kingdom over the whole civilized earth, as though beneath one temple. Gutenberg's invention, not a lucky accident, but the golden fruit of a well-considered idea, an invention made with a perfect consciousness of its end, has, above all other causes, for more than four centuries, urged forward and established the dominion of science; and what is of the most importance, has immeasurably advanced the mental formation and education of the people. This invention—a true intellectual sun—has mounted above the horizon, first of the European Christians, and then of the people of other climes, and other faiths, to an ever-enduring morning. It has made the return of barbarism, the isolation of mankind, the reign of darkness, impossible for all future times. It has established a public opinion, a court of moral judicature common to all civilized nations, whatever natural divisions may separate them, as much as for the provinces of one and the same state. In a word, it has formed fellow-labourers at the never-resting loom of Christian European civilization in every quarter of the world, in almost every island of the ocean."

As trouble crowded upon trouble in the life of the first inventor of printing, some of those who advanced the art towards its present perfection have been similarly tried.

* See the passage in "The Old Printer and the Modern Press," by Charles Knight.

Printing from blocks was an early stage of that art; and stereotyping is, in one point of view, a recurrence to that method. According to this mode, the page is first set up with letters in the usual manner, and a cast is taken from the page when completed, and ready for the press. The invention of this process has given rise to discussions almost as eager as those which arose out of Gutenberg's, and at least four inventors are named in connection with this branch of the art. It appears, however, that William Ged, a goldsmith of Edinburgh, was the real inventor; and if so, his trials were scarcely fewer than those of his great predecessor. He suggested to a friend that it would be easy to print from plates cast from pages which were composed in moveable type, and soon produced a specimen to establish his opinion. Arrangements were entered into with a capitalist to obtain the necessary funds—it was Gutenberg and Fust repeated, and Ged's troubles soon began. As the man of money failed to fulfil his bargain, the inventor made a contract with a London stationer to embody his invention in books. Here again, however, he was long tried and thwarted, till a third arrangement became necessary. He next proposed to the English Universities and the royal printers, to stereotype Bibles and Prayer-books; and for a time this undertaking seemed, or at least promised, to prosper. Again, however, difficulties arose. In seeking to do good, Ged had to encounter ignorance and prejudice on the part of workmen, as well as hostility from interested parties. Plan after plan was adopted by him to bring his method into operation; but from the typefounder up to the printer, all was hostility, so that no progress was made. For four-and-twenty years he continued his attempts; that is, from the year 1725 to 1749, when he died in London of a broken heart, occasioned by the utter failure of his plans. His son attempted to retrieve the loss, but

met with equal disappointments. Those who at first rejected
the plans of Ged subsequently adopted them, and made
extensive use of his plates; but he himself died neglected
and poor, while preparing to add to the wealth of thousands. His chief memorials are two Prayer-books, printed
for the University of Cambridge, an edition of Sallust, and
the sad memory of his crösses and sorrows.*

Such then is too often the reward of genius. Many whom
the world has at last delighted to honour went to their
graves unheeded, nay, defrauded or oppressed. It is as if
the Author of every perfect gift would plant an antidote to
vain glory side by side with what He bestows. It is well
known that Sir Isaac Newton's own College at Cambridge,
was among the last to admit his discoveries into the goodly
fellowship of the recognised sciences — so keenly was he
opposed where he should have been most prized—and that
treatment of Newton embodies a general law of which this
seems the formula : *Benefit your fellow-men, and for a time
at least, expect their envy and their opposition.* It is thus
that God on high tests and burnishes that greatness which
is true.

But who shall tell the effects of Gutenberg's invention
upon the history of man? The result in one single department may serve as a specimen of the whole. Prior to
his time, the price of books was such that none but the
wealthiest ever saw them. At Oxford, for example, in the
year 1446, it was enacted that no student should occupy a

* Melchior de Stambam wished to establish a printing press at Augsburg,
and employed a year in making preparations for his office. He had five presses;
he cast pewter types; and after thus expending seven hundred and two florins
in preparation, he began working in 1473, but died before he had finished one
book, "heart-broken probably," says Mr. C. Knight, "at the amount of capital
he had sunk, for his unfinished book was sold off at a mere trifle, and his office
broken up." Again, "For some years after the invention of printing, many of
the ingenious, learned, and enterprising men who devoted themselves to the
new art which was to change the face of society, were ruined, because they could
not sell cheaply unless they printed a considerable number of a book, and there
were not readers enough to take off the stock which thus accumulated."

book for more than two hours, that others might not be defrauded. Money was often lent on the deposit of a book, as now upon estates. In 1299 the Bishop of Winchester borrowed a Bible from a convent, and gave a formal bond for its restoration. In 1471, Louis XI. of France borrowed the works of an Arabian physician, from the Faculty of Medicine at Paris, and both deposited a costly pledge, and gave a bond, with a second party as surety, for their safe return. Or, if we glance still farther back, other incidents prove both the scarcity and the value of MS. books. Plato paid about £375 for three small treatises by Philolaus, a Pythagorean. Aristotle purchased the books of Speusippus, which were few in number, for about £675. King Alfred, of England, gave to a bishop as the price of a book, as much land as eight ploughs could till. About the year 1274, a Bible sold for about £33, 6s. 8d., and that at a time when a labourer's wages were only three halfpence a day. Now such gleanings help us to judge of the importance of Guten-berg's invention,—its importance even in the high reckon-ing of eternity. Prior to his times, the way to the know-ledge of God's mind was costly, if not royal; and yet the man who introduced a new era in that respect, was har-assed and agitated till we lose sight of him in the dimness of obscurity! Such voices from the past surely reach us charged with deep significance, if we have ears to hear.

II.—MICHAEL ANGELO BUONAROTI.

1474-1563.

> ' Sovran of Art, imperial Angelo,
> Whose wizard chisel charmed the rock to life,
> And giant pencil bade the Sistine glow
> With frescoed marvels of the final strife
> Where doom awaits the wicked, by thy hand
> All loveliness with awful forms is blent,
> Till Greece's beauty lives in thy loved land,
> And Rome itself is but thy monument."
>
> ANON.

Man's normal condition—Michael Angelo—His birth and training—Leaves Florence—Bologna—Returns to Florence—His works—Rome—Examples of his decision—Trials—Leonardo da Vinci—Contests—Julius II.—Michael Angelo leaves Rome—His troubles—Works at Bologna—Is reconciled to the pope—Returns to Rome—Rivalry—Jealousies—Paints the Sistine chapel—Troubles there—Sent to Florence by Leo X.—Prosecution—Michael Angelo becomes military architect at Florence—A siege—He is obliged to abandon the city—Urged to return—Returns—The city taken—His danger—Fresh imbroglio—At Rome again—Becomes architect of St. Peter's—His conflicts—Griefs—Insults—Yet triumphs—St. Peter's completed—Old age—Death—Retrospect.

 FRENCH financier who had amassed a large fortune, by his labour and his energy, was congratulated, in his old age, on the stores he had heaped up, and might now calmly enjoy. "I would give the whole," he replied, "for the age of fifteen, and a five franc piece," and the saying teems with truth. Among other things, it impresses upon us the happiness which flows from energy, and enterprise, and pursuit. Not the supine indolence of an oriental, but manly persistence and vigorous effort from the normal condition of man, as long as he deserves the name.

And if ever any of the sons of men acted under that law, it was MICHAEL ANGELO BUONAROTI. He was born in the castle of Caprese, in Tuscany, on the 6th of March 1474, of a family which was both ancient and illustrious. His father, Ludivico di Leonardo Buonaroti Simone, was a descendant of a noble house, and allied to the imperial blood, while some of Michael's ancestors had held high office in his native country. Thus cradled amid the associations which generally influence, and not seldom inflate "old families," the boy was in danger of being lost to mankind, or doomed to some obscure dignity by parents who deemed labour a disgrace. He was placed at a grammar school in the neighbourhood of his father's residence, not far from Florence, but his progress there was not remarkable. As he was nursed by the wife of a mason, he had access as a child to chisels and mallets which, he often said in jest, had decided his taste and his lot in life. Every moment which he could snatch from his duties as a schoolboy was devoted to drawing and kindred employments; and hence his first trial arose. The senseless pride of his father was shocked at the thought that *his* son should be an artist; and he tried, not merely by persuasion, but by chastisement, to repress the ardour, or alter the bent of Michael's mind. The attempt was vain; there was something in the boy which propelled him towards the arts, in spite of family pride; the father at last gave his consent; the son became the pupil of the painter Ghirlandaio, and soon made it apparent that the master was only second in the studio.

From his earliest years this youth was bold, decided, and even impetuous. So rapid was his progress in his profession, that some of his earliest productions are said to have been such that even his maturest efforts scarcely surpassed them. He found a patron in Lorenzo dei Medici, who sought to foster the love of art in his country, and provided means and models of study for the most promising of the youth. Michael Angelo was one of the first whom he thus stimulated; nor was he unworthy of the favour, for so perfect were his copies of some of the works which he studied, that they were purchased as if they had been the originals.

We should not fail to notice the painstaking of this youth, from the very outset, in acquiring eminence in his profession. Though gifted above most, and propelled as an artist by strong native likings, he did not regard that as superseding the necessity of care and watchfulness. Even in his juvenile efforts, his studies were elaborate. Wherever he could, he went to nature as his school. For example, if he had to paint a fish, he resorted to the fish-market to study the form, the colours, the fins and the eyes; and so in other cases. This was applying to the true fountain head, and helped to make the young artist what he already was,—one of the chief agents in reviving, or rather in perfecting the fine arts about four centuries ago. There is no royal road to eminence in any department, more than in geometry. The path to greatness must be entered on with decision, and persisted in with energy, for life is like stemming a rapid river. If the swimmer, however strong, cease for an instant from his efforts, the current, that instant, sweeps him down.

Michael Angelo is on the way, then, to a place high up among his fellow-men. He has entered on a path where the creations of his mind, and the work of his hands are to be eulogized as superb, and grand, "without a rival in ancient and modern art." Indeed, what may we not expect from one who frequently rose in the middle of the night, to resume the labours of the day; and who often slept in his common dress, that the least possible loss of time might be caused by necessary rest? What, then, was to be the life-work of Michael Angelo? We have seen how resolute he was in entering upon it. Neither authority nor punishment could turn him aside. By a resistless impulse he made up his mind; and what is that impetuous youth to become? He is to pursue one of the grandest careers ever followed by a mortal. The direct pursuit of a man's eternal welfare *is* loftier than that of Michael Angelo, and such discoveries as those of Watt more directly affect the interests of society, the pursuits or the cares of every day. But next to these, we need not scruple to place the doings of a man who stood pre-eminent, many say first, as a painter, a sculptor, and an architect, while his poetry is ranked side by side with the best of its class. To trace the life-career of such a man must teem with lessons for the thoughtful.

Lorenzo dei Medici had obtained the consent of Michael's father to take him entirely under ducal protection. It had become apparent that aristocratic hostility and parental persecution were powerless when opposed to devoted attachment or the resistless impulse of genius ; and the youth appears to be already on the way to eminence. But Lorenzo died. His successor, Pietro, was as stolid as the patron of young Buonaroti was discriminating or munificent; and the youth forsook Florence first for Bologna, and then for Venice. At the former place he resided for about a year, but as his ardent aspirations were not responded to, he returned to Florence, and resumed his labours there. One of his sculptures of this period was so exquisite that, after undergoing such processes as deception knows how to employ, it was sold at Rome as an antique, though Buonaroti was no party to the imposition. He now, however, proceeded to Rome, still pressing upward with indomitable ardour ; and some of his works took a high place there among the productions of the age. One of them was ad-

mitted into the St. Peter's of that day, where the artist overheard a party of Lombards who were visiting the church,
assign his work to one of their countrymen as its author;
and that he might not be robbed of the coveted fame, he shut
himself up in the temple over night, and chiselled his name
upon the drapery of the group. This little incident is an
index to the man.

While thus working his way towards his lofty place
with brush and easel, with chisel and mallet, and firmly
planting all his steps, Buonaroti often evinced that energy
and decision akin to violence, for which he was signalized
through life. He had painted a picture, which still remains, for a certain Agosto Doni, and asked seventy ducats
for the work. Doni sent him forty. But Michael Angelo
returned them, and as the amateur had not accepted the
terms, one hundred ducats were now demanded, or else the
picture. Doni was scared, and sent the original seventy;
but as he had never yet closed with the artist's terms, he
now demanded either one hundred and forty or the picture.
The ducats were sent, and Buonaroti at once established his
own position as a man not to be trifled with, and rebuked
the chafering amateur.

Hitherto, however, Michael Angelo has been only commencing his life-task. He had difficulties to face when
selecting it. He had risks to run in pursuing it; but
the way had been considerably smoothed by those energies which enabled him, when apprenticed at the age of
fourteen, to receive remuneration for his work, instead of
paying for instructions. Still, however, he had difficulties
to encounter such as few have had to face. The gigantic
conceptions of his mind were mighty impediments to their
own fulfilment; for the state of art in his age rendered such
works as hè contemplated impossible to any but a man like
him. If his mighty conceptions were embodied, he would

distance all living competition; but how embody them?
The difficulties which he had to face would have proved insurmountable to inferior minds; but he faced them. He
triumphed; and the future of his life from our present stage
is little else than a series of heavy trials, and as signal successes; of crosses and thwartings; of mean stratagems, and
petty jealousies such as would have worn away any less
noble mind, but which he, by an energy which refused to
quail, transformed into foils to his own greatness.

One of the first contests which Michael Angelo had now
to wage was of a thoroughly testing character even to his
intrepid powers. He had to compete, on a certain occasion,
with Leonardo da Vinci, who was his senior by more than
twenty years, and one of the most remarkable men of that or
of any age. Mathematics, mechanics, hydrostatics, music,
poetry, and especially painting, had been cultivated by Da
Vinci to an extent which renders credible the traditions
regarding the fabulous accomplishments of the Admirable
Crichton. In optics, in general philosophy, as well as in some
of the lighter accomplishments, he was among the foremost
men of his era—the companion of princes, and one who actually died in the arms of a king! With that man, then,
Michael Angelo had to compete. The Council-hall at Florence
was to be painted by Da Vinci on one side, and by Buonaroti,
his rival, on the other. Each selected his own subject, and by
common consent the latter triumphed. His cartoon became
a study " for the whole world;" and amid all his efforts and
achievements, he never surpassed, some say never equalled,
the wondrous genius displayed in the painting of the battle
of Pisa. It was considered at the time the most exquisite
design that had ever been executed.

After this trial and triumph, Buonaroti was called to
Rome when Julius the Second became pope, about the year
1503. He was soon thereafter employed to execute a monu-

ment for that pontiff, and the conception of it was worthy of the genius of this great sculptor, as well as of the bold and martial pope. Had it been completed, with its colossal figures, its bronzes, its columns, and decorations, it would have been the most splendid monument of its class ever constructed by man. It never was completed, however, though it proved a source of disquietude and annoyance to its designer almost to the end of his days. To begin with, no existing church was large enough to receive it. A suggestion was made that a monument so princely deserved a chapel for itself. The pride of the pope, who was so eager to erect his own monument, caught at the proposal, and as the old church of St. Peter's could not contain the fabric, it was determined that a new St. Peter's should be erected on the same site; and the monument of Julius was designed to adorn the new structure. Hence, the present church of St. Peter's—one of the most stupendous fabrics that the art of man ever reared. Hence, more remotely, the Reformation; for hence, Indulgences to raise money; hence, outraged consciences, and outraged common sense: hence, agonies on the part of the Reformed, and cruelties on the part of Julius, or at least of his successors, which may well make the ears of them that hear them to tingle. In the providence of God, the most splendid edifice which Popery ever reared became the means of shaking the religion of the pope to its basis. Michael Angelo, it has been said, laid the foundation-stone of the Reformation.

Having received the pope's instructions, the artist began with characteristic ardour to work out his plans. He spent eight months at Carrara selecting marble. Some of the blocks were forwarded to Rome, and others to Florence, that when malaria prevailed in the former, he might retire to the latter, and proceed with his work without interruption. His figures, chiselled often under the eye of Julius

were admired by crowds; but envy as well as admiration
followed. On the one hand, the pope's favours conferred on
Michael Angelo offended many. On the other hand, his
own impetuous and impulsive temper rather increased than
smoothed away these difficulties; and this was the beginning
of sorrows. Some of the pope's dependants chose to put a
slight upon the sculptor in connection with funds for his work;
but as long as Michael Angelo believed that such things
were not the doings of Julius himself, he bore them without very much pain. At length, however, he broke up his
establishment at Rome, and retired to Florence: he would
not bear the insolence, accompanied as it was with the refusal of funds, while the envy of those who surrounded the
pope gave energy to one who was already sufficiently decided.

In those times of papal awe, when a pope was actually
God, this was a bold measure even in such a man. Five
couriers were in succession despatched to recall him; but he
refused for a time so much as to reply. At length, however,
he declared that as he had been repulsed with ignominy, he
had determined to retire from a service where such a thing
was possible. The pope next applied to the Florentine Republic, and sent a Brief to recall its great subject. Even that
Brief, however, did not move Buonaroti; and not till letter
after letter came, couched no more in the language of
friendly request, but of authoritative command, was he
moved by the applications. But when he did think seri-
ously of them, it was to determine to proceed to Constantinople to serve the Sultan, not to Rome to honour the
pope.

Such are the perils, and such the penalties of greatness.
Michael Angelo is now in collision with the most dreaded
power which then existed. If he would not be at once defrauded and insulted, he must resist the authority even of a

pope. He had subsequently to confess that he could find no rest but in solitary woods, away from the haunts of men; and the events which brought him to that state of mind have begun.

But by the interposition of friends this feud was healed. The pope and the sculptor met at Bologna, and were reconciled. While residing at that place, Michael Angelo executed a bronze statue of the pontiff holding, as Julius himself desired, a sword, and not a crook, as he knew more of the one than of the other. But as the Bolognese disliked the pope, they seized upon the statue as soon as they were at liberty, melted it, cast it as a cannon, named it Julia, and so annoyed both Buonaroti and the pope.

When the great sculptor returned to Rome, he was thwarted by the ealousy of another rival, Bramante, the architect, who persuaded Julius that it was ill-omened to prepare his own tomb, and so impeded Michael Angelo's operations. Moreover, the same jealousy contrived to induce the pope to employ the sculptor in painting the Sistine Chapel in fresco, and that in the hope that Buonaroti would fail in that department, so as to diminish his influence in others. He struggled hard to escape from such a task, and be allowed to continue his congenial work upon the monument of Julius. But the impatient pope had set his heart upon seeing his new Chapel painted. The monument can wait; the frescoes must be executed, and Buonaroti must submit with what grace he can. His demands for money had been troublesome; his manner was too unbending or decided to suit the liking of one who was surrounded by sycophants and adored as a God; but the weak must succumb to the strong.

When the work became inevitable, Michael Angelo was not the man to do it by halves. He gave himself to it with all his heart, and began by inventing a new mode of scaffolding.

He had, in truth, to learn the art of fresco-painting, where
the colours are laid upon damp plaster so as to penetrate the
substance, instead of merely decorating the surface, and he
encountered many difficulties in executing the task; but
they were surmounted by a strong will, and an indomitable genius.   The pope hovered constantly about him,
urging forward the work, impatient as a child for a new toy.
Even tho impetuosity with which Buonaroti wrought was
scarcely a match for the anxiety of a self-willed old man, as
resolute in his sphere as the painter was in his.   But when
the day of unveiling came, the artist's triumph was complete.   The mean jealousy of rivals had overshot their mark,
and he became as distinguished as a painter as he had formerly been first among sculptors.   In spite of some attempts to persuade the pope to set him aside, he was employed to complete the painting of the Chapel.   Indeed, so
impatient was Julius to see the work finished, that he once
threatened to throw the artist from the scaffold if it
were not speedily completed.   And yet it was never finished.
At the end of twenty months, the pope insisted on per-
forming high mass in the chapel.   The scaffolding was removed, and Buonaroti refused to resume his labours.

But only the half of his difficulties as an unwilling
painter in fresco has been named.   He had called in the
aid of some painters from Florence, but they could not embody his grand conceptions, and he undertook the work himself.   His first step was to destroy all that his assistants
had done, and his next was to lock himself up in the Chapel,
and proceed, as none but such a man could do, without asking help or tolerating trouble.   He had at this stage to be
his own master; but had not proceeded far with his first
compartment when he saw the whole defaced by the damp-
ness of the wall.   He was disconcerted at the discovery,
and hoped that the pope would now free him from his task-

work; but he must proceed. By a skill as great as his resolution was unmoveable, he triumphed over all his difficulties. Writhing in mental pain, under a complication of
adverse events, he yet rose buoyantly above them ; and the
appalling frescoes still remain as if embodying the struggles
of his own vast genius.

It is no part of our design to offer any opinion here regarding this stupendous production. Enough to say that
of part of it, at least, the opinion is on record that it is " the
finest group, ancient or modern, ever designed." But it is
not difficult to imagine the fever and the fret of that majestic mind as it struggled with difficulties, or warded off the
attacks of envy, while, at the same time, it was chafed by the
choleric importunity of a restless old man. Julius, indeed,
had a great favour for Michael Angelo, but he not seldom
treated his favourite with harshness, with insolence, and
caprice. Indeed, the artist was disgraced again and again.
He could ill brook the impatience which stung him so often ;
and as he sometimes resented the indignities which he received, he had to suffer for his independence. Not a single
case is known in which a genius so colossal was so habitually
fretted and annoyed by the importunities or the cross-pur-
poses of weakness.

The pope's death drew near. Michael Angelo was instructed to complete the tomb so often interrupted, but on a
diminished scale. He was again thwarted, however. Julius
died; Leo X. succeeded, and he requested the sculptor to
proceed to Florence to finish one of the churches there. The
will of a new pope was law, and once more Buonaroti was
separated from the great work on which his heart was set.
Even in tears, he proceeded to Carrara to procure marble for
his new task, and there again troubles and crosses befell.
Nay, during the entire reign of Leo X., or about eight years
and a half, this admirable man, whose genius was equal to

any result which Art could undertake, was employed upon
works which an ordinary mason could have performed
perhaps as well as he.   He had to superintend the process
of quarrying, and even to make roads to the quarries.   He
was frequently at war with the agents of the pope for
funds to carry on the work; and with one so gifted as
Michael Angelo, and at the same time so conscious of his
powers, it is marvellous that he bore with such galling or
such petty harassments. He was once much pressed by
Julius II. to undertake a work which he was determined
not to perform, and resolutely exclaimed, "No, never.
That is employment fit only for idle persons or women,"—
and he might often have used the same language when employed by Leo X.

Michael Angelo's troubles increased with his days, as in
the case of weaker men. The Duke of Urbino, nephew
to Julius II., was fretted by the delay in completing
his uncle's tomb, and called the great artist to account
for large sums of money alleged to have been advanced
to him.   It was afterwards made plain that the charge
was groundless; but the high-minded sculptor, who had
been oppressed by a pope, and unjustly pursued by a
duke, found no rest for his weary soul. The Duke of
Florence interfered, but only to retain Michael Angelo in
his own power for his own purposes; so that one of those
whom the Supreme had made a prince among men was
made a mere pendant to those whom superstition had
exalted, or birth made rich. He resorted to Rome to effect,
if possible, an adjustment; but the feeble Clement VII.,
who was now pope, was taken prisoner by the Constable
Bourbon, and the following is the dreary account of Buonaroti about this period:—"Up to this time he had only to
contend with the perversity and injustice of his patrons,
and the jealousy and opposition of his rivals; in addition

to these he now found himself involved in the troubles of contending parties, and without coming to any settlement with the Duke of Urbino, he determined again to leave Rome for Florence." . . . Is he not like a general in the face of a pertinacious enemy; or rather, is he not making good his title to rank among the gifted, by trials and endurance like those inflicted upon pilgrims on the way to some favourite shrine? He is like a man climbing the holy stairs at Rome—one of the impostures by which men are duped in that city of superstition.

Wars next arose among the Italian States. Florence was to be fortified, and Michael Angelo must be the military architect. It is new work, new danger, and a new trial. His darling pursuits were suspended; but during the siege the patriot displayed as much skill as the painter had manifested genius. Doubting the good faith of some of the besieged, he took precautions against that danger. But here again he was thwarted, and withdrew from the city. He was treated there with contumely, and as he saw no prospect of benefiting his country, he was compelled for these reasons to withdraw.

But the men who had treated Buonaroti with contempt could not dispense with his services, and he was invited to return. Reparation was offered for the indignities to which he had been subjected, and he removed from Venice to take his place once more among his townsmen. But Florence fell at length, and the great architect was obliged to be concealed for some time in the Campanile of one of the churches to escape from the fury of the pope. When he came forth from his hiding-place, his safety was guaranteed only on condition that he should finish some monument which that pope—the imbecile Clement VII.—was eagerly bent on seeing completed.

Again, however, the Duke of Urbino was loading the

sculptor with unjust reproaches for his delay regarding the
tomb of Julius. Change after change was introduced;
indeed the whole plan of the monument was recast; and
after much vexation and unjust treatment, a compromise
was made, according to which Michael Angelo was to work
for four months of the year at Florence, and the other eight
at Rome. It was as if he had actually been the serf of those
men—a chattel; and instead of being free to choose for himself, his time, his energy, his genius were let out, by a dire
necessity, at the dictation of what was to him a grinding
despotism. Few men ever paid so high a price for celebrity
as Michael Angelo did.

Nor was this sore discipline as yet near a close. Pope
Clement gave the artist one set of orders which he was
obliged to obey. But the pope died before they were fully
executed, and Michael Angelo gladly hastened to his ever
favourite work, the monument of Julius. But another cross
was in store for him. Paul III., the next pope, wished to
take possession of him, as if he had been private property;
and when the artist pled a contract to finish the monument,
the self-willed Paul demanded that document, and declared
that he would "tear it in pieces." His victim was compelled by this importunity to make arrangements for retiring
to Urbino, there to work in peace; but the pope would not
suffer him thus to escape. He went in state to inspect the
artist's works, and out of that visit there arose an arrangement with the Duke of Urbino, according to which Buonaroti was to supply only three statues for the tomb. Paul,
accordingly, now got sole possession of the artist, and he
returned to his work at the Vatican. At the age of seventy-
five, he finished his last fresco there. A pension had previously been settled on him by Paul; and as the aged artist
felt that he was not what he had been, he longed to be set
free from such works as those which had long wearied and

harassed him. His rivalry with Da Vinci—the competing claims of successive popes, six, or seven of whom he had served—the haughtiness and injustice of the Duke of Urbino; and perhaps above all, the uncongenial work of painting in fresco, had gone far to add discomfort, or even misery, to a career so renowned. Nor was it, perhaps, the least of his sorrows to witness that decline in Art which had begun even while he was unfolding the grandest of all the styles.

But though now advanced in years, Buonaroti was not near his rest. On the contrary, he is just about to enter on a new, a vexatious, yet triumphant career. In sculpture he was beyond challenge the first; in painting he was, in some respects, as unquestionably foremost; but now he is to erect his own monument in the construction of St. Peter's. That building had been in progress for more than forty years. Bramante, Raphael, San Gallo, his uncle, and Giacondo da Verona had all been employed upon the structure; but for Michael Angelo was reserved the honour of completing it.

Yet this honour also was to be purchased at a great price. As soon as he was appointed architect, detraction began. Insinuations against him were poured by his enemies into the ears of Julius III.; and though that pope sought to befriend him, his detractors pursued their measures with most determined hostility. A committee of architects was appointed to inspect his work. Objections the most frivolous, dictated by ignorance which was very profound, now galled the still ardent old man. Every step he took seemed to be a woe. He had to appeal to the pope amid his crosses, and on one occasion exclaimed, " Holy father, you see what I gain. If the machinations to which I am exposed be not for my spiritual welfare, I am losing both my time and my labour."

These enemies succeeded, however, in displacing Michael

Angelo from another work which he had begun—the building of a bridge across the Tiber. An incompetent, and more
time-serving architect was employed; but the fall of the
structure was predicted by the discarded one, and in five
years the prophecy was fulfilled : the Ponte Rotto still
attests the ignorance of the adversaries of Michael Angelo.
The caprice, or the despotism of popes—of aged men advanced to power at a period of life which compelled them
to make the most of their time, was not enough. The
genius of the great artist must be further annoyed by the
rival pretensions of inferior men. At one time neglected,
at another overtasked—hugged to-day—and to-morrow
threatened to be thrown from a scaffold—these were the
vicissitudes through which he had to pass in his triumphant,
yet much tried career. The last woe, however, was the
heaviest. Cardinal Cervino had long been the declared
antagonist of our artist. He had thwarted him, injured
him, plotted against him, and when at length he became
pope, as Marcellus II., in 1555, Michael Angelo had to encounter the open and undisguised opposition of the despot-
priest. He even determined to leave Rome, but the sudden
death of his mitred enemy altered his purpose.

Paul IV. was next elected pope; but he had few sympathies in common with Michael Angelo, and accordingly
deprived him of the chancellorship of Rimini without
assigning any reason. But the culmination of the artist's
grief was occasioned by this pope's proposal to whitewash the walls of the Sistine Chapel, and so efface the
frescoes which adorned it. Amid such chafing incidents
he determined to withdraw from Rome, and sought rest
for his jaded mind amid the wild scenes around Spoleto.
He benefited by his retirement there, but his return to
Rome was the signal for fresh annoyances. Indeed, he
seems to have been one of those whom trouble follows

as a shadow.   It was the antidote, or the alloy of his greatness.

When Michael Angelo undertook to finish the building of St. Peter's, he did it avowedly upon religious grounds; and this may introduce a view of his religion.   Of course, he was a Romanist, and entirely devoted to the creed of the popes. It is probable that the errors which lie at the root of their system prompted the undertaking—it was perhaps a work of merit.   But, however that may be, he would not be moved from the twofold condition on which he accepted the office of architect; first, to superintend the work without fee, and secondly, to do so from a principle of devotion.   Carrying out his purpose, he returned a hundred golden crowns, the salary for a month, which the pope sent to him; and though the artist thus incurred the anger of the pontiff, he was not to be moved from his purpose—he "*worked for the love of God.*"

But Buonaroti was a man of deep thought, as well as of lofty genius; and there is reason to believe that long ere his life drew near its close, eternity had been much in his mind. Even to hoary hairs, his antagonists continued to treat him with superciliousness, and his very assistant at St. Peter's thought himself at liberty to act in that spirit towards the greatest genius of his age.   In truth, Michael Angelo had become disgusted with some of the pursuits which had once enchained him, and was roused to indignation when he saw the liberties which some took with his plans.   Even while solemnly meditating on the close of his earthly pilgrimage, he was thus harassed; and if he had not been borne up by the conviction that he was doing what he deemed a duty, his life would now have been a dreary one. His nature was loving and tender; his friends clung to him with a fond tenacity; and when the closing scenes of such a man were beclouded or embittered, as Buonaroti's were, we read in the whole a significant comment on the troubles to which man is born. "Many people say I am a child again . . . . ." "I should esteem it a most kind office if you would lay these my feeble bones near those of my father;" were some of the sad words with which this man approached the tomb. A great artist in our country could say, "I feel a self-congratulation in knowing myself capable of such sensations as he intended to excite, ... and I should desire that the last words which I should pronounce . . . . from this place might be the name of Michael Angelo."* Another could say still more strongly, "I bless God that I live in the times of Michael Angelo." But, notwithstanding, he passed on to the narrow house amid crowding annoyances from a hostile faction; and the spirit which prompted them followed him even across the line which separates the seen from the unseen, the living from the dead. It was not criticism—it was vituperation that sometimes assailed his memory.

Pius IV. had become pope in time to cheer the declining days of his greatest subject. It was the artist's expressed determination to "employ his abilities to the honour of God;" and though his enemies continued rancorous to the last, he resolutely resisted their aggressions. Though he was now too feeble to contend in person, his plans and principles were upheld by his friends, till, after making his Will, and resigning his soul to God, he passed away on the 23d day of February, 1563. He closed that brief but solemn deed with an exhortation to his friends "to remember, in their journey through life, the sufferings of Jesus Christ." If these were his hope and stay, we understand the secret of his strength in repelling the assaults of so many.

While many make the love of Art an idolatry, it may be interesting to know the estimate which Michael Angelo

* Sir J. Reynolds.

formed of it, when death and eternity were near. That may
be distinctly ascertained from one of his sonnets, which
gives no uncertain sound regarding this vital point. When
glancing across the narrow strait between time and eternity,
he says,—

> " Well I know
> How vain will then appear that favoured Art,
> Sole idol long, and monarch of my heart,
> For all is vain that man desires below.
> And now remorseful thoughts the past upbraid,
> And fear of twofold death my soul alarms,
> That which must come, and that beyond the grave;
> Picture and sculpture lose their feeble charms,
> And to that Love Divine I turn for aid,
> Who from the cross extends His arms to save."

As this is not a biography, little has been said of this
artist's habits, except as he had to struggle with difficulties.
His generosity was remarkable; for example, on one occasion
he gave his servant 2000 crowns, to save him from the
necessity of entering the service of another at his master's
death. And one of his friends has recorded that he never
heard him speak in any way which did not tend to repress
and extinguish all that is lawless and impure. His views
of human life, and its grand ulterior, were as lofty as his
genius; while his poetry is placed side by side with that of
some of the most gifted men of his day. But it is first, in
his ardent struggles for greatness as an artist, and then in
the persistency with which he upheld what he had reached,
that he is here presented. "The Homer of sculpture;"
"The salt of Art," as he has been called, had to struggle like
other men through all his nine and eighty years. Though
one not much accustomed to praise has said, that "the
world has many kings, but only one Michael Angelo," yet
all did not save him from the onset of rivalry, or the
struggles of life. And if it was thus even with *him*, who
need wonder at the contests, the falls, or the disappointments which meet *us* in the upward way? If the man who

has been likened to Dante, and Tasso, endured such contumely, such injustice, such despotism, does any strange thing happen when *we* are crossed, impeded, thwarted, in pursuing the good and the pure? Nay, applying to himself a portion of one of his sonnets on Dante, we may close with our eye resting on his memory, as that at once of a model and a beacon :—

> " How shall we speak of him; for our blind eyes
> Are all unequal to the dazzling rays?
> Easier it is to blame his enemies
> Than for the tongue to tell his lightest praise."

In one sentence, Michael Angelo would not submit to the haughty dictation of ignorant men, and therefore he must suffer. He would not forego the free use of his great powers, and again he must suffer. He would not bow before baseness, or act as if meanness were honourable, and once more, nay, through all his life, he had to suffer. His progress was signally by antagonism. Not a few of his triumphs had to be wrung from envy.

III.—BERNARD PALISSY.

1510–1589.

" And yet poor Edwin was no vulgar boy;
  Deep thought oft seemed to fix his infant eye.
  Dainties he heeded not, nor gaud, nor toy,
  Save one short pipe of rudest minstrelsy:
  Silent when glad, affectionate though shy;
  And now his look was most demurely sad,
  And now he laughed aloud, and none knew why·
  The neighbours stared and sighed, yet blessed the lad;
  Some deemed him wondrous wise, and some believed him mad

  BEATTIE.

Michael Angelo—Palissy's birth—Early habits—Selects a pursuit—Follows it—Poverty presses—Failures multiply—Indomitable perseverance—Fresh efforts—And failures—Resolution still unbroken—New perplexities encountered—And mastered—His children die—The attributes of genius—Streaks of light—Duke de Montmorency—Palissy's studies—His philosophy—Removes to Paris—Successes there—His religious life—Persecution—Imprisoned at Bourdeaux—Set free—The Massacre of St. Bartholomew—Palissy escapes—Continues his works—And holds fast the truth—Is cast into the Bastile—Visited there by the king—Is left in prison—Dies there—De Lamartine's opinion of him—Dumesnil's—Conclusion.

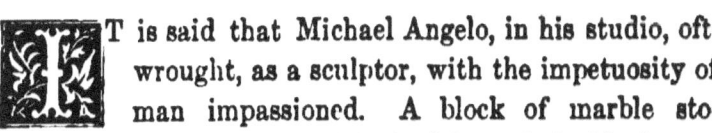

T is said that Michael Angelo, in his studio, often wrought, as a sculptor, with the impetuosity of a man impassioned. A block of marble stood before him, and in his mind he had formed the ideal according to which it was to be chiselled; but as the unfeeling material was slow to body forth what the artist so vividly saw, and so laboriously strove to create, his efforts were at times fiercely violent. Some of his statues are said to bear the marks of this violence, in overdone blows and consequent blemishes. His efforts, when seventy years of age, still surpassed those of youthful artists; and the vehemence of his labours, urged by the vividness of his perceptions, carried him onward over difficulties where feebler men would have sunk. In consequence of this, Michael Angelo's grandeur of soul appears equally in his statues and his frescoes. He is vast and majestic, though sometimes rugged; and a kind of awe still accompanies the works of his hands, or takes possession of the mind, while we gaze upon them.

And we are now to study the life-work of one who, in some respects, resembled Michael Angelo. He was a man of lowly birth, and lived as a peasant for half his lifetime; but genius, and the power to sacrifice self-indulgence for the sake of the useful or the good, are not confined to rank; and though he who is now to supply us with a model was both humble and poor, he yet takes his place far up among the true heroes of humanity. He was one of the men who stand before princes, and overtop the most of them.

BERNARD PALISSY was born about the year 1510, at La Chapelle Biron, in Perigord, and of parents so poor that his scholarship included only reading and writing. To these acquirements he subsequently added some knowledge of geometry and architecture; but too little is known regarding his youth to enable us to indicate the stages of his acquirements, or rather the depths of his neglect.

After serving an apprenticeship to the trade of glass making, some say of pottery, he became a travelling workman for nine or ten years. He resided for some time at Tarbes, among the Pyrenees, and there acquired, or nurtured, that rapturous love of nature which guided him all through life; there, also, he received impressions regarding the religion of the Scriptures, which were then becoming known again, which occasioned both sorrow and joy through the long period of his pilgrimage. Palissy visited Flanders, Germany, France, and other countries, gathering knowledge as he journeyed from every available source—from quarries, from mines, from natural caves, from river banks, from forests. The slight notices which are recorded of such ex-plorings are somewhat like hints gathered on a modern geological tour, though they refer to three centuries ago and more. His school was nature, his master was experience; and, amid his industrious scrutiny, he was in training for something more than the work of a glassmaker.

About the year 1538 or 1539, Palissy settled at Saintes, in the district of Saintonge, on the Charente, a town which was then somewhat famous chiefly in its ecclesiastical rela-tions. He was at that time about thirty years of age, and was employed in various ways—as a painter, a glassmaker, and otherwise, as opportunity served or necessity compelled him, for he was poor, and as he was now married, he had a family to support. Indeed, about this period in his history, Palissy had much to depress him, much to gall and chafe a mind so restless and progressive as his. As his family in-creased, his work, or its remuneration, did not increase in the same proportion, and he began to be in straits. The picture of these is touching, but it was in the midst of them that he entered on the work which was to signalize him.

Palissy, then, had felt the pressure of poverty, but while in that condition an article of vertu in enamel happened to at-tract his notice. The art of enamelling in the style of that article was then unknown; it had been lost; and it occurred to Palissy that if he could re-discover it, the knowledge of such a secret would raise him above difficulties, or turn his poverty into a competence. He resolved at least to attempt it, and from that resolution arose not a few both of his troubles and his triumphs, his sorrows and his joys. In truth, that discovery became the pole-star or the helm of his whole career as a workman, so that in this man's case, we see another example of what has happened in ten thousand others—the germ of great things lodged in the mind by some little or some trivial incident. It is the acorn just planted. It is the little rill just welling up from the earth, and hastening to form a majestic river. It is the little child just born, but soon to occupy a throne, and influence the destiny of empires.

But when Palissy's choice of a pursuit was thus made, few would have supposed that it would end where it did—in raising him to greatness. Yet it did so, in the hands of One who sees the end from the beginning. Experiments had to be commenced in a manner which appears almost hopeless, even after we see those efforts crowned with success. Palissy, we have seen, wished to restore the art of enamelling, but he had no furnaces, and no knowledge of colours, in their chemical properties. Neither had he the means of purchasing what he needed even for the wants of his home, and still less for his new undertaking. He was not, however, a man to be daunted by difficulties. He had chosen his path, and against a thousand obstacles he would persevere. He was entirely a self-taught man, and his very efforts to instruct himself made him invincible, while the failures which he had to encounter developed a patience which never wearied. Though his sacrifices and toils were long unrewarded, he persisted in what he felt he could accomplish; and his perseverance ended in a triumphant success. He hoped and laboured, and laboured and hoped. For sixteen weary years that was his manner of life, and one of his biographers * thus sums up his condition : "To prosecute his new art, he must know the different kinds of clay, he must be taught to construct furnaces, he must learn chemistry with his teeth, that is to say, he must subject himself to cruel privations, approaching the want of daily bread; he must be prodigal of his vigils, of his money, and his health. If he be disappointed in trial after trial, he must yet take courage at the least gleam of success, and at last having wearied fortune, after sixteen years of strug-

* BERNARD PALISSY, *Le Potier de Terre*, par ALFRED DUMESNIL.

gling and of anguish, he will create the art of enamelling earthenware in colours." Such is, in truth, the programme of his life.

Palissy's manly energy was equalled by the accuracy of his study. Urged on by an insatiable thirst for knowing, he examined with exhaustive care the minutest thing that came under his notice, for example, the structure of an insect's wing, or the tints and tracery of the smallest flower. In the spirit of the Bible which he loved, it was Bernard's joy to walk with God in nature, and trace a Father's hand in all the forms of beauty. This poor man was consequently rich in joy, though sorrow after sorrow had to be faced ere he could command even his daily bread. He was, however, indomitable, and failure in one instance only taught him a wiser precaution or more determined perseverance in the next.

But all this is too vague. Examples will best exhibit the skill and the energy of Palissy.

His first aim was to effect a perfectly white enamel, and in seeking it, months rolled away, and years followed, without success; indeed, failure just crowded upon failure. At the same time, his domestic sorrows thickened; care kept tugging at his heart strings; but as he had read in his favourite book that God called men of old to devise curious works in gold, and silver, and precious stones, our potter trusted that a similar blessing was in store for him, and laboured on in hope. When his resources were utterly exhausted and more, he was employed to survey a district near Saintonge, in connection with a tax upon salt, which the Government of France designed to impose on those parts where that article was made. That work occupied Palissy for about a year; and with the money which he was able to treasure up he returned to his search after a white enamel with an eagerness which was augmented by delay. He had formerly employed a common potter's furnace, but he now had recourse to the furnace of a glasswork, as supplying a more concentrated heat, and for two years and a half did that persistent man travel to and fro to tend his work there, in the hope of seeing the art of enamelling at length re-discovered. He was on the eve of losing hope, when out of about three hundred articles which he had placed in the furnace, one was really found to be covered with something like the desired enamel, after an exposure of about four hours to the heat. " That caused me such joy," he says, " that I thought I had become a new being," and this glimpse of success furnished a new stimulus to hope.

But Palissy was precipitate in his conclusion. He was ignorant still of the proportions which were needed to secure a repetition of the happy experiment. It had been rudely made with merely broken bits of pottery, and he now formed earthen vessels with a view to repeat his process. He built a furnace for himself like those of the glassmakers, and had to be his own mason, his own plasterer, and his own water-carrier. He had even to transport bricks on his own back, as he had not the means of employing any one to aid him ; and seven or eight weary months were thus employed by this indefatigable man. For another month he was busy preparing the vessels which he hoped to enamel in his new furnace. For six days and six nights he kept the heat aglow, but no enamel appeared, and Palissy was reduced to despair. He proceeded, however, to rectify what he supposed was wrong in the proportions of his enamelling matter, and keeping his furnace still glowing, he prepared other vessels to be passed through his process. But wood failed. He burned the paling of his garden ; to that he added the tables and the flooring of his house,—but his own words must describe his condition at this stage : " Such was my anguish," he records, " that I know not how to describe it ; I was quite exhausted and withered up by my toil, and the heat of the furnace. For more than a month, my shirt had never been dry, and yet for my consolation, I had only mockery; even those who should have aided me proclaimed over the town that I had burned the wood of my house. Others said that I was coining base money,—an evil which made me pine away upon my feet, and I walked the street downcast, like one ashamed." He was himself in a furnace side by side with his enamel, and might have sat to him who said:—

> "We know the arduous strife, the eternal laws
> To which the triumph of all good is given,
> High sacrifice. and labour without pause
> Even unto death; else wherefore should the eye
> Of man converse with immortality ? "

But Palissy knew of a strong tower. After rallying a little, and with some glimpses of success, he soliloquised thus:—"Why be cast down when thou hast already once found the object of thy search? Work on, and shame thy detractors." At the same time this heroism had one bitter alloy. He was utterly destitute of funds: nay, he was in debt. He had a wife and children to maintain, and four or five months must still elapse ere any profit could result from his labour. A ray of hope, however, again revived him. From a friend he obtained means to employ a workman, and for six months more they toiled and laboured together at their task, but Palissy had then to dismiss his assistant, and to drudge again alone. He had, moreover, to demolish the former furnace, and construct a new one, as well as to procure materials for fresh enamels. He ground them in a mill which would have required the force of two strong men to turn it, but earnestness gave him energy. Like Michael Angelo, he wrought with violent impetuosity,—and he is on the way to success: such sacrifices cannot be lost. If the art of enamelling be discoverable, this man will discover it.

His trials, however, are very far from being over. His

determination has been tested by delays, by poverty, by ridicule, by charges of madness, and other forms of slander. In defence of his plans he had to brave every species of antagonism that could reach him in such a sphere as his; and such were the effects of his toil, increased by these assaults, that he became so wasted and haggard amid his operations, that his clothes would not suit his meagre, emaciated frame. Still, however, if this earnest man is to extort one secret more from Nature, he must himself be further tested; and, accordingly, renewed failures were before him. In building his furnace some pieces of flint had been mixed with the lime. Under a strong heat the flint exploded with violence, and the result was that much of Palissy's enamel was utterly destroyed when just about to take effect. As the pieces thus damaged were numerous, the disaster was like an utter overthrow,—it seemed to extinguish hope for ever. The furnace had cost him one hundred and twenty crowns. He had borrowed the means of procuring the wood, and the matter which made the enamels. He had lived upon credit during this one trial more, and led his creditors to hope that all would be paid by the present batch. They, accordingly, hastened to him as soon as he began to draw the articles from the furnace; but all was blank disappointment to them, and confusion to him. Never was poor man more completely struck down. The object which appeared to be within his grasp has vanished, perhaps for ever, and even hope for a time forsook him.

Yet not for long; Bernard Palissy was not to be driven from his pursuit. On the contrary, he would resume it yet again. Some of his neighbours wished to purchase the damaged articles at a diminished price. But, needy as he was, he regarded that as sure to bring a stain upon his honour; he, therefore, broke the whole in pieces, and took to bed in moody chagrin. He had not the means of supporting his family. At home he encountered only reproaches; instead of comfort, he received maledictions. His neighbours called him a fool; his sorrow reached a crisis; for a time he was ready to succumb, and not without reason.

He recollected, however,—and he tells his own story with characteristic simplicity,—that if a man has fallen into a ditch, his first duty is to get out of it; and, acting on that conviction, Palissy rose from his bed of sorrow; he commenced some paintings; sold them; raised a little money by the sale, and began with fresh ardour to attempt the work of enamelling. Learning wisdom from his past failures, he was now careful in defending the articles from such accidents as had already disappointed his hopes, by the explosion of flints, and other causes. Trials, however, still befell. His enamelled articles were either too much or too little baked in the furnace. On one side the enamel was right, on the other it was wrong, so that he had to battle with disappointments for many weary years. "When I learned," he says, "to guard against one danger, another came which I had never thought of. Sadness and sighs were my portion."

His ignorance of chemistry was a fruitful source of Palissy's disappointments, and before he surmounted that difficulty, he says that he felt like one at the gates of death. One colour he could have enamelled; but how to enamel green, blue, yellow, white, all at once, perplexed him to agitation. At the same time, the continued poverty of his condition, the ridicule of his townsmen, and the murmurs of those whom he loved, enhanced his grief; and as he wandered among the meadows around Saintes, he was one of the most abject or forlorn of men, though on the eve of a great discovery, nay, though in effect he had already made it. Never in a sphere so humble and so poor as Palissy's, was a more memorable example seen of the throes and the anguish which are needed to work out any good in our distempered

world. True, some of his enamelled works, his rustic pieces
and his statuettes, began to be admired; he had discovered
not merely a white, but, moreover, a jasper enamel; but all
the money which he acquired by these means was absorbed in
pushing forward his experiments; in extorting new secrets
which might have continued unknown for ages more, had it
not been for his genius and his resistless enterprise. Sar-
casms were heaped upon him; he was steeped in poverty;
yet he laboured on, and so indomitable was he that if he
fail, it must be when he falls into the grave.

He toiled on, then;—he tried; he failed; and tried again.
In tending the operations of the furnace, Palissy was sometimes exposed for whole nights, without shelter, to the rain
and the storm. He had no help and no sympathy, and
heard only the screech-owl on the one side, and howling
dogs on the other. At times he was driven from the furnaces by the tempest, so that his labour was lost; and when
he retired to rest on these occasions, at midnight or at day-
break, he was drenched like one who had been dragged
through the mire of the streets. His grief and his toils
sometimes made him stagger like one who was intoxicated,
while in the retirement of his home he encountered an opposition from those whose means of support he was consuming in his furnace, far worse to bear than the hostility of his
neighbours. It was natural that those whose comforts he
was abridging, or indefinitely postponing, should murmur
against him, and he felt it acutely, yet still held on his way.

And indomitable resolution like that of Bernard Palissy,
when directed to a right object, commands success, and deserves it. He was teaching men to experiment; he was
manifesting the force of persistent labour, and of manly
courage amid trials, and the long deferred event was perfect
success. He was in quest of a white enamel and nothing
more at first; but his discoveries overpassed his aims—en-

amelling in colours, and a wide-spread influence for good
constituted his reward at length. It was toil, agony, privation, persecution, leading, as ever, to triumph, when the
Supreme Wisdom presides over all. The enterprise of
Palissy, though conducted in poverty, and amid screeching
owls, and howling dogs, and descending torrents, was the
real pathway to success,—rugged at the outset, but opening
into prospects which become both green and goodly as we advance. It were wrong, however, not to record the guiding
maxim of this suffering man. There were some, he said, who
would not let the Holy Scriptures be named; but as for
him, he found nothing better than to follow the counsels of
God. In consulting the Sovereign Will, Palissy learned that
He had commanded his people to eat their bread in the
sweat of their brows, and to multiply the talents with
which they were intrusted. The potter of Saintes read
these things; he obeyed them; and the God whom he consulted did not leave him to shame.

During his experiments and struggles, Palissy lost some of
his children, and that added to his woes. No fewer than
six of them were laid in the grave; and as some of his most
exquisite productions were modelled from the doings of his
little ones, whom he fondly loved, the anguish occasioned by
their death, added to his other griefs, at once pierced and
crushed his spirit. But in spite even of such trials he
persevered. His success had been such as to cheer at least
his ardent mind, and he continued to experiment with a
firmness of will which carried him over every obstacle.—
It is the attribute of genius to rise with the difficulties
which it encounters. Bruce penetrated to the fountains
of the Nile, in spite of a thousand gainsayers. Watt persevered with his discoveries against hordes of opponents.
Kepler conjectured, failed, tried again, and succeeded; and
so in a thousand cases. Now Palissy deserves a place among

these sons of genius. Indeed, his perseverance appears as the very chivalry of invention. One so lowly and obscure, with a heart so fixed, yet encountering hardships unutterable in the pursuit of Nature's secrets, may surely be pointed out as at once a model and an encouragement. He saw that all God's creatures wrought, and so would he. Ocean, earth, and air,—the rivers, the mountains, the valleys, all fulfil their allotted task, all were active night and day, and shall man alone be indolent? Palissy would not. One friend or two came to cheer him amid his long struggles; but he dwelt for the most part alone; and though he did now cherish hope, it was a hope deferred which often made his heart sick. Still the visions of his mind began to be embodied in the fabrications of his hand, and he, so far, rejoiced.

But we now approach the period when light began to streak the path of Palissy. In the ducal family of Montmorency, more than one red-handed persecutor have been found, but that did not prevent them from being patrons of the arts. The duke of that day, though a stern, remorseless bigot, was led to admire some of the productions of Palissy. That Constable-duke was employed in quelling a tumult in Saintonge occasioned by the oppressive tax imposed upon salt. While visiting at a mansion where Palissy was at work, he admired the potter's handiwork, contracted an affection for his person,—and *now* the struggling man has succeeded. The persecutor who, without compunction, ordered his victims to the gibbet or the wheel, has actually become the patron and protector of Palissy, whom he employed to decorate one of his castles, that of Ecouen, about four leagues from Paris. Some of Palissy's labours there are still preserved, and both in the chapel and the galleries of the castle, the effects are described as brilliant beyond aught that had been previously accomplished; they rival the richest of modern productions. The sufferings of the Saviour through their different stages, were represented in sixteen pictures, of which only engravings remain ; but the taste and beauty of the whole are described as exquisite. A fountain of rustic work was also constructed by Palissy, adorned with ornaments derived from the neighbourhood in which his taste was formed. The animals which sported there were frogs, lizards, serpents, fish, and similar creatures,* and these he enlisted strangely but beautifully as decorations. But as a devout Huguenot, Palissy took advantage of the structure to point men to a nobler fountain by far. In stones of various colours he placed conspicuously upon a rustic frieze the words, " Ho, every one that thirsteth, come ye to the waters !" The word of his God was then a sealed book, but a portion of it was open enough there.

For sixteen years, then, this man of firm will has struggled against obstacles in nearly every form that could assail him. Deep in his own mind the conviction was rooted that he could accomplish a certain result. That object was ever-more before him, now appearing to be near and anon far away, but never lost sight of; and he now began to discover that in all labour there is profit; it became manifest that no sacrifice, when guided by right motives, and directed to a right aim, is ever lost. The man who had sacrificed everything he could command to one darling pursuit,—who had passed whole months alone beside his furnace,—whose garments were at one time never dry for weeks together,—who had lived and laboured at the mercy of wind and rain, of sarcasm and sneer, of poverty and all its sable followers,

* " Nature gave all their freshness to these works; for Palissy seized as they passed the impressions which she made. Thus, upon his manufactures, it was the ivy which crept around the walls; it was a cray-fish extending its long feelers which formed the cover of a dish; the handle was a lizard which contracts itself as it climbs. In many basins, reptiles lie in the centre upon a bed of sand, separated by shells, while all around, amid living water, fishes swim ; on the margin, lizards and tortoises creep or lodge amid ferns and marine plants."— *Dumesnil.*

triumphed at last over them all, till he became celebrated
for his handiworks. The taste displayed, the peculiarity of
their structure, and the inimitable beauty which signalized
them, placed them, we have seen, among the chief ornaments of some of the French castles. Specimens are still to
be found in some of the galleries of Paris; for example, in
the Louvre, and the Museum de Cluny; and they are so
beautiful and unique that they are said to be worth their
weight in gold. In all labour, we repeat, there is profit;
and Palissy began to feel the force of the truth.

A sentence may describe the elements of beauty which
rendered Palissy's ware so attractive. Wherever he wandered
he studied. No object to which he had access escaped his
scrutiny. A flower, a fish, a lizard—the inhabitants of the
marshes near his home, the very pariahs of zoology, unseemly to others, but clothed in beauty for him—were the
objects which he copied. Rocks, rivers, seas, meadows, and
forests, as we have already remarked, had long been
Palissy's study; and these he transferred to his enamels,
till they seemed instinct with life itself. The admiration of
such things, no doubt, buoyed him up during many an hour
of sadness, and his imitation of them at length became a
marvel. He had the figure of a dog so perfectly imitated
that other dogs sometimes approached it, where it stood in
his workshop, as a live one, and some of his other triumphs
were similar.

Nor was Palissy merely an artist; he was at the same
time a philosopher, and some of his views in geology anticipated the findings of the modern investigations. Besides
that science, botany, chemistry, agriculture, and other
branches were studied by this toil-worn man, whose intrepid
soul refused to succumb to a thousand difficulties. He
found the book of Nature lying wide open before him, invit-
ing the study of all. Not a leaf, not a line was there which

had not beauty in it. Palissy read; he seized the treasure, and with it in his possession, took his place among the master minds of the past.

He was now in circumstances for removing to Paris, and was there engaged to decorate some of the royal palaces. Catherine dei Medici, the Queen Mother, was then projecting the erection of the Tuilleries, and the man who was lately a struggling and despised operative, was commissioned to adorn them. His wife and six of his children were in the grave; but he and two surviving sons lived and laboured at Paris for a period of at least ten years. They were years of terror, such as have rarely passed over any city; but Palissy was as ardent now as when bent on discovering the art of enamelling. The Castles of Chaulves, of Nesles, of Reux, and other places were decorated by his taste. The ornaments were sometimes grotesque, but they were of a beauty which was then unmatched. Statuettes, vases, tiles, plates, and other articles, in great profusion, were formed; and when purchasers are invited now to compete for some of these relics, the price which is sometimes paid would have amazed the man who strove so long without money, without friends, without everything but genius and hope, to discover the art which taught him how to make them. In his private cabinet he had amassed many scientific specimens, especially in mineralogy, and this helped him to become the precursor of some of the modern sciences. But take him all in all, and Palissy appears at once as a model and a marvel—a model, because no difficulty daunted him, and a marvel, that one so long the victim of nearly every form of trial to which flesh is heir, rose triumphant over it all. Such are the men who enable their biographers to say, as one has said of Palissy, that their works form part of the wealth of monarchs, they help to ornament a kingdom. Some tell us now of the dignity of labour, and surely we have an example of it here.

But, hitherto, little has been said regarding this man's religion. A continuous narrative of his experiments, his failures, and success, has been submitted, and it is time to turn attention to what is greater still than Palissy's achievements in art; he was as remarkable for his sufferings in the one, as for his trials in connection with the other. About his time, the religion of the Scriptures, as opposed to that of Rome, had begun to demand attention from men. Calvin had at one time found an asylum in Saintonge, and others of the Reformers made their influence felt in the district. Missionaries preached there. Philibert Hamelin, an early friend of Palissy, who spent some time at Geneva, became the evangelist of Saintonge, and the potter was not slow to welcome the reviving truth. He became one of the hated Huguenots of France; for his ardent soul rejoiced in the prospect of man's emancipation from the terrible bondage in which he had groaned for centuries. Amid perils not a few he helped to found a Reformed Church at Saintes, but persecution soon arose to scatter the infant community. It was dispersed by ruthless hands, and death for the truth's sake became rife. Women were stabbed in the act of praising God. Some tradesmen were broken on the wheel for their religion. It was a reign of terror; and perhaps the second reign of that name in France, about two centuries later, was a fruit of the former. Palissy, however, was devoted, resolute, and fearless as ever; and eager still for the right, became himself a preacher. He knew the truth; he felt compelled to spread it, and he did so at the hazard of his life. He even went so far as to remonstrate with the persecutors face to face. Friends were torn asunder—the fires of persecution blazed, but he was just nerved the more firmly for his work. "His protecting Chief and Captain, Jesus Christ," was his refuge and shelter; and the devoted Palissy laboured and taught, with characteristic energy as if for life and death. Heavy irons, grated

windows, dark dungeons, and death closing the vista had
no terrors for such men—they endured as seeing the Invisible; and even when they died, they triumphed in their
death as their Lord had done. Victim after victim was
dragged to execution, most of them the personal friends of
Palissy. Robin, the preacher of St. Denis, in the isle of
Oleron; Nicole, another preacher of the truth from the same
neighbourhood; and Gimosac, who also preached from time
to time, were among the first to be sacrificed. Palissy was
present when they defended their convictions against truculent men; but nothing could save them from condemnation
to the flames. It was indeed "the beginning of sorrows" to
the town of Saintes; and after being there paraded in mockery and exposed to the gaze of crowds whom they could not
address, for they were gagged, the three martyrs were
thrown into prison till they could be sent to Bourdeaux.
Robin escaped from prison, but his two companions perished
in the flames. Such sights, we repeat, nerve men. They
nerved Palissy. They have no power over the soul that is
born from above.

And the potter was not held inviolate by those men. He
had the protection of the Duke of Montpensier, and of the
Count de Larochefoucauld, as well as of some others; but
fanaticism was not to be appeased, and his workshop at
Saintes was rudely broken up. Under shelter of the night,
he was dragged from his prison to Bourdeaux, far from his
powerful friends. His works were destroyed; all that
religious hatred could dictate was done against him; and
it was only the interposition of some of the greatest
names in France that saved him from a violent death—
such a death as some of his co-religionists had already
faced for their convictions. He was favoured, not because men were willing to uphold liberty of conscience,
but because the French grandees needed Palissy to deco-

rate their castles : his enamels, not his faith, proved the
means of safety.   The Duke de Montmorency appealed
in person to the queen·mother on the persecuted man's
behalf, and she procured his liberation because she was preparing to build another palace. He was appointed one of
the king's artists, and that rank placed him beyond the
power of the persecutors of Bourdeaux, who had him in
their grasp at the time. He held, in their simplicity, the
grand and Scriptural truths which are the medium of conveying salvation into the soul, and because he did so he had
been doomed to die; but God had work for him to do, and
he was rescued.

When he removed to Paris the celebrity of Palissy grew
great; but he still held fast the truth,even amid the atrocities
of St. Bartholomew's eve, when thousands of Protestants
were butchered for their faith. He was absent from Paris at
that time, executing a commission at Chaulves. His soul had
thirsted for the truth amid the troubles which he had borne
at Saintes, and, in spite of danger, he would not forego it
even in Paris.   Nay, wherever he found an opening he
sought to spread it, and was as resolute in his faith as he
had been indomitable amid difficulties of another kind.
Supported as he was by that mighty though unseen power
which trust in a Redeemer enlists, Palissy was dauntless;
the occupant of a throne, and the terrors of a scaffold were
alike unavailing with him. He had been warned by some
of his friends that his new religion would bring him into
trouble, in spite of royal or of ducal protection; but that
could not alter the mind of such a man. He knew the
effects of God's truth in his heart. He had witnessed
its power upon the peasantry and people of Saintes, and he
therefore held fast his integrity; he would not let it go. In
his own words, he " could better afford to be poor than to
be damned;" " he would rather speak truth with a rustic

tongue than lie in rhetoric." He, therefore, spoke the truth, and stood by all the consequences.

Yet he was long spared. At times he gathered round him the elite of Paris, and put to the proof the views which he entertained on various scientific subjects; and these reunions are among the first on record—the precursors of our Societies, and Institutes, and Schools. At the age of seventy he published the results of his studies in natural history, and thus, perhaps, retarded the evil day; but his time to suffer came at last. His religion could no longer be tolerated in Paris, and the Bastile became his abode when he was about seventy-five years of age. A decree had been passed forbidding the exercise of the Reformed religion, and giving its professors only the alternative of abjuration or exile Mothers were then torn from their children; multitudes were banished, but Palissy stood firm, and was therefore imprisoned. Some of his friends were put to death, and he himself must have perished had it not been for the connivance secured by some of his friends in power. Even the king, Henry III., visited him in his cell, and strove to turn him from his steadfast purpose, but in vain. The potter of Saintes knew of a strength to which that king was a stranger; and the seductive suggestions which were addressed to him were manfully repelled. Two of his companions in prison were soon to be burned, and the king reminded him of their doom; it might be Palissy's next. But still he was unmoved; he told the king he would never bow the knee to images, and was as immovable as when he bore the pitiless storms beside his furnaces at Saintes. "I am ready to yield up my life for the glory of God," was his answer to the blinded monarch. "You say you feel pity for me. I should rather pity you, who confess that you will be compelled to give me up. This is not language for a king; and neither you nor the Guises with all your people, shall compel me, for I know how to die." It was the martyr's spirit. Had it been allowed free scope, it would have made the magnificent empire of France the noblest in the world. But that spirit was stifled as far as mortals could, and from that day France has been, morally, among the basest of the nations.

Palissy died in a cell of the Bastile, about the year 1590, after an imprisonment of three or four years, and when he must have been about eighty years of age. D'Aubigné says, that he died "of misery, want, and cruel treatment."

Such was the life of one who has been called the patriarch of the workshop. It is a life which shows that everything is possible to firmness of will, when guided by right principle, and directed to right ends. By his energy this man rose to be the counseller of dukes, the architect of royalty, the favourite of princes. In art, in literature, and science he is signalized—all because he did not weakly yield to difficulties, but firmly resolved to master them. And, towering high above all, Palissy's religion was of that type which defied the persecutor, and could speak the truth before kings. God had made him noble—and the humble man asserted his nobility by unflinching loyalty to Him who made him what he was. In return, he has eulogies pronounced on him in many lands.

De Lamartine has said concerning Palissy, that he exercised some influence on civilization, and deserved a place among the men who have ennobled humanity. Though he had remained unknown and inactive in his father's pottery; though he had never purified, moulded, or enamelled, his handful of clay; though his living groups, his crawling reptiles, his slimy snails, his slippery frogs, his lively lizards, and his damp herbs, and dripping mosses, had never adorned those dishes, ewers, and salt-cellars, those quaint and elaborate ornaments of the tables and cupboards of the sixteenth century, nothing, it is true, would have been wanting to the

art of Phidias, or of Michael Angelo, to the porcelain of
Sevres, of China, of Florence, or Japan; but we should not
have had Palissy's life for the operative to admire and imitate. It is as a model of triumphant industry, of genius
struggling out of obscurity, in spite of crowds of difficulties,
into a position at once pre-eminent and brilliant, that he is
held up before us.

Haller spoke of him as a man "born for the greatest
achievements." And Dumesnil has said, "In our day all
the ideas of Palissy have been revived in the minds of
philosophers. . . ." His theories regarding springs, minerals,
and other things have been confirmed. Mineralogy, geology,
paleontology, hydrostatics, physical geography, organic
chemistry, have now become sciences; but Palissy long ago
took firm possession of as much of them as he had discovered,
and we can now say, that if true glory be slow, it is sure.
For Palissy it consists less in empty honours, or in statues,
than in the love of those who desire to see more and more
of the light of God from day to day.

And is not this man of humble birth, yet excellent in his
achievements, another model? He had his place among
men assigned to him in an age when the modern times were
just beginning. It was an epoch of struggle and of combat,
of great wrestlers, of soaring souls, and intrepid sufferers.
Artists and philosophers, travellers and discoverers, citizens
and men of science all saw the new truth, and many reve-
rently bowed before it as the sunlight of the soul. Palissy
took his place high up among those lights; and whether as
the fearless preacher of truth at Saintes, the sufferer for it
in the prison of Bourdeaux and the Bastile of Paris, or the
associate of the most cultivated minds of that capital, his
career is equally wonderful. He has recorded his sufferings,
and that as pictorially as were the ornaments which he
lavished in other departments, but not with the design of

murmuring; rather to show what he had to encounter, and
what he was enabled to surmount. A humble worker in
clay, untaught, unfriended, poor, reviled, persecuted, for
forty years of his life having no occupation but that of the
most lowly, he at length took his place among princes; and
one part of his secret he himself described, when he said,
that man should be *all his life an apprentice.* It was so
with Palissy. He was ever learning, ever observing, ever
treasuring up, alike in knowledge human and divine; and
the man who shall imitate his example may at length sit
down by his side, or at least at his feet. Indulging what
has been called "his fierce probity," he told his king that
he knew how to die for the truth. That was because his
life had been guided by it; and the way to the many-man-
sioned home is more easily found by the earnest, because
they have such examples as lights by the way.

But in contemplating the efforts and struggles of such a
man, we can scarcely help asking the question, why such
struggles at all? If God, only wise, be presiding on earth,
why was this man doomed to toil and to suffer as he did?
He was aiming at the good and the right. He was a devout
God-fearing man. A prison had no terrors, and royalty no
attractions for him, when he felt that he was upholding the
rights of conscience and of truth. Why, then, had one so
noble to endure as Palissy did? By what law was he constrained to take his place among the ten thousand times ten
thousand, and thousands of thousands, who have waded
through tribulation here below? Sin has polluted, and by
polluting has distempered our world—that is the key to the
whole. Here the first are often last, the best are often as
the off-scourings. But for three hundred years Bernard
Palissy has made his home where all that is distempered is
put right, and all that is chaotic is reduced to order. The
first are there the first, the last are there the last; and if he

has now exchanged crowns with the king who tried to bend him from his steadfastness, that may explain to us the struggles which Palissy had to endure. He was to be prepared for his crown. He was to be burnished into a celestial brightness, and his toils and tribulations were employed for that purpose. He might have been one of the ignoble of his day—as worthless as the minions of the French court, or as hateful as the most malignant of the French persecutors. But he chose the more excellent way, the only way to glory, that of firm adherence to the truth of God—a humble yet manly determination to fear Him, and have no other fear. God helping him, he kept his resolution inviolate, and now his memory is blessed. He rises above the men who persecuted, ensnared, and imprisoned him, as the spiritual body will rise, at the day of resurrection, above that which is sown in dishonour and corruption.—Go thou and do as he did, that thou mayest be as he is. Never forget that

> " Kind hearts are more than coronets,
>   And simple faith than Norman blood."

The balance of the sanctuary will work a strange revolution at last in the opinions and among the deeds of men. For that the believer, like Palissy, can afford to wait; he knows in whom he has believed.

IV.—JOHN KEPLER.

1571-1630.

" Where finds philosophy her eagle eye,
  With which she gazes at yon burning disc
  Undazzled, and detects and counts his spots? . . . . .
  Where her implements exact
  With which she calculates, computes, and scans
  All distance, motion, magnitude, and now
  Measures an atom, and now girds a world?"

COWPER.

Fallacies—Kepler's birth—His training—A servant to his father—Sent to school
at Maulbronn—University of Tubingen—Family feuds—Kepler adopts
the Copernican system—Appointed professor at Gratz—His life-work—His
mode of study—Publishes—Attracts the notice of Tycho Brahe—Becomes
his colleague—His labours—Tycho's death—Kepler succeeds him—The
advantages of his new position—His three great laws—Examples of his
labours—Objections to his discoveries—Errors—His faults—His devoutness—His trials, domestic, pecuniary, and professional—Persecution from
Romanists—His deep poverty and neglect—Family griefs—Removes to
Linz—Trials increased—The Inquisition and Kepler's books—Some of them
burned in Styria—The Jesuits—Kepler's removal to Silesia—His death—The
Great Sufferer.

HEN we contemplate any admirable work of art,
for example, a statue by Michael Angelo, or the
church of St. Peter at Rome, we lose sight of the
artist's struggles in admiring the product of his genius.
All seems radiant beauty, and we forget the throes or
the sufferings amid which it was created. In the case of
Michael Angelo, for instance, we forget his contendings with
popes before he could wring from them the funds which
were requisite to enable him to execute their commissions.
Alike with Julius II. and Leo X. he was obliged to proceed
in this manner, for both the impetuosity of his own disposi-
tion, and the tardiness of the pontiffs to remunerate the

great architect, sculptor, and painter, chafed and fretted him from day to day. More than once, as we have seen, had he to retire from their employment, and leave them to shame and their own meanness; and what he thus experienced has been the ordinary lot of goodness or of genius—the path in which it moves forward to its place is at once steep and thorny. We have studied some examples of that general law, and are now to contemplate another—oné which is both very signal and somewhat humbling.

It is the life of JOHN KEPLER, who has been spoken of as one who "constructed the edifice of the world," and as "second only to Sir Isaac Newton." He was born at the imperial city of Wiel, in the kingdom of Wirtemberg, on the 27th of December, in the year 1571. His parents were both of noble lineage, but had been reduced to poverty by their own misconduct. Kepler, the father, for some time served his sovereign in the army, where he wasted his patrimony; and his son John was prematurely born, while his father was absent with his regiment. The child was in consequence feeble for some of his early years; indeed, he never became robust.

Henry Kepler was at last obliged to sell the whole of his patrimony, and became a tavern-keeper at Elmendingen, where his son was for some time his servant. Even after he returned to school, which was in 1585, his health was so delicate that he was debarred from mental application, so that his progress was much retarded.

In the following year he entered a school at the monastery of Maulbronn. It was designed as a gymnasium to the University of Tubingen, to which the Maulbronn students went up, according to the peculiar laws and usages of the place. But even thus early, young Kepler was subjected to difficulties and drawbacks, so that his progress continued to be much interrupted. Family feuds of a vexatious kind, and of frequent occurrence, both disturbed the studies and marred the peace of the future philosopher. His father at length separated from his mother, whose habits appear to have been beyoud endurance ; but, amid impediments so grievous, young Kepler graduated as Bachelor in 1588, and as Master in 1591, his eminence then giving some presage of his future position. In academic honours he was the second student of his year.

At Tubingen he studied under Professor Mœstlin, who was one of the first to adopt the Copernican system of the universe. The student early became dissatisfied with the incoherences of other systems, and welcomed with a kind of transport the new doctrines, as propounded by his master. He even wrote thus early in defence of the diurnal rotation of the earth.

Kepler's first promotion was to the chair of astronomy at Gratz, in Styria, in the year 1594. He was compelled, he records, to accept of that office, for at first he displayed no special aptitude or preference for that department of science. With characteristic ardour, however, he threw himself upon his new duties, and began some brilliant, but, as it proved, some baseless speculations regarding the orbits of the planets.

Here, then, we have Kepler addressing himself like one who has the dew of youth upon him, and with the fresh fervour of a recent convert, to his life-work, and what was it ? Discovery—discovery in the loftiest of all the walks on which man can enter regarding things material, that is, among the stars. He has set before himself as his grand object, the detection of some general laws which shall reduce the apparently chaotic heavens to order, and he never once lost sight of the objects of his search. He sought them in devious ways indeed. He even groped for them where they could not be found, and his errors were as great as his labours. For a time, he plunged into speculations which fatigued and bewildered him, and deepened the confusion. At length, however, like another Archimedes, and not by chance, Kepler reduced the skies, or rather man's conceptions of them, to order and beauty. He laid the foundation on which Newton reared his own glory; he constructed the system on which Galileo shed light.—Such is the man of whose doings and sufferings a glimpse is now to be presented—the man of whom Delambre has said that "his perseverance was such that it must triumph over all difficulties but those which are insurmountable."

And first of his doings. As the imagination of Kepler was bold and discursive, he sometimes revelled in theories which only deluded him. He entered upon calculation after calculation, ever seeking a remedy for the acknowledged errors or defects of all past systems of astronomy. But as he gradually discovered that some of his juvenile views were untenable, he abandoned them as frankly as he had ardently pursued them. Over one of these he exulted for a time so intensely, that he declared he would not renounce the glory of the discovery, though he were offered the Electorate of Saxony as a bribe. But he soon found that that discovery was no discovery at all. It was the brilliant vision, however, of a noble mind, though akin to some of the world-making systems which had long prevailed. But the spell was broken at last, and Kepler was led into far more sober paths to greatness.

In 1596 he published a work in which he wrought out some of his wild and wondrous problems. That volume secured for him the friendship of Tycho Brahe, who had been astronomer to the King of Denmark at Uraniburg, in the isle of Huen. Kepler's income from his professorship at Gratz, was small. He was now married; but his wife's fortune did not add much to his resources, and he soon be-

came involved in pecuniary difficulties.   By the advice of
Tycho, Kepler became more observant of facts, and somewhat less prone to theorize.   His friend had removed to
Benach, near Prague, being driven from Huen by the envy
of some Danes, and by the reluctance of others to continue
to pay him his salary.   He invited Kepler to join him in
his new sphere, under the patronage of the Emperor of Germany.   The young astronomer accordingly paid a visit of
some months to that place, in the year 1600; and on his
return to Gratz he resigned his professorship, owing to
troubles which had arisen there.

Soon after that period, Kepler joined Tycho at Benach;
and the Emperor, to whom he was presented, appointed
him to the rank of Imperial mathematician.   He now
assisted Tycho in calculations connected with an extensive series of observations; and while thus laying the foundation of his own future discoveries, Kepler assisted in the
construction of the Rudolphine Tables, named after the
Emperor, and designed to facilitate the labours of future
astronomers.   But Tycho died in the year 1601, in the fifty-
fifth year of his age, when Kepler succeeded him as principal
mathematician to the Emperor.   His salary, which was
ample, was to have been paid partly from the imperial
treasury, and partly from the States of Silesia, and it seems
as if he had now found a haven; but the ample astronomical
observations which his predecessors left behind, proved a
nobler endowment than kings or emperors can bestow.
Brahe had been, what Kepler was not, a careful observer of
the heavens; he had actually made observations regarding
one thousand stars, and thus left to his successor a mass of
facts by which to test and to correct the theories which
were current—the cycles and epicycles which even Copernicus had been obliged to continue.

Though it was Kepler's confessed tendency to "hunt

down" his hypotheses as they arose, and substitute another and another till he approached the truth, he had learned a greater sobriety of procedure under Tycho Brahe. He gradually began to deduce his opinions *from* nature, instead of bringing them *to* it; and *now,* he is on the path which leads to truth. In various departments of science connected with his master study, he led the way in useful discoveries. The eye, the theory of eclipses, of the tides, and even, in a sense, the principle on which the telescope is constructed, were explained more accurately than ever before by the fine genius of Kepler. But it was by his great discoveries, the laws which pass by his name, and which are really the foundation of the modern astronomy, that this man became famous. When he went to reside with Brahe, in the year 1601, Kepler had obtained, for the first time, the means of correcting his brilliant but often baseless hypotheses. Patient observation signalized Tycho; a soaring but unsteady genius formed the peculiarity of Kepler. The one thus acted as a counterpoise to the other; or, if Kepler still loved to walk among the stars, in the hope of extracting from them the secrets of the sky, he was steadied or curbed, guided or illumined, by the long-continued observations of his friend.

It was in consequence of this help that he was led to doubt the view of Copernicus, which assumed that the heavenly bodies move in circles. Kepler discovered after many trials, calculations, and conjectures, that they move in ellipses; and that fact once ascertained, the system of the world was soon no longer a secret. From certain facts he deduced one grand law; and as it was established by observations which could not be gainsaid, it became a key to the mechanism of the skies. It is difficult to convey an idea of his laws to those who are not familiar with astronomy, and it must suffice to quote them. The highest

authorities in science are loudest in their praise; and they
confessedly place Kepler in the very foremost rank of scientific discoverers.   These laws are,—

1. The orbits of all the planets are ellipses, in whose common focus the sun is situated.

2. Equal areas are described round the sun by the planets
in equal times; that is, the radius vector, or the line joining
the sun and the planet, sweeps over the same space in the
same time, at whatever point of its orbit the moving body
may be.

3. The squares of the periodic times of any two planets are
to each other in the same proportion as the cubes of their
mean distances from the sun.

The mere announcement of these laws, we repeat, is
enough to show how difficult and how lofty were the pursuits of Kepler.   And it was not by any happy guess that
his vast mind extorted such secrets.   On the contrary,
he had to labour with an assiduity, and persevere with an
indomitable zeal, such as could be repaid only by discoveries
like his.   Unless we were to follow him through all his
processes, as has been elaborately done by Dr. Small in his
Account of the Discoveries of Kepler, it would be impossible to explain how much science owes to the power,
and posterity to the persistent example of this astronomer.
For instance, it cost him the toil of twenty years to compare
the observations of Tycho, and calculate their results.   Men
speak of the working classes as if they alone embraced the
children of handicraft.   But, in truth, the brain-workers are,
in many cases, the workers by pre-eminence.   It was so in
the case of John Kepler; for he had to struggle with un-
flagging energy along every stage of the path by which he
rose to greatness.   It soon appeared that he must either
labour and strive, and *do*, or take his place among the
nameless crowd, who are born only to die, or live only to be

forgotten. But he chose toil, and he is great in spite of both poverty and neglect.

One example may suffice to exhibit this man's labours. It had long been the opinion, as already noticed, that all the heavenly bodies move in circles. Even Copernicus retained that opinion. At first Kepler did not challenge it. But in making some calculations regarding the planet Mars, he found it impossible to reconcile some of its observed movements with the idea that it revolved in a circle; and not till he had computed such motions with prodigious labour did he discover that the celestial bodies move in *an ellipse.* That led him to other and yet other discoveries, which ended in the establishment of the grand laws already quoted, by which He who is higher than the heavens has bound the planets in their orbits. That man of lofty aims felt that these laws were secrets, but secrets which might be found out.

" Looking forward, fixed
On something which he saw not, solemn, strange,"

he pressed upward, now guessing, now calculating—now stumbling, now rising, till he made us acquainted with the mysteries of all the planets; and philosophers tell us that Kepler's errors and successes, his hypotheses and calculations in working out his results, " excite a feeling of astonishment nearly approaching to awe."

But this does not exhibit Kepler's painstaking labour with sufficient vividness: the following particulars may render it more clear. Arithmetical calculations were then carried on at a vast expense of labour when great accuracy was required. In each of seven calculations regarding the planet Mars, Kepler covered ten folio pages with figures. He repeated each calculation ten times, so that the whole for each of these trials of accuracy occupied one hundred folio pages; seven hundred for the entire series, or a ponderous folio volume filled with sheer calculations.

At times, amid these efforts to arrive at exact truth, the astronomer was perplexed by his own fancies. His love of truth was a passion, but he sometimes sought it where experience has taught that it is seldom found—amid hypotheses and theories. He learned, however, to cast these aside with great magnanimity when he found that they impeded his progress; so that industry which refused to be fatigued, decision which would not be swayed by any promising assumption, as well as genius which could penetrate the secrets of the very sky, presided over his doings; and competent judges could say that everything hypothetical was at length cleared away from the science which Kepler adorned. Some of his discoveries involved results which even he could not fully anticipate; and though he carefully registered the day on which they were made, it remained for the astronomers of future time to profit to the full by the toils, the sagacity, the demonstrations and discoveries of Kepler. Of one of these days Professor Playfair has said, that "perhaps philosophers will agree that there are few days in the scientific history of the world which deserve so well to be remembered" as the 8th of May 1618.

But were the astronomers of that day as grateful as Playfair and the moderns? On the contrary, Kepler's discoveries were objected to because his problems were too difficult. Because the Creator has wrought on a scale of magnificence which man's arithmetic can scarcely calculate, Kepler's astronomy was assailed on account of its very grandeur. He extorted secrets from the heavenly bodies by profound and laborious research; but after extorting them he had to defend them against those who could not walk from star to star as he did by calculations, and Galileo by his telescope. But though the effects of Kepler's discovery were not all confessed at first, it soon became apparent that what he had discovered bound the whole heavens into one vast family of suns and stars. Sir John Herschel says that "they are bound up in one chain, interwoven in one web of mutual relation and harmonious agreement, and subjected to one pervading influence. . . . ." Yet the man who first unfolded that mighty secret had to defend his discovery as if it had been imposture and deception ! The calculations which filled a folio volume of seven hundred pages could procure no exemption from the tax which is exacted by littleness from greatness.

With all this, however, it is to be confessed that Kepler still clung to some of the fallacies of his day. Though he had a glimpse of the true cause of the tides, he continued to hold by the wild fancy that the earth is an enormous living animal, and that the tides are the waves produced by the water gushing through its gills. Though he discarded some of the idle superstitions to which astrology gave rise, and deemed its supporters quacks and charlatans, he yet retained some modified opinions upon the subject unworthy alike of science and of the man. In one of his most remarkable productions, "The Harmonies of the World," which he dedicated to James I. of Britain, the great Kepler appears pleading for—what seems a wild supposition—the influence of the solar and the lunar rays over the human soul. Such is man! But in hours of happier inspiration, and when he spoke or acted as a philosopher, not a dreamer, Kepler laid all time under deep obligations. His works are numerous in spite of much bodily weakness, and troubles more than fall to the lot of ordinary men. Between the years 1594 and 1630 he published thirty-three separate books. His MSS. occupy twenty-two volumes, including seven volumes of his letters.—It was an industry which makes modern activity seem indolent, as his daring genius renders modern discoveries tame.

Moreover, Kepler was not one of those cold-hearted beings

whom mathematics, and diagrams, and calculations endless, transform into recluses. Nay, he enjoyed intensely all that was grand and beautiful in the world. Though vehement, he was generous; though too easily provoked, he compensated for that failing by his frank acknowledgments when he saw that he was wrong, and public confession followed a public offence against a friend. His own views, we have seen, were at once abandoned when he saw that they were wrong, so that the blemishes which attach to his character are over-balanced or over-laid by his grandeur or his genius. Above all, he was profoundly reverential towards Him who created the heavens and the earth. Coleridge once said, and lived to deplore the saying—

> " Of whose all-seeing eye
> Aught to demand were impotence of mind;"

but not so Kepler. He never entered on any undertaking without prayer to God for his guidance. His was not the shallow knowledge which inclines man to atheism, but the profound acquirements which can everywhere trace the vestiges of the Creator. Hence lowly reverence marked all his ways. It was an elevating spectacle to see one whom science places next to her high priest, Newton, kneeling submissive to the Father of lights for wisdom, guidance, and success; and yet never was he in a nobler attitude. It explains the secret of his successes and his triumphs amid unrequited toils, and pressing want, and griefs such as would have ground down a nature less trusting than his. "The secret of the Lord is with them that fear him," and Kepler was borne up by resources of which many are willingly ignorant.

Such were the discoveries of this astronomer. But reference has been made to his troubles and his crosses; and to complete our view of this earnest labourer, we must next consider these, and that with some care.

It might have been supposed that a mind engrossed with

pursuits so lofty and serene as his would pass through life unruffled. His own noble science unveils to us a region where no clouds are formed—where all is tranquillity and rest. Earth is the sphere of vapours and tempest—the upper sky is ever untroubled; and did not Kepler dwell there? As he moved from planet to planet reading off the laws of one and all, was not his case an exception to the rule that man is born to trouble?

It was the reverse. Sorrow upon sorrow crowded his course; and on a review, it is surprising that amid pursuits like his, the crosses which befell did not utterly unman him. Passing over long troubles occasioned by the friends of his wife, we find Kepler and her at one time utterly dependent on the bounty of Tycho Brahe. Pecuniary difficulties arose immediately after his marriage, for his income from his professorship at Gratz was inadequate for his support. Moreover, he was a Protestant, firm and unfaltering. But the Romanists of Gratz raised a clamour against the co-religionists of Kepler, and threatened to drive them from the city. He was obliged to flee into Hungary, where he appears to have occupied himself with literary labours. In the year 1597, however, he was recalled to Gratz by the States of Styria, but the factions which still divided that city made it no safe abode. Fresh troubles occurred, and Kepler resigned his professorship. He had to begin life anew.

Even when the Emperor Rudolph, at the instance of Tycho, had settled a salary on Kepler, it excited the jealousy of some mean minds, so that a new source of disquietude arose. He possessed an elasticity of spirit, however, which bore him up amid all these disquietudes; indeed his broad humour, amid all his griefs, seems sometimes to pass due bounds: he indulges his love of merriment alike in the presence of an Emperor, and in discovering some of the sublimest laws which are known to man. Whether in refuting the Epicurean theory of creation by atoms, or explaining the virtues of a salad at his table, sallies of fancy broke forth. He was as remarkable for these as for his sagacity and his power.*

Life, however, is not a jest to any man; and least of all to Kepler. Though the Emperor had assigned to him an adequate salary, the imperial treasury was so exhausted by war that it was always in arrear, and such was the pressure which that occasioned that Kepler spoke of himself as perpetually begging bread from the Emperor. He was in consequence compelled to suspend some of his nobler pursuits, and betake himself to the composition of ephemeral books to earn a morsel. "I have been obliged," he says, "to compose a vile prophesying Almanac, which is scarcely more respectable than begging, unless from its saving the Emperor's credit, who abandons me entirely, and would suffer me to perish with hunger."—Such was the position of one whom men of kindred genius would place side by side with Newton, but who must first sit side by side with Job. Yet though such things impeded his progress in discovery, they could not quench his ardour; and, on one occasion, when one of Kepler's grand demonstrations was complete, he could say, "Nothing holds me; I will indulge in my sacred fury; I will triumph over mankind by the honest confession that I have stolen the golden vases of the Egyptians to build up a tabernacle for my God, far away from the confines of Egypt. If you forgive me, I rejoice; if you are angry, I can bear it. The die is cast; the book is written, to be read either now or by posterity, I care not which. I may well wait a century for a reader, since God has waited six thousand years for a discoverer." †

* His preparations for his second marriage are described by Kepler in a style that is grotesque. See his life in "The Library of Useful Knowledge," or Sir David Brewster's "Martyrs of Science."
† Sir David Brewster's "Life of Kepler."

But family griefs were added to pecuniary embarrassment. Kepler's mother was a woman of dissipated habits, and that often shocked him. She was at one time charged with poisoning one of her friends; and that occasioned sorrow upon sorrow. While the Emperor's exchequer and his hand were equally empty, the "starving astronomer's" home was full of grief. And yet not full, for it *must* hold more. His wife was seized with fever, and other diseases, in the year 1610; his three children were at the same time invalids. His favourite son died; Prague was occupied by hostile troops, and Kepler's home, already sufficiently tried, found the Bohemian levies a source of constant annoyance. Then the plague broke out in the city; and while the astronomer was attempting to obtain a professorship at Linz, in the hope of securing an income, his wife was seized with consumption, and soon afterwards died.

But there must be other troubles still. When Kepler resided at Linz, as professor of mathematics, he was denounced by the Romanists for some opinions which he had expressed regarding the doctrine of transubstantiation. That did not encourage him to remove, though he was invited, to Bologna as professor of mathematics. Some of his books were placed in the Expurgatory Indices of bigotry; and Kepler was too independent in soul to brook a position where man may not utter what God has been pleased to teach. The arrears of his income continued unpaid. One ruler died, and then another; but it made no difference to poor, defrauded, and neglected Kepler. He was destined, above most men, to feel how broken a reed imperial patronage may be, and to discover how unerring is that truth which warns us not to put our trust in princes. He was invited to settle in England. But under the charlatan king, James I., would Kepler have been better there? At all events, he declined the suggestion of the British ambassador;

and even the pressure of want could not induce him to leave
his country, cold and inhospitable as it had been to him.
"While the fire eaters and astrologers of Rudolph were
basking in the sunshine of imperial favour, Kepler . . . . .
passed his life in extreme indigence;" and that was the
reward which a monarch bestowed on brilliant discoveries—
on genius unsurpassed, and a moral heroism that would
quail before no difficulty.

But his troubles have not been all recounted even yet.
The States of Styria ordered some of Kepler's books to be
burned, for some affront to these States, which it was alleged the works contained. To one who loved truth with
an immoderate passion, as Kepler did, and who was ever
ready to confess his own errors, and proclaim his own failures,
this was galling. It was perhaps forgotten, however, amid
some gleams of light which now broke through the darkness.
In the year 1622, the reigning Emperor, Ferdinand, ordered
all Kepler's arrears to be paid; and he seemed at length on
the eve of accomplishing some of his most cherished designs
—the man who has received the lofty title of "the Legislator
of the heavens," is about to be set free from poverty. But
the Jesuits were in the field. The persecutors of Galileo
were also the persecutors of Kepler. His library was
actually sealed up by their order; and it was only his
official connection with the Emperor that saved him from
personal durance. The rancour of a dark superstition
thus added its influence to the hardships of poverty. The
Grand Duke of Tuscany might forward a gold chain to
Kepler, in token of his applause; but what is either imperial patronage or ducal approbation when Jesuitism assails
a man who said, that he "always took the view of religion
which seemed to be agreeable to the word of God?" In
this case men tried to quench the light of science, as they
try to extinguish revelation; for the instinct of self-

prescrvation may everywhere tell the Jesuit that he and light, or he and progress, cannot co-exist.

To the last, then, Kepler's troubles continued. Albert, Duke of Friedland, invited him to take up his abode at Sagan, in Silesia, and religious strife and the pressure of poverty induced him to comply. He removed to Sagan in the year 1629; and that was to be his last, as it was also his most comfortable home. But even there he could not recover the arrears of his salary, now amounting to eight thousand crowns, and he proceeded to Ratisbon, to make one effort more to wring them from imperial hands. Harassed, however, by care and vexation, and weary of his long solicitations, he was seized with fever, and died at Ratisbon on the 5th of November 1630, when under sixty years of age. He was interred in that city; and on his tombstone it was recorded that the "mathematician of the whole Christian world," "piously died in Christ." But even the grave of Kepler was not respected like that of most men. The tomb was soon desecrated by the ruthless hand of war, and not till the year 1803 was any structure raised to his memory. Such treatment almost justified the bitter sarcasm of one of his admirers, who said that Kepler's countrymen first refused to give him bread, and then would not grant him even a stone. His monument is a temple, built near his grave, surmounted by a sphere, and containing in the interior a marble bust of the great astronomer. At the time of his death the sum of twenty-four thousand florins was due to him by the Emperor; but his family, who were of course left in straitened circumstances, never received more than a part.

And such is another life-study. It is strange, eventful, eloquent. No doubt, the afflictions which befell Kepler the astronomer, helped to burnish the graces of Kepler the Christian. He had a great fight to maintain, and there is

reason to believe that he maintained it with patience, and
well. But that does not diminish—it enhances—the shame
of those who doomed him to neglect. The story of "the
starry Galileo, and his woes," was repeated in the case of
Kepler, for intolerant superstition troubled and beclouded
the life of each. In that of the latter, a poverty which
was well-nigh abject pressed down his spirit; and even
when he was exploring the furthest ranges of creation,
or announcing the laws which bind star to star, he was
the victim of imperial neglect—tantalized, deceived, and
starved. Yet he persisted. It was not merely for the smiles
of crowned creatures that Kepler lived and laboured;
he knew of a joy with which their frown or their neglect
could not intermeddle. By that joy he was cheered, till at
last he found an asylum where the wicked cease from
troubling, and the weary are at rest.*

His path through life was chequered, if we should not say
all dark. It was at least as dark as man can make it;
and Kepler is one proof more that the man who would
do good to his fellow men, who would shed light upon their
darkness, or train them to soar instead of grovelling, must
often be prepared for hardships, for persecution, for contumely or neglect. One wondrous Benefactor came to our
world from a better. He never saw a sorrow which he was
not ready to soothe, nor a want which he was not willing
to supply. He held out his hand to help, and what did
man do? He seized that hand and nailed it to a tree. It
was a premonition—loud, deep, and touching—of what
awaits all who would do good to ungrateful men.

* Kepler left a brief epitaph, in Latin, for himself, which was incorporated
with a longer inscription on his tomb. It was this,—
  " Mensus eram cœlos, nunc terræ metior umbras:
    Mens cœlestis erat, corporis umbra jacet."

V.—JAMES WATT.

1736–1819.

" Wealth, worldly glory, rich array
Are all but thorns laid in thy way,
O'ercovered with flowers laid in a train—
All earthly joys return in pain.

DUNBAR.

The claims of genius—Honours of Watt—His birth-place—His school-boy days
and trials—Was his genius precocious?—His life-work commences—His
acquirements—His passion for mechanics—Proceeds to London—Becomes
known in Glasgow on his return—The university—Its advantages—And professors—His employments—A retrospect—The Newcomen steam-engine—His
resolution exemplified—A glimpse of the inventor—His first inventions—
Want of means to push them—Accepts of other employment—His health
a wreck—A rival inventor—Resolves to invent no more—New Inventions, and
fresh troubles—Results—The Clyde—His honours—Westminster Abbey—
What were his religious views?—The close.

HE claims of genius are not always recognised
during the lifetime of its possessor. The effects
of envy dominate in some, and they will not
acknowledge what might otherwise seem too obvious to be
challenged. In others, indifference; in others, ignorance, or
stupidity; in others, conflicting interests, and rival claims,
operate to the prejudice of the gifted. They are not seldom
left to poverty and neglect, and sink, perhaps, into the grave
unnoticed and unknown. They are often advanced to their
proper position only after their removal from the scene
where envy not seldom supersedes admiration, and cold
neglect robs the benefactor of men, not merely of the fame
which is his due, but of the more substantial rewards which
it should be our joy promptly and liberally to pay.

It once seemed likely to be thus with JAMES WATT, at
whose inventions and life we are next to glance, as illustrating the necessity of decision and earnest concentration in
the way to eminence. During his lifetime he rose at length
to competency and more, even to ample wealth; he was in
circumstances to show that he could be munificent as well
as inventive, and to encourage struggling merit, as *he* had
not been encouraged. But the marvellous benefits which
he bestowed on man, the mighty revolution in every department of life, which he was the means of introducing, attracted
little public attention for many years. It is true that George
III. honoured Watt with his notice; some of the allied sovereigns, who visited this country, also visited the great inventor when near the close of his career. But only after
the grave had received him did the public mind wake
fully up to the gigantic results which were sure to follow
from the inventions of James Watt. He had to defend his
achievements by nearly every form of lawsuit, up to the
highest. He had to struggle for years with most inadequate
means. He had to encounter the attacks of unprincipled
pirates; and years elapsed ere the brilliance of his discoveries was adequately comprehended by men. At last,
however, the eloquence of the highest minds was taxed to
do him justice; and never, perhaps, before has a homage
more profound been offered to genius. Men who lived in
the shadow of royalty, and were charged with the government of empires, combined with the noble, the eloquent,
and the learned to do justice to his memory and name. He
was placed at once, and far up, among " the starry lights of
genius." His inventions were hailed at length as peaceful
revolutions in many departments; while the lapse of nearly
half a century has seen the celebrity of Watt placed on
a foundation from which no time can ever remove it. What,
then, were the stages—what the powers or mental peculiari-

ties by which he was guided to his lofty place among the benefactors of the world? Can we trace his footprints, for our guidance, along the rugged ascent where he climbed so nobly and so high?

Watt was born at Greenock on the 19th of January, 1736. As his parents had already lost several children by death, he was watched over with care, and he required it: from his earliest years he was subject to ailments which often interrupted his career as well as saddened and distressed him. His father was a magistrate in his native town, and was in easy, if not affluent circumstances; and traditions are current which tell that the home of his parents, as to its decorations and its comforts, was in advance of what was common in Greenock a hundred years ago.

At school, the boy Watt was rather victimized by the more turbulent of his class fellows. His shy and retiring habits, his frequent ailments, and other things provoked attacks, which are said to have fallen "thick and heavy on the ethereal, yet passive spirit of the gentle boy." Indeed, the ordeal to which he was exposed appears to have been unusually severe, and the depression of mind, occasioned either by physical pain, or mental anxiety, or both, caused young Watt to be regarded at school as chiefly remarkable for stupidity and supposed want of sense. No one would have ventured to predict the eminence which awaited him.

In consequence of these things, the early history of the boy is given in very different terms by different biographers. Some have denied that any precocity or peculiarity appeared in him, except that of dullness and reserve, and the facts which are detailed regarding his early studies are viewed by this class, for the most part, as myths. At the same time it is confessed that even thus early, he had a small forge constructed for his own particular use. It is believed that even as a boy, nautical and scientific instruments passed through his hands for repair, such as the young are rarely permitted to handle.[*] Others, again, have recorded that when he was only six years of age, he was found stretched on the floor of his father's house, struggling to solve a mathematical problem from a diagram which he had drawn with chalk. Not long after that period, the future mechanician constructed a small electrical machine. He repaired the toys of his companions. He made juvenile experiments on the condensation of steam; and was scolded by a thrifty relative for his idleness, though he was then, as we are told, catching the first glimpse of a bright idea which, after making his own fortune, has made the fortune of thousands. If these things were so, then Watt has indeed decided early as to his future path. With the certainty of instinct, he has entered on his life-career; he is beginning, no doubt without plan or purpose, but actually, nevertheless, to be the benefactor of the world in its material interests.

There can be no doubt, however, that James Watt really woke up to his true vocation in his thirteenth year. In this he has been likened to that other giant of Timnath when the Philistines were upon him. The commencement of the study of mathematics was the occasion of this intellectual birth. He then got possession of the power which was to unlock to him some of the secrets of nature, and spread out before men the means of growing rich beyond the power of computation. But along with that, other branches of knowledge were acquired; chemistry and chemical experiments occupied much of his time. Medicine and surgery were not overlooked. Botany, poetry and literature in various departments were cultivated by Watt; and while delicate health compelled him at times to seek its renovation among the

* It is alleged that about this period Watt fabricated a "punch-ladle," for one of his friends, out of a large silver coin, as he is known at a future period to have constructed a guitar, which is still in existence, for a female relative.

wild uplands around Loch Lomond, and in other scenes, he was treasuring up stores which made the great inventor, when he became such, an accomplished and a lettered man. What he did, in short, he did with all his might, and no man ever rose to eminence or stamped himself upon his times without doing likewise. "Give thyself wholly to these things," is a maxim of profoundest wisdom, as of highest authority.

His passion for mechanics, however, at length overbore all other pursuits. In quest of higher skill and finer manual training than he could acquire in Scotland, he proceeded to London, in 1755, and there spent a year in learning some of the more delicate processes of practical mechanics. The construction of some of the most delicate pieces of work in his trade, such as Hadley's Quadrants, Theodolites, and others was there learned. Whether it was his father's failure in business and other reverses, which took place a year or two before this period, or whether some other cause helped to propel young Watt along his favourite path, we do not tarry to inquire: enough that another step was taken in the direction in which his genius urged him on. At the expiry of a year he left London and returned to Scotland; and as he had been often rudely treated amid the tumults of the school-yard, he is now to find that that was only an introduction to similar treatment upon the broad arena of the world. If he had been tended with gentle care in his father's house, or if his juvenile pursuits had been quiet, retiring, or sometimes even sombre, he is now to enter on a career which will test, and strain, and task his utmost ingenuity, sometimes his firmest endurance.

His skill in repairing some mathematical instruments which belonged to the University of Glasgow, brought him under the notice of its most gifted professors. But as he was prevented by local laws from commencing business as a mathematical instrument maker in that city, the University

appointed him their agent in such matters, and assigned to
him a workshop within the college. From that period we
may perhaps date the dawn of the greatness of Watt, as from
the time when the study of geometry became his ruling passion, a new charm was added to his existence. "To understand everything" was with him a persistent impulse
which never left him satisfied with half knowledge, or half
thoughts; and when a mind so decided, or so bent on progress
was brought into daily contact with some of the master
spirits of his age, the effects need not be depicted. A galaxy
of names then notable, and now celebrated, adorned the
Western University at that period. Adam Smith was there
elaborating and maturing the system which has so largely
influenced the destinies of nations. Joseph Black was there,
whose discoveries in chemistry gave a strong impulse to what
appears the most rapidly progressive of all the sciences.
Dr. Robert Simson, the restorer of the ancient geometry, and
one of the most eminent mathematicians of that age, was
also a professor in Glasgow; and amid society so congenial,
or in daily intercourse with minds so well fitted at once
to appreciate him, and to be appreciated by him, his views
enlarged, his knowledge grew; it became evident that Watt
was to take the place of a master. It cannot be said, indeed,
that there was any brilliant thing done,—anything to dazzle
or to amaze. But the mind was gathering momentum: it
was slowly feeling its way to that elevation from which its
force was destined to be felt through ages untold. When
resident in his native town, Watt has been known to spend
hours reclining upon his back, watching through the trees
the movements of the stars. The child was father to the
man; and within the walls of the University of Glasgow
the same spirit appeared, for Watt there entered upon the
great work which he was destined to achieve, and though its
achievement was still a great way off, he was advancing—as

the vessel advances over wave after wave to its haven. The
miniature crane-blocks, pumps and capstans, and the more
complex miniature barrel-organ constructed by young Watt
in his father's house, have given place to experiments which
now, though not then, point the way to all the eminence
which Watt has attained.*

His house now became a little academy, where many
of the youth of the city assembled to gratify their scientific
predilections, to consult, and confer with an acknowledged
guide. His own decided bias helped to decide others, and
he became the common referee of those who were puzzled
with scientific difficulties. When any question was propounded to him, it forthwith became the subject of a new
study; he subjected it to an exhaustive process, and either
detected the worthlessness or announced the value of the
suggestion. He could not, in truth, superficialize: he was
thorough; and no matter, one has written, what was proposed, languages, antiquity, natural history, nay, poetry,
criticism, and works of taste—all were investigated, though
engineering was his favourite. At the same time his mind
was both stored and stimulated by the works to which his
position in the University gave him access; and as some
have alleged that a close inspection might enable us actually to see the palm tree growing, we can see this mind
growing, because all its energies were bent on growth,—
they converged, instead of being dissipated. They sought
with all the heart and they found.

It was after or during such a preparatory training that
the incident befell which caused the genius of Watt more
and more to fix upon one single point—steam, and its

* It is known that though Watt was devoid of all taste for music, and a musical ear, he constructed several musical instruments, in particular an organ of
such compass and power that it produced remarkable harmonic effects, to the
astonishment even of professional musicians. This, of course, implies profound
skill in the science of Harmonics, as well as power mechanically to reduce that
skill to practical results.

applications—which had already obtained some attention
from him. The professor of Natural Philosophy in Glasgow
had, among his class-apparatus, a model, a mere plaything,
of the Newcomen steam-engine. It needed some repairs,
and was sent to Watt for that purpose; and from that moment we may regard him as more intensely committed than
ever to his life pursuit. It was a trivial incident, the veriest casualty, and something light as air; but it led to a
train of results such as are not uncommon in the history of
man, and which warn us of the wisdom embodied in the
question, "Who hath despised the day of small things?"
Newcomen's engine was little more than a steam-engine in
embryo, if it deserved even that title; but its very imperfections helped the better to develop the powers and display
the ingenuity of Watt, in his attempts to remedy them. He
experimented, failed, and experimented again, and ended in
becoming the benefactor of nation after nation—or, rather,
in leaving his impress upon all the coming ages.

It is not our purpose to detail the various stages by which
Watt elaborated the grand idea which now began to possess
him—that of improving the applications of steam as a motive power. It may help, however, to show how decided
and how concentrated his mind had now become to mention, that he mastered the German tongue in order to be
able to read a treatise on Mechanics in that language. To
that acquisition, and for a similar purpose, Watt added
the knowledge of Italian, about the same time, threading
his way through the theory of sacred harmonics, that he
might be qualified to construct an organ, as has already
been noticed. These and similar pursuits on the part of
one who was still only a working mechanic, although ex-
quisitely ingenious and accomplished as a workman, evince
a power of concentration, an entire devotedness to the
thing in hand, which renders it easy to predict what that

mechanist is likely to become. He has chosen his path well: he holds by it decidedly, and will yet stand in high places.

We get one glimpse of this inventor amid his experiments and discoveries, upon which his friends have dwelt with delight. Professor Robison has said of the period when the "Separate Condenser," Watt's first great result, was discovered: "I came into Mr. Watt's parlour and found him sitting before the fire, having lying on his knee a little tin cistern, which he was looking at. I entered upon conversation on . . . . . something about steam. All the while Watt kept looking at the fire, and laid down the cistern at the foot of his chair. At last, he looked at me, and said, briskly, ' You need not *fash* yourself any more about that, man. I have now made an engine that shall not waste a particle of steam ; it shall be boiling hot : ay, and hot water injected, if I please.' So saying, he looked with complacency at the little thing at his feet, and seeing that I observed him, he shoved it away under the table with his foot." Such is the account which is handed down to us of one of Watt's brightest discoveries, and, therefore, of one of his brightest hours. That "little thing at his feet" was the representative of a mighty power. It bridged over difficulties which even Watt could not surmount till then ; and from that germ the world has been filled with wonder, while the power of its population, in some lands at least, has been multiplied many hundred-fold. Most probably, the unromantic mind of Watt did not at that moment anticipate the mighty results of "the little thing." Yet who can doubt that his joy was then as deep, though not so tumultuous, as that of the orator amid his popular triumphs, or that of the poet amid his highest soarings?

The progress of Watt amid these experiments was like the struggles of freedom, apparently lost, but really won. He was at times baffled and tempted to abandon some of his instruments, or regard them merely as toys. A less decided mind would have ignored his life mission, and yielded in despair. But his genius impelled him to grapple with difficulties, and his mind converged the more upon a subject in proportion to the effort which it cost, till success at length crowned and encouraged his labours. He had now, as we have seen, accomplished his grand discovery of the "separate condenser," and had formally registered his patent for a method of lessening the consumption of steam, and, consequently, of fuel, in fire or steam-engines, the results of many watchful hours, many unpromising experiments and deep speculations, such as only Watt could conduct. If we add to these that he had enrolled in Chancery a threefold specification of an effective steam-engine, a high-pressure engine, and a horizontal rotatory engine, we have enumerated discoveries which have not merely rewarded his diligence and his sleepless nights, but have placed within man's reach those resources of productive power which have immeasurably added to the riches of our globe.

But ere the time for the full expansion of these inventions arrives, the inventor must be further tested: even yet he has other difficulties to surmount. Has he patience, determination, and decision to surmount them, and to feed on hope for a quarter of a century more?

At this point, Watt was often checkmated by the want of means to push his various inventions into notice, so as to take advantage of the results of his skill and perseverance. Some of his earlier experiments had been conducted under most unpromising circumstances from a similar cause. Apothecaries' vials, a glass tube or two, and a common tea-kettle, were his chief apparatus in arriving at some very important conclusions. By attaching a glass tube to the spout of a kettle, he conducted the steam into a glass of water, and upon that founded a result which helped him materially in some of his future discoveries. His contracted resources thus limited his efforts, but could not damp his zeal, though the same impediment continued for many years to haunt him. He could extort secrets from nature by appliance added to appliance, and embody his discoveries in machines which were to guide as well as expedite the circumnavigation of the globe, and change the whole face of society; but he shrank from the occupations of the mere man of business. He disliked the scramble for money in which the world takes delight. He could grapple with difficulties such as scarcely any other man could have mastered, yet recoiled from a conflict with ignorance or prejudice in vulgar minds. When his reputation was attacked, his originality denied, and his right to the work of his own hands contested, he was under strong temptation to abjure the course he was pursuing amid the unprovoked assaults of the malignant or unprincipled.

But some fresh glimpse of nature's secrets lured him on, though for a time he had to diverge from the path of his fame. He accepted of other employment than invention, and was for several years engaged as a Civil Engineer. He made a survey of the river Clyde and the adjacent parts; he constructed maps, traced out the course of canals, and superintended their formation. He had involved himself in considerable debt by his attempts to perfect his inventions, and secure protection for them in a legal form. His three great inventions already mentioned— the improved steam-engine, the high-pressure engine, and the rotatory steam-engine, for which letters patent were obtained in 1769, had not merely cost him time, thought, and labour — they required more substantial means for their completion, and, as a result, Watt had a burden of debt to bear, with all its attendant drawbacks. It was

more difficult for him to raise £1200, for that was about
the amount, than to mature what could make him and
tens of thousands rich; and, in these circumstances, he
gladly availed himself of other employment for maintaining himself and those dependent upon him—canals,
docks, and harbours, for a time engrossed his attention,
and added to his reputation for scientific skill. Indeed, to
have competed with the Brindleys, the Smeatons, and the
Rennies of that day, and that in their own peculiar sphere,
was itself a fame, and furnishes another proof at once of the
power and perseverance of Watt. It deserves, as it has
obtained, the encomium of a kindred mind in France. "At
this stage of Watt's career, we see," exclaims M. Arago, in
his *Eloge*, "the creator of an engine destined to form an
epoch in the annals of the world, undergoing without a
murmur the undiscerning neglect of capitalists; during eight
years, lowering the lofty powers of his genius to the getting
up of plans, to paltry levellings, to wearisome calculations
of excavations, and embankings, and courses of masonry."
Everywhere, however, and in all employments, he was still
James Watt—facing all the difficulties with which genius
could compete, and shrinking only from those in which less
gifted minds feel no embarrassment, but rather congenial
employment. His genius found both an outlet and a stimulus in the one, an incubus, or a cross in the other.

Nor should we fail to notice, that amid this battling with
adverse circumstances, the health of the great inventor
often seemed a wreck. It unfitted him for activity, or exertion of any kind, insomuch that he could only sit in solitary sadness, musing, if capable even of so much, on the
obstructions which seemed to block up his path. It was a
portion of the price which he paid for fame—the tax imposed upon greatness in our distempered world.

Still, however, the inventor could not be supine. Though

the events of this period were painfully ruffling to one so
natively serene, and so fond of what was tranquil and
domestic, they could not overmaster the ruling passion.
The eye of his mind was fixed on one great, though apparently distant, object. From that he might be diverted for
a time; but true to the life-work which he had to do, he
evermore recurred to it—he turned to it as to some radiant
spot, and the more distant its completion might appear, he
was sometimes just the more bent on seeing it performed.
Plan after plan was therefore adopted: friend after friend
was appealed to for means to escape from pecuniary difficulty, and all that by a man who was "suffering under the
most acute sick headaches, sitting by the fireside for hours
together, his head leaning on his elbow, scarcely able to
give utterance to his thoughts." Zealous, however, as ever,
and to induce a friend with whom he was in correspondence, to assist him in launching his inventions, Watt erected
one of his engines at Kinniel, on the Forth, though portions
of the machinery had to be conveyed thither in secret, to
avoid the risk of piracy or premature disclosures.

Nor were such precautions unnecessary. Referring to a
rival patentee, who appeared just when Watt seemed near-
ing the goal of all his aspirations, he had to confess, that
"of all things in life there is nothing more foolish than inventing. Here I work five or more years contriving an
engine, and Mr. Moore (his rival) hears of it; is more awake;
gets three patents at once; publishes himself in the news-
papers; hires two thousand men; sets them to work for the
whole world; gets a fortune at once, and prosecutes me for
using my own invention!" Such were the impediments
which obstructed his career: such the difficulties with which
he had to compete, while "he continued a slave" to what
he called his "present hateful employment" of civil engineering. To a mind so delicately formed as his, all this

must have been a species of martyrdom; but his whole
life had been concentrated on his inventions, and he is
not to be thwarted when so near the goal. It is well known
that a coral reef surrounds some of the islands in the Pacific
Ocean. Outside that reef the sea may surge in wildest commotion, till it is impossible for any vessel to live amid the
terrible breakers. But once inside, all is serene: it is like
the very home of the halcyon. Now, Watt had long been
among the breakers, but he is at length about to enter the
lagoon.

And yet the remark must be modified. Even at this
stage, it seemed not unlikely that he might be wrecked after
all. Pecuniary difficulties on the part of those to whom he
had made over the larger portion of his rights, occasioned
fresh delays, so vexatious and chafing that he had occasion
to say, "I am resolved, unless those things I have brought
to some perfection reward me for the time and money I
have lost on them, *if I can resist it*, to invent no more.
Indeed, I am not near so capable as I once was. I find I
am not the same person I was four years ago, when I invented the fire (steam) engine, and foresaw, even before I
made a model, almost every circumstance that has since
occurred. I was at that time pressed on by the alluring
hope of placing myself above want, without being obliged
to have much dealing with mankind to whom I have always
been a dupe. The necessary experience in great measure
was wanting; in acquiring it, I have met with many disappointments. . . . . . . I have now brought the engine near a
conclusion, yet I am not, in idea, nearer the rest I wish for,
than I was four years ago. However, I am resolved to do
all I can to carry on the business, and if it does not thrive
with me, I will lay aside the burden I cannot carry." The
fame of Watt is great—and will continue while this world
endures; but did he not acquire it at a high price? Is

there not truth in the sarcasm which speaks of this benefactor of men, as exposed to "the martyrdom of an English
patent?" Though faint, however, he was still pursuing.

"I am resolved . . . . . . *if I can resist it*, to invent no
more." Such was the announced design of Watt, amid the
difficulties which now environed him. He wisely, and in-
stinctively, however, inserted the condition, "If I can resist
it"—and he could not. He was under a law, a kind of
mental necessity to invent, and must cease to live ere that
law be set aside, or that necessity evaded. Watt accordingly continued to invent till his closing day; but that should
not prevent us from noticing the pain which he endured on
the way to eminence, on the one hand, or the triumph which
he achieved, on the other. A man of fiery temperament
would have adopted some bolder device than patience for
bringing his discovery into play. But he—calm, retiring,
and serenely philosophic—was not propelled by any impulse, or borne up by any excitement. It was the steady
persistency and invincible power of his genius, and not any
spasmodic efforts that made him what he was; in short, as
the material benefits which he was about to bestow upon
the race were perhaps unmatched, the basis on which they
were to rest was prepared with toil and self-sacrifice; a deep
and difficult foundation for a lofty structure. Another inventor says of such a man, in speaking of this period of
Watt's history: "He elaborates a great invention, or per-
fects a great discovery, and a wasted frame, an empty purse,
and, perchance, a starving family measure the labour which
he has expended." It is "the cruel infancy of invention,"
"the first sufferings of a man of genius, whom Providence
has raised up as a benefactor to his country and his species."
Strange that it should be so in a world where omniscient
love presides! But that love has not left us ignorant of the
cause of such a state of things.

We are trying here to trace some of the effects of decision of character; and, to show how much Watt needed it, we next observe that so many years of his patent had expired ere his machines came into operation, that he petitioned parliament for an extension of his privilege. It was conceded for twenty-five years; but was opposed even by Edmund Burke. That was done on behalf of one of that statesman's constituents; and for such reasons, Watt was to be deprived of the fruits of his toil, his anxiety, and his genius,—the hope deferred which had often made his heart sick, was to sicken it still longer. Kindred genius has stood amazed at such opposition from such a quarter, but it evoked one proof more of two things—First, an inventor must contemplate, at least, a moral martyrdom; and secondly, Watt had both to contemplate and endure it.

We have just seen that he once determined to invent no more "if he could resist it." But the power of his genius bore down all resistance, and he proceeded to heap invention on invention, to add patent to patent, and augment the sum of his benefits to man. This, however, was not accomplished without still encountering the resistance which has ever waylaid or tried to thwart the good and the great. After Watt had brought his inventions into practical operation, by an engagement with a wealthy English engineer, and after the application of his machines had begun to open up the way to wealth to all who employed them, he had still to defend them from aggressors; nay, at one period he had to uphold his patents amid the pertinacity of vexatious lawsuits, even till he had reached the highest court in this kingdom which takes cognizance of such matters. Some of those to whom he had furnished engines, conspired to get rid of their obligations to the inventor, and fresh annoyances hence arose. His patents were formally violated, and Watt had no alternative but to succumb to robbery, or appeal to law for his defence. He was successful; but it shows how much his calm persistency was needed, to know that not merely had he thus to conflict with obstruction upon obstruction while completing his machines, but had, moreover, to defend his rights against unjust assailants, even after he might suppose that the result of his labours should be quietly his own.— If the oak which is most exposed to the storm be also the most deeply rooted, we see an analogy to that fact in the assaults which beat upon Watt.

After all, however, only a minute portion of the inventions of Watt has been here described. Amid his feeble health, amid conflicts which he could ill brook, and surrounded with difficulties to which he was at times disposed to succumb, he persisted in his researches and experiments, sometimes even with the ardour of youth. There is reason to believe that he was the first discoverer of the composition of water, at least he disputes that honour with Henry Cavendish, one of the most accomplished philosophers of his day. Among his miscellaneous doings, he invented a machine for drawing in perspective. Early in his career he invented and constructed two micrometers for ascertaining distances. In 1780 he took out a patent for a press for copying letters, and while the mightiest results known to human power were not beyond the range of his genius, he also invented a flexible tube for conveying water into our homes, and devised a method for heating them by steam. Nor did he stop here. The momentum of his mind, like the power of his own engine, extended its influence alike to the majestic, and the miroscopic; he devised a new mode of constructing light-houses; an arithmetical machine which could perform the processes of multiplication and division, and another machine for copying in miniature all kinds of sculpture. Further, he invented the screw propeller; he constructed a

steam carriage of some size, and gave occasion to a remark
quoted by Sir David Brewster, that "steam would become
the universal lord, and that we should, in time, scorn post-
horses.   An iron railway would be a cheaper thing than a
road on the common construction."   That was in 1813.

Such, then, are some of the achievements of Watt.   It
has not been attempted to give any continuous narrative of
his life, but only to indicate, by a series of particulars, how
he selected his path wisely, and persisted in it decidedly, in
the face of such opposition as might have quelled the boldest ;
and it is needless now to add that the results have been
colossal in proportion to his perseverance.   If it be true
that one half of a man's wisdom consists in discovering
what he can do, and the other half in doing it, the effects
which have followed the doings of Watt prove him to have
been one of the wisest of the sons of men.   It were superfluous to dwell at length, and in general terms, on the results
which have followed his inventions.   Genius has vied with
genius in pronouncing Watt's encomium, or describing his
achievements—poetry and oratory, philosophy and science,
art and literature, have all laid their garlands on his tomb.
He was not the first to suggest the application of steam as
a moving power, but he distanced all rivals by the inventions which brought it under the control of man, and it is
now no hyperbole to say that there is scarcely an individual
—certainly not a land—on the face of the earth which does
not profit by the inventions of Watt.   Every comfort of life
is augmented by its means.   The tears of the mourner may
be dried by its help, for he may rush to a last farewell to
the object of his affection.   Nation is linked to nation by
ties which every ten years which pass will render it more
difficult to snap.   The follies of kings, and the haughty indifference of rulers will yet melt away before this amazing
elevator of the people.   By the foot of mechanism—Sir David

Brewster has written—by the foot of mechanism is trodden the wine-grape to cheer man's heart. By its hand is ground the farina that is to nourish him, and moulded the dough, the staff of his life. The scholar's alphabet, the poor man's Bible, the daily gazette, the idler's romance, and the page of wisdom, the elements of man's moral and intellectual growth, are all the cheapened products of steam. At its bidding, too, the materials of civilization quit the dark places of the earth, its coal, its iron, its silver, and its gold. The instruments of peace, the loom, the ship, and the plough, are all fashioned by its cunning hand, and even the dread engines of war, the machinery of death and destruction, owe their origin to the same universal power. Such were the effects of a single worker.

For honours, we have seen that Watt was not overlooked by learned and scientific bodies. Few could foresee the illimitable expansion which his inventions were to give to the wealth, the intercourse, the commerce, the social and moral condition of the world; but none who were capable of understanding his improvements could be blind to their intrinsic beauty, or their scientific value. His early buffetings, and his persistent perseverance in his peculiar walk, were, consequently, honoured and repaid by the applause of the like-minded. He was elected a member of the Royal Societies of Edinburgh and of London, and also of the Batavian Society. He was created a Doctor of Laws, and named first a Correspondent, and then an Associate of the Institute of France. His name is perpetuated in the British navy and elsewhere, by the majestic vessels which float it over the deep. In short, whether we consider the man, his work, or the wonders which have followed him, we know of few of the sons of men who can stand side by side with James Watt; and to see him bearing up and pressing on, in the face of all opposition, till he had mastered every difficulty, or made it tributary to his skill, reminds us of one of his own steam-winged vessels beating up against wind and tide. "Never despair," becomes more and more the maxim on which men should act while they trace the efforts, the triumphs, and the benefits of Watt. The fixed resolution to be deterred by no difficulties, on which he acted all through life, gave him an object for which to strive—namely, successful invention ; and a motive in the struggle—namely, I have succeeded before, why not again ? And he thus walked forward, from invention to invention, calm, though not unfeeling—resolute, though never contentious. It was the momentum of his character that helped thus to bear him on ; and when his friends laid him in his Gothic sepulchre at Handsworth, or placed his marble statue in Westminster Abbey—while a hundred other places hastened to imitate the example—it was a fit sequel and consummation to a life which had done so much for the good of man.

As we wander along the aisles of that Abbey, where so many of the illustrious repose, or are commemorated, poets, warriors, statesmen, nobles, commoners—many whom genius made great, or philanthropy beneficent—we can scarcely help rejoicing that we are Britons. The "sceptred dead" still rule as from their urns. Yet may we question whether among them all there is one who has wrought such changes, or bestowed such blessings as Watt, the indomitable labourer, the improver of the steam engine. His industry scarcely knew repose ; his firmness refused to be turned from his selected path, and, altogether, his powers place him in the very foremost rank in the great family of man. His genius may have been all his own, and a century may revolve ere there be room in the world for another Watt. But his calm intrepidity amid opposition, his earnest struggle against neglect, indifference, ignorance, or hostility, render him a model. His example, as well

as his inventions, he has bequeathed as a rich legacy to all
time.

Yet amid all the admiration which the life and the
labours, the genius and the firmness of Watt display, we
confess to one melancholy feeling associated with the history of the great inventor. We might, with others, desire
more knowledge of him than we possess, as a husband,
a father, or a citizen ; but the general tone of Watt's character is a sufficient guarantee for these. Those who knew
him best loved him most; and it is only when we approach that sacred domain in which the immortal spirit
communes with God that a blank is felt, and aching desires rise up in a believing mind. It were wrong rudely
to intrude into that domain ; and in many cases there
has been somewhat too much of such intrusion. But between that extreme and the other, of utter silence upon the
loftiest of all subjects—subjects deserving and obtaining the
homage of creatures transcending man—there is surely a
middle way; yet Watt has not given any proof that he
walked in it. On that subject his history seems blank.
His letters show, indeed, that he gratefully recognised an
all-wise Providence, to whose goodness he owed the blessings which he enjoyed. His best biographer, moreover,
has told us that on contemplating his death in 1819, " he
calmly conversed on that and other subjects with those
around him, and expressed his gratitude to the Giver of all
good, who had so signally prospered the work of his hands,
and blessed him with length of days, and riches, and honour."
But was that—were these all? Was there no Saviour, no
sin, no revelation, no judgment before him? Why so uncertain a sound, or rather, why such utter silence upon the
most solemn of all subjects—and that in a man in his eighty-
fourth year,—one of the sagest and most sagacious that
had ever walked our world? Were his hopes for hereafter

founded only on the basis to which he looked when speaking of a departed wife? "If probity, charity, and duty to her family can entitle her to a better state, she enjoys it." These things are right, they are essential, between man and man; but, alas, for poor humanity, if such a foundation be all! Has not Inspiration said, "Other foundation can no man lay than that which God has laid, which is Jesus Christ?"

On such a subject the mind gladly takes refuge in what one of Watt's biographers has beautifully said,—"Let us cherish the hope that the calm which rested on the spirit of the pilgrim as he approached the confines of the dark valley, and which enabled him to be, himself, the gentle and affectionate supporter of his sorrowing family and the friends who surrounded his couch, was one which caught its radiance from a far higher sphere than that of the purest human philosophy—even from a simple and child-like reliance on the infinite merits of Him whose name is the Wonderful." Apart from that hope, the close of the life of James Watt was sad beyond endurance; and from such a contemplation we gladly turn away to think of the result of his inventions in helping on the time when at the name of Jesus every knee shall bow, and every tongue confess.

The main object of these remarks has been to fix attention on the grand results of determined perseverance on the part of Watt, in spite of a hundred obstructions. These results, we have seen, are already well-nigh world-wide, and are increasing from day to day. The sweep of his influence ranges from the mightiest human production down to the most minute. The Alps cannot withstand the power which he has taught man to wield, while the very ocean is rendered more smooth as the highway of the nations. In the right sense, liberty, equality, and brotherhood have all been unspeakably advanced by the inventions of Watt. It is often remarked that in former ages, the events which occurred in God's world were the result of long elaborations, whereas now, all is proceeding with eager rapidity to some great consummation. How much of that is owing to the labours of that mind whose life-work we have been trying to trace! How deeply has hè left his mark upon man, and in the world where he sojourned, toiled, and struggled, or where he suffered and enjoyed for eighty-four years! Is another Watt needed prior to the final consummation, when the purposes of the Supreme shall all be wrought out? Or has he unconsciously placed within our reach the great renovator of our poor world, as far as material means can promote such results?

At a time when difficulties encompassed him, Watt was invited to settle in Russia, and offered a fixed annual income of £1000. He declined the offer and clung to his country; but what might have been that country's present condition, or what that of Russia—of Europe—of the world, had Watt consented to transfer his genius to the empire of an autocrat?

Few things can indicate more clearly the power of a present God than the mighty results which often flow from feeble or speck-like commencements. What seems so insignificant, we ask once more, as a word? Perhaps it is the utterance of a little child; but even though it be that of some mighty mind, how puny it seems! A slight impression made upon the air—an impression slighter still upon the ear, and that seems all—a thing more fleeting than a flash. Yet, such a word may become like the very power of God; it may be life from the dead—the birth moment of glory, honour, and immortality.

Or even less than a word may suffice. A mysterious Sufferer once stood at the tribunal of truculent, time-serving men. While there, one of his professed adherents denied him, and that with reiterated imprecations. The Mighty and Innocent Accused then "looked upon" the man, and that look went right through the conscience, the heart, and the whole soul; there is reason to believe that he walked humbly till his dying day in consequence of that mere look.

—Among the Alps there are spots where the traveller must advance in silence. He may not utter a syllable; and the reason is that his mere words might so agitate the air as to detach the sharp-poised avalanche, and launch it with death and destruction in its mass.

Now it seems one of these little incidents charged with immeasurable results, to notice how the repairing of Newcomen's engine, in the University of Glasgow, became the pivot on which Watt's history turned. It directed or developed, though it did not create, that tendency of his mind which is now diffusing its effects round a globe. And surely it were alike unphilosophical and unreasonable to overlook the All-wise, or decline to recognise the operation of his hand in such a case. None so mighty as they in whose weakness his strength is made perfect. None so wise as they to whom he is a counsellor. None so prosperous as they whom he crowns with his blessing. None so steadfast or decided as they who seek their sufficiency in him; and, none so woe-worn, so baffled, or so wretched as they who are ignorant of the grace and the glory of Him who is the Father of lights, the Author of every good and every perfect gift.

THE END